A

HUNCH

BACK

Named

Katchy

By Marshall B. Thompson Jr.

Trafford rev. 02/12/2014

 www.trafford.com

North America & international
toll-free: 1 888 232 4444 (USA & Canada)
fax: 812 355 4082

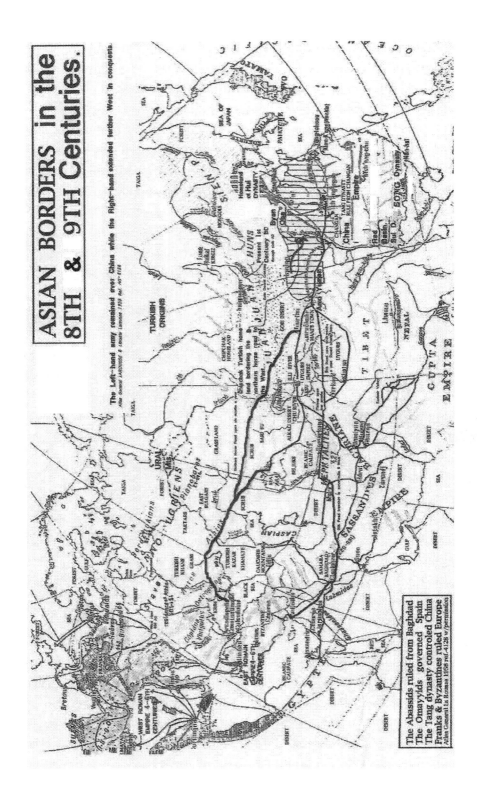

ASIAN BORDERS in the 8TH & 9TH Centuries.

The Left-hand army remained over China while the Right-hand extended further West in conquests.

The Abassids ruled from Baghdad
The Omayyids governed Spain
The Tang dynasty controled China
Franks & Byzantines ruled Europe
Atlas General La Roman 1958 ref 4128 w/permission

TABLE OF CONTENTS

CHAPTER * * MUSIC * * ILLUSTRATIONS * * PAGE

THANKS TO FRIENDS

Writing books is not easy at any age, but as age increases additional difficulties appear. Fortunately I found friends ready to help. They are too many to name. However, my thanks go especially to one who rescued me from the tedium of endless corrections. My dear wife Hazel Fay has been a constant help and encouragement in the production and printing of this Grey Wolf Series.
I needed a publisher who would handle original material.
I found the needed qualities in Trafford Publishing. I went through numberless author's helpers and contacts, but eventually things got done the way it was supposed to be. My thanks go to all of them.
"Thank God from whom all blessings flow" is not just an old saying, but a present reality. There are things in life that can not be done by man-power alone. My thanks go there for many favors continually received.
My thanks go to you my reader. I hope this effort to provide original entertainment from historic sources will satisfy both our needs. Read and enjoy!   Marshall B. Thompson Jr.

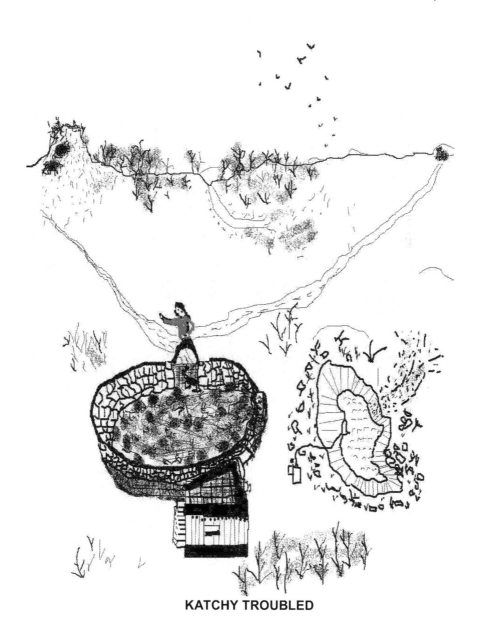

KATCHY TROUBLED

9

AUTHOR'S OPENING

The characters are braided in to play a part in the intertwined three stories here: Katchy, the brazen hunchback; Sulema and the Sheriff from the village; Erly, a Tuzlu guard; Baja the smugglers' aunt as well as a Fergana mare. They bring new attitudes and situations. It turns out like painting with water colors, the edges blend into the other strokes. Early characters that become less prominent see their decisions carried forward by others. Crossing borders changes the characteristics of culture and expectations making problems with adjustments necessary in each person's situation. Personal and collective reactions range from enthusiastic to violent. Decisions affecting their future must be made. All exhibit different values that affect their actions.

Time lines seem to merge or in contrast, to stand apart; agonizing delays or hasty forced choices are demanded. A new awareness of fallibility and caution enters their lives anew: when confidence wanes all become worried and irritable. The person with strong convictions and yet open, friendly attitudes seems to triumph; though not always with a whole skin and full wallet. There is a price for winning through.

The Gray Wolf Secret Society is active planning assassinations and riots. The wolves' head, a schemer, is always present in every society and at some stage of every life. He will attempt to control every situation as bully or seducer for his own perceived goals. He does not flinch at damage to or destruction of others. He always prefers to stay hidden and yet seeks dramatic moments of display to turn any situation to his gain. He commands wealth and obedient servants, yet is always short of his desired aim, even when he wins. His soul can never say hold; enough. Those who unknowingly serve him are without number. His existence brings into play the basic theme of creation. Even planning predators have their limits. In the hands of the Creator all can be turned to good and a well done to those who trust. I write for your pleasure; read, learn and enjoy.

TREASURE ON HIGH

MID-ASIA TIME LINE

At the beginning of the ninth century of the present era the empires East and West were in a state of recuperation from the previous internal struggles. Upheavals in the East with the expulsion and successful restoration of the Tang dynasty brought China into a retreat toward earlier traditions. In the far West, Barbarians: Teutonic and Slavic were being converted as they settled into parts of the old Roman Empire. Byzantium suffered many religious quarrels, political riots, and drained resources, due to Islamic aggression.

Islam had its own upheavals in civil wars. The first division was between Shia and Sunni. War brought separation of the Umayyad dynasty, ruling Spain and the Abbassids in Baghdad. Korasan had become the seat of power in the expansion against the Rajput's frontier marches beyond the Indus River. Northward Islam found their progress blocked by the formidable Turkish tribes in the grasslands of Central Asia. They could hardly hold the agricultural areas and the Turkic Uigurs resisted strongly on the east of the dividing Tien Shan or Tanra Dah range of Mountains. Everywhere, wars were perennial, but success in conquests was small. Warriors were in constant demand. Life expectancy was low. Consumption exceeded production in every sector of that world.

In all these circumstances religious affiliation was a part of the conquest structure. Yet, as always, the personal element was present to speed or retard the process. Each empire had an official language, religion, law, and ruling capital. It was dangerous to oppose the ruling dynasties and their opinions. Yet, then, as now, minorities continued to exist and follow those things dear to their hearts and traditions. They practiced such in secrecy or publicly at a high risk and material cost to their group. Their successes and occasional prosperity was often penalized by the pliant majority at the behest of the ruling classes. Force, in all its human guises, was prevalent then, as now. It was often maintained even in the face of logic, compassion or need. Virtue was as rare a commodity then as it is today, both personally and collectively.

It is our purpose to explore such a world and understand its ancestry to our own situations, both in Central Asia and around the world. We are living with the results of these encounters and their ideological positions as a result of historic clashes. The resulting defeats and victories have proved to be durable in nature. The game continues, however. God has yet to lead the *finale* that brings down the curtain on uncertainty and striving; to take His children home for a toasty snack and warm bed before the awakening to a new day. MT

PEOPLE, PLOTS & PLACES IN CHAPTER 1

Ayden bey: comes to Goat Hill seeking fugitives.
Ilhan: seeks rewards for criminals captured or killed.
Kynan: a fugitive who seeks to take Leyla to her tribe.
Kerim of the East Bulgars: the assumed name of Kynan.
Katchy: a hunchback youth caring for his goats and hill.
Leyla: rescued daughter of Khan Erben is torn by thorns.
Umer: seeks to avenge himself on Leyla and her rescuer.

GLOSSARY:
Bayan: a title for a Lady, used before the name.
Do'er: Stop! Halt!
 gel: come; accompany me; this way.
ketchyler: goats.
ketchylerjik: diminutive form, 'dear little goats'.
kuru yemish: dry fruits, nuts and powdered foods.
Salaam alaykum: Peace to you; Arabic greeting in Islam.

Note: The glossary and foreign words are *italicized* and spelled to
help readers of English. They are not spelled so in their dictionaries.
                                                                    MBT

KYNAN FINDS A HILL

The first light of dawn brought a quiet hum of recognition among the large flock of goats and sheep in the stone corral. What a shuffle of motion there was as those awake pressed against those still sleeping and murmurs of protest were voiced.

From the entrance a figure rose on two feet and slowly stretched arms to the sky. A sweet tenor voice issued a yawn and then the cry, "*Allah hu Ekber*" in full voice. The corral echoed the call with loud bleating. The refrain was repeated: "God is great!" The choir agreed with renewed vigor. The third time the animals nearly drowned out the cry. The boy turned toward the valley and shouted the name "Kooskoo bey" and turning to his flock shouted "*Kechylerjik.*" The chorus voiced their approval of their being called 'dear little goats,' but they reserved their last and loudest approval for the affirmation made by an ugly, shaggy, hunchback to the growing light. Raising one hand with the other on his breast he affirmed the chief focus of his personal world, his name and purpose: "*Kechy, Katchy* cat*ch 'em*! I'm the ruler of them all!"

He ducked into the corral and started milking the nannies. They were vigorously crying to their kids, who were penned-up by a separating barrier inside the main corral. The nannies were all beside the foam-rock wall, nosing the openings, to be as close as possible to their kids. The boy hurriedly milked the nannies. Then he collected the milk, after drinking a fresh bowl-full warm.

He released the babies to their mothers to have their breakfast. He placed the jug of collected milk into a stone covered depression over a small spring. The little spring seeped under the rock and trickled into a collection pond below the hill. The thorn brush grew thick about it. After storing the milk he ran to reconnoiter the pond. Seeing no predators, he then hurried to the gate. He released this bleating, noisy crowd to drink and eat.

He watched his troop of animals drinking their fill and turning to search for bits of green for breakfast. They were his charges, to care for and keep for his master. He was leader and guide. He patted his chest and sang of his importance and place in the world. His tenor voice was loud and clear.

> I'm the leader of the goat herd.
> I'm director of the band.
> I'm the teacher of the kids and
> Nannies' counsellor I am.
> I'm smart! Yes, I am. Yes, I am.
>
> I arrange 'most every marriage,
> I deliver all the kids.
> I'm the doctor for all wounded,
> Warrior, too, 'gainst wolf or bear.
> I'm there! Yes, I am. Yes, I am
>
> I'm the tax-man to the living,
> Milk and wool they must supply.
> I'm the judge, who will condemn some,
> For I know who ought to die.
> I'm high! Yes, I am. Yes, I am.

I'm the salesman of our produce:
It's the best that can be found.
I'm the maker of great cheeses,
Finest leather seen around
I'm sound. Yes, I am. Yes, I am.

I'm the ruler of the thorn lands,
Khan of all that you can see.
I'm protector of a hundred,
All their lives depend on me.
I'm He. Yes, I am. Yes, I am.

YES, I AM

I'm the lead - er of the flock here.

I'm dir - ec - tor - of the band.

I'm the teach - er of the kids and

Nan - nie's coun - sel - or I am.

I'm smart! Yes, I am! Yes, I am!

He jumped to the top of the stone gate posts outside
his little corral and did a pirouette and victory dance.
There he overlooked all his band and water hole below.
He smiled his mastery and surveyed the thorn land, all
his except for the landlord. Then, remembering, he
frowned and growled.

15

Now he craned his neck to see from the high spot the sight that had troubled him the evening before. Tiny black dots were sprinkled like dust on the far horizon where the valley lay. Something big had died. The hungry birds had gathered. Someone would be in trouble. He shuddered; if it belonged to Kooskoo bey there would be trouble for everyone everywhere. The demanding owner was a tyrant in Kathcy's small kingdom; the man collected a part of his small hoard of coins every season. A man to avoid!

Then he discerned a figure nearer. A single rider was coming toward the corral. He shook his head in fear. He did not want to see the angry Lord now. He must hide the herd: disappear.

> - - - - - >IN THE FOAM ROCK THORN-LAND > - - - - - >

Kynan rode all night and carried the girl he had rescued from the menace of two fugitives. He was determined to return her to her tribe, but it had to be done by night. His disguise as an East Bulgar adventurer would not stand up to close scrutiny. All local authorities were searching for an escaped war prisoner named Kynan; changing his name to Kerim was a thin ruse. Leyla would be safe with the people of the Khan's champion: Twozan. However, his father was an enemy of her father and her clan would know that. He had to proceed with caution, yet he dozed. Dreaming, he again witnessed the great tribal event: the marriage of a Khan's son. Abundant food and drink had welcomed the travelers to the site. As colorful as spring flowers on the steppes, women moved among the throng. Music punctuated by conversation, or colorful comments by some enthusiastic drinkers spiced the moment. The bride's moment of glory came. He sighed, remembering. He was only a boy at the time, but he recalled every word.

The wedding song was sung by the women as they paraded the veiled bride to the place of assembly and ceremony. Drums and flutes echoed in his mind. The smell of perfume touched his heart. He sighed again and repeated the words of the song.

16

THE DOVE

1. See the bright dove soaring o'er us?
   She's flying far. There she'll make her nest.
   Storm clouds will come
   With great wind and thunder.
   She'll warm her nest 'til the sun breaks through.

Refrain:
   Glad hearts singing, music ringing,
   Love is bringing joy to everyone.
   Beyond measure marriage pleasure
   Holds life's treasures truly.
   She'll be a dove all her life with you.

2   See the bright face smiling o'er us?
     She's going far from her father's home.
     Troubles will come
     With great stress and wonder.
     She'll guard her yurt 'til the sun breaks through.
Refrain:

> - - - - - >THE SEEP MEADOW HILL> - - - - - >

Kynan noticed in first light a green hill before him. He drove his black horse and the bay mare up the slope and prepared to spend the day hiding.

Kynan dismounted carefully, not wanting to wake the girl, but she moaned and started crying. He laid her down upon the grass to unsaddle and hobble the two horses. He took the saddles and bags to the top of the hill and returned as she started to scream. He knelt down and covering her mouth with his hand. He slowly took her into his arms as she quieted. He muffled her moans with his shoulder and carried her to the top of the hill where the thorn brush was green, screening them from view. There he built a little rock wall the size of a yurt around girl and goods for defence. He placed his weapons at hand, then, he began to inspect her scratches applying a medicine he took from the pack. The sun slowly rose over the desert, painting the sky from magenta to pink, warming the earth and its creatures.

> - - - - - >KATCHY'S CORAL> - - - - - >

Katchy started to move the mob of goats away into the wilder parts. He shouted as he turned and saw there were two horses on the seep meadow. Over an hour away and higher up, they were grazing his field! Indignation swept over him. That field was reserved for hay now and spring lambs later. The loss of hay would thin his winter flock. Hastily he ran shouting to gather his flock and drove them toward the high meadow. His clear voice imitated the sounds of his dependants; the mature baa of the lead goats from the column's head to give direction. With accurately thrown small stones he hurried the stragglers

18

and straying. When he looked again at his destination the horses had moved out of sight, but he heard the sound of screaming. Someone was hurting a woman!

> - - - - - > NEAR THE AMU VALLEY > - - - - - >

Umer, the fugitive, cursed the dawn; so much need for distance and he must pass the day hidden. He was only a night's travel from his vengeful pursuers. His horse was flagging. He had passed two nights without sleep. Red eyed and befuddled he drove on searching for a hiding place. Then he heard it. A scream penetrated his weariness. He knew it now, like his own voice. It was the girl who had caused his troubles. He hissed his hatred.

"I hope it hurts. Perhaps he's collecting his due for carrying you off. But you still owe me and I intend to get it all and settle with him too." His hand caressed the knife in his belt and he snarled in anticipation.

On the hill ahead he saw dust bathing a corral. The animals had moved off in a cloud of sound that retreated before him. The empty, rock walls of the corral offered defence and cover, but would be sure to draw the attention of searchers. He studied it carefully.

"They'll be all around me by noon." He murmured to himself, but coming to the little stone topped spring and the little pool below he decided to risk it. He staggered down. "It might be the last place they would search with care." He drank first and moved the stone to discover the milk and cheese guarded there. There was dry pide bread and *kuru yemish* in the saddle bag. He made a meal, fed his horse and counted the money in the bag. It made a substantial pile. He grinned. "I can trade the horse and buy a uniform and equipment if I get to Samarkand, but first I must find the Turk and the girl." He hid the horse in a wadi behind the corral and collapsing in the shade of the wall, slept.

> - - - - - >ON SEEP HILL TOP> - - - - - >

"I'm sorry I had to gag and tie you, *Bayan* Leyla, but you were delirious and there are searching eyes and ears

19

around. When you screamed, I had to gag you. When you fought I had to tie your hands and feet."

She squinted up into the morning sun to make out the face of the man. She shook her aching head and tried to clear her thoughts. She attempted to reply, but couldn't move or speak. Kynan removed the gag.

"Who are you? Where am I? What has happened?" She groaned as she tried to move her arms and legs. She looked closely at the scratches and thorn punctures she had received when fear pressed her back into the trees. Kynan thought she seemed to ignore him, her captor. He answered carefully.

"I'm Kerim of the East Bulgars. I promised your father I would look out for you and get you to the tribe. We are a night's ride away from the valley and pursuit is close at hand. We may have to fight."

She seemed preoccupied. "I must look frightful. This medicine – what's it made from?"

He was unprepared for this change of subject. "Why – it's horse medicine, - for scratches and bug bites." She started giggling, but it became a moan. She still did not look at him.

"I'm wretched and sore. Where's the water? Oh, I see. Why don't you leave, Kerim? I need privacy." Her cool tone distressed him.

"Please." Her word came as an after thought, but he stood. Dismissed, he looked around outside his rock wall. The sounds of herds and horses caused him to crouch behind the thorn brush. A herd boy was moving toward the hill sniffing around the spot where he had dismounted. Two horsemen approached on the horizon. He strung his bow.

> - - - - - >BELOW THE SEEP HILL> - - - - - >
"*Kechy gel*, come goats." The herd moved forward while Katchy stopped on the trail up the hill. Here were the tracks again. He stooped to smell the ground and picked up several broken thorn spines. They showed stains of blood. The horses, well grazed and hobbled,

were sleeping among the brush. The tracks led up the hill. The female was there. He could detect small changes in the rocks above. The man had altered things, for defence no doubt. Only his accustomed eyes could detect the difference. Looking back over his shoulder he saw that the two horsemen were closing to his position. He stood up hastily and uttered urgent bleats.

"Baa, baa!" It was the sound of distress made by baby kids in danger or hurt. The female animals rushed to the sound. The billy goats milled around on the outer edge of the flock looking for predators. Their hooves over printed the soft meadow earth and obscured the larger prints made by horses and people. As the approaching horses drew up, the herd formed a thick line between the herder and the new visitors. Ayden Bey rose on his stirrups. "*Salaam Alaykum*, peace to you. We search for two or three criminals. They would have travelled most of the night. Have you seen them?" The shepherd made a negative, don't know, kind of gesture.

This irritated Ayden Bey. "You have or you haven't? Make it clear. There's a reward for information." Still the herder hesitated. "Here's an advance, damn you. Tell us."

A copper coin flashed through the air. Like a cat the boy leaped up and caught the gleaming metal. He flashed a broad smile and pointed, hand high with drooping finger, beyond the hill to the north east where the mountains lie beneath the horizon.

"They double back to get to the mountains. We should get the reward by cutting them off!" The other, Ilhan, cried. The two men were off in a cloud of dust and pumice rock.

Katchy spit after them as a gesture of contempt. Then he smiled as he polished the coin on his ragged sash and tucked it away with satisfaction. He patted his chest proudly and boasted. "It was no lie. I pointed where the people are." The herd had started to drift now that the intrusion had passed. Katchy sat under a bush to plan.

Above them Kynan unstrung his bow while Leyla

21

sleepily continued her tidying. She called him over to get some thorn scratches doctored on her back.

Kynan was finding his task increased his emotion and desire. He did it gingerly, dabbing the ointment on the red discolored spots, while his face worked and lips pursed.

> - - - - - >IN THE SEEP MEADOW BRUSH> - - - - - >

Katchy crouched under a bush peering through a crack in the wall in the afternoon haze at the girl dozing in the shade behind the rock shelter. The man was out of sight, Katchy could do as he pleased, yet he waited for some event, uncertain and uneasy. Then it happened -- a thrum of arrow string with the thump and death cry of a young billy. Katchy leaped with a screech to the top of the rock wall from where he could see his flock below. The alerted girl had her four inch utility knife out and pointed in his direction. The man below was claiming his prey. Katchy's flock milled about in distress voicing their disapproval, calling for help.

Ignoring the girl, who was up on her knees now ready to stand, the boy jumped down and seizing a hand size rock. He flung it with great force and accuracy at Kynan's head. Surprised, Kynan dropped his prey and barely deflected the stone with his leather wrist guard, as he sprang away. He drew his steel scimitar and armed, shouted a warning as the boy rushed him. "*Do'er*, stop, I'll pay you and we'll eat it together."

The boy ignored the man and rushed to the yearling. Gathering it in his arms he moaned tearfully rocking from side to side. "Kooskoo bey, what will he say? Kooskoo bey, how will I pay?"

Kynan looked on in confusion. Leyla too, ran down the slope and gathering both boy and animal, began to wail and cry, joining the mourning. Kynan stood ruefully rubbing his bruised wrist hoping for an explanation. Ignored, he finally gathered dry branches and prepared a fire. Come what may, a man must eat. He returned to quietly pull the young goat gently from the relaxed hand of the youth as Leyla rocked him, crooning tunelessly.

Umer went through the goods in the saddle bag again. The money, divided between two pouches, would be needed later. He saved the dried meat and poached wheat, provisions for the trip, but gave a few handfuls of oats and barley to the horse. The beast would travel hungry. There would be no grazing where sheep and goats had lived. He watched the lowering sun hopefully, impatient for its darkening. He had a score to settle. Also he must be gone before the herder returned with his flock to discover his losses of cheese, milk, and black olives. He had eaten what would be a week's meager supply for the boy. The herdsman was bound to his flock and not to be feared, yet Umer did not want to be seen and identified for others who would pursue him.

The two searchers had ridden past the corral that morning. Others had appeared in the distance, but none had come to investigate the site. He had slept much of the time and was rested. He was ready to go when the sounds of a moving herd were detected at a distance. He left in the opposite direction and circled to move toward the distant hill still gleaming in the sunshine. He tested the edge of his knife with a finger and smiled grimly in anticipation.

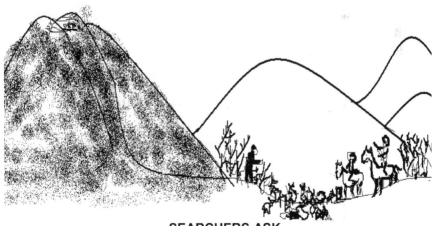

SEARCHERS ASK

PEOPLE, PLOTS & PLACES IN CHAPTER 2

Abdullah: a big man with experiences to match.
Atilla: happens to meet his stolen horse and the thief.
Ibn el Ari: veteran and hero of the late Arab Civil Wars.
Katchy: prepares to hunt a thief by moonlight.
Kynan: finds danger caring for a Khan's daughter.
Leyla: finds respect and comfort in hurt and loss.
Magazi: must learn to follow and fight Turks.
Mansur: son of el Ari wants to destroy an invading army.
Umer: finds deeper trouble than he ever imagined.

GLOSSARY:
babam: my father.
hazer ol: ready; prepare.
Salaam Alaykum: Peace to you; an Islamic greeting.
Tan'rum: My God!
you rue': walk; move on; make room.

UMER RECOGNIZED

"The meat was rich: barbecued on the spit. I didn't know a man could cook that great a meal." Leyla smiled her thanks at Kynan and prepared to mount. For all her care, she still showed dark shadowed eyes and a worn, wan look in her expression: a woman afraid, desperate and lonely.

"You have never travelled with a war party. The boys have to cook under the supervision of one of the old men of experience. The East Bulgars taught me well. My blood brother and I became the top pupils." He carefully girded his saddle on the horse and put on the saddlebags.

"My father thought your leaders too ambitious." She stated.

"Because they defended the forest tribes? Erdash Khan wished to dominate them. He set Kaplan bey to rule them. I spent time with both and prefer the East Bulgars."

His tone made her decide to change the subject. "Poor Katchy, he almost cried when you gave him the coin. It would have bought two goats. You're generous." Her voice was warm.

Kynan shrugged and replied with a deprecatory laugh. "When you spend another man's money you can always be generous. This was gathered from a bet made by a friend. I did his foot work and collected. I must use it as a loan to get you to the tribe."

He held up his hand suddenly and they listened to the quiet. Then, below them a horse blew and a kicked stone sounded. Someone was coming! He crept to his rock fence, drew his bow and notched an arrow. Below on the slope a rider appeared, Kynan knew him. A muffled whimper beside him told him that Leyla had recognised him too. He reluctantly drew his arrow and waited for the man's approach; the moment of a sure hit and maximum penetration. His prayer was calm, but urgent.

> - - - - - >MERV OASIS SOUTH OF THE AMU VALLEY> - - - - >

"With racing camels we can overtake the cursed Turks before they cross the mountains below the Kara Kum, the Black Sand Desert," the Youth concluded.

Ibn el Ari sat cross-legged drinking Yemeni coffee with satisfaction. His certainty was challenged by his son, Mansur who was concluding his military training.

The boy had an after thought and added: "Unless they take boats across the Caspian sea there."

The Sheikh Ibn el Ari laughed cynically shaking his head in derision. "They are strangers to salt seas. The day the Turks take happily to the waters, they will rule the world."

The son continued, "We must settle the score. We are the founding race of Islam. The Persians are our clients, the Turks, our slaves. We must maintain our prerogatives and privileges. Without our province of Khorasan's war power the Abbasids would have lost the recent wars."

The sheikh again signified his satisfaction. "Well said, Mansur, my son! You will do that. But it must be planned for a complete victory."

The son snorted his ire. "The recent division of the Toozlu tribe assures victory. The smaller group returning home are to be dealt with by their Seljuk friends in the government, but the larger must be annihilated as a lesson to these accursed people. We can't allow them to

26

take service with our Caliph. It will seem a reward for their audacity in trespassing in our land."

The Sheikh Ben Ari smiled his approval of the boy's bravery and zeal. Social rank and status were of great importance. Allah ordained them through the Holy Koran and they must be maintained.

> - - - - - >BELOW THE SEEP MEADOW> - - - - - >

As Umer faced the slope up the hill he was startled by the approach of the man on horseback who came up behind him unperceived.

"*Salaam Alaykum*, fellow traveller, can you help me?" The rider said, riding forward.

"*Hai, Allah!*" Umer screamed, spurring his horse round and down the slope.

"Wait, I - why, - that's my horse! You stole my horse! Stop thief!" Atilla bey dropped the lead rope to his pack animal and whipped his new mount into action. Both men thundered down the rise and across the desert as the sun sank into twilight. The lead horse was weak and tiring rapidly and the new mount was in good condition having worked only since noon that day. Slowly but surely Atilla bey was gaining ground on the thief as they entered a section of thick thorn woods.

Atilla's heart was filled with joy. To catch the fleeing murderer and recover his goods would satisfy justice; re-establish his reputation with Tewfik bey, the local Kaymakan, and the whole community. His trip to the capital would be without penury, he would have money to spare, surely a reward, too. Everyone would hear of his exploits. The Caliph in Samara would invite him to the new palace. He thought of the words he would prepare for such an occasion, and so thinking rode past the point where Umer had cut back and paralleled his trail.

Umer dismounted in a deep wadi where the walls cut the sound of his horse's heavy breathing. Atilla rode on the empty trail, his mind preoccupied.

Darkness halted pursuit. Atilla, cursing his luck, sat and brooded over his loss. Umer slowly continued to back track toward the hill. In a few hours the moon would be up, the hunt would continue.

> - - - - - >AT KATCHY'S CORRAL > - - - - - >

Katchy got his flock into the corral and milked late. It was just before last light when he heard the sound of two horses from the hill running parallel to the wadi and then he heard only one continue. Finally, in the dark, all action stopped. He spoke to the older, wiser goats that led the others and helped him see to their welfare.

"He would not be pursuing her. Kerim was respectful and caring of *Bayan* Leyla. She would not chase him. Who then? One or another of the younger lambs commented with a baa, but the wise ones kept their mouths shut. He was not sleepy, he had slept after that full meal of meat and pide bread. There was time till moonrise so he decided to put away the night milking. As he went to the covered spring his bare feet walked on olive pits. He hastened to lift the stone. Reaching in he found there was nothing there inside. The morning milk, cheese, olives - everything was gone. He remembered the horse and rider he had taken for Kooskoo bey. Ayden bey had said that criminals were loose. He drew his knife and nosed around outside the corral. A stranger had come, stayed and robbed him. He sharpened his knife on a stone as he waited for the moon.

> - - - - - >ON TOP GOAT HERDER HILL > - - - - - >

"*Tanram*, My God, that was close." Kynan breathed a sigh of relief as Atilla's horse ridden by Umer plunged down the hill and away with his friend, Atilla, screaming insults in pursuit.

Near him Leyla wept. "Why didn't you shoot?" She cried, "I could have been free of him forever."

"I don't think he'll ever bother you again. Atilla will chase him to the moon and back for revenge. You'll not see him again." He mounted his horse to go down the hill where a bewildered pack horse stopped in the twilight. She mounted and reluctantly followed. Kynan checked the familiar pack and separated a small heavy bag of money.

"We'll need the food we packed for the trip. He can buy more with this purse. We get the goods and he keeps the money. We won't have to risk buying food. Where do I put it for his return? Katchy is spry and will find and keep anything in easy reach."

Leyla looked around and spotted a high thorn branch silhouetted above a clump nearby. She pointed upward and suggested its use. "Spry he may be but he's not thorn proof. Can you reach that fork of branches from your horse?"

He leaned back smiling and stood up on the saddle clicking his tongue. The horse walked forward slowly and he could reach up and touch the branch. The purse fit and the branch bore the weight and remained swaying in position.

"It will be easy for Atilla to get and hard for Katchy. I'll leave three coins here below for him. He's heard the chase and when he investigates he'll find the money here on the ground." He took the halter rope and rode around the hill to go north-west. She urged her horse ahead. Then she stopped and gasped in fear. "Listen, the running has stopped."

He came up beside her. "Keep moving but don't run. It'll make too much noise. They'll be playing a hide and seek game now. We'll listen in while we move away from them."

She followed the path while he came after leading the pack animal. She shivered in the chill breeze that blew over the plain. She felt the smart of the healing thorn pricks and cuts. Fear welled up in her heart. She again wondered about this stranger who seemed familiar. Why had she feared to ask about her father? Why had he not told her about his life and family? He had spent the time with Katchy talking about the local roads and Kooskoo bey. He had asked nothing about her. Was she really safe? She touched her utility knife for reassurance. Did she dare go on with him? What did he know?

"Are you going to accompany the expedition?" Abdullah's question was direct, but almost whispered to his dear friend and confidant, Magazi. Their faces were inches apart and each spoke to the other's ear.

"Yes, but no gain. No hope of loot there or golden reward here. These are nomadic Turks going to the Caliph. They have been contacted, but not paid or even placed under protection by any kind of agreement."

Abdullah nodded his understanding and replied. "They will fight like demons if we catch them and it's a waste of good horse flesh and time if we don't. Why must our Lord, Ibn el Ari, insist so?"

"With great position goes great pride. The older and richer the family, the more stubborn the desire is to play Allah's helper."

"All for the death, under doubtful circumstances, of a cousin, killed while protesting the battle orders of his general? The commander who must have caused his death is here, close and although well guarded, available. Why seek revenge elsewhere?"

"The qualities of the hunting dog are best shown in the chase. The father would show the qualities of the son. So, we have a convenient need of revenge." Magazi smiled in a superior way.

Abdullah protested. "But they are already leaders in Khorasan and have the Caliph's ear. Why the need of this expedition? I must go as a client family."

"To remind the Turks that they are servants, not masters in Khorasan. The old families of Merv wish to teach an object lesson." Abdullah looked around the tea house. It was late, most customers had long since left. The owner was busy with preparations to close. No one was in a position to overhear. He spoke angrily if quietly.

"Then they should reprimand the Caliph who buys them for his palace guard and permits them to settle within the frontier."

30

"Is this not the best manner of showing the Great Shadow of Allah, peace be upon him, that his troops in Khorasan, who won the civil war for him, can beat anyone, even the Turks?" Magazi moved back and crossed his arms.

Abdullah however shook his head slowly eyeing his beloved friend. The little man was dressed in fashion and neat as a pin with a small trim beard under his moustache.

They took their last sip of tea and big Abdullah stroked his full beard, and smiled as he concluded. "I remember now that you have never fought the Turk. You see the rough exterior and despise them. I know them; it is well that we go together. I will be your book and shield tomorrow."

> - - - - - >CITY BARRACKS > - - - - - >

"Hazer ol. Ready. Up and out. Form up around your company's colors. Get to the banners now." Messengers scurried up and down the length of the field. Shouting at the tents and buildings where some were already out.

"*You rue,* Move! To horse everyone! Up, lazy bums! The last'll be flogged. You sons of camels move your tails." Salty language accompanied the calls and orders as the officers moved the ranks to action.

The barracks were difficult to rouse before dawn. The veterans were there to wake up the new, inexperienced, younger men. The commanders were fully equipped and some were waiting. Each company sat their horses in groups before their commanders. As client or dependent families they were obliged to serve without pay. Food was provided by the land owners who managed those whose villages used their land. Great lords wielded the power to combine companies and to use the whole host, the *ordu* against the enemy. A mounted band, rich in cymbals and drums, played loud music. Representatives of towns and villages came with families to see them off. Each group straggled up to the edge of the field.

31

Mansur Ibn el Ari, son of one of the greatest families, dressed in flowing robe of gold with black tunic and gold belt, posing gracefully on his black horse, riding back and forth shouting orders, was obviously in charge. His aging father, a hero of the Civil wars, rode up to observe proudly. He, too, wore the Abbassid colors and carried the black banner of the dynasty. An authority of the city greeted him cordially.

"Allah be praised! It is a good day for beginnings. A late moon makes for an early march. Taking advantage of it they will soon catch and punish the culprits." Proudly the elderly lord and land owner nodded in return.

"Allah wills it and we shall be His hand of vengeance against the ungodly foreigners. My son will be His sword to bring them to the true faith and scourge out their alien ways." The black horse thundered by and was suddenly reined in, reared and turned. The son dismounted and saluted his father, bowing before the father could embrace him.

"Here is Allah's blessing to me. He will add greater luster to our name." All the arriving people came to stare and admire the youth.

"Father, none can rival your victories in the Civil war and you made firm a throne and dynasty as God willed. I will show the strength of our blood and punish those invading infidels." A roar of approval came from the pressing mob. The troops too beat their swords on their shields, while the horses plunged and whickered, to raise a din of enthusiasm. They were sure that the God who showed his approval by victory was with them. The son embraced and was kissed by the father. He mounted to command the formation of the column as the sun rose.

> - - - - - > AT GOAT HERDER HILL > - - - - - >

Umer had led his horse back to the hill. The sound of his pursuer still told him he was safe and undetected. That might soon change with moon rise, but it gave him the time he needed to find his goal. From the hill he had gotten the smell of his prey and the faint sound of horses moving north. He had counted on the fact that animals make noise as they travel at night. Progress would be slow in the dark. But if he followed the sound, by moon rise he might have a chance at them and close the gap. He led his horse and walked north stopping to listen from time to time. He could hear the sound of the horses, a hoof striking a rock, the snort of fear as some clump loomed or animal darted before them. The sound of leather strained as the horses moved over hill and dale. They were riding, but at a walking pace. They had more than two horses. He remembered the pack animal and grinned. This would be revenge with profit indeed. Then he heard the murmur of quiet talking. He knew they felt safe. They were ahead to the left, but he did not try to make up the distance. There would be time for that later.

Behind him came muffled sounds, the fool followed no trail floundering about. He shouted challenges to the dark and getting no answer, cursed and ranted of how terrible his revenge would be. Umer laughed to himself. He need not waste his time, but he congratulated himself on how easily he could have killed that buffoon.

Suddenly he was transfixed by a woman's shriek. "*Babam*, poor father dead? Not so!" When the crying and wailing gradually ceased he was much nearer and could hear some of the words. "Don't cry, I promised to take care of you. We'll go to the tribe and return home." All the foolish words men use to comfort women in distress.

Umer laughed to himself again, how quickly men presume on the unknown future. Dropping his reins, Umer crept forward, knife in hand. Before him loomed a dark blob and the horses snorted, sensing his presence. The sobs came from the farther horse. He moved toward the nearer hoof steps. With knife raised, he rushed forward with a blood thirsty cry. Now he'd finish it.

PEOPLE, PLOTS AND PLACES IN CHAPTER 3

Abdullah: alert to find fault or wisdom in his leader.
Atilla: poses as the generous patron and host.
Ayden: is angry for being set on a false trail.
Aziz: a smuggler whose house in the village is raided.
Bolben: leads refugees to a secret tunnel.
Ilhan: warns the goat boy of his danger, if he lies.
Kadir: a guard for the band of smugglers.
Katchy: lets greed put him in peril of harm.
Kynan: discovers new difficulties caring for Leyla.
Leyla: finds one guard is not enough to care for her.
Magazi: follows in the army, but doubts its success.
Manish: the Manichean Uigur guide is caught.
Mansur: leads an army on a glorious enterprise.
Maril: the frail daughter of merchant refugees.
Umer: finds deeper trouble than he ever imagined.
Yavuz: an aggressive partner is nearly caught.

GLOSSARY:
gay bert': slaughter; kill; massacre.
hazer ol: ready; prepare.
kadun'muh: Is that a woman?
on'basha: corporal; leader of ten soldiers.
sea'r-seary: tramp; drifter; bum.
Soos: Hush; Quiet; Silence; Calm down!
you rue': walk; move on; make room.

TREASURE HELD

"*Gay-bert-e-jaym - sear-seary*, die Turkish tramp!"
Umer shrieked as he plunged his knife over the horse's
back to the place of the rider. He met no resistance. The
saddle was empty! His swing threw him off balance. He
fell as the startled animal jumped forward. Snarling with
rage Umer stumbled up to spring again at the other
horse, but the startled pack animal blundered into him.
Again he fell. His scream pierced the night, as the
frightened horse stepped on him and ran to the length of
its tether causing the other horses to run forward. The
light of the rising moon didn't help him. The horses were
gone, still running. He nursed his bruised thigh, crying
with frustration as much as pain. He remembered there
was a man hunting him, so he wept silently.

"What happened? Why are we running?" Startled, Leyla clung to Kynan's neck. She had previously slept in his arms. Now she hung on desperately.

He was trying to slow the pack animal at the end of the tether. The saddle horses caught up with it. Reassured, they calmed down and slowed together. He looked down at her, the treasure on his saddle. "I don't know. Someone or something frightened the horses. I was half asleep."

She sat up before him, half turned, to state worriedly. "I heard an angry oath and then a scream." She shivered in fear. "It sounded like Umer."

He looked around distractedly. "I'll go back and see."

She caught him close and hung on. "No, don't go back. Whatever he tried failed. Tanra has saved us. It's only moon-rise. You won't be able to see anything. He might hide or hurt you. Don't leave me. Never leave me."

He listened with joy and offered generously. "You would be safe here. I could finish him off."

Her head shook. "I'm only safe with you. If he's hurt badly enough the others will find him. We need time to get farther away."

He relaxed and nodded. "Yes, they would kill me as gladly as he would. We should make contact with the tribe in a few days. There you'll be safe." He tried to reassure her. Then he felt moisture on his neck, he touched her cheek. Tears? But they were safe! He leaned forward to hear her whisper.

"My dear father, he won't see them. He won't see my happiness. He won't see his brother in the north lands. To be murdered and buried in a foreign land." Her body shook again and he pressed her close, soothing.
No sound came from before or behind. The horses plodded on wearily hour after hour. Too soon the dawn would come and the need to hide another day. Water and grass would be lacking for the horses. They slept again.

> - - - - - > GOAT HERDER HILL > - - - - - >
Katchy glowered angrily over the mix of trails near his spring and pastured hill. The man who had robbed him

had come to the foot of the hill and then ridden away at a run. Leyla and Kerim had ridden away north before or after, with an extra animal. They had not followed the thief, but someone else had chased him. The good man, for so Katchy esteemed him, had arrived with two animals but used only one for the chase. He knew by the sounds that night that the chase stopped abruptly and in the quiet someone stalked another. He snorted his disgust. He remembered his fear lest the thief return. He had not known the true extent of his loss until morning light. He would have to skimp on food.

He was contemplating following the tracks to their conclusion, when the bag above the thorn clump swayed in the dawn breeze. He knew it immediately: money! Did Kerim pay the good man for the pack horse? He had paid Katchy a fat price for the kid. The purse bulged with more than the price of a horse: surely enough to recompense him his losses as well. Then as he searched for the right stone he saw the three coins beneath the tree. With a shriek of joy he pounced on the trove. He drooled over the beauty of the copper, shined them with spit. He held them up for the admiration of the flock that moved slowly past. He looked up at the bag again and slowly lowered his hand. What he had was so little and above him was so much. He knew the message that Kerim intended for him to understand. He put the coins away, but he was not content.

He picked up a sharp edged rock and threw it. The sound of coin on coin followed the rock's impact. Katchy smiled in anticipation. He retrieved the rock and threw again with force and accuracy at the same spot. A silver sparkle arced out and down in the early sun. Katchy cackled with delight as he pounced on the coin. A well paid man had no need of revenge, let the thief go. His next throw brought a shower of coins from the enlarging cut. His noisy shouts stirred the goats into voice. He immediately threw again to bring more coins; to make the hunt worthwhile. He was so preoccupied with gathering the booty amid the thorns, that he failed to hear the sound of approaching horses. His arms were reaching between the thorn branches.

"The little man has struck gold it seems. Someone pays well for silence." Ayden bey's voice struck fear in Katchy's heart. He bleated.

"Now he calls for his flock to help him, but they are neglected and scattered. So who is the goat?" Ilhan quipped as he put his horse between the boy and the flock. Ayden drew his bow to ready and warned.

"Don't try to duck under the horses' belly to escape. We have to talk. We need information."

Katchy stood slowly and carefully his hands still filled with coins. He opened his hands and let the coins slide away to fall to the rocks and red dust. The men smiled appreciatively.

"That's better. We talk as men without the distractions of gold. You sent us to the mountains; did the man go to the west?" Ilhan asked.

"The evil one robbed my food while I was gone. A good man came at dusk to chase him away and they ran south. This morning I came to track thief and found good man's money bag."

Ayden laughed and sneered. "Then you rob the good man to recompense his goodness and join the thief in supplying your needs from what is not yours."

Katchy pouted and then suddenly looked around. The sound of an approaching horse alerted them all. A weary Atilla bey came round a thorn thicket on a tired horse. His smile became broad as he saw his friends of the chase.

They exchanged looks of surprise and suspicion. "Atilla bey? How do you get here? What news?" They queried.

Atilla promptly rode up and put on a brave air. "I continued the hunt, for I knew that we were close. I found the murderer just here at the foot of the hill - on my horse, if you please. Since I buy nothing but the best, I was hard put to overtake him. When he was near to being caught he pulled into bush and gully country and hid in the dark." He shook his head sagely. "We played hide and seek for hours and I know I nearly had him twice. Oh he's a slippery devil and dangerous too, but I'll have my horse back yet."

"This little thief sent us on the wrong road and we returned to find him robbing your purse. That is, if you are the good man he talks about who left it here?" Ayden prompted while Ilhan scrutinized them.

"I planned to return here and spend the day to rest and start again tomorrow. The boy would help provide meat and find the trail. I'll owe him tonight. Perhaps he would have bought supplies for me? I'll stay and settle with him unless you men have something more."

Ayden spoke again. "If you stay here you'll have company for tonight. We met a party coming this way. A cart with an old woman and three boys is traveling west. They got off the main track and needed directions, or so they said. Your hospitality will be stretched."

Atilla bey shrugged and lifted his hands eloquently with a proud smile saying. "Allah supplies for guests, none of mine have ever complained. With a mother's cooking and three hearty men to talk adventure we will have a great night of it." The men pulled their horses to one side, but Ilhan pointed at the herd boy with a stern message.

"Please Allah, you made an honest mistake sending us east, but I'll talk to Kooskoo bey. If there's treachery in you, we'll know how to repay you." The men departed swiftly. They returned to Sheriff Tewfik to report on all they had met and seen. There was still a murderer loose.

> - - - - - >TANRA DAH ARMY BASE > - - - - - >
"Open the door, smuggler. We know you just arrived with illegal goods. Unbar the door or we'll break it down. Do you hear?" The pounding increased in volume waking the village. Pie dogs barked, scavenger cats howled, babies woke to cry. Women screamed and men shouted for quiet as they tried to hear where and whom the authorities were threatening.

"One trip too many, I didn't want to go again, but you would have it so. Now the base commander intends to dig us out." Big Aziz stood up from the food covered breakfast table to complain to mean, little Yavuz in a fierce whisper. Kadir, the guard inside the door, whipped out his sword and moved a trunk before the buffeted door. He made a motion with his head to the rest.

"Get out the roof window, they'll have the house cut off and surrounded soon. Be quick!" Yavuz scampered and was up to the window in an instant. Young Korkmaz grabbed some bread and food, put it in a bag and followed. Kadir went out next and Aziz strained to get his mass through the small window. Kadir pulled him from the roof and the great bulk gradually passed as the door crashed in below. Noise and chaos followed inside. They descended the roof at a low corner that was built into a wall. They dropped over into the neighbor's land and ran to a low brushy ditch that carried them to the edge of the village. Several guards saw their movement from a distance, but made no outcry. They would collect their reward later, for smugglers paid well.

"Split here, we meet tonight at the rock cave." Aziz growled as they started each for a private hiding place.

"*Allah korusoon,* God protect you." Each faithfully repeated the invocation as they moved in different directions.

> - - - - - >FRONTIER VILLAGE > - - - - - >

"Bolben Bey, soldiers are here." The home owner shouted as the door vibrated with blows to break the bar.

"Quick, to the tunnel! Jon, follow me." Jon and Sesli were in the room breakfasting and resting. Maril had retired too ill to eat more than a bite. Manish, too, was elsewhere.

Bolben ran to the kitchen where a low wooden barrel stood. The cook opened the top, she lifted out a bin of flour and set it on a low table and Bolben jumped down inside. His head was still visible and he motioned to Sesli and Jon to follow suit. They followed as his head disappeared down the ladder. They jumped in and the woman replaced the flour and top as the soldiers forced the door with a crash.

The soldiers pushed through the door and spread out to search. The onbasha seized the owner and was shaking him vigorously. "Smuggler, leach, we know you have people in the house. Where are they? The commander wants them."

A surprised Manish came into the room. Manish spoke as a soldier searched the owner, roughly patting him down.

"I'm here behind you. I'm a shepherd from the hill country here to buy for my master." The onbasha pushed the owner to one side and turned. Manish tried to look calm.

"A Uigur? What would a boy from the land of war want in the land of peace?" A scream echoed through the house. It was Maril. The onbasha reacted and ran to the bedroom door.

"*Kadun-muh*? a woman? Don't molest her! Bring her here." He turned to the homeowner, smiling lecherously. "Bringing in entertainers for the troops, huh? Let's have a look at this one."

Manish spoke quickly. "She's the daughter of a rich merchant just returned from Tang China. She was lost from the main body and I guided her here. I hoped for a reward from the family."

A distraught and exhausted Maril was pushed into the large room. She tried to run to Manish, but was restrained. He walked over to stand beside her. The onbasha was unimpressed; she lacked the outstanding attributes and proportions that troops expect in entertainers. He looked at his men as they returned from the back.

"Anything in the kitchen?" Two guards bounced their noses up in a negative gesture. One spread his hands and answered. "A meal was prepared and eaten, but only the cook is there."

The onbasha scowled at the table where bits of dry fruit were scattered over its top. His annoyance surfaced. "There should have been more than these four. Go over the house again. The commander will not be pleased with only a skinny girl and a shepherd boy. Open the trunks. Look for hidden holes or storage places. I know a lot of the smuggler's arts. There'll at least be money and goods these thieves have brought to Dar al Islam.'"

> - - - - - >TANRA DAH ARMY BASE > - - - - - >

Sanjak's arrival at the base caused little stir, few would know or care that he had led a caravan of expelled refugees from Tang China. There was too much excitement to notice a new officer.

The village was alive with the stories of the smugglers and captured goods. A girl too, the daughter of a rich merchant, was now sheltered in the Commander Onat's harem in his mother's care - held for ransom no doubt. The Uzbek shepherd boy was in prison with several surly smugglers caught with foreign, untaxed goods. The village had little else to do. Frontier posts that serve the army always fluctuate between boredom and animated speculation. They have entertainment and excitement by night but little else than gossip to occupy their days. Except when away on a trip with the excuse of business or relatives; each villager eked out a living in boredom. This made the act of smuggling an addictive passion for the thrills it automatically provided as well as the needed revenue that neglected army posts lacked.

Another Turkish officer was of little importance because migrants and converts to Islam were the usual reinforcements on the cold, northern frontier. Arab troops were in elite squads in the south or east, in climates much like their own. There the

41

cities and commerce of empire flourished. In the north a Turkish frontier loomed. That line with the nomadic tribesmen was then manned by Turks enticed for many reasons toward the southern civilized lands, but employed in the preferred occupation of their people: as soldiers. As long as the line did not move, all was well. Each side could raid occasionally and defy the other in thievery or good natured rivalry, but any real drive for the Turkish tribal homelands would result in heavy desertions from the army and determined resistance by hordes of angry nomads who could well endanger the southern cities. Thus the frontier remained stable from the first conquest. The main income for all was not from the spoils of war, but by the smuggling of goods and some honest efforts toward trade of salt, felt, hides and meat. Wood and stone work existed for a few artisans. Story telling and music were the common sources of entertainment. The tea houses were full of soldiers, hungry for diversion after another day like all the others of army life.

> - - - - - >IN THE SMUGGLERS' VILLAGE > - - - - - >

Bolben groaned his complaints as they sat in the dark cellar in the chill air. The atmosphere is great for the preservation of fruits, vegetables and other goods (whether legitimate or smuggled) but cold enough for it to be uncomfortable for the hidden refugees. Sesli sat shivering in a corner.

"We should be able to get back to the house as soon as the soldiers leave, shouldn't we? Why don't they come call us?" Jon asked worriedly. Bolben shrugged.

"They may have posted someone in the house to watch. They also may be probing the walls and floor for tunnels. It's common enough. We must wait till they call." Sesli moved in the corner and called out to them, patting the ground on either side of her.

"Come here, I'm cold and I want to sleep. You must keep me warm." Her tone was angry and demanding. Bolben spoke to the dark surroundings with a sigh.

"None of my village will ever believe that I slept with the escaped harem girls."

> - - - - - >ON THE ROAD TO BAGHDAD > - - - - - >

Mansur Ibn el Ari was tired and angered. It had taken hours to get the mass of men into an organized body of moving columns. His adjutants, young men like himself, had been of little experience or help. A few of the old hands who served with his father had been able to help the body of cavalry to strike out ahead. However, since the adjutants had overestimated the speed of the infantry and the distance to be covered, the exhausted men were still straggling into camp in the dark. Hungry and tired the youth sat in his tent waiting for the men to be fed first. He was following his father's advice and stories of hardships and leadership to the letter. He wondered if a well fed commander might not show greater leadership and ingenuity. News of the nomads attack on a farming village had just come in. He decided to divide the army into two sections. A large, fast advanced group of light cavalry scouts with horses and camels as baggage carriers to contact and harrass the enemy until the slower column of men and supply carts arrived. The adjutants and old timers could get the army into shape while he gained the glory of first blood with the tribe. İt was Allah's justice that they be punished for attacking the village and stealing the store of food. The area Kaymakan would be grateful and his own ability and leadership lauded in all Khorasan. His father -- no, the whole of Islam would see his greatness. He went out to the cook's tents where men were still eating. Two men watched his progress toward the tents.

"Look here, our little lamb appears. Will he give us bile or honey for our day of turmoil?" Abdullah asked Magazi.

"It's for us to listen and measure the heart of our commander. We begin the process of becoming one in purpose, or of division and distrust. On this hinges the battle."

"*Soos*, hush, he's speaking!"

"Come men, I will sample your food and enjoy it with you. We fight together and gain glory for Islam together. Let us share in this too." His wise words thus gained the approval of his men. It earned him a quick meal. In a few weeks he would want to use their vigor against the alien Chipchak mercenaries.

PEOPLE, PLOTS & PLACES IN CHAPTER 4

Tayze: is anxious about Erben and Leyla's safety.
Fatma: must marry a man she does not love.
Gerchin: greed moves him to seize wealth and beauty.
Ishmael: decides to play fast and loose with love.
Kaymakan: this official keeps order in the villages.
Kemeer: can only protest violation of the peace.
Kerim of the East Bulgars: a fugitive's assumed name.
Kynan: finds protecting a princess arduous work.
Leyla: decides men aren't to be trusted anywhere.
Sevman: the cripple is anxious to get the correct road.
Sulema: a village girl chooses the road to trouble.
Umer: is still full of tricks seeking survival.
Yeet: finds danger in exploring and helping.

GLOSSARY:
Allah: God of the Muslims.
Allah korusun: God protect you.
Bock: look.
Booy roon: behold; look around; here it is.
Emdot: Help; Rescue me!
hanjir: sharp pointed knife to make sewing holes.
howdah: a box for passengers mounted on a camel.
Kim siniz: Who are you? Who's there?
setch: choose; decide.
Tanra: old Creator God of the eternal blue sky.
yetishin: help; give me a hand.

LEYLA STRIKES

"We've traveled all day and still not got to the goat corral or the hill spring the troopers talked about." Sevman complained, "Yeet, you ride on ahead to look for it. There are two on the horizon, see which one is the right destination." The two wheeled cart squeaked slowly ahead.

"Okay, I'll get things ready for you and gather the water from the seep. Look for the red signal cloth on the hill top." Yeet was glad to be away from the glum group who were lost, yet looking for the tribe that was supposed to be somewhere in this vicinity. Not daring to ask and seek directions directly they wandered ever westward, ever dryer, seeking what they only hoped was there.

Yeet looking ahead split the difference between the two peaks thinking it would be easier to spot a bit of verdure being closer to both. The midday sun was focused, but the coming winter tempered its bite. He rode on and on.

"*Kim siniz*? Who are you? Answer me. You have nothing to fear." The horse he had heard whickered again. Looking about carefully Yeet found a lonely black horse wandering riderless. It was both hungry and thirsty. It was still saddled and bridled, but, evidently, lost. He came wearily toward Yeet dragging his reins. Yeet dismounted to examine the animal more closely. There were some oats in the back pack and a water bag. Yeet first watered the beast, filling Sevman's leather Kirgiz hat with the short brim and after it had drunk twice poured some of the oats into the hat. He loosened the cinch and fed and watered his own horse so he wouldn't be jealous of the new comer. Then they walked.

"This should fix you up. You'll feel better soon. Now, you wouldn't have run away in the state you're in, so you must have lost your rider some other way." When people were not present, Yeet talked to animals. The silence was absolute from the nearby thorn and rocks so Yeet started looking for hoof prints to back track the animal. He feared the rider would be in the same or worse condition than the horse had been. Together they all started back as Yeet followed the dim trail. After an hour Yeet stopped in disgust, he had lost the tracks again.

"I wish I were a better tracker. You came on your own, but I can't trust you to find your starting point. We are between the two hills now and I can't see much difference from here. So what are you doing here? I wish you could talk. Hi, Tanra, what am I to do?" They rounded a large thorn thicket where to Yeet's amazement he found a highway of tracks. Three or more horses had been this way, running! He stopped, puzzled.

"Which way to go? Back or forward? How can I find the one who needs help?" He stood for some time, head cocked listening.

"Look over here under the thorn bush, herdsman." The dry and cracked voice penetrated the silence causing both surprise and unease.

"Why didn't you call for help, I would have come faster." He made out the dirty face of a man only some years older than himself, sheltered in the shadow of the bushes. Yeet tied the horses to a bush and took down the water bag.

"You might have been the man who injured me coming back to finish the job. Are you Kirgiz? You wear the hat." Yeet walked toward the youth with the water bag in his hand.

"*Booy roon*, See here, this water's from your saddle. Drink." The boy took and drank. "Your horse took most of it. Let's see where you're hurt." He stared at the boy closely and startled back, gasping in surprise.

"You're Umer! From the quarry! You blinded Kardesh."

"*Hi Allah*, Yeet the knife thrower, aren't you? I didn't think you looked Kirgiz even with the hat. So you told me what you would do if we weren't careful. So now you can do it. You have your knife."

Yeet stood with his mouth open. "You want me to kill you? You show no mercy, so you expect none?"

Umer snarled and pulled his tunic open at the neck tearing it, exposing his chest. "I'm not afraid to die. I've killed. I'd be a coward to fear you, little knife thrower. You don't like to get too near or feel the blood spill on your hand. You'd be afraid to face me knife to knife. Better throw while you can." Umer crawled forward from the bush and tried to stand as he drew his knife. He fell back dropping his knife and exposing a blue and swollen thigh under his torn shalvar. He lay exhausted, with his eyes closed tight, grimacing. He cried out in a tense voice, "Oh Allah! Kill me Yeet. Let me die like a man!" Tears tracked down his dirty face.

"Is your leg broken then? No escape by horse or by walking? No hope? Slow death?"

"Keep your pity, use your knife."

Yeet stood shaking his head slowly. "I prefer to leave you to *Yesu*. Meditation with pain sharpens the sense of justice and judgment to come. You might find salvation."

Umer glared. "I blinded your friend trying to kill him, killed a rich old woman, got two friends killed and I'll add you to their number if you don't get me first."

"Tanra has not made me executioner or judge. I leave you to justice by God or the law as He prefers. I'll keep your place and condition secret. You have a little water and time." Umer turned and wiggled toward his fallen

47

knife. Yeet stepped and kicked the knife away and stood just beyond his fingers.

"You have caused others pain and death. You will now have time to face them both and God. I'll go." Yeet walked to the horses. Umer twisted around to see.

"The Turk, he robbed a packhorse that I wanted back. He killed a khan and stole his daughter. I tried for the horse, but got stepped on. There's a reward for the girl and the gold's in the pack. Follow their trail, they'll lay up by day, they can be yours if you're brave." Yeet released the horses and mounted his. He looked over the trail carefully and started toward their source.

Umer groaned. "Don't go Yeet! You can bring the searchers. I'll tell the judge everything about the robbery. You would be a hero. Don't let me die alone. Show a little mercy." Yeet stopped and released the lost horse's reins and the animal halted and remained when Yeet started. Yeet spoke first to the horse.

"You will stay with your rider so he won't be alone. If he can't ride, you can come down this trace later where there's food and water."

He looked at Umer and spoke angrily. "You must eat what you've gathered, so don't whine. No one made you do these things. Isa said, 'ask and you will receive.' You ask for mercy which you have never shown. I'll grant you a small mercy, the company of your horse. A larger mercy, come to our camp and we'll feed you both. You can ask Kardesh's pardon for his eyes. He'll probably forgive you. The choice and effort are yours to make. May you, too, learn how to show mercy." He rode off, up the trail toward the high hill that showed some signs of green. He did not look back as Umer started crawling painfully toward his weary horse.

> - - - - - >BETWEEN HILLS WITH LEYLA> - - - - - >

"Kerim, what are you thinking about?" Leyla lay beside a thorn bush enjoying the warm feeling of sun on her back. Her scratches still hurt, but she was content. Kynan lay sprawled with his head on the saddle which was on the ground near the horse-pack. He stared into the sky lazily after sleeping most of the morning.

"Wondering what I'll say to the Toozlu leaders when we meet the tribe."

She tossed her head indignantly and observed sharply. "That you have rescued the Khan Erben's daughter. You return her to her people. What else would you say?"

He yawned and put on a grin. "I could ask if they really want her or how much she's worth."

She kicked out at him and managed to touch his foot.

"I'm wounded in my proclamation of truth." He moaned and nursed his pretended injury. She stared him down, half amused half annoyed, nearly laughing. Then she let out a little titter and relaxed. She again reached out the foot, this time to rub his leg as if to sooth it.

"Bey, you'll get a reward you know. Everyone will be very grateful. I..." She couldn't go on. She drew her foot back coyly, waiting.

"I can only be your protector now. Your tribe will not accept me. To them I'm an enemy. They may drive me out."

"We've had no wars with the East Bulgars recently. We've exchanged youths with them to be educated in their court."

"Yes, we exchange hostages, youths to learn foreign ways, but what standing do these youths have in your camp."

She was puzzled. "I don't know, I saw a few working the herds. They served the warriors in the bachelor halls and ate with them."

"Exactly, no status and abused by those they served. The fate of all who go on exchanges. I know it first hand."

She frowned and sat up, folding her arms she spoke decisively. "Yes, we need to think this through and decide on how to proceed when we meet them. It might be good to watch a day before making contact. I wonder if Twozan or Gerchin will be in charge.

49

"It won't matter, their attitude will be hostile. After they have you in their control, they will turn me out if they don't kill me first." She looked at him sadly and shook her head. She spoke hesitantly.

"We don't have to go to the tribe. We could return to your country. They would receive you, wouldn't they?"

He moved his head up in a disdainful negative. Then he gave a little laugh. "They would take you away from me, princess, and marry you to one of their own princes. Then they would have power with the Chipchaks. A chance to mix in politically and gain points."

They lay quietly. Then he added, "You are grateful, yet endangered, no one could interfere if I took you by force. No one would blame you, but any of these people, here or there, would kill me for violating a princess. There is no hope, only temptation in this, our present situation."

They turned away from each other. There was nothing left to say. And each, pretending to sleep, considered their predicament. His face was lined with worry, her face wore a pout.

> - - - - - >IN THE THORNBUSH > - - - - - >

After the long dry afternoon, Leyla's curiosity was piqued. She felt as if someone were talking. Yet she heard nothing. But the evening wind seemed to pick up and blow murmurs and whispering to her ears. Secrets and laughter mixed in her mind as she restlessly fidgeted and medicated her bruises and healing scratches. Kerim slept again. 'Men are such sluggish brutes', she sighed, gazing at him longingly, wishing he would awake and talk to her. Again she felt rather than heard another whisper. The giggles started again in her stomach and moved to her mouth. She quickly suppressed the sound and smile. She quietly arose and moved toward the high hill that towered in the near foreground. She walked as one stalking prey, moving from cover to cover, pausing to listen and watch. She tied her horse.

Now she did hear something: a tinkling of metal; a muffled shout; the spontaneous tittering, and the splash of water. Her throat felt its dryness. She wanted to rush to the sound and plunge her face in the water, but she stopped to watch and wait, pressing close to the ground.

Then she saw in the distance on a rocky prominence on the west side of the hill, a village of mud buildings, which were protected by cliffs around the base. A narrow trail led up to the crags guarding the little village.

The seep springs above gathered in a tiny pool below the cliff. A few girls were congregated around the pool, some with water jars on their shoulders. The pool was enclosed in stone work and the source protected. The overflow plunged over the lip of a carved stone to run further down the hill. Small orchards lined either side below the tiny brook. The spill was used on the orchards until it was between the fields and thorny desert.

The girls would go home before dark. Leyla decided to wait and take water back with her to present to Kerim when he woke: her surprise and gift. She listened to the banter.

"You must be counting the days now Fatma." One girl exclaimed and all giggled exchanging glances.

"I hear he is quite rich. You will never have to go to fetch water." Another suggested.

Still another quipped. "You will get all the village news second hand. What a pity."

Fatma sat by the stone spill-way that filled the line of pots, but said nothing in return. This silence irritated the girls who renew their attempts to get a reaction from her.

"Riches have their price you know." Said the first. "I hear the widower has gray in his beard. And you will be number two for him, not the first beloved."

"A man of experience, why won't you be happy with the arrangement?" The girls exchanged glances and encouraged each other in their goading of their companion. "Would you prefer a closer poorer match?" Laughter followed the question. And another made the statement. "She has already been as close as it's possible to get to him." At that moment the girl sitting silently beside the fountain erupted in a passion of fury.

She launched herself against the body of the accuser and carried her to the ground, pitcher and all, in a flurry of blows and screams.

"Stop this disgrace, now!" A powerful male baritone cut through the shrieks of the girls. A turbaned man pushed through the thronged watchers and pulled the girls apart one in each hand shaking them vigorously. He scowled at the offenders and at the open-mouthed children and girls.

"What are you doing here so near dark? Your mothers are waiting for water. Get it to them. Go!" Mounting jars on their shoulders, they went in a wordless rush up the slope.

"Now, you two, what have you to say?" Fatma took a seat by the fountain's edge again. She spoke first. "Your pardon Kaymakan bey, I could not bear the insult. I ask your forgiveness, but not her's."

"Sulema, why did you insult her?" Sulema looked bleakly at the official. She ducked her head and whispered. "I repeated what I heard my big sister say. I thought she knew all about it."

The Kaymakan's eyes narrowed. "You repeat the gossip and wonder that you are attacked?" His eyes hardened, he shifted his gaze to Fatma. "Is there truth in this accusation?"

She had lowered her veil and met his eyes for a moment, shaking her head. "My family would be disgraced if I met him alone."

He nodded agreement. He motioned Sulema up the slope and she filled her pitcher and left. He waited a long minute. "I heard her words. Let there be no truth in it, now go quickly, your mother is fretting with worry by now." The Kaymakan continued by the water, listening and waiting. Finally he turned and made his way up the slope.

Leyla breathed a sigh and led her horse to the water. She filled her leather water bottles and buried her face in the cool flow. Then she put her head under and rubbed her hair vigorously. She reached into her waistband where a small bag was tucked away. Out of it she drew a leaf wrapped lump of soap. She occupied herself with the washing in the twilight darkness. When she finished she used her waistband to dry her hair and folded up the soap. Turning she found her way blocked by a man with his hands on his hips staring at her.

"Why would a tribal maid linger two days behind her people? Are you lost little fool?" From behind on the path came the worried voice of a girl running, out of breath.

"What is it Ishmael? Is someone there?" He turned and caught her, pulled her before the confounded Leyla. It was the girl Sulema. He laughed as the two stared.

"See my luck with women, Sulema? First the prudish Fatma who loves, but resists me. Then yourself, a willing slave to all I want. Now variety comes to add the spice of resistance to my conquest. A tribal wildcat lagging behind her people. I shall have sport tonight." He pushed Sulema forward into the face of Leyla. He caught Leyla's wrist as she raised her hands. Twisting Leyla's arm behind her he caught the other hand searching for her knife. He shoved the girl to the ground, throwing his weight on her body as she twisted beneath him.

Sulema ran and bent protesting to him. "You love me! What foolishness is this? Why take from her what I'm willing to give? You dropped Fatma for me. You swore it."

He looked at her face an instant and laughed. "Fatma loved honor more, you love what I give. I love what I'll do to her. Here, pull down her *shalvar*. Her face is down so she can't bite."

Sulema drew back in anger. "No, I'll scream, the men will come."

"Ruin yourself and your family. The men will join me after I'm through with this damned nomad. Go to her feet, pull the shalvar down." She stood indecisive, then turned away moving toward the path. Leyla, spitting dirt and getting her breath, turned her face to shout; "*Emdat*, help! *Yetishin*, rescue me."

Ishmael with an elbow shoved her face in the dust again and pressed her down. As he bent an arrow tugged the jacket on his back making a metal click on something in his sash. With a shout Ishmael released both wrists and pulled his *hanjir* pressing it to Leyla's neck as he pulled her over before him. He shouted loudly. "Down the bow or she's dead." Silence followed Ishmael's threat. Sulema forgot to go up the path. Leyla lay still as death, waiting. Ishmael strained his eyes to see.

"Did you hear me nomad? Down the bow or she dies." The sound of a horse moving rapidly toward the fountain made him turn, but the riderless, running horse continued, stopping only to drink deeply of the water beside Leyla's horse. Its saddle was empty. Sulema gave a little cry and moved toward Ishmael.

He cursed and commanded. "Why don't you scream now? Get the men down here." She walked to him and bent over him, trembling. He felt the prick of a knife at the base of his skull and a man's urgent whisper.

"She lives, you live. If she dies, you die. *Setch*, choose." Sulema, now freed, gave a little moan and kneeling put her head on Ishmael's shoulder. She reached over and gently took the knife from his hand. Ishmael sat back up with his empty hands open to show the man behind him.

Leyla, now free of all restraint, suddenly moved with the speed of a striking viper. She whipped out her utility knife and plunged it upward under the man's ribs to his heart with a savage twist, wrenching the point in an arc. A shocked "oh," escaped Ishmael's lips and he slipped backward to the ground. Sulema, sobbing hysterically, tried to hold him up. In one bound Leyla was beside her horse. Mounted, she plunged into the brush, her horse's full stomach of water gurgling with each stride. The noise of her going reached to the village.

The man beside Sulema left without a word, running for the horse still drinking at the fountain. He hastily un-slung his water-bag dipping it into the pool and pulling it back immediately. Mounting, Kynan drove his reluctant beast into a run.

Sulema's blood covered hands marked her face as her keening voice rose in sharp ascending notes to alert the village.

Rather than follow Leyla's race toward the tribe, Kynan turned toward the camp where he had left the thirsty pack horse and travel goods.

> - - - - - >RUNNING IN THORNLAND > - - - - - >

Stomach sloshing with water the reluctant horse plunged on in the night. Leyla hoped that Kerim would soon overtake her and speak words of comfort to her heart. As strong as the attachment had become she could not turn back to that hideous village and its people.

Leyla slowed her horse and cried as they walked through the night. She dismounted and let the horse rest while she thought. If the tribe lay ahead two days she could catch up. Let Kerim come as he would. He was denied to her anyway. She would find her people.

Behind her there was a sudden burst of noise. Fear clutched at her heart, she was too close to the village. Something evil was coming behind her. She had to hurry. The horse snorted. She took the reins and started running before it on foot. Her father had taught her that an hour leading and an hour riding would overtake drovers in a day. She would find the tribe first and be among friends. Everything would be solved. She put Kerim out of her mind as she sped through the night. She was going home where she would be safe. She repeatedly sang of her intentions through the night.

> I am going home now, I am riding home;
> Halleluya, I am running home!
> Going home, I'm so glad.
> Friends are waiting for me there.
> I'm going home. Yes, home!
>
> All expect to see me there,
> When I get back home.
> They will celebrate the day;

When I get back home to stay.
I'm going home. Yes, home!

Everyone will visit me
When I get back home.
Laughing we will sing and play;
When I'm safe back home to stay.
I'm going home. Yes, home!

GOING HOME

Refrain I am go ing home now, I am riding home.
Hal-le-lu-ya, I am running home. going home. I'm
so glad. Friends are waiting for me there. I'm go-ing home.
All expect to see me there. When I get back home.
They will cel-e-brate the day, when I'm home to stay Yes, home!

> - - - - - > ON THE ROAD TO BAGHDAD> - - - - - >

"*Bock*, Look, a caravan with a body guard, *Tanram*, how much
wealth they must be carrying. The camels are loaded. See how rich the
tunics and harness." Gerchin mounted on his fierce black stallion was
impatiently leading the tribe westward out of the Kara Kum, meaning
the black sand desert. Gerchin smiled in anticipation, while Kemeer
looked over the scene carefully.

"There are women in the *howdah*, It looks like a wedding to me:
there's a bride, her women, her dowry and guards. They go to that
great valley we crossed two days ago, perhaps they come from
Meshed." He motioned south.

"You were a killjoy in the valley but you won't stop me from my fun now. This is an occasion we won't miss."

Kemeer motioned angrily. "Don't be a fool, we have animals and can't move fast. You'll have the whole district down on us for robbing a wedding procession. The Caliph will have your head."

Gerchin laughed his contempt for all wishes but his own. He whipped from his saddle bag a flag and raised it on his sword, to signal 'rally round'. He pulled out his horn to call them.

Kemeer's face was set in anger, but his status in the tribe was not sufficient to challenge their hero's quick decision. The men riding with them raised a shout. One lifted the pole with the tribe's symbol of Yak tails displayed. At their cries the warriors of the tribe assembled. The very young and old took up their posts guarding the animals while the others drew up and formed a mass of men and horses.

The wedding caravan commander saw the danger. The horse guard drove the cargo animals ahead to form a shield of protection at the rear. The drivers beat the beasts to make them run away from the forming mob of tribesmen. They ran toward the valley.

Like wolves on a herd, the ululating warriors ride down the fleeing band. A steady stream of arrows drive the guards before them, while the small advancing horns of the attack drive around and in, to separate the choice animals and their cargoes. Gerchin and his guard smash into the center where the *howdah* was shielded by the troops. The commander of the guards goes down and the troop collapses. Gerchin with a whoop of triumph takes the bridle of the *howdah* animal while screaming occupants cry for mercy from Allah. Gerchin takes his prize and runs off through the scattering horde. The guards continue to flee while the attackers loot any of the goods they can overtake. Drivers dump their cargo packs to escape. All discipline is lost on both sides. Groups stop to pick over the packs and rob the dead. Shouts of triumph, fear and death fill the air.

STEPPE FLOWERS

PEOPLE, PLOTS & PLACES IN CHAPTER 5

Abdullah: protests the management of the army.
Atilla: meets people who enjoy adventures.
Baja: the sister of Aziz loves her nephew Korkmaz.
Chichek: helps her mistress plan the wedding.
Gerchin: reacts angrily to conflicts over his actions.
Katchy: hears a rider, but doesn't know he's a friend.
Kaymakan: the village authority cares for the wounded.
Korkmaz: hides a friend and picks up supplies visiting.
Leyla: runs to join the Toozlu, hoping Kerim will follow.
Manish: feels better after a prison interview.
Mansur Ibn el Ari: follows a trail of destruction.
Nooryouz: stops hiding to save her baby's life.
Onat: interviews his prisoners.
Seerden: sets a trap while obeying the Gray Wolf.
Setchkin: Shows off her plans and sparks envy.
Sevman: tries in vain to protect his friend.
Umer: finds people to rescue him in his distress.
Yeet: seeks friends, but finds much more on arrival.

GLOSSARY:
Aslan Atlar'um: I'm of the Lion Horse Tribe.
ben'de: I, too; I am.
Boo rah dah yam: Here I am; I'm here.
Dekot: Attention; Careful; Danger!
deli kan'la: youth; young people; crazy blood.
Emdat: Help; attend me!
hivan: animal; contemptible.
kaymakan: a village or regional authority.
kim oh: who is it: who's there.
pida: a flat bread that travels well.

UMER'S ARRIVAL

"Help, *imdat*, help me, please. The nomads have destroyed me. Hear me, someone, Allah, Allah, hear my cry." An immediate hubbub of voices responded to Umer's cry, as his horse followed the guiding sound of trickling water in the darkness.

"Someone's hurt!"

"Careful it could be a trick."

"Who goes there?"

"The horse stumbles."

"Someone clings to the saddle."

"It's a body over the saddle."

"The horse won't stop!"

"Let him get a drink, then he'll stop."

The crowd gathered about the drinking horse. "I'm Umer, set upon by nomads, my leg's broken, be careful." He gritted his teeth over a cry as they lifted him down from the horse. They laid him down beside another body. The smell of blood caught Umer's attention. He gagged for a moment, then, he spoke. "They caught you unexpectedly, did they? Killed your people?"

"The main body passed two days ago. They gave no trouble, but tonight there were stragglers or stalkers and they killed Ishmael," the village kaymakan responded.

"They attacked me and I was trampled by their horses and left for dead." A murmur of sympathy spread through the crowd. One man shook his fist in rage.

"We should go after them and make them pay, life for life." Many voices agreed.

"We stand no chance in the dark, they are animals. We will stay, care for this man, and report it to the military. They will know how to proceed," the kaymakan stated. "We must care for the victim now."

Sulema spoke up "There is room in my brother's house. We can provide for his needs." There was a pause of uncertainty, then as men considered the offer and their own situation, agreement.

"We will consider your offer, but first let us bind his wounds and give him water. Judging by his horse they have traveled dry." The kaymakan's words set men into action.

> - - - - - >SMUGGLERS' VILLAGE> - - - - - >

"I hear you made a big haul this trip over," said Baja, the doting Auntie to her young nephew, Korkmaz.

"Enough to make for more arguments and protection money," smiled the boy. "The two inseparable partners reached new lows with threats and insults, while Kedir and I got things done."

" The room burst into titters and guffaws of laughter as the aunt shook her head. "It is a scandal that such men can carry on like that. You must not learn their ways. Tanra does not love such foolishness in men of station and responsibility." The auntie was very tender to the fate of orphans and wished to protect her nephew.

Korkmaz had passed the day visiting friends and relatives with news of the latest moving of goods. As a local boy he had no trouble with questioning by authorities who knew he was active, but whose laws required catching him with the goods. At each place visited he steadily acquired items he needed and secreted away in a bag: dry food, squares of cotton or wool material, a utility knife, a flask of spring water, a small felt jacket, a few skins and quilted coat, even a small bag of yogurt to make ayran. He brushed aside the praise of others to ask for the needed items or simply to help himself.

He wanted to move out of town near sunset at the changing of the guard. He watched carefully as the Onbashas drew up their squads. Some men were owned by the smuggler's guild others were troublemakers anxious to acquire by seizure more that they could obtain by bribe or payments. The stationing of the guards was of vital importance to any nighttime movements. Especially with the new commander's zeal for suppressing the traffic and disregard for the prosperity of the village.

> - - - - - >TRAVELERS' HUT > - - - - - >

"Boo rah dah yam, I'm here, look what I brought you." Korkmaz waited at the closed skin door on the desolate hill until the count of five. Then he tried again; no answer. He slowly straightened up and searched the dark landscape around the hump of stone and earth.

"I'm Korkmaz, we came over the pass last night. I have brought more food." He waited again for a slow count. He heard a slight noise of pebble or movement in the bush to his right.

"You're safe. The soldiers are on normal duty again. The search is over for now." Again he waited and then quietly opened the door and swept the inside with his hand. Next he entered and felt behind the stone top. Nothing remained behind except some old, worn wool clothes. He sat on the stone inside the door and looked out as the stars began to appear. He thought through the night and day of travel and hiding. She would have slept most of the day. She could only have a small lead on him. Where would she go? He stared out the open door. Below the village he could just make out a grove of trees where a water source issued in a tiny stream. It would be the obvious choice of any thirsty person. She would avoid the village but make for the trees and water. There was a trough where the water ran out. Women went there with pails and jars, but after dark few would venture out. Still it was a risk for her to go there and he left the little shelter hurriedly taking the short cut through town.

At the fountain, out of breath he stopped, listened and uttered the low whistle of a night bird, waiting the count of five again to repeat it. Nothing! He started up the slope behind the stone facing of the water source. Perhaps she had not arrived yet.

"*Gel,* come, it is I, your friend Korkmaz. Come to the *cheshme* and drink. I will help you like I did yesterday. Is the baby all right? I worried about him. Please answer."

"What do you plan to do with me?" The voice came softly, hard to locate.

"There is a summer hunting lodge high in the mountains, we use it sometimes. It will take two days to get there but you can hide tonight in one of our caves."

"*Git ah mem,* I can't go, the baby is sick; he has fever. I need another woman, one who knows medicines and plants." Korkmaz felt a chill of anxiety and uncertainty.

"But the village is dangerous and the women don't go out by night. It's a soldiers' town. They frequent the tea houses and bordellos for entertainment," he explained.

"Then I must go in; the women are safe indoors, no? Do you know a wise woman who cares for babies and women?" Her voice trembled as if she were going to cry.

"But everyone in the village will learn about you, nothing can be hidden from them; word spreads among the families." He protested. Her voice was still elusive and seemed to fade. Korkmaz was seized with a fear that she was going away, leaving him.

"All villages have secrets. I'll find a way, if you won't help me." Grass hissed as she moved.

He protested, "*Olmaz,* it can't be. You don't know the dangers. I have an Aunt Baja; she can be trusted and is good with the sick." The voice became urgent, as she came closer.

"Let's go then, we have little time to spare." Her hand caught his arm fiercely; her nails like claws digging into his flesh and he found himself running before her, breathlessly, through the village streets.

> - - - - - >GOAT HERDER HILL> - - - - - >

As the horse drew near the hill, Yeet could see the green amid the brown of the thorn brush. A faint wisp of smoke curled up from the far side of the pasture. The bleat of goats and sheep wafted to his ears on the evening breeze. He hoped that the fire would be cooking Tayze's good bulgur with the day's game. His mouth watered. A faint whirring caused him to check his horse and look to his right as a speeding rock clipped his left earlobe. Yeet screamed out in pain as his startled horse jumped forward. Katchy came leaping out of the brush and was again loading his sling for another throw. The horse, however, was moving at a run toward the smell of water and grass. Yeet seemed to be only partially aware of his situation, bent over on the saddle clutching his blood-soaked head. Katchy shouted in triumph. "Thief steal cheese, bread, make Ketchy poor. Now pay big!"

The group around the campfire stood and strained toward the distant conflict. The horse continued to run toward them and Katchy continued in pursuit whirling his sling around his head. Sevman shouted in dismay as Katchy shot.

"It's Yeet! Stop, Katchy, he's a friend." The others joined his cry.

"Don't hurt him."

"This is a friend we're expecting."

"Don't stop him Katchy."

"Leave him alone."

"You've hurt him."

"Why is he so wild?"

"Why is he attacking people like that?"

The startled horse redoubled his pace and Katchy, angered by his near miss, loaded another rock. The hubbub continued. Atilla Bey mounted his horse and sped toward the tired mount carrying a crouched figure.

Katchy stopped, frustrated by his panicked, scattering flock and the shouting. He sulkily turned from his pursuit and let the stone fly past the nose of the distracted lead ewe, causing her to turn back upon the flock and stop. He kept his distance while the cart party attended to the fainting Yeet.

> - - - - - > BAGHDAD ROAD> - - - - - >

The road traveled by the army from Merv was easy to follow. Broken ground and shrubs or grass were like voices crying: "See, here it is. A thousand men came this way." The trace would remain for years marked by the weight and waste of man and beasts.

Seerden hardly paid it any mind. He rather wondered what Tewfik would think of his lie. Would he really expect

63

him to go north? Was the man an agent or more to the Grey Wolf? What did such a high placed man know of the stakes? It was truly a game in the dark. He decided to avoid the obvious trail and run south into the desert where word would spread more slowly and eyes drawn to the army might miss. With four changes of horse each day he would soon out pace the army. He needed time to organize a barrier at the high pass to the Iranian Plateau.

> - - - - - >OUTSIDE THE TOOZLU CAMP > - - - - - >

It had been a long dreary day driving north with few animals. They had made better time than drovers, but with women and children it was still a matter of slow and steady. So, reluctantly, the Toozlu Clan returned to an uncertain fate in the homeland. The guard, Erly, leaned against his tired horse and let his mind wander. They had traveled far into the south, but had failed to see the cities of wealth. He had neither seen nor gained any of it. He half regretted the decision to return. The *deli-kan-la*; the crazy young warriors had left them for the adventures in the West. Had he been younger he might have joined them, but with his wife wanting to see relatives and go home; he had surrendered the opportunity. The men of his wife's clan would take care of his family if the Toozlu clan was destroyed by Khan Erden.

He sighed, but thought of the coming day. They would remain for a day or two here at the water where a wedding would provide diversion and feasting on the few strays they had encountered beyond the village two days back. The marriage of the Khan to the widow of Erdash was a significant event. Kaplan would be the father-in- law. The Tiger was a big man in all the north. He wondered how the father would take the news. He was never a friend of the Toozlu. They had camped early and his wife would doubtless be preparing for the feasts of the great day. He might get back in time to get a pre-dawn sample of some of the special dishes. He sighed again and rubbed his hands on his arms for warmth.

His horse whickered and moved, ears pointed forward. The guard quickly sniffed the breeze smelling the scent of dust, a sweating horse and the sound of movement. In one liquid movement he stepped behind his animal and had strung his bow and armed it. He remained hidden in the shadow of his horse and waited tensely.

He detected one person only, but it could be a scout for more. From his hill vantage he scanned the horizon in the darkened light and then sought the source of the noise. It had stopped. His whickering horse forestalled the intruder. All was quiet. Calmly he stepped forward then mounted his horse in one leap and plunged ahead charging down the hill.

He caught a glimpse of a tired horse standing alone, the lead limp beside its head. Then from a bush nearby came the victory cry, the ululating voice of a woman. It was the familiar sound of encouragement that women make sending their men off to war. He pulled his horse up sharply beside the new mare and gathered the lead. He looked for the well hidden female and demanded.

"Show yourself. *Aslan At lar um*, I'm of the Lion Horses." The reply came softly.

"*Ben de*, I too." Behind him the form of a girl arose from the shadows and moved forward confidently. He whirled tensely. Now the voice commanded in firm definition.

"Perhaps you do not know me, but I am the princess Leyla, the daughter of Erben the Warrior Khan. I must see your leader." She moved forward and took the halter from his hand mounting with confidence while the man watched passively.

She raised a hand. "Now lead. I'll follow." He produced a horn and blew a call; then he led her uphill as an answering call came from the camp, a squad was coming to help.

> - - - - - >ON THE ROAD TO BAGHDAD > - - - - - >

"Let the world know that the army of the Caliph comes in peace." Two heralds had entered the pillaged village announcing the entrance of the army. Mansur Ibn el Ari had taken the lead into the deserted village hoping to find news of his sought after prey. But no informers had appeared. The people had vanished from the countryside or gone into hiding. Few had seen the nomads, only heard of their passing, those who had seen them were still in hiding.

No news was not good news for the searching army. Food supplies diminished and the villages had little to demand and confiscate to re-supply a hungry column of men. Farmers from the Persian parts of the empire were rarely happy to see Arabs who had little compassion for the problems of agriculture. The army concluded by taking what they found and moving on through an ever diminishing supply base.

There was the puzzle of a missing bridal party with many goods reported lost. After that, nothing, no news. Could they have moved into the deserts? The Great Salt Desert stretched to the south and the Kara Kum, black sands to the north; only a corridor of fertile mountains and valleys connected east with west, yet this lay in ruins. One tribe, armed for war, could have its will among the defenseless farm villages. They were passing outside the jurisdiction of Khorasan, the frontier province, and were trespassing on the jurisdiction of others who would doubtless be well represented in court at Baghdad. Yet his men were not paid in goods of conquests nor spoils of war. The house of Ibn el Ari would suffer loss without the compensation of glory.

"*Kishi var*, someone's here." The call came from one of the heralds. Mansur rode to his side and stared at the covered bundle of rags. He kicked the bundle and a tearful wail rewarded his effort. A woman half-concealed in the dark burka sobbed hopelessly.

"Where are your men? Where are the villagers?" Mansur demanded.

"Look sir," The herald intervened. "There's a child in her lap. I think its dead."

"Bread, Sir, give me food. I'm starving, help me." Mansur drew back from the hand.

"Where is your husband? Answer me." She made a vague wave toward the hills. The tribe has sent the people away without food. I was too ill and weak to follow. They dare not return. There is water, but no food here." Mansur waved to the heralds and officers to turn away from the village and continue past it.

"There is no help of food here or men to recruit. On to the pass." He angrily determined to push on.

Abdullah groaned and whispered to his dearest friend as they rode. "May Allah curse the ambitious and clever leaders. They disregard rewards and ease to exhaust their friends so that their pride and name might be inflated." No answer came as they passed the neglected woman to drop a handful of pide bread in her lap.

"We will correct his notions at an opportune time."

"Yes, by ending his power to hold them."

> - - - - - >TANRA DAH ARMY BASE > - - - - - >

The dungeon was dark and cold. The sounds of the streets had quieted. Quiet comes with fear to dreary places. The Uigur shepherd boy, Manish, huddled against the wall with the thin blanket wrapped around his small, trembling body. After questioning he had sat nursing his bruises and wondering what would happen next. Would his friends manage to stay hidden? How much would the garrison know of the search for them by the Uigur village at the bottom of the mountain? Would they not know of the harem escape? A sound came from the corridor. A door slammed nearby. Keys rattled at his door. Noise too, brought fear. A tall powerful figure entered his cell. He drew back in fear.

"*Korkma*, don't be afraid, I know you have traveled far. I brought you a felt shepherd's cloak such as you use. The boy gratefully received the heavy material and was soon nearly lost in the folds. The man sat on the floor next to him and nodded approval.

"You are very brave and we will send you home after you tell us your story. Do you know the Uigur village was destroyed? The ones who chased you?" He waited.

"You help no one by being silent. You wouldn't want me to send you back there? They would be angry. They know you slipped by them. I can get you home another way if you tell me the truth." Slowly the boy shifted position beginning to warm. He hesitated and then thankfully reached for the bread offered him. It was travelers' bread; carried for long journeys. He decided he could trust such a man and replied in a hoarse whisper.

"You will send Maril to her people?" The answer came warm and quick.

"My mother cares for her now and will not easily give up one she is spoiling. But I will send her to her family this week. She answered my questions. I know there are more than two. The ones from this village will be dealt with today. You cannot help them. The others will be safer in our hands." The boy tucked his chin down and replied.

"You will not send them back to Uigur lands? You will let them go as they will?"

"I am here to keep the border open to honest men and trade. Holy Law applies to all equally. You are in the land of peace now. The land of war lies behind you. You may remain or return as you like. We are not at war with the Uigurs at this time, but we would not return your travelers to them so you can rest assured. We know you followed a band of smugglers over the pass and know nothing about them. They are local people. We will know all about them from local sources. Now tell me about your friends.

> - - - - - > A TOOZLU RAIDER'S YURT> - - - - - >

High on the mountain in a small, but protected valley, the yurts were placed in the traditional order and the animals cropped on the dry grass cured to hay on the frosted slopes. The yurt of the tribe's master was quiet with tension. A sullen wife pretended to be busy about the fire while a timid, sobbing girl huddled in a corner. Gerchin sat handling and admiring the newly acquired goods, ornaments, satins and money piled near the door. He and some tribesmen admired the accumulated goods. They laughingly joked.

"Our yurts are full, but here you have garnered the best treasures, my Khan. How did you manage to gather this while enjoying the pleasure of a second wife?"

He smiled. "A true warrior never disappoints a woman's expectations. She was to get a husband and have a good romp and she did."

Another said: "Her companions went fast enough, but there weren't enough for all."

"The biggest hands gather the most."

"The slenderest fingers pick the jewels."

"The knowing eye discerns the hiding place."

68

The wife spoke: "The biggest fools make hasty choices." There was a shocked silence then the men excused themselves and left.

Gerchin turned to his angry wife, his face severe. "You could not wait to trumpet your anger. You must insult me before my men?"

She pushed her face up toward his height and stormed at him. "You take this child and make her equal to me? You make me a laughing stock in the tribe. She knows nothing of our ways; our language; our life. She would be difficult to train even as a slave. But no, you must take the little bride and run off to the mountains. You must forget your past, your God, your present situation here in the land of Islam among these villagers. Kemeer is right, you are a fool!" She reeled under Gerchin's slap and recovering stood on the other side of the fire. Now two voices had begun to sob.

He stood tall and menacing, hissing. "He has become my enemy and opposes all I do. He wants to be the Khan."

"He knows what the tribe needs and he knows that the Sultan will not permit his people to be robbed of goods and girls. If you want to stay Khan you should listen to him." Her eyes blazing she drew near him again. She whispered as she pointed her finger. "He was careful not to take anything on this raid, when the troops come he can be clean handed. He thinks ahead. Listen to him and be Khan. Dispose of him and you lose everything."

He sneered down at her, his hands on his hips, lips curled. "I know you fear to be replaced or reduced in the tribe. Status, not love, drives you. I will win a fearsome reputation with the Sultan; then he will pay gold to pacify me with agreements and territory that we may send him warriors for his guards and his palace. Others before us have done this and others will do it after us. City people become tame and weak. Farmers are clods who know nothing beyond their lands and climate. A taste of war sends shivers down their spines and embassies to make peace."

Her mouth turned down as she looked away in contempt. She nodded toward the sobbing girl. "War is one thing, the stealing of a bride is another; both bring different results, even though they both cause fighting. You will repent your folly."

> - - - - - >AT THE TOOZLU CAMP > - - - - - >

"Look! They come." The people came out of their yurts to see the arrival of the squad of horses. There was a new one, a girl, one of themselves by her dress and riding. She drew up before the Khan's yurt.

"*Hoe sh geldinez*, welcome," Twozan bey greeted her. Then he gave a start of recognition, and hand on heart, stepped forward to greet the daughter of a khan. She dismounted, but swayed as she stood. "*Hoe sh bul duke*, I find you well," she retorted, but she stumbled forward.

"You have come far, princess Leyla, You must rest now with the tribe," Twozan replied. He opened the door flap that she might enter. Several women pushed forward to help her to rest comfortably at the place for honored guests. Servants rushed about serving ayran to the horse guards and guest. Kumiss was given to the men who crowded in to hear the story of the new arrival. She drank thirstily, listening.

"We celebrate your timely arrival; you will grace my wedding ritual as khan of the Toozlu and the widow of Erdash of the Chipchak Brotherhoods. Be our welcome and honored guest. Talk or rest as is your pleasure, you are at home."

"My father lies far to the south on the field of battle, where I too would lie but for the ferocity of a valiant hound and a brave warrior." She began her recitation while her mind dealt with the fact that her families' rival, Kaplan the Tiger, who planted the upstart Setchkin, his daughter, in the khan's bed, was now in the process of another victory. This marriage to one of her dynasty's faithful followers would change everything. Those who came to make her father khan of the tribe were being brought under the influence of the slut who had soiled and smudged the lines of inheritance. She was stealing her rights. Her voice droned on while her heart raged.

"I stood with my back to the thorn thickets facing the men who pursued us as the hound took the one and the warrior the other. The man had buried my father and hastened to my aid. Kerim of the East Bulgar fulfilled his oath to Erben, son of Erdash, twin brother to the present ruling khan Erkan. He led me through numerous attacks to the last village where we were again attacked by vile men and separated in the fray. I alone have gained the tribe." The listeners' heads nodded happily, here was entertainment for the coming winter nights. The details and embellishments would fill many tedious hours under the constraints of weather. Anticipation would whet appetites and delay would not damage interest. She saw the opportunity of postponement of details for the needs of food and rest.

"I have run for a day and two nights and have need of food and rest, I ask your indulgence. You will have more of the past on other occasions." She begged.

"We have other duties and pleasures this day to prepare for tomorrow's celebration. We rejoice that you will grace the occasion being present. Peace and rest be yours now in the heart of your tribe." Twozan's voice conveyed sincerity.

> - - - - - >IN SETCHKIN'S YURT> - - - - - >

"I got this blue velvet two weeks back, it was given by a tribesman of our people, a merchant here in this land. Do you like it?" Peri hanum asked.

"It's the color of the everlasting blue sky. Many still say its luck to wear it." Setchkin's voice held excitement as she held up the soft, lustrous fabric.

"The colors of Mary, mother of Yesu," said Chichek her attendant, reaching out to touch it. "There's a blessing in it."

"This should be the coat and the pink beneath for the blouse, hidden yet peeking out." The women exchanged knowing glances and smiled happily.

"There must be red for wedded happiness and children."

"That will be the trousers."

"But it will over-power the pink."

"Should it be white?"

"That is for the broad cummerbund with the gold dagger; the white is a wall against the red."

"And the gold a defense of virtue," completed Peri hanum her nurse smiling agreeably.

"What think you of the princess?" Chichek ventured, nodding toward the still form sleeping on the divan. "Her story of the Bulgar warrior? He did not try... to entice...?" She blushed.

Setchkin smiled archly, knowingly, "My brother was hostage among the East Bulgars. They're not as other men." Her helpers looked horrified.

"I have heard it so," said her old nurse in agreement.

"My brother, Kynan, returned to us completely changed. He had been a bold fool before, he returned a complete coward, a friend of the Crow and ones like him." They shuddered, and one crossed herself.

"Perhaps she did not find herself sought after and so was happy

71

to leave his company." They laughed lightly and continued with their plans while Leyla, not asleep, grimaced and bit her lip on the couch.

"Well, I have the real man and warrior of this tribe and I will trade him for no one or nothing under heaven by the everlasting blue sky," she vowed. The women paused as if in reverence for her sworn oath. Her old nurse gave a small secret smile, then all continued to spread the fabrics for inspection. The planning of the wedding became their joyous occupation.

> - - - - - >SEERDEN AT THE HIGH PASS> - - - - - >

The command forwarded from the Grey Wolf, had supplied another piece in the puzzle of his identity. Seerden had ridden hard since leaving the search for the murderers with Tewfik bey. The discovery of Erben's body had eliminated any threat to the eastern realms of empire. The dead dog and victim had supposedly ended the search for the murderers. Tewfik could tie up the loose ends and finish the case. The split tribe and the pursuing army were now his special care. The Caliph, the shadow of God for the faithful, had his plans and projects and they were abetted or crossed by the mysterious plans of the Grey Wolf. Seerden smiled his contentment. A double agent has the excitement and pleasure of playing two ends against the middle. He must please both, yet gain his own ends by doubling credit or gold with his sponsors. These thoughts produced a smug smile of confidence.

The Caliph owed too much to the armies of Khorasan to allow more victories and greater political weight to the arrogant men of that province. But how do you save the reckless followers of Gerchin, an unhinged tribal leader? Here was a problem worthy of Seerden's talents.

His route took him south of the mountain corridor, on the northern edge of the Salt Desert. There, caravans traveled and information was easier to come by.

Using a new horse at each caravansary, he gradually pushed ahead of army and tribe. Arriving where the mountains grew rugged and higher, the Caspian Sea replaced the northern desert. Passes were narrow and steep. There he paused to consult local leaders. They were the wild men of the mountains above the narrow Caspian plain. The houses were forts located wherever springs of water and mountain peaks or crags were found together. Impregnable points of defense and attack, they dotted the landscape. However severe their appearance, the interiors were luxurious with the spoils of war and tolls taken from countless passing caravans and armies. The keeping of the passes was a profitable responsibility. They knew their worth. Banditry was controlled and those passing were taxed to pay for policing. Guards have to be paid and security does not come cheap.

"You know of the Tribesmen that come to work for the Caliph. Have you heard also of the men of Khorasan who ignore the Caliph's commands?" Seerden asked.

"They are near, only a mountain separates them. We are watching both. If they make war we will gain much spoil. It matters not who wins," the chief replied.

"If it matters to the Caliph, it will matter much for you, his faithful dependants. Do you long for the return of the men of Khorasan?" The chief spat into the fire. No further word was needed. They enjoyed a long silence together while tea was served.

Afterwards Seerden spoke again. "I wonder if you would consider this idea of mine as a possible solution."

MARRIAGE PLANS

PEOPLE, PLOTS & PLACES IN CHAPTER 6

Atilla: is tracing Yeet's and other's trails north.
Aziz: feels all his troubles come from his partner.
Baja: helps those in need, loves all her nephew does.
Gerchin: gets an ambassador he expected, but what?
Kadir: forgets to guard when the quarrel is hot.
Kemeer: sees the surprise the ambassador brought.
Korkmaz: must persuade his Aunt to keep silence.
Kynan: must follow his enemies to gain freedom.
Leyla: is home, almost, and unhappy at a wedding.
Manish: feels the failure to protect his friends.
Nooryouz: has gained a nurse for her sick baby.
Sanjak: finds trouble on arrival at his assignment.
Sevman: must ride in spite of his lameness.
Tash: finds trouble wherever he goes.
Umer: suffers dreams from his crimes.

GLOSSARY:

Alay kum salaam; to you peace; a Muslim response
aptes'hane: outhouse; toilet; urinal.
emdat: help.
esen lay aniz olson: may peace be yours; tranquility.
hoe sh geldin: welcome.
jezve: a small, long-handled, copper coffee pot.
kumiss: a clear alcoholic drink of mare's milk.
salaam alay kum: peace to you; a Muslim greeting.
yetishtir: give me a hand; help.

UMER'S DREAM

"Blast you fool! Yeet, don't! Allaaaah!" Umer found himself wide awake from a dreadful dream. It had to be a dream he told himself. The details remained vivid in his mind. Yeet had leaned down, accusing him beneath the thorn bush. He held a fire above him and was setting the brush into a blaze. He could feel the heat consume him. He tried to push past the face, but something powerful held him there beneath the burning bushes. His face roasted! His eyes streamed tears. He tried to plead. Mercy! Anguish filled his mind and the pain became unbearable until he screamed and called the name of Allah. Then he woke sobbing, drenched in sweat and tears. The dried mud-cast holding his dislocated knee in place, now held a throbbing, swollen, mass of flesh pressed against the confining walls.

> - - - - - >GOAT HERDER HILL> - - - - - >

Katchy sat with his flock scowling at the group gathered around Yeet, they had pastured the horse, with others on his green hill and they were eating his grass. He sulked and refused to join their campfire but returned to his corral to hunker in his habitual place at the gate. There he brooded over the injustice.

Yeet reported his trip to the family. "When I saw Umer I knew he had been up to no good and yet he lay defiant, angry, cursing us all; wanting death as much as he wanted to inflict it before." They all clicked their tongues in disapproval. He would answer to Tanra they each reasoned.

Kardesh spoke quietly. "You did not grant his request, Yeet?" Yeet closed his eyes and sighed. "At that moment I remembered my mother's teaching and I could not act against it. I just couldn't do it!"

Sevman agreed. "Evil destroys itself. Balance must be restored. Why take on the weight of his sin yourself?"

At the fire Tayze carried another damp, cool cloth to place on Yeet's lump on the side of his head and his lacerated ear. She fed him where he lay: bread dipped in the common pot by hand, bite by bite.

"You are in no condition to travel until the bleeding and swelling stops and color sets in. This kind of wound is more serious than men think. You must stay awake now otherwise you might not wake up." She lectured him.

"Oh, that I had caught the clever jackal the other night! I would have finished the matter for everyone's satisfaction. Such men sow only evil and must be destroyed. Come Sevman join me and we will hunt down the rabid dog." Atilla bey was up and pacing impatiently.

Tayze spoke. "Wait till morning if you would search the roads. What would you find at night among the thorn thickets? A knife in the back!"

Atilla snorted his disdain for knives or other dangers.

Sevman spoke calmly. "We are called not to war, but to serve. My friend is wounded and I must stay tonight. Tomorrow I will ride with you, if you so desire, Atilla bey."

The man smiled broadly. "I must not be impatient for success. Others also wait for revenge." He nodded toward Kardesh. "His eyes demand it."

"Four eyes are better than two. I will go and help protect you, but not to kill. That is the role of Jehovah, the old God of vengeance and law," Sevman explained.

Atilla looked carefully at Sevman. "I had always thought the Manicheans were but followers of another prophet of the same truth and law, but you are as widely different as the eastern Tang." He sat down and picked up a mug. Taking the long handle he pulled the *jezve* from where it rested among the coals to pour a cup of coffee. Cradling the mug between his hands he stared at the dark liquid and smiled at his new friends. "Let's not talk of revenge or lives as if we were some agent of the High Unknowable One. Rather let's consider tomorrow a hunt. Yes, a hunt for a jackal that raids the flocks."

> - - - - - >AT THE TANRA DAH ARMY BASE > - - - - - >

Tash wore his new dignity like a coat of armor, He sat with his back to the wall looking over the men who huddled over tables sharing tea and anecdotes of their lives: likes and dislikes, frustrations and joys. He had passed his training as military police with commendation. He had a place and practice that he enjoyed. He got pay and even special gifts when he could ferret out news that his sponsors needed. Onbasha Tash knew his unique importance and wanted others to recognize it also. What his years lacked, his rank was to compensate for. In short, he was a kid looking for trouble. He despised this poor village and its inhabitants. He was from the centers of civilization further south. He had visited a caravan city for Ali bey. Now he would fulfill his task for Onat, Ali and the shadow which he knew would order his boss to new ventures for some hidden plan.

His present duty demanded a patrolling of the streets every hour to clear all army personnel to their barracks away from the houses of pleasure. Only the tea houses were neutral ground. He started to the *aptes-hane* to relieve himself before the next patrol, but stopped when he caught a whiff of alcohol. Someone was drinking lions' milk as the deadly brew, *kumiss*, was jokingly named.

Tash followed his nose to a small room where a group of men indulged themselves with a bag of fermented mares' milk; the stimulant of bored soldiers. Prudence and regulations suggested a return for help from his squad, but pride and the hope of glory prodded Tash into folly.

"Who is in charge here?" he demanded. A young Yuzbasha stood and motioned him to come in. He was a tribal Turk by the look of him and Tash felt his antipathy grow.

"*Hoe sh geldin*. Welcome, Onbasha, come have a drink on me. I have just arrived from the south and am washing away the dust from my throat. I have found new friends who will share my life here in this garrison."

"Alcohol is forbidden in the tea house, bey, and I cannot excuse your breach of Binbasha Onat's regulations."

A grizzled veteran laughed, and stood to look Tash in the face. "You're playing Onbasha games, boy, I've been broken from your rank a dozen times and I match you in anything you've got."

Tash looked at the Onbasha's drunken face with disgust, but he was now surrounded by belligerent faces. As he backed to the wall, he panicked and yelled for his squad. "*Em dat*, help, *Ye tish tir*, come to me here." He tried to push past the old man, but struggling, they lost balance and he was pulled with the falling veteran to the floor.

The yuzbasha Sanjak's voice cut commandingly in the scramble. "Stop men, that's enough, let them up." It was easier said than done. Someone's boot caught Tash in the face and all went dark. He remembered no more. The old veteran laughed in derision as he smashed a fist into the limp form of the policeman and gained his feet. He kicked at the still form and turned to run from the room. The squad came too late to catch most of the men, but after some arrests and pursuits they took their new onbasha, battered by kicks and fists, to the doctor. Sanjak was detained. Regular patrol duty was suspended for at least two hours.

"Quick, down this path, someone's coming," the boy whispered. Korkmaz had plotted a course between the various centers of attraction that brought the army men out every night. Nooryouz followed blindly clutching her little bundle in her protective arms. Once they were forced to stop and hunker while several men came running down the paths that served as streets. They were laughing in grim satisfaction. One yelled to the other. "Hold, they won't catch us now."

"No, you don't want to be caught after what we did to that smart-ass kid."

"Nobody drew a knife, he'll live."

"Ain't that too bad, he could finger us."

"That was the patrol, they won't be out here."

"Hell, I'm spent. Where do we go now?"

"Closest pleasure palace will do." They shambled down the path to disappear.

Korkmaz stood and led Nooryouz toward a fine house on the edge of the town. "Come, there was a fight, we are safe for a while. Here is my aunt's house." He indicated the structure.

Nooryouz was trembling with fear and exhaustion. "We must hurry, time is short," she cried.

> - - - - - >CASPIAN PASSES TO IRAN > - - - - ->

"*Esen ley aniz olsun*, peace be yours." The tall, mounted, gray beard awaited the scouts of the Toozlu band with only one outrider and greeted them in Turkish with great dignity. The men milled around them after they had blown the horn of warning to alert the main column. The squad of tribesmen eyed the strangers' garments with avid admiration. Both the boy and the old one were rich.

"Remember, I saw them first," proclaimed one to his friends.

"But I took the lead and challenged their presence," another hastened to add. The visitors ignored the greedy remarks.

"We come in the Sultan's name; we have followed your progress and now come to greet you into the land of peace." The voice of the outrider shouted the message in Arabic and Turkish, too loud to be conversational: it was a proclamation. This statement had an immediate effect on the milling riders. They withdrew to one side and awaited the presence of their leaders. Kemeer arrived first and after a brief word with the scouts continued to meet the visitor. At that time Gerchin appeared with a squad of young warriors sporting the yak-tail standard, insignia of the tribe.

Kemeer paused, then, he spoke. "*Hoe sh gel den iz,* Your arrival is welcome, sir. You have come for a special time with a message from our sovereign?"

"Our royal ambassador will speak to the Khan of the Toozlu," the boy shouted. Kemeer, however, persisted. "I and my wife are Muslims and pledge our lives to our Sultan's pleasure. We come to serve his cause. You have but to ask." The gray-beard sat silent and unmoving. The boy herald too, sat awaiting the approach of the standard and squad. Kemeer, humiliated and ignored, withdrew to the scouts and was joined by others who raced out to see the men that blocked their road toward the greening slopes. Angered, Kemeer pressed up the hill behind the waiting men. As he reached the top of the pass he glanced at the descending slope and gasped; an army of hundreds of warriors were drawn up in battle formation and were spread before him filling the valley, all the way to a huge stone fort on a hill facing the pass. He whirled and raced back to the scouts, but the group with the standard had reached the ambassador. He knew they were trapped. He could only wait for the conclusion of the parley. He rode gingerly forward to join the warriors grouped about the standard to hear the Sultan's proclamation. He knew that the Sultan, the shadow of God on earth, held them in the shadow of death.

> - - - - - >BAJA'S VILLAGE HOUSE > - - - - - >

Aunt Baja looked solemnly at her nephew and the frail, frantic girl and returned to her ministrations to the infant before her. She finished wrapping the child in the toasty hot wool sheets taken from their hanging place over the stove. "This will take a,way the chills and fevers from our little man. The ointments will penetrate and cure the cough." She looked at the girl, well dressed under her shepherds wool and cloak. "We need to feed you, little lady, and hear your story. You, nephew: get the stove stoked up and be quick about it. We are safe enough from nosy neighbors now, but by morning we had best be through here and have her safely away. The old garrison is being reinforced and under the new commander they're no longer lax. A new yuzbasha arrived last night, another Turk." She sniffed contemptuously, "My mother said that in her mother's day they were all in the wild north lands and only civilized people lived here on the borders. Like our Uigur kin down below the pass we are ruled by newcomers who limit our traffic. "

The boy stood hesitant before speaking. "Baja, I have heard tonight that there are fires burning below the pass. We hear of people coming over the pass, refugees from army attacks."

The aunt straightened up. "The Uigurs are a civilized people. They would do nothing so foolish. They are not at war. There has been some accident and the fire spread, nothing more. There are always people coming over the pass." Korkmaz listened respectfully, but Nooryouz was asleep on a cushion.

> - - - - ->IN A SMUGGLER'S CELLAR > - - - - ->

Bolben's whisper was full of excitement as he returned from the kitchen entrance. "Jon, we can leave, there has been a brawl and the guards are called in." Sesli squealed her joy and was promptly shushed by all. They moved to the tunnel.

"Quick now, we must scoot out before they return." Jon knelt to let Sesli walk up his back and stood to lift her on his shoulders to the shaft and she popped out of the barrel on to the floor. Jon was foot-lifted by Bolben whom he in turn handed out of the narrow hole. Those who had offered refuge urged them to greater speed.

"We can't know how long they will be gone. There is a refuge below the village, away from the pass where they will expect some of you to return." A figure whose face they never saw, motioned them out of the house and down one of the paths that served as streets. As light as a blown leaf the figure swept before them motioning and moving; stopping, listening and then waving all clear, moving on again. He swept them out of the village into the rocks and dirt of the margins of the inhabited, into the outer areas away from danger into the unknown. After what seemed like hours of groping, scrambling through the dark the guide lit a lantern and led them to a cave. Kadir was guarding the entrance. Within, raised in shrill discourse were the voices of two men in heated argument. Yavuz screamed his impotence, shaking his fist in Aziz's face.

"You mangy camel you had people following our trail. Imported new women without telling me, your partner. Now one slave girl is caught and the alarm is out for more. Our profits are gone," Yavuz shouted in anger.

Aziz snarled his frustration and clenched his fists. He stood over the little man menacingly. "They were not mine, not one of them. Who arranged this stupidity? You cur, it smacks of your kind of deal. Bordello trade, selling women's bodies."

Yavuz stood on his toes and shrieked back in his face. "You lie, I am an honest smuggler. It's you who always bend our rules. You're always watching the pretty girls." Aziz turned his back in disgust, and walked to the entrance.

"I didn't do any slavery, but by Allah, I'll kill the one who got us blamed for it." The voice of Yavuz followed him. "It was to be our last trip in partnership. You betrayed me and brought more for a big gain that you have kept secret."

The shadow leading the group had stopped outside the cave and waited while the argument continued. Bolben, panic stricken, whispered to the guide. "We're not going in where those men are fighting. Take us further on to another place."

Jon joined them and pleaded: "There will be problems if we take Sesli in there. Those men will think she's for the trade."

The guide motioned a direction and faded from sight and the fugitives followed. Sesli fell over a bush with a cry. They helped her up almost carrying her in their haste.

"*Kim orada*? Who goes there" Aziz yelled the challenge past the bemused Kadir who had stopped to listen to the argument. He turned quickly and darted out. He could hear the sound of running.

CAVE DISCOVERY

82

"I will tell you everything, Baja, but you must not tell Uncle Aziz; you know what he would do." Korkmaz spoke quickly.

Baja smiled. "You know your Uncle Aziz has no teeth, but tell me the truth and we will face him together if need be. Your foreign lady is very pretty, how did you come by her?" She settled herself on the shelf bench at the wall but a tapping at the barred door brought her back on guard. She went to the door and tapped a response.

Some one whispered. "Baja, there was fighting tonight, we are under orders to remain at home all day. Anyone on the streets will be arrested. I must tell others. Keep your door barred. Refugees are coming over the pass." The aunt responded and the messenger retreated across the street to another house. Thus the news was spread in the pre-dawn night.

"We have time now," breathed the Aunt, "Time for all the details and time for the child to heal. Now start from the beginning and don't leave anything out. Do you understand? I know you started down to the cave. Then what? Where do this praying lady and her sick child come from?"

> - - - - - >TO THE HILL VILLAGE > - - - - - >

The two men rode slowly, Sevman's leg did not allow for fast or easy riding. They spent the day following the trail. They discovered the place where someone had rested under a thorn thicket and a drag trail where someone had left broken earth and horse tracks. Farther along, they followed the trail of three animals to a camp where one track of two horses went north. Then, the trace of horses to and from the camp to the high perched village and then one track away to the north from the village. Atilla descended to drink at the fountain, water the horses and wait for women to come and draw water before night.

As he helped Sevman to dismount he noticed what looked like blood stains near the trail up to the high village. He saw a furtive movement above.

"*Salaam alaykum,*" he called, "We need to buy provisions and water our animals. We come in need of direction. We have lost our trail."

A veiled girl with a jar on her head approached slowly. He could detect her fear and hesitation. "*Alaykum salaam*," she returned, and looked down at the stains where he stood. Her eyes filled with tears and her voice keened. "Oh Allah, my friend died here. Yesterday he was buried. A warrior's death!"

Sevman heard with a shiver. "Health to you and yours," replied Atilla quickly. The girl stayed above on the trail and did not approach them. She awaited others; perhaps unfriendly help?

"Was there a wounded man as well?" Atilla asked.

"What wounded man? A tribesman?"

"No, Umer, from the quarries. We seek him. Did he come this way yesterday?"

"The tribesmen left, that way," she pointed north. "Others followed later."

Sevman could feel the hostility growing in her voice and manner. But Atilla spoke. "The man we seek has done great damage to others and may be a murderer or an accessory to murder. Tewfik bey seeks him. He is dangerous and clever."

"How do we know such words are true? Where is your Tewfik bey? Perhaps you are the murderers." Sounds of many coming down the path stirred them as Sevman strained to remount. Atilla bowed cordially and mounted his horse. He spoke sadly as they turned back.

"You're angry with me. I only favored you with a true warning of danger. We will leave with regret. Peace be to you and your village with Allah's blessing."

> - - - - - >TRACKING THE TRIBE > - - - - - >

Kynan was careful to make his trail visible and easy to follow for half a night, leading away from the trail of Leyla and then he took his horses down a dry stream bed in a zigzag course to circle back and cross her track. There he waited through the day but no pursuers appeared. So the next night he followed on in her track. He read the signs of fatigue and confusion in her trail. But he kept to it, slow but sure. As he went he made his plans. The Toozlu would not welcome him. His sister might still be among them. She despised him, and would not be happy to have

84

him back as brother or as captive. There was no need for a strenuous rescue attempt; that could be done by the offended relatives when they entered tribal lands. The Toozlu were moving the right direction for his escape from any of his jailers in pursuit; the size of the force would hinder all but an attacking army. He could travel near, but not too near to gain his own land. He sighed and wondered how his Princess Leyla would fare among the tribe. She had forgotten him to run for them, perhaps it was for the best.

He took two days to follow her while guarding the trail from pursuers, but there were none. Now he slept by night and followed by day. He was but an hour on the trail when he detected changes. He felt a presence. He felt danger. He started back from her trail and descended into a dry gulch. As he did he heard an alarm horn blown from the top of the hill. Help would be coming soon for the guard. He would be hunted relentlessly. The extra packhorse hindered his escape, so he dropped the lead rope. A horde of warriors would be all around him in a few minutes. Turning, he urged his horse into a run.

ATILLA WARNS

PEOPLE, PLOTS & PLACES IN CHAPTER 7

Ambassador: offers conversion or destruction.
Atilla: seeks a criminal or a friend and finds both.
Gerchin: finds his recklessness controlled.
Kemeer: ignored by all, sees the dilemma ahead.
Kerim: the name which most of Kynan's friends know.
Korkmaz: cares for new friends, guard's old ones.
Kynan: whatever his name, is caught by the Khan.
Manish: finds prison life hard for a shepherd boy.
Mookades: the priest knows his tribe and people.
Onat: is determined to bring discipline to the base.
Sanjak: is blamed and punished for his men's fight.
Sevman: finds travel and trailing, tiring and puzzling.
Twozan: traps an intruder whom they expected.

GLOSSARY:
Allaha ismar la dick: God wills it; Farewell.
affet beni: pardon me; excuse me; forgive me.
barish: peace.
belki de: perhaps; maybe.
bock: look; see.
booy roon: see here; behold; consider this.
mookades: holy; set apart; reverend.

KATCHY'S CONCERT

"There are only two possibilities here, either the man Umer is in the village and they have taken his part or this trail north is the one our murderer made," Atilla reasoned.

Sevman listened carefully and nodded thoughtfully. "This trail will put us farther from our friends."

Atilla laughed. "There is no glory at all in neglecting a trail, nor are the jackals disposed of by allowing a scent to grow cold. The village will remain and can be revisited with Tewfik bey."

Sevman shook his head and objected. "What if the man damages or kills in the village?"

Atilla chuckled. "Those who extend refuge to the stranger must take their risks. They have been warned and more than one heard the last statement I made. Nothing is secret in a village that small." He shook his head. "They'll know."

"Is it enough? Isn't there something more we could do?"

"You can scarcely force people to be sensible. Only hard experience teaches fools. I think he is in the village, but we must not be negligent. He will not slip away in a day or two, nor will we relax."

They rode swiftly for the track was plain and easy. But later, two more horses had joined the trail.

"Bock, look, the horses from the camp have joined up." He got off his horse to look closely at the tracks. He shook his head and remounted. "It is my pack horse and my friend's, the East Bulgar, Kerim's. Has he stolen my pack? He left me the gold, but took the travel goods. Would he need them? If he is the escaped prisoner of war he will need them."

Sevman looked doubtful but continued following on the tracks. "It would seem more likely that the murderer stole the horse and took the other person a prisoner, or travels with an accomplice."

"We caught one of three and it is possible two escaped, but why throw away the gold? Thieves don't ignore the thing they kill for. Besides, there was a report of a man killed by a dog, and another ambushed, while I was detained. Yeet met only one, Umer." Both men traveled in silence. Neither suggested returning.

"I was leading my pack horse when I met him at the green hill. How could Kerim have taken it? He was with me at the chase. We were going west, together." Both paused to watch the trail, two horses had obviously continued, but the original track was lost. Atilla stared hard and turned back to hunt for a dividing of the rider's trails. He did not find it.

"The horse from the village has vanished, perhaps covered by our decoy? Also the first track seems older than the rider's and the pack horse."

"Could the two be tracking the one? How could he lose it?"

"No, the two are covering the tracks of the first. We must find it." They backed until they found a place where the two had left prints, but the first track was brushed over and fresh sand spread over the hoof marks.

Atilla nodded, he indicated the erasures with a laugh of triumph. "I will follow the one. You will follow my pack animal. I will sound the horn at sunset and you'll answer. We'll spend the night and tomorrow we will find our prey." At sunset they were surprised to find their paths cross again; the three tracks became as one as they went north, toward the border.

> - - - - - >ARMY BASE PRISON > - - - - - >

Manish sat cloaked in his shepherd clothes not eating the last of the bread left by his interrogator. The pasha was much more lenient than he had a right to expect. However, guilt consumed him. He sighed. He had told on his friends with only a promise of freedom to tempt him. He had imagined himself dying for their safety, loyally silent. The kindness had undone him. He was braced for threats and pain, not sympathy. He prayed to the Jesus of Light and the prophet Mani for his need of forgiveness and understanding. He could not think of any way to atone for his weakness and betrayal. He cringed at the thought of seeing them again. What if they were imprisoned here? How could he ever face them? He wondered if ending his life might not bring a better rebirth and better opportunity to show truer loyalty, but he hesitated. What if, after this betrayal he was to come back in an inferior form? His merits might be so small as to gain no advantage for him. He hung his head and only the thoughts about Yesu, innocent yet crucified by the Jehovah of law, hate and revenge brought him any comfort. Tears made their courses down his face.

>- - - - - - - >ARMY BASE HEADQUARTERS > - - - - - >

"You come to a new posting and immediately get drunk, disorderly and into a fight. The poor onbasha is battered."

"I take full responsibility, Onat bey. I let the men voice their resentment of the onbahsa's abrupt manner of speaking."

"The onbasha is very young and newly assigned here. He does not have the moderation that experience brings.

I understand, but cannot condone the incident. So, Sanjack bey, you will spend this week in supervising the prisoners and degraded ones, including your own men from the fight. You will share their swill for food, their bed and their labor for occupation until further notice. Remember I will not tolerate slackness here."

"*Evet Binbashum.*"

"Dismissed, lieutenant."

"*Allah ismar la dick*, farewell sir."

>- - - - - - - >AMBASSADOR'S CONDITIONS> - - - - - >

"The Sultan welcomes you under these conditions that I explained to you. You can turn back if they are unacceptable, you will have to fight the army that follows you closely. Ibn el Ari will be happy to gain a victory for the men of Khorasan. Even should you win you are far from home and new recruits to replace those who fall."

"We can beat any army our size or larger." Khan Gerchin bragged.

"*Belke de*, perhaps, but your service to the Sultan depends on your troops and their abilities. Would you waste them to fight without need?"

"We came to fight for the Sultan, what are his conditions of service?"

"As I said, you must take an oath of loyalty and become Muslim, surrendered to Allah. Then you must release the imprisoned bride, her party and her goods, beyond that the Caliphate will make restitution. You will be fed and cared for by Turkish slaves of the royal house. You will be trained for royal guards. Your quarters will be far superior to your customary dwellings. No one who comes to us ever wishes to return to the wild life in the land of war beyond Dar al Islam."

The tribesmen surrounding the two nodded in agreement, happy to trade God and past glories for an unknown but attractive future. They had surrendered the past when their Khan had failed to appear after the big fight in the desert. Prosperity in the old homeland was now impossible.

"*Booy roon*, here we are, we're your men. Tell us what to do now." Khan Gerchin gestured to his men to form up the troop and placed himself at their head.

The little outrider announced to all in his loudest voice: "Form a column and leave your weapons in piles according to the type: bow and arrows in one; lances and spears in another. Keep your knives sheathed at all times. Fighting men will proceed over this pass before the women and children. We have rear guards for your safety. Separate from yourselves those pertaining to the bridal party and leave them here in the pass."

Kemeer had spread the word of the waiting army. All the clan now knew that they were caught between two armies and could be destroyed. Better to live and be soldier-slaves to the Sultan.

A Royal Guard yuzbasha stood with the veiled bride and her women and stopped each wagon or camel to reclaim their goods. There was no resistance.

> - - - - ->OUTSIDE THE ARMY BASE > - - - - >

"Quick this way, there are more caves further down the slope." He helped Sesli over and out of a dry stream bed. Bolben was all nerves. He had recognized Aziz and Kadir in the light from the cave interior. As a bird reacts to the silhouette of a hawk so he too, took to cover in the dark. He vividly remembered the death threat shouted in anger: "The next time you cross my path in my territory, I'll crush you like the worm you are." He had known at the time that he was outside the law of state and community, for even smugglers had their code of right and wrong. He was too ashamed of his transgression of double dipping and fraud to admit it to family or friends, so he made excuses for dropping out of the traditional commerce of the villages on borders and had taken over the horse herd until he met the escaping Christians. Helping them he had transgressed the prohibition of one of the big kingpins of the border operations. He was a dead man if he met any of the organization.

Jon waited for them to catch up and whispered excitedly. "That was some blow up in the cave. Don't they allow slaves to be passed over this border?"

Bolben put his nose up, "Part of the village keeps the old Manichee faith which does not approve pandering to the flesh.

91

The Uigurs are an influence and the smugglers try to keep peace with them by not offending."

"Where are we going now? We need to stop and make a fire in this cold." Their guide had stayed closer to them and saw all were tired.

"There is an old deserted monastery in the hills about twenty minutes from here. You can make fire safely there. Villagers think its bad luck to visit it." Jon nodded his willingness and all pressed on.

>- - - - - - - >TRAILING LEYLA > - - - - - >

Kynan dropped the lead to the pack horse and spurred his mount into a run over a hillock into a dry stream bed. A shout of discovery and the sounding of horns followed him. His horse was tired from a day's travel and ran reluctantly; heaving and blowing his distress. Whipping his horse past a thorn clump and bend he suddenly found himself facing two men with drawn bows. He drew up his horse and let the tired animal pause, panting. Caught out, he dropped his reins and slowly placed his hands on his head.

"We expected you yesterday, Kerim bey, your horse is out of condition and dry. We will water him and you, if you come in peace."

Head bowed, Kerim studied them carefully. He knew the Khan from his boyhood days. Would the men know him? He did not remember meeting him face to face after his return from his hostage years in the west. Chipchak lands were too wide for everyone to be instantly known, especially between rival houses in the far flung nomadic communities. He decided to speak with an accent like the East Bulgars.

"*Barish*, peace, yes! I wasn't sure. How could I be sure of a good welcome?" They lowered their bows and sheathed their weapons.

Twozan rode closer and inspected the captive. "If all that the princess Leyla has said is true, you are very welcome."

"The princess is gracious and more of a talker than a listener, so I can't know what she has said. I do need both fresh horses and a clear road."

"You're returning to your own land then? We are short handed now, could we persuade you to go north with us? We will provide food and horses and send you on your way with style when we get home."

The question froze Kynan's mind: how could he answer this friendly overture? His silence caused Twozan to turn and give an order to his companion.

"Go fetch Mookades. He knows the Bulgar's dialect. Have him bring the pack horse with him. Set the other men to intercept the other riders that follow." The man left and Twozan rode his horse closer to Kynan's and scrutinized him. He kept silent and Kynan lowered his hands to the reins.

"Riders that follow?" Kynan spoke without accent, as the warrior rode away on his mission. "I am followed by the villagers?"

"That remains to be seen. Our visitors are diverse and intent on their missions lately: my estranged son; merchants selling cloth and bringing pigeons for the informer in our camp; two government agents; a princess, the daughter of the man I strove to support for the ruler of the tribe; my new bride's brother or perhaps my brother-in-law, as I believe you must be."

"I wondered if you would know me. I escaped my prison and came here going home. I found Leyla in distress and brought her this far."

"The least you could have done to recompense the damage you caused with your pursuit and attacks. If I take you into camp some will want quick revenge."

Kynan nodded understandingly and grimaced. "I know, that's why I was trying to avoid direct contact; to pass by."

"I knew you were probably not all she said, infatuated women exaggerate and make over the rough exterior of things. She would not say so, if you had mistreated her in any way."

Kynan agreed readily. "She's royalty. I confess to nearly offered pledges that I would be unable to fulfill. She could have gained any. I'm glad she arrived alone."

Twozan nodded and added. "Well said, a princess requires time to adjust. She will be happy later, I think."

KYNAN CAUGHT

"She must be with my sister then, Setchkin has special talents. An ..." He stopped abruptly, after a silence he continued. "*Afet beni*, pardon me, you said, new bride, you have married her then? My congratulations not insults should be your due. As a brother I can say she is very beautiful, talented and ..."

"Willful, capricious and wavering." Twozan interposed. "I well understand her nature. She has come willingly, I can ask no more." Both men thought of the Tiger, but deemed it unwise to say more. A noise above them announced the arrival of Mookades, the priest of the tribe. He came leading the packhorse, whose reins he dropped and rode on to the two men.

"The horse, my Khan, has been watered." He looked carefully at Kynan. "You are the Kerim we waited for, but you are not Bulgar. I know your father. Come now, water your horse." Obediently Kynan dismounted, took off his leather cap and held the two ear flaps while Mookades squeezed the bag to fill it with water. His horse drank it dry immediately. The packhorse moved into reach, hoping for more. The men chuckled and looked at each other. "How like us are the horses!"

> - - - - - >GOAT HERDER HILL > - - - - - >

Katchy glowered at the party around the fire. The good man who paid had been gone for two days. No money would replace the grass he had lost in these days. His flock would go hungry if they stayed another day. He knew what he wanted, but did not know how to say it. He took the time to return from the corral, leaving his flock that night, to the stranger's fire and shouted at the top of his voice from the top of the hill. He felt safe in the dark.

"Good man gone two days. You go too. Eat all my grass. You no pay nothing. If you not gone in morning. I bring sling, bang you plenty on head." He watched the figures below move and talk. They threw on more wood and made the flame bigger. He grinned in his satisfaction. It made the targets brighter. He thought of finishing it immediately. Then he thought of the bey: he would come and might take him away. He sent one stone over the cart and into the bush with a bang. It was enough. The people moved a box into the cart. He chuckled. They were showing their intention to move. He could go back to his flock and sleep. He had his victory. He had a familiar little song that he had practiced on his flute. He sang it loud enough for the strangers to hear. He wanted them to know how smart and ready he was, to save his flock. He was their hero even if people thought little of him.

Come my lovelies, come and be happy;
Your food and water I'll supply.
Come you beauties, dance and be glady;
You know your Daddy is close by.

Come you Kechies, come love your pal-ys;
Here in my valley, safety lies.
Grow big bellys, bear little fell-ys;
That is God's way to multiply.

When rich man come, he see you prancing;
Playing and dancing, my flute by.
He pay Katchy, plenty of money;
With bread and honey he'll supply.

KATCHY CAN DO

To Katchy's disappointment the people paid no attention. They continued loading their cart.

PEOPLE, PLOTS & PLACES IN CHAPTER 8

Atilla: finds all he's looking for, with boasts to hosts.
Erly: has a chance to show contempt for the outsider.
Kemeer: has second thoughts about his new beliefs.
Leyla: finds her expected hero will not arrive.
Sevman: finds rest after the humiliation of capture.
Twozan: expects more visitors as they move north.

GLOSSARY:
Allah ismar la dick: God willing I go; permission to go.
aksham: evening; prayer after dark about 6 pm.
bayan: title for a respected lady; ma'am.
do'er: stop; quit; leave off.
evet: yes.
gear: enter; come in.
gel: come.
goo lay goo lay git: go happily; goodbye.
Hi'er: no; not so;
kalk: get up; stand up.
kechy: goat.
kafir: unbeliever; pagan.
koot'lu ol son: congratulations; be blessed.
shirk: polytheism; worship of beings as Gods.

THE AMBASADOR

Sevman and Atilla came to a sudden halt. The trail of the two horses had resumed only to split again. One stopped, while the other veered frantically as it ran between the thorn thickets. This trail they followed until it was intercepted by several others. Atilla reined in and motioned with satisfaction.

"He was caught here, see. One stands and the others come and go. The Turks have him." Sevman rode past to the other side of the clearing and painfully dismounted. Atilla rode to him and stopped.

"Rest a while, the trails go north together here, but some go back east from where they came. What about us, east or north?" He dismounted and squatted beside the now prostrate form of Sevman.

"Go satisfy your curiosity. I'll rest here until you come again. If I'm asleep or dead, don't disturb me."

Atilla laughed heartily. "Sleep then, little one, I'll fix supper after *aksham* prayers tonight. You'll be too sore after two days of riding." He urged his horse north on the trail of the man whom he suspected of being his friend.

> - - - - - >OUTSIDE THE TOOZLU CAMP > - - - - - >
Sevman groaned, but again it came, a sharp boot dug into his ribs with force. He rolled painfully over and looked up at the face of his

tormentor. A strange, savage countenance glared back at him. The boot made of horse skin, taken from the hock and foreleg sewn together at the end, was drawn back for another blow. He rolled to avoid it and felt a thorn in his back. There was no more room to maneuver. The man grinned nastily and feinted with his foot as if about to kick and Sevman again backed into the thorn and cried out.

"*Do'er*, stop, I give up! I have no weapons." The man laughed and showed him his knife and horse standing beside his own mount.

"*Kalk, gel*, get up, come." The man's voice was rough, coarse, but the meaning was clear. It held the contempt of the victor over the careless bungler. He was caught napping and losers have to be taken in. He looked around hopefully as he hobbled to his horse to mount. He was deliberately slow in mounting.

"Your friend is already in our camp, he will not save you." The old man sneered. "I could have cut your throat and you wouldn't have known it. Let me see your medallion I saw it while I decided what to do with you" Sevman took off his medal of the cupped hand holding the flame. The guard examined it closely and started off. Sevman followed although the man paid him no more attention. It was the hour of *iftar* when they arrived, but no one was praying. The women walked about open faced doing the work of the camp. The men sat in groups waiting to exchange their views on the events of the day. A group was waiting around the large central yurt where Atilla's horse stood eating a bit of hay. Sevman ignored his captor and rode to the yurt to dismount. He swayed as he touched ground.

"This one is sick, he should not be allowed in camp," his captor announced to the world as he rode in.

"*Gear*, enter," the voice of command came and Sevman stumbled toward the entrance. The smell of food rocked his body and his stomach rumbled. He looked hopefully toward the fire in the yurt, but there were no utensils or food. The cooking was in a neighboring yurt. A meeting was in progress in the Khan's yurt.

"Here then is your friend, does he know the man Kerim, the East Bulgar, whom you pretend to seek?" Twozan inquired lightly.

"*Hi'er*, no, I met this young man several days ago after my friend Kerim had left me. We joined a hunt for murderers and although I caught two, one escaped to a place near here. I needed a companion and pressed this youth to accompany me. He is unaccustomed to ride in the search. He's a city boy."

Twozan smiled triumphantly. "You must be a man of great ability, to risk so much with so little. Could not the authorities of the hunt have provided you with better?" His eyes reflected a sardonic humor. "Your friend Kerim flees the law and you came short handed to capture or speed him?"

"I came from friendship and curiosity. The murderer also came this way. I would like to know if they have met or if there is news. There was blood spilled at the village two days back and I want to find my friend for news of the events." Atilla's frustration was rising.

"You would best find such information in the village. Are you afraid of the authorities?" Twozan leaned forward.

"I was dismissed by the hunt authorities and I followed my friend who was on the trail of the man they had lost. There was blood near the fountain at the village, but the woman thought we were in pursuit of a wounded villager. There was too much blood for just a wound."

Behind them near the door a hysterical voice rose. "Kerim saved me, but I killed the devil who would have taken my honor. His blood fouls the fountain. Kerim was to follow me here. Where is he?" The princess had arrived after Sevman was brought in. She had been listening.

Twozan rose "Princess, you come unannounced, forgive our carelessness."

"Well, where is the friend this man was following, do you know?" She glared imperiously at both the men who now stood together beyond the fire. Silence was absolute.

"My lady," began Twozan, "he has continued north toward his land, after learning of your safe arrival with the tribe, of course."

She stared in disbelief at the two men, finally forcing Atilla to confirm. "*Evet bayan*, yes lady, I saw the place where his trail went on north, after the other tracks turned back. It was there they caught me."

The beautiful, if scratched, face of the girl seemed to collapse and she turned quickly to dart through the door.

"Her soul remains with the man who saved her. If it is true that you are a friend, you can catch him in half a day and tell him. I fear she will not rest without him. I am detained by my marriage today."

"This is news indeed, Allah's blessing: a new wife.
I will ride and tell my friend that we may come to be blessed by this event."

The Khan moved his head up in the negative nod and explained. "Your Kerim knows, but has reasons not to return. Go seek your friend. Leave the boy here, he can only delay you. The food tent will give you supplies to carry for the trip." They left the yurt.

Atilla exclaimed, "*Allah ismar la dick*, as God wills, goodbye, I'll bring news."

"*Goo lay goo lay git*, go happily, we await your return."

"*Koot'lu ol son*, congratulations," Atilla finished.

> - - - - - - >IRAN MOUNTAIN PASS > - - - - - >

Kemeer felt his great opportunity had come. Here at last before the authorities he had the chance to tell them his adventure of faith. His wife had explained the ways of Islam, surrender to Allah. He had accepted what he understood of this and had conferred with no others. Opportunity offered few chances to expand his first knowledge. He had many questions to ask, and the moment had come. The imam was Turk in origin and language: that made things so much easier.

The greeting at the door of the mosque office was effusive and warm. The Imam was proud of the station and prosperity he had found in this village in the mountains just out of the desert. The visitor was a tribal convert who was just emerging from the darkness of ignorance. The imam anticipated the observations, jokes and boastings that would come of such a rich encounter. He greeted and seated him.

"Praises be, Allah has brought you from darkness to light and into the richness of Islam. Allah's plan and blessing will now be manifest in your life. What great changes He will bless you through."

"Praises be, Allah has shown me a new prophet and a new way of understanding my life as a servant of God. My tribe has been a servant of God through the teachings of Yesu for six hundred years, now we will learn the ways of Allah through Muhammad."

"May he rest in peace," the Imam stated as Kemeer stopped. "Yesu, you must realize, was a prophet of God who predicted the coming of the last and greatest prophet of all, May he rest in peace."

Kemeer happily agreed, "Prophets are humans whom Tanra has commissioned to carry a message to a people in error. Most of the prophets of the times of Israel were single. It amazes me that ours should have so many wives, surely that was a mistake on his part."

The imam protested. "King David was a prophet after Allah's heart, he had six wives. The majority of the women of our prophet were widowed by his defenders. He owed support and protection to them and their children. It was an act of charity. Besides, the prophet is beyond criticism. It is forbidden by the Sharia and all four schools of interpretation of the law. You must not say things like that again. The people will be angry; you would die needlessly. You must learn prudence and hold your tongue here."

Kemeer nodded slowly. "You make your prophet perfect then, and his ways beyond criticism. My wife says the People of the Book are privileged to know something of the truth of Allah, but the fullness of revelation has come in the Koran delivered through Muhammad by recitation."

The Imam now looked somewhat more discomforted and spoke sternly. "You must say, 'may he rest in peace', when you mention the name of Muhammad, may he rest in peace."

Kemeer looked surprised and then thoughtful. "All the saints of God rest in peace. Why should we wish our prophet what all who do the will of God must have? To do the will of Tanra is to have peace. Why mention it, unless there is doubt?"

"It is custom and has been for hundreds of years while your tribes were steeped in superstition and the way of the ancestors."

"I have said that we are Christians and well spoken of by even our enemies. I thought your religion held new truth."

"The truth is as old as Abraham, in his day there were neither Jews nor Christians," said the Imam.

"That faith that obeys God, whatever the world and the outward conditions approve, is the faith that changes the world. It has value like gold. Money is valued by the metal it bears whether the image and inscription are in Arabic, Greek, Hindi or Chinese. Value is not found in the writing. Could the coin of true godly character be written in the metal of faith with the cross on one face and the crescent on the other? The apostle Paul speaks of the faith that responds to the offered grace of God through Yesu."

"It is the faith of Abraham that we espouse. God is One and to elevate a person to the level of Allah is *shirk*, blasphemy. The greatest of sins is to confuse lesser spirits or persons with Allah. This is the sin of the Christian: polytheism. You pray to saints and virgins to find your answers in prayer." The Imam was severe.

"We wish to be like the saints, so we ask for their faith and guidance in our lives. Christians believe in Emanuel: God with us. God shares human life and bears our sins. God is one, but a complex one: Creator, Living Word and Spirit. Three parts of one true reality, Tanra."

"You said you were a Muslim when you came, but you lied. You are a Christian and a renegade. You must die. You are not allowed to renounce Islam. You are not allowed a Muslim wife; she will be taken from you. You will be detained and executed."

"I thought you were a man of God who would talk of the deep things of God. But you talk of laws and ancient practices, just like some priests do. Now you threaten me. What new light is this?"

Both men were standing belligerently face to face now, their voices raised and shouting. Several men came to the door to listen.

"You are *Kefir*, and insult our holy prophet, peace be upon him. I will see you dead," the Imam shouted.

"I thought you had new truth, but I was wrong. I let my wife persuade me. Much has been revealed since the time of Abraham. To go back to that simplicity is to forget all that was revealed after his time. Each prophet had a different purpose in coming."

"But the same message is for all: Return to Allah and you will be forgiven. Allah is merciful, He pardons."

Kemeer shook his head. "Men resist God in their hearts. Yesu died and rose again to ransom the souls of men. Forgiveness is brought in by His blood sacrificed."

"He did not die, but was taken up to heaven. Allah cannot be defeated by His enemies. He put another in his place. Yesu will come again."

"We both agree on something at last. He then will judge if your prophet is right or wrong. I now see where I was wrong and I'm ashamed. I must remain a free man, and leave you and your Islam. Forgive my disturbing your peace." He pushed out the door past the stunned hearers.

"Infidel!"

"Blasphemer!"

"Renegade!"

"Spawn of Satan!" were the words shouted after Kemeer as he mounted his horse. Several gathered stones and others shook clinched fists at the *kafir* as he rode away at a gallop.

KEMEER STONED

103

PEOPLE, PLOTS & PLACES IN CHAPTER 9

Atilla: finds the friend he was following.
Aziz: has intrusion, betrayal and changes to face.
Baja: learns about and shares news with her guest.
Gerchin: finds that surrender means everything.
Kadir: can identify one of the cave's intruders.
Kardesh: finds special guidance in prayer.
Katchy: calculates his gains and plans his future.
Kerim: has a wedding feast far from the bride and groom.
Kynan: is hated by many in the Toozlu clan.
Leyla: must attend a wedding she doesn't approve of.
Maril: hopes to find her friends and go home.
Nooryouz: learns the fate of a special friend.
Setchkin: anticipates her wedding with joy.
Yavuz: is afraid that someone will steal his profits.
Yeet: gets special treatment while he recovers.

GLOSSARY:

Allah razza olson: God willing; may God desire it.
bashanuza saluck: health to your head; be comforted.
bismillah: the Muslim grace, said after a meal.
dun'en: come back; return.
Ema: Arabic for Mother.
namaz: the act of worship; bowing toward Mecca.
Soon-et'je: the professional who performs circumcisions.
soos: hush, be quiet.
Yesu gel: come Jesus; God help me.
yetter: enough; no more.
yok: nothing; eliminate or make something vanish.

TRESPASSERS?

Having strangers blunder into their secret, storage cave produced anger and panic in the smugglers. Quickly drawing weapons they rushed outside the cave. Aziz led the charge screaming. *"Dun'nen,* come back, bastards, spies, you thieves won't get any of our goods."

Yavuz came out after it was obvious that the area was now clear of the intruders. He was frowning and suspicious. "You recognized them. You can identify them, right? We'll put out the word and offer a reward, okay?"

Aziz looked at him in contempt and walked back to the cave and the light. He paused. "There was a woman whose voice I have never heard, but the other, the man, was someone I know, but not from here."

"Think man, think, who was it? Don't just stand there, speak."

"Silence, by Allah, you donkey! Stop your braying." Aziz turned to lean over his excited companion, his hands on his hips. "Hold your peace man! How can I think with you shouting in my ear?"

Kadir entered the cave still catching his breath, gasping: "I almost caught the girl. She's new around here. The man caught me off balance. They got away, but I recognized him."

"Who is bringing in new girls?" Yavuz yelled angrily. "They can't move in on my line. The bordellos won't buy them. They've sworn."

Both Kadir and Aziz stopped open mouthed and stared at Yavuz. "You kept talking about me smuggling girls, you were protecting your interests and using my partnership as a cover. Don't say any more Kadir, don't tell him anything. I hope someone else will break his big dirty game. I'm an honest smuggler, I don't deal in vice like this little vermin."

Yavuz waved his arms and cried. "Let me explain. It's not as bad as you think. I only handle other men's stock. I don't buy in on the merchandise."

Aziz picked the little man up by his coat collar and held him at eye level. "Yetter, enough of your lies: you disgust me. The partnership is ended. Kadir will give you your part when I calculate it. I don't want to see your ugly face again. If I do I'll mess it up for you. No one will ever recognize your face again. Understood?" He threw the little man against the side of the cave and stalked out.

"Be reasonable, you fool! There's big money to be earned," Yavuz cried after him, but he paid no attention to him. He was out in the dark where only a smuggler would know the paths by memory and habit.

"Kadir, you can tell me the name of the man. The one you saw."

Kadir made the negative sign with his head. "I work for Aziz, He says no. You don't tip me for the trips. My lips are sealed."

Yavuz dusted himself and smiled broadly. "Aziz will come around in a few days. You'll see. Tell me." Kadir laughed and moved out of the cave toward the path home.

"Wait, you can be my new partner. I'll give you a part in all my dealings. You'll be rich." Kadir was lost to sight and did not answer a word. Yavuz remained alone.

> - - - - - >MOUNTAIN PASS IN IRAN > - - - - - >

Gerchin listened with care to the instructions of the ambassador, who necessarily spoke through his outrider and page who translated. His tribe had surrendered weapons, confiscated goods accumulated from villages, and to his wife's relief the foreign bride, her goods and people. Weaponless, between two armies, grace and mercy were their only hope. They were the Sultan's men, only he could save them.

"His Excellency wishes you to know that the Sultan has need of such men as you. Men who know how to fight, but have no political ambitions that endanger the Sultan's freedom to administer justice."

Gerchin nodded his acceptance of this situation and added. "We are such men and for this reason accepted his calling when we were still among the Seljuks near Khorasan. For this purpose we decided to come: to protect the Sultan and offer our lives for his safety. Some of the villagers refused us hospitality, but we have persisted in fulfilling our calling."

When translated the man shrugged and continued his listing of conditions of employment.

"You'll all become Muslims, surrendered to Allah, of course. You must choose circumcision now, for the land you enter is pure and must not be contaminated by heathenish ways. You must learn how to worship, do the *namaz* five times a day. We have an imam to teach you these things. He will live with you and come with you to the capitol; to the quarters appointed you there. You will recite the five columns of Islam within the week. You will live and dress like Muslims, but you must not mix with the general population. You must stay outside politics, but guard against those who disturb the peace of the Sultan by guarding His person and palace."

Gerchin inclined his head slightly. The ambassador did not deign to ask for acceptance of terms.

"The ambassador says that the *soon-et'je* will be here tomorrow," the scribe announced. "All males above twelve years of age will be circumcised. After a week you should be able to move toward the palace." On this note the meeting terminated. The delegation rode back to the yurts with the news.

> - - - - - >GOAT CORRAL > - - - - - >

Katchy counted his coins again with an expression of greedy excitement on his face. He stroked his downy face growth thoughtfully. Surely he could buy four nannies of the flock with his trove: three anyway. He would chose them when his master came and they would all be pregnant, but only one would show noticeably. One of three with a kid he would argue with the man. Surely he could give him one expecting. He hugged himself with glee. Even if the man insisted on a young female he would make sure she was soon due. The good man's bounty would soon have him on the road to prosperous independence. He would sell his cheese at the village. He

107

would not need a male until he went off into the brush farther from the rivers and found his own seep spring and grazing range. He nodded his head agreeably.

The cart people would move on and the good man would come back and perhaps need another young goat before traveling on. The crippled boy would follow with his horse until he reached the cart. He might want cheese for the trip. They could graze their horses for a day before continuing. If they waited a week to come, there would be fresh grass. He would have to move away in two years. The master would not share his grass with his own increase. It would be lonely out farther in the desert. He did not have a bride price. Who would be willing to give a daughter to a goat herder? The people of the cart would say: *Yesu gel.* The people of the village would say: *Allah raza olson.* Katchy wondered what he could do to please so great a One. God would have to provide answers.

> - - - - - >WITH THE CART PEOPLE > - - - - - >

"I was praying when the heavenly voice said – 'You must leave now.' Then I heard Katchy shouting when Tayze put the first chest in the cart. After he hurled the rock I knew the voice was warning us not to stay. Yesu loves and protects us." Yeet sat beside his friend Kardesh listening, as the cart rolled slowly forward. Tayze had mounted Yeet's horse and was leading the cart animals, picking a way forward through the scrub, going west. They had become used to obeying the sweet voice that directed Kardesh after his prayer times. Yeet was still pale and weak and Tayze refused to allow him to ride the horse or load the cart.

"She treats you like you were a little girl." Kardesh teased.

"Tayze is tender toward you, as well," scoffed Yeet, "are you becoming a girl?" The cart rolled gently forward tilting them as they rolled among the thickets.

"I don't know what I'm becoming, Yeet, the voice says I'm to be strong and not to fear, God must be taking me somewhere for a purpose. He doesn't say what for or where."

Yeet sighed and asked. "You don't know where to find your father or sister now. Will the voice tell you?"

Kardesh lifted his nose in a negative sign. "*Yok,* nothing, Yesu says not to worry they are kept safe in his purposes and plans. I feel so guilty at times. I treated my sister badly and disobeyed my father. I doubted Tanra and left off praying."

"Tanra is good and will pardon those who are sinful and rebellious."

"Yes, when they repent and turn again. But we also reap the seeds we have sown. My harvest is a rough marred face and weak, useless eyes."

Kardesh flinched when Yeet moved his hand before his face.

"Don't you see anything more than dark and light?"

"I see objects without details, I see the motion with dark against light or light against darker, but things have no edges. No one has a face, only a form and a voice." His voice was sad.

Yeet replied. "We have life, food and a cart to go adventuring. Allah is merciful."

"I wonder how long it will take Sevman to catch up."

"I wonder what stories he will have to tell us then."

> - - - - - >TOOZLU CAMP > - - - - - >

"Come, why the gloom. It's bad luck to frown on a wedding day, especially mine. Forget the ungrateful Bulgar. I'll leave you my old nursemaid tonight, when I move to the Khan's yurt. She can and will name you every eligible male of standing in the tribe. A princess must marry appropriately, so you will know what surprises await you when we return north. I have experienced careless youth and age. Believe me a man of maturity and experience is the best. That's what I've got. Tanra, I can hardly wait. I've got the shivers and giggles with a bonfire inside." Setchkin primped before a brass mirror held by Chichek arranging a headband of green silk with small gold coins dangling around the edge. She sighed with satisfaction as she had her hold the reflector at various angles.

109

"I have heard that the Caliph's mother has a mirror that reflects her whole body at one time - such luxury - I can scarcely believe it! How I would love that kind of magic. Tanram, if he doesn't have a heart of stone he'll melt when he sees me. Look Leyla, this is what a man likes on a wedding day." Leyla did look, but could hardly smile. She knew what her own scratched face looked like and she was still uncomfortable with the thorn poisons in her wounds. She did summon up enough pleasure to sincerely wish her hostess well.

"I pray that blessings and children will follow this union. Will your parents approve? Do they know the groom?"

Setchkin laughed. "You have been away too long. My father will curse and rave, but will find a way to use the arrangement. Twozan is loyal to friends and to the Khan, nothing will change that. Yet I bore the child of promise for the tribe, guardianship will make both men happy and important."

The old nurse stood behind Leyla and murmured, "If they would but be content to share that importance." Only Leyla heard and thought she understood.

> - - - - - >SMUGGLERS' VILLAGE> - - - - - >

"Korkmaz is back watching the door, but the village is under an order of quarantine so we will not be able to move in the streets until it is lifted." Nooryouz smiled in relief, there would be time to recover.

"I had friends who were to climb the pass as well. How could we find them?"

Baja shook her head in wonder and thought out loud. "The village below the pass has been burned, perhaps because of plague and the people scattered. That is the purpose of the quarantine. Illness has spread with them and there is danger of it infecting other villages."

"There was no illness in our band. We came shepherding and were strong and healthy up to the border. We were four girls and two guardians plus a guide for the mountains."

Baja turned curious to ask. "Who was the guide?"

Nooryouz did not hesitate to answer. "I think it was Bolben. He kept the horse herds on the high hills away from the village. He made the offer once."

A look of shock registered on Baja's face. "Oh, my dear, you mean he came here? That may be a terrible mistake. Aziz and Yavuz have had trouble with him. They exchanged insults and death threats when they last met. They will kill him if they find him here. Are you sure they're here?"

110

Nooryouz shook her head. "I don't know, they could have been captured and returned to the harem. Dahkool led the pursuit away from me. I don't know what happened after that."

Baja looked thoughtful and asked, "One was taken dead to the village. Did she have a scar on her lip?"

Nooryouz's nod caused a look of sympathy to shadow Baja's face. "Some say she was the reason why authorities burned the village. Others say plague."

"She tried to protect us, the baby was her delight."

"*Bashanuza sah a luck*, be comforted, God wills it." They embraced and cried. Nooryouz turned and left the room and went to look at the baby. After a long time she tiptoed out of the room where the baby slept and sat in the patio under the grape arbor, she needed comfort and sought the Yesu of her husband. He would understand.

> - - - - - - ->NORTH OF TOOZLU CAMP > - - - - - >

Atilla was amazed. He had scarcely ridden a half hour before he spotted a small fire hidden in a dry water-course. He announced his arrival laughing boisterously as he rode to the fire and dismounted.

"I surrender, you caught me easy enough." Kynan shouted, laughing at his friend.

"You refuse their hospitality, but stay close enough to hear the music. Or perhaps to be hear the girl you've deserted. "

Kynan shrugged, but smiled at Atilla, dismounted and after a hug started to unpack some of the special wedding foods taken from the band.

"I see you have gotten your banquet before the ceremony. How did you manage that?"

Atilla laughed again and laid down the food. "I thought a Muslim guest might chill the party. But I left a young Manichee to recover and a heretic may be considered a bad omen. Now, Kerim of the East Bulgars, if it's not life threatening nor an imposition I want to hear your whole story."

Kynan smiled his amusement. "You followed me all this way from curiosity or to recover your goods?"

Atilla pointed to the food now laid out on a square of cloth. "I feel grateful enough to say the *bismullah*. Come, the bridal feast is prepared, but you have left your bride behind, was she not satisfying?"

Kynan's smile turned sour and he shrugged. "This band is on an opposing side to my people, the leader is marrying my sister tonight and it would cost me my life to witness it. She desires the marriage, but doesn't know I'm here. We were never close, so I don't think it would matter to her."

Atilla looked grave. "To your health, now we will eat and you will enjoy the festivities for I have brought lions' milk to wash away regret and to make a fountain of joy as a gift of my Allah and your Tanra."

"They will be seeking the same source of joy plus special additions that we'll miss. Come, I'm in a mood to talk. I'll tell you a story that will keep you at the center of every festival you ever attend."

"And nobody will believe that I tell the truth, no doubt, always my fate. Tell away, my friend Kerim, I'll be your best advocate."

> - - - - - >BASE PASHA'S HOUSE > - - - - - >

Korkmaz stood at the Commander's door. The old servant stood to attend his master's business and was very annoyed by the boy's insistence on talking to Onat bey's mother. When the lady came he extended a package of cheese from his aunt Baja in appreciation of the commander's reception and care of refugees, who were, after all, relatives of the people living at the base. She thanked him and carried it to the kitchen where she laid it on the table. Maril was there helping the cook as helpfully as she had her own mother. She was given the run of the kitchen because they saw her skill and knew a girl of her sweet temperament could be trusted there. She was a busy, happy helper and the new mother had resolved not to part with her, no matter what her son, the commander's opinion. The girl's family was, after all, traveling and hadn't been heard from in a year. Maril was safe with her.

"Just see what Baja hanum has sent us. Sheep cheese just made, so fresh." She smelled the round cake appreciatively. "That nice boy, Korkmaz, has brought it. They say he is following the family business. Which is a pity; he would make a good soldier."

"What is the family business, *Ema* Onat?" Maril, an exshepherdess, was staring at the cheese and its cloth wrapping as if her soul were in her eyes.

"Smugglers, as most are in this place, but always of quality goods. They have kept aloof of alcohol, drugs and slave girls."

"Oh, I've heard some stories this week that you wouldn't credit, bayan." interjected the cook in a confidential, secretive tone.

"*Soos*, hush, we have tender ears here. Keep your gossip to yourself. Besides, I already know where these lies started. Yavuz bey, the double dealer, is behind it all." She marched off self-righteously to deposit the gift in a cooling cabinet.

Maril whispered to the cook. "You can tell me about it later, it's our secret." Cook nodded, smiling slyly.

> - - - - - >TOOZLU CAMP > - - - - - >

Setchkin woke in a mellow mood. She giggled for it was Twozan who blew in her ear to waken her. She looked up hopefully. "*Evet*, yes, whatever it is, the answer is yes."

He chuckled, "You had better be careful, it's a ride I'm waking you for. We will ride ahead and watch the dawn together. The horses are ready."

"I can think of other things for a wonderful first night, but I'm yours to command. Let's stage our first dawn raid together." He pulled her up and handed her a shepherd's cloak. She held it up.

"You will appreciate it more when we are out in the wind." They both laughed together and she rapidly put on riding clothes. The horses were waiting beside the yurt door and mounting they left in the dark before the early rising neighbors were up. He led out.

"Wait up you maniac, you can't see the trail," she yelled. He paid her no heed and thundered ahead. She forced her pace because she was determined not to be left behind. She was irritated and mystified by his behavior. He always stayed just ahead so the trail was never missed. She was thoroughly annoyed when he suddenly turned left and stopped, laughing at the top of his voice. She caught him.

"What in the world are you up to, running ahead like that?" Without answering he dismounted and held her horse so she could do the same. She saw the dull glow of a nearly quenched fire. Dimly, in the growing light she saw two figures rising up from the ground. She caught her breath, suddenly afraid of the new situation.

113

PEOPLE, PLOTS & PLACES IN CHAPTER 10

Abbassid Ambassador: has soothing words for hurts.
Abdullah: plans the future for himself and friend.
Atilla: meets the lady whose wedding they celebrated.
Bolben: hides from enemies, soldiers and his past.
Deputy: makes more trouble than he's worth.
Erly: must always guard the perimeters of the camp.
Katchy: tries to get money from the wrong people.
Kerim: the Bulgar is ordered out of the perimeter.
Korkmaz: uses cheese to pass a message to people.
Kynan: sees his sister at last for a moment of memory.
Magazi: skillfully plans a man's death.
Mansur Ibn el Ari: son of 'the son of the bee' gets stung.
Setchkin: shares her husband's view of beauty.
Sheriff: works for the Kaymakan, but has poor help.
Twozan: shows concern for the bride's visiting family.
Yeet: suffers from wounds and loss as he goes west.

GLOSSARY:
barish, arkadash: peace, friend; I mean no harm.
bayan: mrs; miss; ma'm; (used before the name).
evet: yes; definitely.
hanum: lady; madam; (used after the name).

DAWN RIDE

"We're looking for a boy from the quarries, name of Yeet. He was reported to have come here four days ago." The village authority questioned Katchy around mid-day. The boy grinned and waited for inducement to be offered. He nodded his head, but said nothing. The three men were from the village, he recognized them.

"Come now, don't protect the guilty. He is accused of robbing and refusing to render aid." Katchy nodded enthusiastically, but silently. They bought his cheese sometimes.

"You must tell us what you know." Katchy extended a hand palm up. One of the men grunted, swore and slapped down the hand.

"The goat herder is an idiot, sir. What can you learn from him? They are not here and the tracks lead west."

The sheriff protested, "I'll not follow a cart three days gone. Not for the few coins the boy could have gotten from the other one." He turned to Katchy again. While the other men rode over to examine the camp site.

"When did they leave boy? Speak up, you are nearly a man and have hair on your face, surely you can talk."

Katchy pouted, "I talk plenty. They go, no give me any coins. You come, no give coins."

"I think this fire is from last night, Sir, they can't have gotten far."

The leader shook his head and rode up calmly to the spot. "There are tracks of at least five people here, seven to nine horses have passed or stayed here. The tracks go three directions apart from those to the village. You're going to follow them all?"

"No sir, just the wagon," came the reply.

"And if the quarry boy took off on a horse? He had one when he met Umer, according to his complaint. The cart may have nothing to do with this Yeet fellow. No, deputies, we waste time and energy for a few coins." He rode back to Katchy followed by the deputies.

The sharia law requires the loss of a hand for stealing. Both these boys hail from the same quarry. We don't know the particulars of why one boy, who knows another, doesn't help and may have stolen. It's all vague and hearsay without two witnesses. I'm letting it go."

"I guess you're right Sir. We would have to feed the rascal too, but I think this boy here needs a lesson. He doesn't want to help. He wants money to talk. Can we lay a few on him?"

The leader looked doubtful, but then shrugged. "He looks spry. You'll have to catch him."

The deputy walked his horse past Katchy and suddenly loosed his whip with a back hand slap that left an angry red welt across the boy's cheek. With a shriek of pain and rage Katchy was off at a run. The man whirled his horse around and raced after him while his companion cut him off. Katchy dived behind a thorn clump and was crawling into a tunnel between plants when the whip caught him on the leg. He howled his hurt and frustration again. The riders first cursed and then laughed as they rode back to the sheriff. The loud-mouth deputy spoke again.

"Well, I guess he'll remember this for a while. It'll teach him more respect for authority. We should take a little kid with us for our trouble. We'll call it a fine for harboring a criminal."

The sheriff put his nose up. His deputy was calling too many of the shots. "You'll have the owner down on our necks. The judgment would go against us. Leave him be, he's had enough."

"You're missing an opportunity to apply the law. He may have been paid by this Yeet fellow to keep mum."

The sheriff ignored him. They rode away, only one was satisfied that they had done their duty.

> - - - - - >AT THE IRANIAN PASS > - - - - - >

"The Sultan extends to you his personal thanks for your valiant pursuit of the invading tribe. These Turks have surrendered to the Sultan's mercy. They're being taken to Baghdad as prisoners of war. Your service to the Shadow of Allah, our Sultan, may his name be praised, will be rewarded." The ambassador's words rolled like a silk spun garment, bright, shining, but offering little substance or weight.

"We have pursued and harried the tribe into your ambush and capture. We claim the right of spoils from the tribe and the possession of some of their principal men as trophies and signs of victory to display in our homes in Khorasan."

Mansur Ibn el Ari held in his anger: determined to gain some significant goods or honor from their fruitless pursuit and expense. A promise of recognition was not enough. His mind darted in many directions, but met stone walls on every path. The ambassador and wall builder was again speaking softly. He appeased, offering soothing oil for the wounds.

"The men of Khorasan have ever proved their worth to the Abbasid dynasty. From the rebellion until today, our Sultan has never failed to reward the men of the Eastern Battle Ground. All men must answer to the truth before Allah. You are not neglected, for his eyes are ever on His valiant men of the East. Rewards will come. You are ordered to return to your city and have a victory parade. I deliver to you an Abbasid black banner bearing a gold medallion on the staff. Go in honor. Go happily to your families."

117

The audience was terminated and poor Mansur was conducted out while still trying to protest. Outside in the camp two dear friends conferred over their new future.

"You see how the Abbasid palm off any eastern prosperity by conquests or government opportunity."

"The sun is setting in the east and shines best and longest in the west. We must follow the Turks. Grazers say the rains come out of the west, so we will go forth to meet the larger opportunities there."

His companion nodded agreement. "The el Ari family will make no honey out of this expenditure. They'll keep only the most faithful of their retainers, others will be left empty. We must find a scribe to write the letter to our parents, to tell them of our decision."

Abdullah smiled happily. "A few like us will desert the ranks, but many will remain to share our leader's blame for the present lack of Allah's blessing."

"Well placed words will fan the fury of those who feel defrauded. You have the gift of words that would serve to that end."

"Yes, and I know just where to start and who pays."

> - - - - - >NEAR THE TOOZLU CAMP > - - - - - >

Two figures were in the act of standing. Setchkin smelled the alcohol as they rode nearer the fire.

"You celebrated well last night," Twozan stated in an amused voice, "I hope you are clear minded enough to meet the bride."

The first light was beginning and she could make out two men standing, rather disheveled, open mouthed, about ten paces away.

"This is unexpected. You have done a noble thing Twozan Khan, I will never forget it."

She gasped and moved forward, unbelieving. "Kynan? You are Kynan? How did you come here?" She looked about, suddenly worried. "Is father here?" She paused.

"*Yok*, nothing like that, I have one friend here, Atilla bey this is my sister Setchkin hanum, now happily married."

Atilla replied, "I'm privileged, Bayan, to meet you."

She nodded distractedly and walked to Kynan to touch his face and look closely. "You are different, what has changed? Why are you here sleeping in the scrub? What has brought you south?"

He laughed, "One question at a time please. As a commander of troops chasing you, I was captured by the Caliph's troops and imprisoned. Tanra helped me escape and I arrived here with the help of my friend Atilla. I sleep here because it isn't possible to enter the camp."

She could wait no longer and broke in interrupting the explanations. "You should have come. They are Toozlu, a sept of our people."

"I have shed Toozlu blood, they could shed mine. I would not be welcome in camp, I prefer to travel ahead."

She shook her head. "Are you, then, this Kerim of the East Bulgars?"

He nodded, "You have heard, then, my alternate name?"

She chided him, "That poor girl loves you so. She talks only occasionally and always of you and how you saved her." He hung his head. "You must see her again. She's still healing from the shock and thorns." She shook him reproachfully. "Why won't you understand? You men are so stupid about women."

"That's why they attract and fascinate us so," Atilla said. "You women are a beautiful, never completely solved puzzle." The men, laughed uneasily.

Setchkin humped and retorted sharply, "At least you think you know an answer. I wish my brother had gotten that far." She paused and moved closer to Twozan. "Be sure she will try to teach you as fast as you are willing to learn."

Twozan looked down at her thoughtfully and smiled gently. "Something you are willing to teach me I'm sure."

She smiled. "We both will have much to discover." She moved to her horse, "Come, my lord, we must finish our ride. The camp will be awake and search parties or sentries will be out along the perimeter soon."

"Out to track the exiles or the newly weds?" asked Kynan.

"Both, our people are boldly curious and find distraction in minding other's business," she countered.

Twozan added. "The sentries will speculate on our meeting here, the whole camp will be in the know by noon."

"I hope they will let me enter the camp when we have finished out here." Atilla hastened to say, "I have to pick up Sevman to return him to his people"

Twozan embraced Kynan and mounted. "You both have immunity, and Atilla, you have permission to enter the camp. Only the Bulgar is excluded. I can't guarantee his safety from one lady there."

Both men acknowledged the reply. Setchkin rode to Kynan and leaned from her horse to embrace him. He smiled up at her and sniffed appreciatively.

She laughed and turned to Twozan. "You can't imagine how he used to tease me. 'You smell like you've been into our honey supply, I'll tell mother. You smell of birch, what did you do in the woods?'" They laughed and rode off.

"What did she smell like today?" Atilla asked still watching them.

"Fresh cut hay and meadow flowers," Kynan answered softly.

> - - - - - >AT THE IRANIAN PASS > - - - - - >

"You took this step long ago, Kemeer bey, all the tribe knows, now we are forced into the same, it goes with the job. We must become Muslims to work at the Caliph's palace. They will be here to cut us short tomorrow. We rejoice with our wives tonight, who knows how long it will be again? Gerchin had relented a bit, adjusting to the new reality.

"In theory, what my wife told me sounded different and good, but when I talked to the Imam it sounds like we surrender to slavery of religious men rather than surrender to Tanra. Their prophet is treated like the Christ, beyond criticism. He is not a man, a human messenger, with men's weaknesses, but like a word from heaven with no flaws. He

120

says it is death to mention the weakness of the prophet for women: the vanity of dying his beard; the injustice of wholesale condemnation and executions of tribal religious opponents. Even today any objections are treated as blasphemy and as a crime deserving death. You should have heard him curse me."

Gerchin heard him out. "I felt like that toward you when you announced your conversion to Islam in the tribe. I thought it was a political move to split us."

"I was trying to look forward to our new status as members of their Dar al Islam, a religious empire. I was ambitious, I admit it."

"As Turks at home we were a free people, now we are war prisoners of the Sultan. They will kill you if you don't return and repent to the Imam. You must confess your error and accept what he says. Never again must you admit doubts to any outside the tribe. Be comforted in this one thing, we will be rich and powerful as guards of a Sultan that dare not trust his Arabs again."

Kemeer heaved a sigh and shook his head sadly. "It goes against my pride to admit a fool of a puppet is right, when my experience and logic say he is wrong. I lose my freedom."

"And you gain wealth and importance. You should thank the Saints for that advancement." Gerchin stopped and considered what he had just said. He smiled at his mistake and added to his fellow. "We will no doubt continue to honor the Messiah Yesu, whom they call the prophet Isa; in ways they would never understand or appreciate. What we have been is not changed in a day. Only the exterior will change tomorrow, but within we will still be Turks, free of soul if not of body."

Kemeer nodded and rose from his place. "I'll return to the Imam and eat quince, a bitter humiliation."

"Yesu teaches that the humble gain Tanra's approval."

"We were not very good Christians, I wonder if we will be any better Muslims?" He walked away without the usual farewells.

"If we can gain gold by fighting, we will excel them all." Gerchin murmured to himself, "An empire awaits us and we will wrest it to ourselves."

> - - - - - > OUTSIDE THE TOOZLU CAMP> - - - - - >

"Here we merge with our old trail," Twozan stated. "We'll angle off toward that high hill. It will look like it was our original destination and that we were distracted for a moment to visit the Bulgar and his friend who stopped by the camp yesterday. We must keep your brother's identity a secret shared between us only."

Her smile was radiant now. "Married one night and already I share secrets with my new husband. How delightful!"

He grinned over at her. "It's a basic need of every family: silence and solidarity in some private matters."

She laughed back at him. "That's the kind of marriage I've always sought, not a pretty, 'play time girl' or a 'political toy'. I'm a partner now, we have secrets."

"That's what it was supposed to be, until men changed it. Adam was given Eve as part of himself." She rode so their legs met.

"I'll love being part of such an important man. You'll be proud of me." She tried to suppress the sudden attack of doubt; could she really make him proud? She had spent her life hiding her true feelings. She had feigned, with an agreeable face, to obnoxious arrangements that others planned and imposed on her. She had become a habitual liar, loud and demanding when she wanted her own way. She had become increasingly unreasonable, frequently flattering or insulting others for advantage. Could she change? She hesitated in her mind, fear chilled her. She must make him proud. 'Oh Yesu, let me make him proud.' She found herself crying, tears dropped off her chin. They stopped at the hill top.

"See there are the yurts just over there. You can see the spring and well on the north." Smiling, he looked at her expectantly. Then he saw her tears. "Setchkin, my love, why are you crying?" She dabbed her eyes and sought an excuse, directing her horse toward the ravine below.

"Wedding night leftovers I suppose, I'm not sure how to please you, so, I yield to the obvious." She dismounted where the ravine widened and a bit of winter grass lay brown. She spread her shepherd's cloak over the grass, sat and held out her hand invitingly.

> - - - - - >OUTSIDE THE CAMP> - - - - - >

Old Erly rode out for sentry duty rather late, for celebrations tended to relax the camp routines. He grinned as he followed the tracks of two horses, whose tracks he knew, heading to the high hill ahead. He knew the drive of all new couples to find or show off beauty in places blessed with wide vistas. They could parade their right of mutual possession. The joys of coupling, free of the sneaky, hidden actions of those feeding lust and passions unacceptable to parents and society. Respectability, yes, and contentment too, came with commitment.

Erly glanced at the Y in the trail, the pair had visited the Bulgar and his friend. Erly paused, undecided a moment, but curiosity won, he entered the camp quietly. He peeped around a bush and found an arrow pointed at his eye by the Bulgar. The other man had drawn his scimitar which rested at ready over a shoulder.

Erly gulped, "*Barish, arkadash*, peace friend, I come from the yurts."

"Unannounced visits, show bad intentions," quoted Kerim the Bulgar. "Why would you sneak into our camp?"

The long pause showed that the intruder had no ready response. He explained. "My name's Erly," He held out his lunch. "I thought you might like a bit of the celebration. Our Khan has a new wife."

Atilla took the package and a medallion fell with the gift. Erly eyed the piece sadly and then said. "The medallion belongs to your boy. I guess you can return it to him." He turned to go, "You need to move out. We're ordered not to bother you, but you must stay outside the camp perimeters" Erly rode out irritated with himself. He had lost his gains through sheer carelessness. He wondered why the East Bulgar looked familiar. Some of their boys had served in Chipchak camps in youth exchanges. Perhaps that was where he had seen him. He rode past the hill top, but was too annoyed and occupied in thought to notice the horses in the gully.

> - - - - - >MONASTERY RUINS> - - - - - >

They huddled in one of the ruined rooms of a hermitage. It was built against and on a cliff, but largely roofless and broken by time. The guide, Jon, Sesli and Bolben were chilled and although out of the wind they were still cold. The small room had a partial shelter of wood placed on rocks that helped enclose their corner. They shared the bread brought from the village and shivered under their thin blankets. Jon addressed the reduced and discouraged group.

"We need to find out what has happened to Manish and Maril, They were taken I'm sure and may be hurt or imprisoned." No one stirred.

"I feel so terrible, Nooryouz and Dahkool were lost on the other side of the border, and now two more are gone. Can't we wait for news here?" Sesli begged.

123

The guide looked at each face before he started whispering. "I must return to the base before I'm missed, but I'll tell you what I know." The new commander is strict but fair. The girl is with his mother and will be sent to her family, when they pay, some say. The shepherd boy is held in confinement and eventually will be sent back to his master. I took Nooryouz to my aunt's house. She's safe with the baby there. She told me about you. I came looking for you the next night. I didn't know Aziz and Kadir would be at the cave. I'm sorry about that."

"That was a scary moment. Do you think they'll report us?" Jon asked.

"No danger there," Korkmaz replied with a laugh.

"Did they recognize me?" Bolben asked.

"Kadir is sharp; he doesn't miss much. He may know us both now. We'll have to wait and see what he does with it. They'll be busy covering up and reducing inventory: moving stock out. They could lose it all otherwise." Korkmaz paused then continued explaining.

"The Wigers are at peace, but the border is now full of refugees from a drastic police action. They burned a village, claiming that the men raped a harem girl. Villagers say she committed suicide, others say she was murdered. The base is on full alert, they are watching the passes. You should be safe here for a couple of days, I can bring food, more and better, if you have money." He held out his hand.

Bolben spoke up. "I have friends here who will pay for us. We escaped just before the troops arrived. I saw the dead girl, they did not molest her. I was there to make sure. She was beautiful, even dead." He ducked his head sobbing. "I wish it had been different; I wanted to hear her voice. I would like to be sure she's the one I knew and loved. I needed to hear her speak. Oh, Yesu of light, I'm in pain."

> - - - - - >PASS TO IRAN > - - - - - >

"There's a demonstration planned for tomorrow, the tents are full of rebellion." Magazi whispered to his dearest friend. "Have you found the slinger yet?"

Abdullah answered with irritation. "I could have found a dozen archers for the one David and at a better price. Why do you insist?"

His friend touched Abdullah's mouth softly, moving his own head back in a negative gesture. "*Soos!* Hush! Those sweet lips must be for other things. An arrow proclaims murder, and an urgent investigation with punishment. Rocks proclaim anger and an accidental death and, perhaps, involve some fighting by the guards. Mob action equals generalized retaliation, a few cuts and bruises and cracks on the head, nothing more. A very regrettable situation everyone will say. However, as a safety measure you can contract one archer since they are cheap and we never know how a situation will work out. The Sultan has a debt of gratitude to the father, so, he will be sorrowful yet glad to hear of the son's demise at a moment of glory. The flag and medallion will comfort the family."

Abdullah kissed his friend. "Forgive me for doubting you. One of our men was a shepherd, now grown tired of herding. He feels doomed to feed goats for the rest of his life and has little future. His price is high. He wants it all in advance, he doesn't trust us."

"*Ee-ye*, good, stay by him with your knife handy. Make sure he throws until the man is down and dead or near it. If the effort fails, kill him: you'll be protecting Mansur, the army commander."

Abdullah nodded, laughing. "I silence a witness against us and gain status as a hero, very neat!"

"But leave the money as evidence, to confirm his commitment to murder."

THE CONSPIRITORS

125

PEOPLE, PLOTS & PLACES IN CHAPTER 11

Baja: convinces neighbors that a relative is visiting.
Derk bey: a secret agent who is hunting the Gray Wolf.
Leyla: is still looking for any word of Kerim the Bulgar.
Nooryouz: must learn Baja's family's history for safety.
Sanjak: observes Manish talking with Korkmaz.
Setchkin: has problems answering questions.
Sheriff: sends word to Kooskoo bey and others.
Umer: complains and schemes while recovering.
Yeet: finds an old friend to relieve his lonesomeness.

GLOSSARY:

aja chekten: you hurt me; that hurt
Allah ha ek ber: God is greater; God is great!
Alaykum salaam: Islamic response, And to you peace.
Bowzkurt: Gray Wolf - also the head of a secret society.
Hi'yer: no; negative, with an upward jerk of the head.
Salaam alaykum: Islamic greeting, Peaace to you.

THE FERGANA MARE

"You left the camp this morning before dawn. Where did you go?" Leyla lay applying medicine to her many scratches and pricks with the help of the old nursemaid, who squeezed points that were headed.

Setchkin stopped to watch and consider the question. She answered, "We rode to the tall hill you see to the north. You can view the river valley from there. We shall have to cross it."

The helper spoke. "Princess Leyla, don't fidget, this has the thorn point still." She shook her head in exasperation and sighed. Then she started again. She was kneeling, working on the princess' lower back.

"The stranger, Atilla bey, did you see him?" Leyla continued.

Setchkin pondered how to answer this for she knew what would follow. She went over to one of the trunks to check its contents. "Briefly, we warned him to move out of the camp's perimeter."

"But you saw Kerim bey as well, didn't you?" She squirmed.

"They had been drinking. They had a celebration to match ours" Setchken was busy checking the contents of the trunk and trying to measure, before the question, how much to tell. This was a test. She had a secret to keep. "They were disheveled but able to converse."

Leyla stopped her primping and looked at the busy bride. "Did they mention my name?"

Setchkin shook her head. "I think I mentioned you and they asked about your health."

"How did you come to mention me, if they didn't ask?"

"I said that you were recovering somewhat. That you needed attention to recover."

Leyla looked annoyed and shook off the helper. "Why should you volunteer such information if it was not requested?"

Setchkin sighed, but did not turn to face the inquirer. "I scolded Kerim bey for not staying for the wedding and your recovery."

Leyla, only half dressed, stood up. "You were strangers, why should he attend the wedding? I suppose he felt his duty to me terminated?" She allowed the surgery to continue, bending slightly holding a yurt support pole. "How did he answer?"

Setchkin now closed the trunk and turned to look up. "He said that he had to continue north before us. He also congratulated us and regretted that he could not attend the wedding. Said his friend, Atilla bey, would return to camp and take the boy he left here home again. We then continued our ride."

Leyla sighed, "It sounds like him, courteous and helpful. You were wrong to scold him. Why should he think of a scratched and dirty girl with only one change of clothes? A pitiful lost child..." Her words caught in her throat.

"He is such a thoughtless, careless, happy go lucky vagabond."

"How harshly you judge him, Setchkin hanum, How can you?"

"Oh, I know him well enough ... That is, I know his kind. My brother was like that... careless of peoples' feelings." Her face flushed and she felt her pulse race. She had almost let it out. Let go of the secret! What would Twozan think?

Leyla, however, was distracted. "Ouch, *aja chekten*, are you digging for the bone, old one?" she exclaimed.

"Bayan, you wiggle too much. Hold still. Now, I've got it out." She stood and bared Leyla's shoulders "I'll put medicine on your back and look for more points."

Leyla readjusted her meager cover. "Just rub on the medicine, please. Kerim got all the points out."

There was a moment of silence; both women stared at her, wordless. "What else could I do? The thorns points are poison and itch terribly. He was careful."

Setchkin stood and walked over to look at her back. "And tender no doubt? Men do have tender moments, I've been finding out again. You forget how you miss it."

Leyla blushed to her neck and back, then she turned to face them. "I never..." Her voice faltered, so she tried again. "We didn't do that

128

even once..." Tears welled up, and her voice failed her completely. She turned her back which shook with emotion.

Setchkin walked to put her arm around her and to comfortingly whisper again and again. "He won't go far. He will not be far away from us at all."

>- - - - - - > SYR RIVER SOUTH BANK>- - - - - - >

"You will have a long trip north to arrive home and need a pack animal. However, I chose that pack horse you have and paid good money for him and this one I ride." Attila proclaimed. "My old horse was stolen by the murderer I pursued. I intend to get him back."

"I recognize your right to take this one. But how am I to get home if you do?" Kynan protested.

At that moment a herd of horses driven by two men appeared descending the hill. They wore tribal clothes and their hair was braided in queues.

"I guess I'll have to buy you one as a parting gift."

"You've already bought me this black for the chase," Kynan exclaimed. "I refuse to cost you more."

Atilla chuckled, "Nobody knew of our bet, so I never paid. The owners think a fugitive stole it. An escaped prisoner does that sort of thing."

"Why you rascal, you still owe me the price of a horse. I hope Katchy didn't keep your money bag. I left it in a high thorn tree, out of his reach."

"Oh, he had already put a hole in it when I arrived. He's sharp with a sling." They laughed together.

"*Salaam Alaykum*," Atilla shouted to the horsemen approaching the river. "You have fine horses. Do you have any for sale?"

The men looked them over carefully, one then replied, "*Alaykum Salaam*, We're merchants and I take the herd north to the tribes. They are all very special breeding stock."

"Yes, I see you have a beautiful Fergana mare. I don't expect you'll want to sell her?" Kynan asked.

You're right, she's beautiful, but we've been attacked twice in as many nights to get her. They are tracking her, so she's a source of trouble to us."

129

"I've had that kind of experience as well. Will you pay me to take her off your hands?" Kynan suggested.

Everyone had a good laugh. "*Hyer*, but I'll sell her at near cost value. I'll be surer to get home with gold, than with her." Everyone sat ready to enjoy the bargaining.

"She's too fine to carry packs, so I'll have to pay the difference to get another for cargo. But I want two for the price of one. Remember, I'd like to get home whole too," Kynan added. They enjoyed another moment of shared laughter. Then they started to talk about money.

At the conclusion and the reluctant payment of the price by Atilla, the merchants parted with a warning. "The whole valley is in a state of unrest. Quarrels and fights are breaking out everywhere. I'd say: get out of here fast, before it comes to a head.

> - - - - - >WEST TOWARD KHIVA> - - - - - >

Yeet was weary of being bounced in the cart. He took to horse over the protest of Tayze. He even proposed to scout ahead and see if there was an appropriate place to camp that night. With help he had carefully wrapped a turban to enclose, cushion and hide his bandaged but still swollen wound. He knew they were somewhat north of Samarkand and they should strike a valley soon. The wind carried a chill that spoke of winter and the need of shelter. Yeet felt a wish for home and a visit to mother at the rug factory in Kokand. He wondered if the room he had held was still available. The members of the gang were scattered and he wondered what else had changed. Sevman's Manichean community had moved east. The Chipchaks were retreating north and the forces of Ibn el Ari were going west chasing Turks. How rapidly things change. These happenings were talked about by villagers and you wondered if they really understood. If it was all true, the world had changed forever. He concluded that Allah had a restless mind. Yet, each move was the result of someone's idea and choice; they willed it. But, also, Allah willed it. Yet, each choice seemed necessary based on what others were doing. It made his head hurt and he felt dizzy. Yeet brought his horse to a stop. He lifted his hands and his voice to the one he hoped would be able to give him an answer. He needed to get a reply, now.

"Al - la - a - a - a - ah, hu - u - u, e - e - ek - be - e - er." He stopped and waited. Then, he did it again, louder: God is great! He had heard it all his life. His mother, born a Christian, always said: "Listen to the call to prayer. The first words are the important ones. Pray at that time. Saint Paul says we should pray constantly. Pray with Christian, Jew, Manichean, Muslim, or any other God seeker. Don't be distracted by customs or place. Look for sincerity, warmth and humility. In such company God will speak to your heart."

Far ahead and very faintly he heard the prayer call echoed back to him, but the voice was that of another.

> - - - - - >IN BAJA'S HOUSE > - - - - - >

"I have passed you off to my friends as a refugee from the burned village who followed the trace her family had always used to get over the pass and then your story of the mountain hut and the spring and Korkmaz finding you and bringing you home. The word is out and they have accepted it as true. Now we will review a bit of family history that you will be expected to know and we will build a good story of life in the village below."

Baja the aunt, had kept them for three days, during curfew. She loved to talk and Nooryouz knew her day would be full of questions and answers.

Now the post was returning to normal as the refugees were housed and cared for. When the Uigur authorities are prepared to receive them again, they will start to pass over the border and to reoccupy the village. It would require rebuilding to be fit for winter. Some already preferred to remain with relatives in safety.

Korkmaz had visited the caves and learned of the quarrel and angry separation of Yavuz and Aziz. The village was divided on how permanent the division would be. In some circles bets were laid on the length of time needed to reconcile them.

Refugees who had neither money nor relations were scattered about the countryside and were given a food ration from the base. Bolben, as a known villager, also went for a portion 'for his family.'

Corporal Tash was dismissed from the infirmary to resume half time duty as a function fit for a boy with a cracked rib.

The new Turkish captain, Sanjak, was put out to supervise prisoners digging latrines for the post. All military and some civilian prisoners were put under his command for disagreeable tasks. Manish was included in the work details. They were using mattock hoes to dig new latrines below the base and applied lime to the old facilities and filled up some. Such were considered the habitation of jinns, demonic spirits. This made the odious task spiritually dangerous as well as dirty.

While supervising this work Sanjak noticed one of the local boys. He dared to come there. He saw him speak with a young prisoner and gave him something wrapped. After they had exchanged a few words, both vigorously resumed their duties. Sanjak went to investigate and found the wrapped bundle to be cheese, which he let the boy keep. But something was different now. The shepherd boy, Manish, had changed in some way. He was – confident, perhaps even happy? He must find out about the local boy, his name and other particulars.

"Derk bey, what are you doing here?" Yeet was astonished to see his old benefactor in this thorny waste. They embraced joyfully.

"Yeet? Why so far from Kokand? How is your friend Sevman? Is he here?"

Yeet was crying and nodding, yes and no, together. "We've traveled and Sevman is away. We are going west. How have you come here?" Yeet was breathless.

"I visited a group of nomadic Turks and made some agreements and was to go north with a new captain to his base. He left and I changed my mind and am going west also. Where is your group?"

Yeet pointed behind as a cart began to show over the hill. "They are coming now. Erben and Leyla have gone ahead of us. I think they were hurrying to meet the people they were expecting near here somewhere." Derk bey received this news without comment.

"Let's ride beside the cart and you can tell me all that has passed since you left Kokand. Such adventures need to be shared with friends." Derk rode along listening to the accounts of life in the quarries and his heart was heavy. He asked himself –'How do I tell them about the unsolved death of Yeet's mother at the rug factory?" He wondered if the name of the *Bowzkurt*, Gray Wolf, would have any meaning for them. Had Seerden been in touch with them at any time?"

>- - - - - - >IN SULEMA'S HOUSE > - - - - - >

"I'm exhausted, and it hurts so much. Can I stop and rest a while," Umer complained to the old healer.

His tormentor laughed or rather she cackled in cruel derision. "I've never seen such a baby! You whine about everything. We took off the clay cast after four days, just because it hurt and restricted you. The joint was only displaced, not broken. You should be able to walk now with only a little pain. You could run, if your life depended on it. One of our village boys would be out in the fields working by now."

Umer hobbled to the bed and sat heavily. He sighed and reached for a bowl of water and drained it, wiping his mouth with the back of his hand, muttering, "Perhaps there is something else wrong. You made me do leg lifts and foot bends from the second day. You make me bend my knees now, a hundred times twice a day. It is torture."

"They are recovery exercises. If you leave an injured leg or arm without exercise, the muscles always wither and weaken. Unless you want to be crippled for life, you must obey instructions. I want you to go out for a walk every day. Go down as far as the fountain if you can, the climb is good for you."

Umer made an ugly face, but Sulema's brother was master of the house and he nodded in agreement. "Don't worry we'll see he does it. He can start this afternoon."

The healer nodded her appreciation. The family had been feeding the boy for ten days, he should work or travel. The girl seemed a little too possessive of him and her eyes glinted mischievously behind their veil. The family was a small land owner, just enough irrigation and grazing to keep body and soul together. If the father had lived the boy would have been gone from the village by now. The girl might have been of use too, but with the father gone she had strayed and would bring no bride price in the village. His only hope was to get an outsider to take her for a minimal price. He hoped that he would get enough to obtain a bride for himself. They lived a snarl and shout relationship in the house.

"You might take a look at that horse of yours, he needs grooming. You would find a short ride helpful and stimulating," the healer said as she departed. She walked over to the house of the local sheriff. He was home and after greetings she came to the matter. "What news of the accused thief? What was over there on Goat Hill?"

"I found lots of tracks coming from and going everywhere: horses, cart, men and women's signs, walking, running, sitting, lying down, camping and all that go with living somewhere a day or two. It looked like a market had been there, the road over too: full of tracks."

"Any certainty of the things declared?"

The sheriff fidgeted. "Hard to say, I think our boy's a liar, but there was some kind of trouble. There's lots of running horse tracks all around. Some rocks like a wall on top the hill. They're built like a little fort."

She shook her head exasperated. "I had our letter writer send notice to the owner over there. He'll come over to investigate. I know the man."

The sheriff smiled. "That'll put his little idiot on edge. The boy's practically got a beard. I always thought he was a child, but I guess he has been there twelve years or so."

The woman nodded agreement. Then she asked, "Where did the goat boy come from? Did Kooskoo bey get him from the orphan's home or did someone abandon him?"

He shrugged. "There was an old man there and the boy must have come to help him. He's been dead ten years at least. I went over to see them then. The boy was little and cried a lot, but he learned to do the job."

"I guess that's what he'll do for the rest of his life. Never be more than the animals he guards. Allah wills it so," she said.

"This is where the two men crossed the ford. They examined it closely moving up and down stream. Then, they crossed the river again and talked. They met two merchants with a herd. Only one crossed to the other side and the other one went back the way they came."

The farmers gathered by the hill that descended to the ford. They talked anxiously of the approach of nomads.

"They'll take the crops and pull out to the desert."

"Rob us blind in the process."

"If we catch them here we can split them or block passage so the troops can take them."

Some agreed, but others objected strongly. A tall skinny old man yelled at them. "We lost three men five years ago. We still have orphans and widows because of it. Cornered they become fanatical."

"I say hit the rear guard and take their women and provisions. Slaves bring good prices, especially women."

A short stout man disagreed bluntly. "It's our crops we want to protect. Go for their gold and men will be killed for sure. If we make our presence known they won't dare send out raiding parties."

Another agreed loudly. "They came through here this spring chased by our troops. They just want to get home now. Lets make our presence known and I think they'll just go across." There was general agreement.

"Let's do that. We don't know if there are troops to come help us. We need to consult with the authorities."

"They never know. They say they'll protect us, but it's always late, sometimes too late."

The skinny old man shouted for silence. "We'll send two men to the Kaymakan and the rest must come here with arms and neighbors. We'll confront them here."

FARMERS PLAN

PEOPLE, PLOTS & PLACES IN CHAPTER 12

Atilla: leaves a friend, to take one and go to the hunt.
Cornelius: a miller with hospitality and big plans.
Katchy: must invest his coins and buy into his future.
Kerim: Waits at the river's ford, yet avoids the tribe.
Koolair: is happy to stop traveling and be home.
Kooskoo bey: tries to best his herd boy bargaining.
Leyla: takes the lead to find her man at the river.
Sevman: is rested for a return trip to Goat Hill.
Twozan: must pass the river to return to his people.
Yusuf: must face life in Samara on a neglected estate.

GLOSSARY:
barish ve esenlik: peace and serenity; be calm, let's talk.
beckle: wait; hold; just a minute.
booy' roon: behold; look here; regard.
cheshme; fountain; spring; water source.
esenlik; tranquility.
geldim: I've arrived; I've come; I'm here.
geldik: we've arrived; we've come; we're here.
hanum: lady; Mrs. title used after the name.
inshalla: may God will it; I hope.
janum: dear; beloved; my life. a family expression
tabbi: of course; naturally; certainly.
ta'mom: okay; agreed.
soos: hush; quiet.

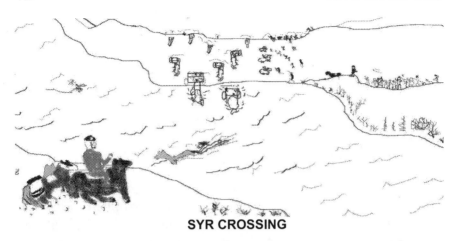

SYR CROSSING

"*Bouy'roon geldim*, behold, I've come," Atilla bey shouted in Turkish as he rode in with the perimeter guard to the main yurt. Twozan came to the door and Setchkin poked her head out to look.

Twozan smiled and called out. "*Hoe'sh geldeniz*, what news Atilla bey? Have you seen the road ahead?"

"We have indeed, Twozan bey. We have marked a path to a little used ford across the river. You will be able to cross, hopefully, without interference from the farmers or troops."

"The government agents agreed on our withdrawal."

"But authorities don't always know what others agree to."

"We will have to trust in Tanra and make our plans. It's the last of the big agricultural settlements on our road north."

"The harvest is cut and drying, the farmers will worry about crop raids. We looked for a place where the hills come down to the river. It's rough and there will be few farmers who irrigate that kind of land."

"I can't understand farmers. It is hard work and so restrictive. You don't go any where or see anything."

"Where is Sevman? Has he recovered in your care?"

"Three nights rest is no cure-all, but he's rested and feels better. I doubt if he's anxious for a long trip yet."

"We'll go back to the village where the trace split and find out where our man hid. The tracks will be over a week old by that time, but cold is better than no trace at all."

Twozan nodded, "The boy told us all he knows about it. We got the story of our Khan's life in the quarry. Leyla told us of the reports of his death and the son, her brother's condition. If the brother will come we can take him and his friends with us. We can't wait, however. He must catch up to us. I hope you can find the one who started all this trouble."

"Allah is a sure guide, we will discover the boy. Stay well."

"Here comes Sevman mounted and ready. Go with Tanra."

"*Beck'le*, wait, where is Kerim?" Leyla hanem shouted as she came from a yurt.

"Across the river waiting," was the parting shout.

> - - - - - >AT THE GOAT CORRAL > - - - - - >

"No Katchy, I won't sell you a pregnant female in the deal. I'll sell you two yearlings that you can resell for meat and make a bit. I'll throw in that old female, she's got years left and still gives milk from the last kid." Both men were hunkered down by the corral drinking milk laced with sultana a tea made from the dried husk of the coffee bean. Coffee from Yemen was too expensive for shepherds.

"Katchy give gold for young black female: easy to see, she favorite, my friend. I sell yearling to good man, he pay, I give you money. Sheriff men talk about fine you one kid. I fight them, they give stripe, face and leg, you see. Men no take kid. I give good value. I sell cheese, give you money. You pay me same all years, but herd grow double size, much work. You give me good value now."

Kooskoo grimaced.   "I'll give you the black, one yearling and a kid for the money."

Katchy jumped up off the ground and yipped. He came down pouting. "I no work more, you get new boy, you hard man, no fair. I buy goat in market, more cheap, good value."

Kooskoo cursed, "Hell, boy you don't have to carry on like that. You do a good job and I'll let you pick out two yearlings now and the black. Will that suit you?"

Katchy looked doubtful, but moved toward the corral. "*Ta'mom*, okay, white spot yearling, good, take her? There black and brown, little fat girl, okay?"

Kooskoo looked doubtful. "I'll keep the black and tan, you take that calico girl."

"Calico runt, no good, I take white stripe or black tan," Katchy insisted.

"*Ta'mom*, okay, you keep the white stripe one. Pay me the money now. When kids are born to your nannies, I get a stud fee. A copper coin each. You don't have a billy, so you'll pay for mine."

Katchy threw the money at Kooskoo's feet and shouted his anger. "You one big cheat!"

Kooskoo warned him. "I can get a replacement for you. You aren't indispensable to me. You have to play by the rules."

"You big fool, white stripe pregnant now, All three I buy, pregnant mine. Black tan fat girl, no baby. You get new boy for herd, many will die and get sick. I save you money. Okay, I stay for winter, but Nevruz festival I go away. You be plenty sorry."

Kooskoo bey got up glowering and moved toward Katchy menacingly, fists doubled. Katchy pulled out his sling and placed a rock. The man stopped, he grunted and turned to go. After he had mounted his horse he frowned down at him.

"You've got your animals. Get out after Nevruz or I'll whip the hide off your bottom and back. You'll pay double for any dead or injured these last months. Understand!"

> - - - - - >TOOZLU CAMP > - - - - - >

"Everything is packed and ready to be loaded tomorrow morning, Leyla hanum. Your clothes are laid out." Peri hanum the old nurse maid advised. "The yurt is ready to be taken down and packed, we leave at dawn." Leyla lay on a narrow bed made up on the top of the trunks. She was stretched out dreamily plaiting her hair.

"Yes. We cross the river; perhaps he will be there to show us the way" She sighed, "It would be as easy to join us there."

"Bees go to flowers, not flowers to bees. Men do not wait patiently for ladies to seek them, Leyla hanum. If they like a woman they seek her. She is the one who waits."

Leyla made a pretty face. "But if duty calls they go before, prepare the way and wait."

"What duty has an East Bulgar to a sept of the Chipchaks?"

"The Gospels say that it is noble and pleasing to God to help - even enemies - and besides he might have reason, Peri hanum."

The old lady whose name, Joy, contradicted her nature, snorted.

"He is Bulgar, they cultivate strange tastes. My mistress' brother was among them, he came back strange. He was a friend of the Crow. I know, you know nothing about the people in your old home, but the Crow and the Tiger are the men to avoid at all costs; men of unnatural appetites." She shuddered and even shed a tear.

Leyla frowned. "Atilla bey is a loyal friend, nothing more. Kerim escaped an Abbasid jail with his help. You wrong them both to air such suspicions. I want no more talk like that. Do you understand?" The lady humped again and blew out the oil lamp.

> - - - - - >SAMARA CITY > - - - - - - ->

The procession of people and animals stopped before the Bowzhun Samara mansion. A weary travel-stained group pounded on the door. After a long wait the door was opened by an old man in worn dirty clothes. He peeped out cautiously.

"Hello, Tomas, I sent messages, didn't you expect us?" The man gasped, a timid maid stood behind him.

"Sir," he stammered, opening the door wide. "We weren't sure." He turned to the maid, "Get the stable boy," he scolded. "He's to scratch up some hay for the animals." She turned to screech, "They're here." Aiming to inform a back building as the travelers wearily entered. The animals and drovers went back and the family turned in at the house patio, where a waterless fountain and pool awaited them.

"*Geldik*, we've arrived, we're here, we'll never have to travel again. Never again, Daddy has promised. He promised didn't he?" Koolair was spinning like a little top: shouting her words and questions to the world. She was too full of joy to tone down her excitement. She spun around and ran among the broken flower pots and neglected foliage plants.

"*Tabbi*, of course we're here and we need rest first and time later to put things in shape to live here." Yusuf bey quietly observed looking at the forlorn desolation.

"Forever and ever!" Koolair added enthusiastically.

Her father smiled down at her, but her mother walked wearily to the center of the deserted patio and looked at the opening doors to more rooms. She shook her head sadly. How she had loved this house in the capital! She could not stand to be left alone and so they had lived ten years in China. It was just enough to be over the shocks of change, learn the language and to have good friends of long standing. The expulsion had ended that and now a new, old world was reclaiming her with work she was less willing and able to do. It was the house she had come to as a bride to live with her mother-in-law and their active family. She was so anxious to please, and had so much to learn. The memory made her smile.

"Bayan, my lady, if we had only known the day we would have been more prepared. We only heard messages of your coming, but nothing certain. We pray you, forgive us."

Yusuf smiled happily, "We could not be certain of how the journey would go. Now, thank God, we're home. You have done nothing, so get us a room and food and we will do things as strength and time permit. Where is father's steward?"

"He is out on a trip, Master; he will be back after a time."

"Exactly when did father die?"

The servant paused thoughtfully, "It was last year, a week after Nevruz, the spring festival. He loved spring and the return of the heat and flowers."

Yusuf nodded happily, "I'll see the orchard and gardens later."

The servant paused, "Sir, the summer was hot and the irrigation... It's a sad sight."

"What happened? We have water rights. Was there rationing?"

"You must ask the steward, sir, it was his affair and responsibility, but..."

"But he is traveling on someone's business now and will return someday everyone supposes, right? No one but himself will know."

"Yes sir, He will have the details I'm sure."

Yusuf sighed. "Father clothed the servants with a new outfit every fall, yet the clothes you wear are old. Do you have your ration?"

"No sir, Moses complained and was beaten." The man started away, and then turned. "Sir, we have only lentils and yesterday's bread. Could we make you a soup, add some leeks and we will buy fresh tomorrow... if you have money, Sir."

Yusuf stared in disbelief. "What ever you have we will share.

141

Tomorrow, I will go to the money lenders Tomas, to check our investments. We will buy all that you have listed for the kitchen. Then, I will check our ledgers."

"Yes Sir. Oh, it's so good to have you back, Yusuf bey. I'll make the list. If we had only known the precise day, Sir. I'm sorry Sir." Thomas bowed and excused his way out of their presence.

The knocker sounded at the door, loud and persistent. Yusuf waited, but the knocking continued and no one answered, so he went himself. A short, ugly man stood before the door. His eyes lighted with delight at the sight of Yusuf, the heir, standing in the afternoon light. He fell to his knees and kissed his master's hand.

"God be praised, you have arrived, Yusuf bey. We waited, hoping, but only heard rumors of your coming. You must come to the mill. You won't believe how much better the new stones are. They have increased our production by a third. We have not finished paying the cost yet, but you will see that it will be paid off in another two months. The books are ready for the auditors and you will see how well the business is doing. I have some plans for expansion I would like you to see. They could double our business." The man entered on a stream of words and after pressing Yusuf's hands to his lips and head again he arrived in the patio. He still happily proclaimed his ideas and good news to all. Yusuf allowed his relief to show, he smiled and even laughed when the little man said he had planted flowers before the mill buildings and around the watercourse.

"It is only a half hour trip up the river and I have brought a picnic spread for the children. You have an older and this young daughter, don't you Master?"

"Yes, the other, Maril, will come later, *inshallah.*"

"You will love the gardens on the premises. We have benches scattered for the customers that must wait for the grinding of their grain. Some say they come for the gardens only" He laughed loudly and slapped his knee. Koolair watched in fascination and Meriam looked less tired and dejected. Yusuf saw the difference.

"Tomas," he called, when the servant appeared he said, "We are off to the mill. Prepare the food for tonight when we return. Here's a silver coin for extras." He turned to the little, enthusiastic director of the mill, smiling broadly.

"Come, I've forgotten your name, tell me about yourself."

"Cornelius, Sir, like the man in the Bible, but I've no Italian soldiers to share the good news with. Just customers, Sir, Mostly Christians, Turks and some Muslims come now. Your good father hired me seven years ago. The mill was neglected and run down, but I had a free hand to build it up again. The steward kept the budget low, but we did it anyway. I've arranged for a Fulton-carriage to carry us there." A horn sounded from the street and the man ran excitedly to the door where he shouted to someone outside before running back again.

"It's him sir, He's anxious to go, if you please Sir."

Yusuf gathered his family and the servants who had come on the long journey with them. He herded them all to the door. He indicated the smiling Cornelius, "Here, we have a man who has prepared for us, let's enjoy his welcome and share the feast together to celebrate our arrival."

> - - - - - >SYR RIVER FORD > - - - - - - ->

"Twozan *janum*, look below! You have an army waiting." Setchkin's alarm was late, the advance guards were waving flags: Enemy sighted. Horses were drawing into a tight formation ahead.

The column of the Toozlu arrived at the hill overlooking the river and they saw below them clumps of farmers with an assortment of weapons both agricultural and antiques from the walls of the families.

"Go back to the baby, hanum, this is men's work." She obeyed, but Leyla hanum moved up beside him. She stood up on her stirrups.

"I see three horses on the far bank. It's Kerim bey!"

"Holding the other bank. Now I must secure this bank safely." He rode forward and she kept pace. He ran his horse past the mustering Toozlu guards and scouts. "Hold your position; we'll parley first." She followed until they were an arrows flight from the farmers. There, he drew to a stop. Leyla stopped beside him. He held up both hands to face the mob. He took off his bow and arrow sheath and handed it to the girl. He then faced the mob and slowly rode forward toward them.

"*Barish ve esinlik*, Peace and serenity, let's talk." His firm words calmed and reassured them somewhat. They waited impatiently.

SAMARA WELCOME

PEOPLE, PLOTS & PLACES IN CHAPTER 13

Atilla: joins the chase for an escaped murderer.
Kynan: is sure of Leyla's love but tries a short cut.
Katchy: finds his thief, but can only pursue him.
Leyla: catches her man and then tries to kill him.
Sorba: fails in his work as steward of the Bowzhun.
Sevman: is troubled by the things he has learned.
Sulema: is taken as a hostage and carried away.
Umer: is caught and accused by his host and runs.
Yusuf: finds much to criticize in his overseer's work.

GLOSSARY:
Allah kah'ret-sin: God curse you: God damn you.
baa-rak' oh nu: leave it; leave it alone.
barish: peace.
beck'le: wait; hold there.
cheshme: a stone structure guarding a spring or well.
dough rue: correct; right; truly.
janum: dear; beloved; my life. a family expression
kahpa chin'niny: shut your mouth; shut up.
kateel'je: killer; murderer.
peach: bastard; no-good bastard.
ser'sery: tramp; bum; worthless man.

UMER ESCAPES

"Sulema, you little witch, why are you sitting on his lap?" Umer quickly pushed the girl off and stood up from his bed to confront the brother; who shouted again. "You can move when you've reason, you viper! You fox! You trick us with your stories and fake injury." Umer could think of no appeasing answer. He and the girl stood frozen for an instant, and then she ran forward while he felt under his pillow.

"Please brother, it was just for a second, a little fun, like when you tickle me. Nothing has come of it. He wants to give a bride's price for me. No reason to be angry." He shoved her aside, walked to face Umer and glaring raised a fist. "We took your part when the two strangers came."

The point of Umer's knife caught the Addams apple and pierced to the bone. Gasping and bleeding, he fell forward on the bed. Umer had wrenched the knife free as he fell and now waved it under the nose of the paralyzed Sulema. He hissed like a snake as he pushed her toward the door. "*Soos*, hush, no noise. Get the water jar, we go to the fountain." Numbly the girl moved forward, shock written on her features. Umer took some water and washed his hands. He sheathed his knife, walked out and got his saddle, and pushed the girl forward.

"Now walk slowly, I'll follow limping. Don't try to run. I'll catch you and ruin your pretty face." She pulled up her veil and carried her jar. The whole village knew by now that Umer was to walk and exercise every day. It was early for water, but she wouldn't make two trips. Shouts had been heard from the house. The brother was moving his guest. They smiled as the solemn pair walked and limped past, descending the path. When they reached the bottom he sat on the fountain edge.

"Fill the jar and leave it. Come help me catch my horse and saddle her." She hoped to get far enough away to scream and run. He wouldn't dare chase her if he had to get away by horse. However, the horses were resting in the afternoon shade. There Umer saddled and mounted his horse. He'll leave now, she hoped. He held an extra blanket. "You put this on one of these. Take the roan mare, she looks strong. Now mount up, we're leaving." He took the halter strap and led her horse. He took them to the path leading south. The neighbors wondered if she had permission to take the Sheriff's horse.

> - - - - - >SYR RIVER FORD> - - - - - >

Leyla rode past the several bands that watched the column, to the river where she urged her horse across. The horse waded forward several lengths. He swam about six lengths before gaining footing on the other side. Leyla fell off in the rough water, but swam holding the tail. She waded out still holding the animal's tail. The man on the black horse had started forward to help her, but seeing she had made shore, he stopped. She mounted.

"Kerim bey, *beck'le*, wait, we must talk." He took his packhorse and mare, to depart at a run. Astonishment, then anger marred her face. She kicked her horse into a run and armed the bow, but the figure of Kerim was fast vanishing. She shrieked her frustration.

"*Ser'sery, peach*, shiftless bastard, you should at least talk to me. Stop, you coward!" He entered a thorn thicket. She followed at full gallop screaming, "You can't hide from me!"

146

"I'm tired! We've been riding three hours without a break. I'm cold! I'm not used to this. We ride an hour out and another back home. Now, I've got no home or brother to go back to. Why did I think you were such a hero and believe every lie you told?" Sulema whined like a baby as the cold, weariness and boredom increased.

"*Kahpa chin'niny*, shut your mouth, another half hour does it. You see this hill we're passing? Just down there is a corral. I spent a day there two weeks ago. There's food and shelter for us there."

They rode in silence for a time when she again began to whimper. "Why are you taking me with you? You've had what you want from me. Stupid me! Why should I have to go with you?"

"Because you, little stupid, are my safe conduct out. They'll spare me to save you."

She shook her head negatively up. "All the villagers despise me, but they're a bunch of hypocrites. They do the same things I do. I got caught, they didn't. My being here will confirm my reputation. They won't care what happens to me now, with my brother dead."

He stared at her frowning, and replied, "If we hide in the groves they might miss us." She suddenly laughed hysterically loud and long, almost falling off the horse.

"The sheriff will follow you to the end of the earth. You took his favorite horse."

Umer gasped astonished, staring in horror at her. "The red roan is his? We took his horse back there?" He looked behind them, nothing appeared on the horizon. He worried, "We have to get another horse."

She laughed more, so he reached over and gave her face a back-handed slap.

She cried, "Kooskoo bey alone has a horse here. The goat boy can't ride."

"Where is this Kooskoo bey? Does he live close by?"

"Nearly four hours south of here, by the river. You can't get there tonight. He's a big man. He can take you apart. I hope he does!"

147

Umer smirked, then spurred his horse and jerked her's forward. "You'll show me the way, if you wish to keep that little nose. We'll ride by the corral and be there before the herd comes back. They may even erase our tracks."

She suppressed a laugh. "They'll search a large circle where they lose them and pick them up again, where the herd stops."

He raised his knife, "I told you to shut up. I'll scratch your face next time." They rode south in silence.

When the corral came in sight Umer spoke: "You get your first stop now. There is a little spring of water and some cheese and jerky near the shelter.

She looked forward eagerly.

"Remember if you try to run you're dead."

She looked at him, her face full of contempt, and she sniffed, her face sour.

He leaned over and touched the point of her chin with the point of his knife. He flicked his wrist up and she felt the prick, even as she squalled. She sensed a warm tickle down her neck. He had nicked her. She was overpowered by dizziness and feared she might fall.

> - - - - - >AT THE HILL-TOP VILLAGE > - - - - - >

"We have made good time, Sevman. The rest did you a lot of good. You'll make a horseman yet." Atilla bey was in high spirits after leaving the tribe. Sevman had learned things that saddened him because he knew they would affect Kardesh. His father's death and his sister's strange adventures; these were motives for sorrow and relief. All this required travel. There were decisions to make, would they join the tribe? More riding! Sevman groaned and Atilla looked at him brightly.

"We are almost to the village, just across this little meadow. It looks like we have a reception committee waiting. Half the village is out by the look of it." As they approached men were saddling horses and women were clustered before the cheshme fountain. Everyone was talking excitedly and none noticed the approach of the pair until they were thirty paces off. The volume rose as one of the men rode toward them.

"You're the men that came a week ago after the death of our man, looking for a murderer weren't you? Well, he's been here and now we have another death. Come help us, they can't be far away."

"They? How many are there?"

The sheriff snapped a reply. "Took a hostage: the man's sister." He wheeled his horse. "He stole my horse as well, damn him! Let's go." Dust flew as they left.

> - - - - - >SYR RIVER FORD> - - - - - >

Leyla pulled to a sudden halt, the thorn thickets were close around her and dense in the hilly sector near the river. The winding path she followed was cut the width of a cart into a little valley tucked into the hills. There was a slight forking of the trail ahead, and beyond what looked to be a small field for grazing, screened by bushes. She had lost track of the time and distance ridden. She was suddenly aware of sounds: men's voices and the squeaking of a cart. They were coming toward her from the right side of the meadowland. She turned left through the open fringe of bushes and the branches clawed at her leg. The voices and cart masked her exit.

"I tell you someone slept by the rock fall last night. The meadow's been grazed. At least two horses," he complained.

"You're jumpy, you hear Turks everywhere you go."

"You'll be seeing them too, in your sleep." Several laughed somewhat uneasily.

"They're crossing the river, that's no dream."

A voice shouted, "Look, there goes a woman, riding." The excitement spread, "Is she alone?" Interest picked up and animated their voices.

"Yeah, but she's got a bow armed. Watch out, she'll shoot." All eyes were fixed on the rider.

She held the arrow at ready as she galloped, but she suddenly saw ahead of her a rider in leather armor. He was bearing down on her. He launched an arrow, but it was far off her right and high toward the cart. She aimed for the area above the chest, but he caught it on the small shield used by horsemen to deflect direct shots. She readied and shot her second arrow at the neck, above the armor as the distance closed. He deflected it also with the shield and now there was no time to turn. She saw his face then and fainted. He swept her off the horse as the animals brushed by. The smack of their bodies gave emphasis to the encounter. He turned his horse and trotted back to lead her mount away. Still holding her tightly he kissed her face and neck. She roused enough to protest. He ignored her with a laugh. She struggled to free herself, but he held her firmly. Grasping the bridle of her horse, he rode on.

She drew her knife and stabbed up. The knife skittered along the leather breast plate until it reached the armpit where it entered. He gasped and slumped.

"What happened?" a surprised voice from the cart asked excitedly.

"I don't know, but I'm not going back to find out. He nearly hit us there." The cart creaked down the path away from the meadow.

"Look, I got the arrow out of the wheel. I'll keep it to show." the youngest affirmed.

"We'll come armed the next time we take this road."

"Turks are a savage race," another affirmed as they hurried away, down the trail.

> - - - - - >SAMARA MANSION > - - - - - >

"I'm sorry we missed your home coming, Yusuf bey, I was off on business and we didn't have a certain date." Sorba, the steward, explained smoothly as he bowed his way into the owner's presence.

"You were away on personal business and I sent you advice as to my probable time of arrival. With the uncertainties of travel I could do no more. You, however, could have done a lot more. I'm relieving you of your stewardship, I've looked over the books and they seem full of omissions and gaps. I want a full accounting before you leave. For this reason I've asked a friend who works with an importer to go over everything with you."

150

Sorba a tall, fat man of 50 with twenty years at his job, reacted with heat and indignant protests. While soft of body he was hard of mouth and stubborn about his position of trust.

"Your father trusted me. I don't see why you should be so critical. I've done all that could be done with what he left. There are receipts for every item sold or received during my stewardship. It's not an easy job. I may have been too busy in your affairs to record everything promptly, but it still has receipts and documentation available. I know how strict you are in money matters and I have always been careful to prepare to give accounts. If your estate has not rendered as much as you desire, it is possible that you have failed to equip and invest sufficiently to make the land or industry more productive."

Yusuf laughed critically. "I leave you in charge; go away for years and now it's my fault that the estates investments and equipping was slack? If you knew I would be demanding, why weren't you prepared for my advised return? Next you'll tell me I spend too much on my own needs and luxuries for the place to prosper. I'm going to the magistrate tomorrow and draw up a charge against you and your goods, which I've no doubt you possess. You have defrauded me, sir. I intend to make you pay what you owe me."

Sorba shook his head sadly and sighed. "Your father was such a great discerner of character. He knew persons for what they are. He trusted me. You have smirched my name by your false accusations. I'll have satisfaction in court."

"You may have been all you say when my father chose you. Men do change, however, many for the worst, with exposure to wealth. Here is a bill for olive oil owed us five years ago, but the receipt is done on new parchment, have you renegotiated the bill? There are several like this."

Sorba drew himself up proudly and replied coolly. "Bills become old and must be renewed from time to time. Other goods or services may make up the difference in the older original agreement. You'll find such negotiations all clear and legal. Stewards have full responsibility to adjust such accounts according to the situation they perceive. All such transactions are within the scope of the job."

"You're doing favors in order to receive favors, aren't you?"

"I've treated your customers and suppliers with the same generosity which your dear father always taught me to show. The mill-Wright has flattered you into seeing his point of view rather than a safer more conservative view of how businesses should be run. He charmed you with flowers and new building plans." He sniffed disdainfully.

151

"The mill-Wright as you call him, is enterprising and honest, his books are in order to the day. Yours are not. He has your job and you will have none if my influence counts in this city. Men who show you honor will get none from me. Let's see if that crimps your favors and renegotiations. Will they loan you money to pay me back?"

There was a long pregnant pause as both men considered the situation. Sorba took a long ragged breath and licked his lips.

"Sir, Yusuf bey, I have spoken hastily and poorly. My pride was hurt. I have offended you and been careless of my words. I must apologize for that and my slackness and lack of attention. I beg you to reconsider. I was an honest man when your father trusted me. I was as much again, when you left for your trip east. But, after your father's death - I lacked the example he always set for me. I confess my weakness. For his memories' sake, please don't take me to court. I will work with the accountant and pay the amount set by him, even if it takes me the rest of my life." He had slowly sunk to his knees.

"It would have been better if you had started on this tone, Sorba bey. I remember your promptness and energy when I left for the China trade. But, now, you're fat and sassy; full of weasel's ways and proud. I doubt I can trust you again, but since my father loved you, I'll hold off till we know the worst of it. I have other anxieties over my daughter's safety so I'll not act in haste."

> - - - - - >GOAT'S CORRAL> - - - - - >

The flock of goats came moving toward the corral. They wanted water and the warmth and rest of a place of protection: home in human language, to fellowship and sleep safely. But they stopped and stared uneasily at the two horses drinking at the sink hole. They were saddled and, therefore, there had to be people, strange people. They milled about uncertainly, bleating, until Katchy came to see the trouble. Then, they complained loudly. Umer came out of the shelter at that moment with jerky, sun-cured meat, in his hand. The two stared angrily at each other. Then, Katchy shrieked loudly, startling the goats into short nervous bursts of running and jumping. Umer drew his knife threateningly, but Katchy whipped out his sling armed it and slung. Startled, Umer ducked, but felt the stone numb his shoulder. Umer ducked his head and ran for the horses yelling for the girl to come. She

152

observed from the shelter where she nibbled a pressed round of cheese. The goat boy was local. She had seen him selling cheese at the village and special fairs. She had laughed at his language, but everybody understood him. She stayed in the shelter, it was safer. Endangered, Umer mounted his horse, reached for the halter of the roan and looked for the girl again.

"*Allah kah'ret-sin*, God curse you, damn bad man. You come back. You eat 'for-sale' jerky and cheese. Rob poor Katchy all time. I fix you good, you see. I break your head like Yeet. I give you big head." He sent another whirling stone after the dodging Umer, hitting the horse causing it to shy. Then it raced up the embankment and ran out of range. The roan followed, but both were water logged now and slow. Being a quarry boy, Umer did not realize the danger of leaving tired horses alone to drink all they could. He also expected the goat boy to look for the girl, or for her to run out to escape this danger, but neither happened. Rather the boy left the herd and ran in pursuit.

"*Kateel'je*, murderer, I fix you like Yeet, more worse! I hear 'bout you, two men come look for you. They no find. Good man no find. I find, I fix you, give big head. You no get away from me." His stone hit the roan causing it to run ahead.

Umer tried to get his horse to keep pace with the other and to get away, but they soon fell back into a walk. Katchy was winded from his running and shouting, so they both settled into a walk. One, not close enough to use his weapon, the other found it too dark to use his sling with accuracy. It developed into a long walking match, sprinkled with occasional shouted insults.

KATCHY PURSUES

153

PEOPLE, PLOTS & PLACES IN CHAPTER 14

Atilla: will pursue the murderer and his stolen horse.
Jon: tries to free his master's daughter from captivity.
Kynan: needs medical attention desperately.
Leyla: tries to undo the damage she has done.
Maril: tries to escape and find freedom to go home.
Marium: tends to the women's' side of the tribe.
Mookades: has remedies to heal body and soul.
Setchkin: worries about the missing Leyla.
Sevman: wants no part of the violent pursuit.
Sheriff: misses finding the horse, girl and murderer.
Twozan: crosses the river with lots of excitement.

GLOSSARY

ahfeder'siniz: excuse us; your pardon please.
ahne: mother; mom.
Allah hu Ekber: God is great; used as a battle cry.
az'un-uz ach'en: open your mouth.
barak'en: leave off; stop it.
dough rue: truly.
he'be: a woven wool saddle-bag or pack carrier.
high'er olmaz: No, it can't be; he can't do that.
kai'makan: a town or village authority.
ko'jam: my husband.
nobet'chiler: guards; those on duty.
o'ra-da: over there.
shim'dy al: now take it; receive it now.
Tanram: my God; my Lord.
yetishtir onu: help him; give him a hand.

WINDOWS WATCHED

Maril hovered near the door. The boy was to deliver an order of cheese today. Would there be notices from her friends? The cloth cover was something saved back from their Uigur harem experience. Such signs were not coincidental. She hoped to get back with her friends and to go on to Baghdad and home. A faint tap caught her attention, as some sound came from outside. She waited one breath, pulled up her veil up and opened the door a crack, there stood Korkmaz who whispered, "You be Maril?"

She whispered an affirmative.

He said: "Shepherdess and baby lamb wait here. Horse village friends wait in country. Put candle in your window when moon reaches zenith to-night, be ready."

"Set the cheese down inside and go," she instructed in a loud voice. The old servant would be annoyed at her taking his task and going to the door, but she hadn't touched the goods or boy, perhaps they would let it pass. She picked up the cheese after the door was closed and carried it past the old servant who arrived to watch her pass.

> - - - - - >PASHA'S HOUSE >- - - - - - >

Light shown from the window of Maril's little room. She lay fully dressed under the cover with a bundle of her belongings at the foot of the bed. She felt like she had been waiting for hours and was now dozing as mid-night passed. Outside there was an unexpected tapping noise. A ladder had been laid beside her window. Then, she heard the voice of Jon, "Maril hanum? Are you there?"

She thrust a small kitchen knife through the bladder window pane and whispered through the slit,

"*Dough rue,* truly, right here, is that you Jon?"

His voice came. "Yes, are you ready mistress?" he questioned.

Her knife cut another pane and she tried to force the bundle through the opening. The carved wooden screen guarding the whole window stopped it.

"*Baa-rak' oh nu,* leave it," he hissed. He held a metal bar in his hand and applied pressure to the corner. There was a loud pop and the screen broke loose and moved away from one side of the window with a snap. The bundle fell through the hole and rolled down to fall to the ground with a thump. The occupants of the house would have to be deaf or dead to miss the noise of the intrusion.

Lights were now being lit in the house and the voice of the Commander of the garrison was heard shouting. A loud gong resounded. They were found out!

> - - - - - >NORTH OF GOAT HERDER HILL > - - - - - >

"We press on till morning, he can't ride all night and day too," the sheriff shouted to the assembled posse.

"We ride south to Goat Hill first and take our bearings from there. The goat boy will have seen them." The cavalcade was launched.

Atilla rode next to the sheriff and asked, "You're sure he's heading south?"

The man nodded vigorously, "He bragged about a brother in Samarkand, a military type, said he would join up, too."

Atilla nodded enthusiastically and said, "We have friends that will help us, down toward the river."

The rest of the ride was done in silence as the sun lowered and shadows grew. Grimly they walked and trotted their horses, sometimes walking or running beside them at a distance-eating pace.

> - - - - - - - >BASE COMMANDER'S HOUSE> - - - - - >

"Quick, here is the ladder. Down you go, run for the woods before the house. Our little friend is there." Jon's voice guided her and she grabbed her bundle at the foot of the ladder.

The voice of the garrison's commander came clear:

"No-bet'chi-ler, Guards, apprehend those escaping. Get them."
From around the property, guards, posted during the night,
appeared.

Maril squealed and stopped abruptly as guards surrounded
them, spears pointed at their hearts. She stepped in front of Jon
and protested, "This man serves my father and came with us
from the Tang territory in China. He is seeking to return me to
my father's house in Baghdad as he is pledged to do. You must
not hurt him. We surrender."

> - - - - - >GOAT HERDER HILL > - - - - - >

After two hours the posse arrived at the hill and the
Sheriff headed for the corral. Sevman, however, went to
the bottom of the hill where he had left the cart. Atilla
found him there staring bleakly at the bare, abandoned
campfire-marked spot. They both shared a silent moment.
Then Atilla bey spoke to his little friend's need. "Don't
worry! Allah will guide our steps, we'll find them."

"I'll go to the hill-top and see if they left any signs."
Sevman's reply came as he started up. "They would leave
some notice here."

Atilla dismounted and lit a torch with flint and iron,
and followed the tracks. Sevman arrived at hilltop at last
light and could make out a pile of small stones for a sling.
Then, looking down hill he saw something hanging on the
top of a thorn thicket below. Puzzled, he returned to the
campsite. "Can you see what's in the tree, Atilla bey?
Something is hung there on top."

Atilla held up the torch and peered at the object. "I'll
get up on the horse and see," he passed the torch to
Sevman. "Allah, Allah, it's my box and *hebe*, the saddle-
bag with my stuff that I left here in the cart. They've left it
for me, hung high so Katchy can't get at it."

Sevman moved closer and held his torch high to see.
"*Shim'dy al*, Get it now. There are sling size rocks piled-
up on the hill. I wonder why? We need to get to the corral
and talk to Katchy."

> - - - - - - - > PASHA'S HOUSE> - - - - - >

The wakened commander stood at the door in his
pajamas watching his guards. He smiled broadly and

157

nodded his approval. He knew that his *Ah'ne*, Mother, would protest, but he now had good reason to send the girl away. If the boy were truly a servant he would have to be sent too. It promised an interesting morning. Now he would have to find and question the messenger boy as well. He wondered what kind of recompense he should give his house servant for his suspicions. Faithfulness deserved its rewards. He entered in high spirits, to have a midnight breakfast with his perturbed mother, while his prisoners finished the night: the girl back in her repaired room and the boy in a cell, alone.

> - - - - - > GOAT CORRAL > - - - - - >

"Sheriff, the goats are locked in the corral, but the hut's empty, and there's no sign of the goat herder," one of the men reported.

"Sure as hell, he took off for the bush when he heard us coming round the hill," the deputy asserted loudly, "He don't want to see us."

His companion agreed saying, "The stinking little coward took off and hid. He doesn't want a whipping."

The sheriff made an angry observation. "That's what I get for letting you boys have your fun, I'd pay for any information now, just to get that horse back."

One of the villagers heard the exchange and protested, "What about the girl, Sheriff? We can't have kidnapping."

"If that's what happened," huffed the sheriff. "No telling what that little bitch has been up to. That brother and her used to fight all the time. You could hear it all over the village. Now he's dead and she's run, and who can tell more about it?"

There was a brief silence. Then the deputy said, "She always wanted to leave the village and go to the city."

"And now she's gone," finished his companion.

"I want her as bad as I do the quarry man she ran off with," affirmed the Sheriff. "The slut's got a lot to answer for. We don't know what happened in that house."

158

The milling crowd of mounted men moved over toward the water tank. Some watered their horses with care. Not allowing too much. Atilla and Sevman joined the group. One finished and observed. "Two horses, moving fast, left here. Ran up this side of the bank. It must be Sulema and the stranger."

"Mount up, men," the Sheriff called. "Which way did they go?"

"South toward the river! I knew it, Sheriff, Samarkand for sure. Let's go get 'em."

The group began to move with renewed enthusiasm as a tracker on foot followed the tracks with torch in hand.

Sulema watched carefully from inside the thorn scrub beyond the hut. The posse was full of men she distrusted from her knowledge of village life. The loud agreement with the sheriff's last words of condemnation froze any words from her lips. These men would not rescue her; quite the contrary. Without her brother she would be at their mercy. Her heart cried out: Allah must help her now! She was saved from going on, but she could not go back. She must wait and see how things turn out.

Sevman stopped and motioned to Atilla as the crowd moved out. "I'm tired, and I don't like the way this hunt is going. I'm not a lover of violence under any cloak. I'll stay back at the campsite and follow the cart tomorrow."

Atilla nodded. "Evil must be stopped by law or it grows, Sevman. I go to see that justice is done and doesn't get out of hand."

Sevman frowned, "But if justice is done with violence, evil is multiplied, and those who do it in the name of justice carry the seeds which may spring up at any time, when law is not on their side."

Atilla nodded his head, "I understand your concern. I'll return to help you find your friends. I must go to kill the coyote, lest more die. Stay well."

"Go well, the Jesus of light shield you."

The farmers milled about in confusion some called out one thing, some another. "No more nomads!"

"Kill the coyotes, they'll rob our crops!"

"Down with the Turks!"

"Don't let them pass!"

"Let'em go and good riddance."

"Don't provoke them."

"Why make trouble now, they're leaving."

"Peace, brothers, peace."

"Cowards!"

A few tried to harangue the crowd denouncing all nomads and grazers. A few grazers were present to protect their animals and fields from exploitation by the nomads, but objected violently to condemnation of their profession by farming types that they held in contempt.

Twozan stood on a boulder giving him prominence over the crowd and allowing him to be heard at least part of the time. Behind them all the line of animals bearing the yurts and goods of the tribe were plodding in file toward the ford in the river. The sight infuriated some to greater protests and they started to move to intercept the line progressing northward.

Suddenly the file of armed warriors stopped riding toward the river and started to move toward the crowd. No one armed their bows, but they brought out the whips which some began to whirl about their heads. Others made the whip circle beside them to one side and parallel to the horse with the butt end coming down beside the horses head in a figure eight. The encroaching crowd stopped at the sight and sound of the nomad's wall of moving horses and whips. Some turned their anger on Twozan who still stood on the rock about waist level above the crowd. He lifted his head and shouted. "We cross the river with the Kaimakan's permission. None of your goods will be touched. Let there be no fighting or damage here."

Those near the river heard, but a mounted attack of grazers and farmers launched its-self from the hills just behind the caravan. They were a noisy, rowdy crowd of young immature boys and old greedy reprobates looking for excitement and loot. Encouraged by shared lion's milk and barley beer they listened to nothing but their brags. They chased the end of the column to the water. Where many were knocked off their horses by the whirling whip butts. With an odd assortment of weapons they managed to inflict an exciting exchange of minor wounds. The blood was worn by villagers for three days as a visible proof of valor.

"*Allah hu Ekber*," the villagers chanted as they fought. Twozan leaped to his horse and rode into the river. He was laughing as he repeated their war cry. The rear guard of Toozlu warriors disengaged and entered the water. Villagers who tried to follow got a bath, none arrived at the other bank. The nomad's carts and supplies arrived safe to the north bank and hills beyond.

> - - - - - >ABOVE THE FORD > - - - - - >

"Wherever is Leyla?" asked Setchkin. "She moved to the head of the column near you," she insisted. She was binding up a cut on Twozan's forearm where a chance arrow had nicked him.

"She crossed the river with the first pack animals, I think. I was distracted as you know," he chuckled. "You're content that my scratch won't get infected?"

She settled the knot, smiled and nodded her approval.

"I'll go look if you're worried," he volunteered.

"Don't bother," she said as she put her nose up. "She's been moping around about 'Kerim' and has probably gone off to search him out. You have more important business, so I'll look for her."

He smiled affectionately and patted her shoulder. "Don't go alone. Too much has happened around here. Get Reverend Kootsal, or his wife to go with you. We can trust them with our secret." She nodded her assent and sighed. That dark cloud again. "It will be a relief to tell someone without guilt," she affirmed.

He laughed and took her face between his hands. "Is it so hard then, to guard your tongue?"

She looked down. "Women are used to sharing secrets rather than hiding them," she confessed. "Only a few have to be kept from your most intimate friends."

"Now you can tell it, but only this once." He turned and strode away, already his mind intent on the needs of the day. Pride filled her heart as she watched him go. "*Tanram*, here, indeed, was a man worth the effort to please. She walked to her horse. The minister should be near the end of the column with the sick and wounded.

> - - - - - >THE END OF THE COLUMN > - - - - - >

The so called sick and wounded were rowdy and full of jokes about the 'gophers' they had dug up. Their wounds were light and the skill of the priest and his wife were great. No one would die and although the chance of infection from dirty weaponry was present, most felt that the possibilities were small.

Ribald comments passed from one to another: "I saw you chasing that little kid who got you with the rock. I guess you were going to fix him good."

"Me fix him ... a little kid like that? I wanted to know where to find his mom so I could fix her."

"You were careless to let that old guy hit you with the sickle, Erly."

"Careless? Hell, I was taught to respect old age. I thought he was out to harvest some wheat."

"He thought he was. Men at that age can't see good. He thought you were an extra large stand."

"As drunk as they come, if you'd given him one more cup he'd have dropped without your help."

"Don't be mean, Onder, we're told to help our neighbors, even if they are 'gophers'."

"Erly helped him to sleep before he drank any more."

"Yeah, but he'll have a worse hangover for it."

"I'd have brought his supply with me if he'd left any." The banter raged on after they were bandaged and dismissed. The old couple cleaned up the instruments and bottles and packed them away in their saddle bags.

"I'm worried about Leyla hanum," Setchkin confided. "She was one of the first to cross the river, but no one has seen her since. She's not been happy these last days."

The pastor's wife nodded. "I think we should go back to the river to pick up the trail, Mookades is a good tracker." They turned the horses back south.

> - - - - - >SYR RIVER FORD > - - - - - >

"Here," Mookades pointed, "she left the track and went right. The others ground out the tracks afterward, but you see the track going into that grove over there." They looked past some small groups of people eating lunch around the banks of the river with a good view of the battlefield. Women and children were present so the trackers did not feel especially endangered. A boy sitting on a cart was playing with an arrow. It was Chipchak. Marium rode over to the boy and asked kindly.

"I see you got a nice trophy. Did you see a woman riding into that grove of trees? She is a friend of ours." He nodded nervously and his veiled mother walked over to intervene. She spoke quickly. "We came to see the excitement and before reaching the river we saw a man who shot this arrow at us, then he captured the woman. We were afraid to stop." The women exchanged glances. Both nodded understanding to one another and they both smiled at the mute boy.

"This is the right track and we need to hurry," said Marium, "we may be needed." She rode with Setchkin while Mookades led.

"*Bock*, look, *o'ra-da*, over there, horses beyond the clearing under that little tree." The cart tracks had matched the tracks to that point where they parted, each going in opposing directions. They saw them there. In the shade near the horses the man lay with his head lolled away and the girl was applying a bandage of rags to a wound under his raised arm, which rested above his head. Riding closer they saw the blood and tear stained face of the girl. The man lay limp and passive as they stopped, dismounted and gathered to her side. She fell into Setchkin's arms crying while Mookades and Marium started to help.

"*Yetish tir onu*, help him," she cried, "I can't stop the blood."

Together the old couple got the leather armor off his limp body and applied the pressure to the cut. Mookades smiled grimly. "We are fortunate the knife was deflected by his ribs. The wound is shallow, but he has lost a lot of blood. He will need water when he wakes."

Setchken poured water into her leather bonnet and began to clean Leyla's face. Marium got clean horse hair from her medicine kit and

163

started to sew the cut closed. She got willow bark concentrate ready to feed the young man. When he moaned she leaned over and put a bit of powder with a sip of water in his mouth. He swallowed, coughed and swallowed again. Marium gave him a taste more of water and he thirstily took the cup.

"He knows what he needs." she laughed, "I'll get some more, if you'll let go of the cup." She walked back to her horse for a bag.

"I'll bet you would like ayran better at this point, salt and milk are a great combination for a wounded man." She took the bag to him, took off the protective cap, and tilted the mouth a few inches from his face to squirt the liquid. "*Az'un-uz ach'en*, now open your mouth," she commanded. When he obeyed she shook and pressed the leather container and shot a short stream of white liquid through the bone nozzle. He swallowed the mouthful with evident relish. Then like a baby bird opened his mouth again. All the women laughed and Leyla jumped to take the bag from Marium. "*Ba-rak'en*, leave off, let me," she exclaimed, her newly washed face bright with relief and joy. The women watched with knowing smiles as the feeding continued. Mookades watered and fed the horses, then he checked the pack.

"He's going to need something in the way of equipment if he goes his own way from here," he stated. The women stopped to consider his words. Leyla, however, was absorbed in her task. "He can come with us, we will be fine. We'll marry and travel with the tribe," she spoke softly as if in a dream.

"*High'er ol'mahz*, no, it can't be," Mookadez spoke firmly. He saw the agony on the face of Kynan or Kerim of the Bulgars as Leyla knew him. "He would be killed as a sworn enemy. His face must not appear in the camp." A look of confusion touched Leyla.

"My brother has many enemies, even those of his own family," said Setchkin. "Come, it is better that we explain the situation to you. It is too much for him now. Let him rest."

Marium took the bag from her resisting hand and Setchkin led her away deeper into the brush. Mookades took the place beside the man and motioned Marium to join the pair.

> - - - - - - >KOOSKOO BEY'S HOUSE > - - - - - >
The posse came to a halt and surrounded the house and corral of the rich landowner, Kooskoo bey. All was dark and quiet until a voice came shouting from the

corral. "Sheriff, here's your horse and the other from the village. Just them, no others. Kooskoo bey must have lost some."

The sheriff tried the door to the house, and, finding it open entered, announcing his presence in a loud, but friendly voice. "*Afa-der'sin-is*, excuse us, we are from the village and seek a fugitive. Bey, bayan, whoever is here, we need information and mean no harm."

A tremulous voice answered from the house. "*Ko'jam*, my husband heard shouting and left, I heard lots more shouting and then horses left running. It was quiet but I was afraid to go out. I shouted from the house, but no one answered.

"We think a man and a girl changed horses here and must have taken yours with your man. You lock yourself in. We'll send someone tomorrow with news." He left when she agreed.

LOVE'S CONFLICT

PEOPLE, PLOTS & PLACES IN CHAPTER 15

Bolben: wants to help his villagers in their trouble.
Dahkool: mountain rose is gone, but remembered.
Derk bey: meets old friends as he seeks information.
Erly: stands guard, but longs to meet the princess' hero.
Katchy: comes home and makes friends with Sevman.
Kerim: wounded, yet strong enough to kill Kynan.
Korkmaz: leaves the village to help the refugees.
Kynan: dies willingly to make a marriage possible.
Leyla: faces new dangers as she guards her lover.
Mookades: buries and marries the same man in an hour.
Marium: attends both a funeral and a wedding.
Sesli: thinks she's the last of the refugees left free.
Setchkin: repeats her brother's eulogy for the tribe.
Sevman: awakes to fear under Goat Herder Hill.
Twozan: finds the searchers: witnesses a decision.
Yeet: learns about reports from an agent.

GLOSSARY:
ba'rok: leave it; quit.
Dee-kot' ol: look out! Beware! Be careful.
ha-key-key: right; just; appropriate.
ha-rik'a: splendid; great; wonderful.
Inshallah: God willing; I hope; may it be.
Ta'mom: okay; agreed.
The Cow: the second and longest surah in the Koran.
yakalada onlar: they caught them.
yap'ma: don't do it; stop it.
yet'ter: enough; sufficient.
Yesu gel: come Jesus; God help me.

WHO WINS?

It was near dark when Twozan arrived at the little clearing. He had left his companion to guard the river entrance where the cart had been, but had taken another way home. The glade was lit by a small fire and four people were seen. One pair of men was near the fire where Marium cooked a meal. The women were whispering, under a tree, face to face: mouth to ear. Both noticed his arrival and spoke quiet greetings. Twozan moved first to the fire and the standing man, Mookades, to exchange news. Then he went to the women and after greetings took his wife aside.

"You realize what must be done?" He inquired.

She nodded, "*Ev'it*, yes, they must ride apart from us. She will not leave him and he cannot ride with us."

He smiled down at her and sighed relief. "I'm glad you accept it so easily, many resent her because they sacrificed so much for her father who disappointed them."

"She is not at fault in this," Setchkin protested.

"*Dough-rue'*, true, but the feeling exists," he glanced at the couple. "Will she be willing to tend and care for him? He doesn't look able to go on by himself."

She chuckled and put her hands up around his neck and drew close. He self-consciously pulled back.

"As willing as I would be to go with you under such conditions," He smiled and took her hands from his neck,

"You must remind me of this conversation when we get to the yurt tonight."

He turned, walked to the prone man and sat. "Will you ride on tomorrow?" he asked.

Kynan paused, "I may sleep over tomorrow and go for a ride late in the afternoon. I've been riding pretty hard lately and it's time I took an easier pace."

Twozan agreed amiably adding. "You might meet less resistance if you allow our priest to marry you here tonight. Then you could go on at a leisurely pace toward home."

Kynan smiled at Leyla and took her hand. "Will you marry me here in this clearing of our first, and I hope last, misunderstanding? I acted without your consent. All men already take me for an enemy of your people."

"Our priest taught us that we should forgive, even love our enemies. I try to obey Yesu's words." She nodded her head, "I accept your plea."

"It can be done here now as you will." Mookades offered.

"That would suit me fine, but who will she marry? What will you tell your people about tonight? They'll kill me tomorrow if they know my real name."

All were silent then Setchkin spoke. "All know she loves Kerim, now she must marry him."

"Then I must kill myself and remain Kerim; Kynan is dead."

A look passed around the group, their heads nodded in unison.

"*Ha key'key*, it's the right thing to do, a true plan that we can all swear to." Setchkin whispered.

"I have seen Kynan die, killed by Kerim who marries the khan's daughter of her own free will and choice," stated Mookades.

"*Bock*! Look! We will bury him here," affirmed Twozan. He dug a hole in the ground under the tree with his knife and then took the rags wet with blood on the point of his knife to drop them into the slight depression and immediately cover them. "Say some words Mookades, a man is dead and buried. Some here knew him well, others slightly. He will have a eulogy we can recount to others."

Mookades cleared his throat and began. "We bring to your remembrance, *Tanram*, our fallen fellow tribesman, Kynan, a brother of Setchkin hanum, son of Kaplan of the Kynaklar clan, friend and protector of the high Khan of the Chipchaks. The youth was hostage to the East Bulgars, later captive of the black banner of the Abbassids whom he defied; escaping out of their lands. Here, on the border of his freedom, he has met his end honorably; admired by all. He was a credit to his family, and trusting in Yesu did all that is right and necessary for the good of the tribe. May his memory be treasured, amen." The circle of witnesses repeated his 'amen' solemnly.

"There is a strange sensation in observing one's own end and burial," said Kynan, now forever Kerim, "I'm sad and yet happy."

"I never knew him," stated Leyla, "I love Kerim. We're going to be married today."

The mood became immediately lighter. "Yes, all know it."

"Have you ever married a man incapable of standing for the ceremony?" Kerim asked Mookades, chuckling. They laughed. "Take her horse back to the tribe. I have a better present for her."

"Now the bride and princess will have guard duty all night to keep you and your goods safe." added Twozan.

Setchken snickered and observed pointedly. "And the guests leave at last light with no lion's milk to make them lose their way home."

Mookades nodded solemnly. "Let's start now. We are in hostile country here about." It was a short marriage ceremony and the guests did leave as the sunset faded.

> - - - - - >SYR RIVER FORD > - - - - - >

"What took you so long?" inquired the nervous sentry, Erly, at the river bank. Twozan motioned the others to ride ahead.

"We had to bury a man and marry another: Kerim, to his lady love." He explained, "She goes to his country with him. His chase was successful, but it has caused wounds that will cost him dear in the future."

The sentry was curious and excited now. "He has fought and killed another man for our princess?"

"Only one can hold her love. He who died could never have kept her; it has turned out right for everyone."

> - - - - - >KOOSKOO BEY'S HOUSE > - - - - - >

Katchy squatted in the brush as the posse rode shouting away. He moaned, caught between two emotions: fear of the posse and the urgent need to bring them to the dead body of his owner Kooskoo bey. Now murdered, and lying in the ditch beside the corral. He was afraid they would blame him for the death. If he had been able to hit the bad man he would have saved Kooskoo, but it was dark. His stone had whistled overhead while the struggling owner was stabbed to death. It was useless to follow the man on fresh horses. Now the posse would do that, but it was two hours and they were crossing the river. The bad man had followed the north bank of the river going west.

"Help widow, save money from deputies," he nodded his head vigorously. "Stay here, give widow coins tomorrow when bury big man." He felt better already. The posse would not come back for the funeral. They would not know that he had untied the dead man's money belt, which Kooskoo always wore in his sash.

Katchy decided to wait out the night and call the widow in the morning at first light. The neighbors would hear and come in the afternoon to bury him. He had put back the sash without the coins. It would be shameful if the bey's shalvar, pants, fell from his fat belly when they carried him. He counted the coins again. So many! He had never handled so much money in all his years. They were more than his flock of goats in number. He wondered if he could sleep with so much to guard. He had left his goats outside the corral. They could forage without him, but he prayed they would be safe from their enemies for the night and day he was away. He sighed, there would be a new owner and all his plans were blown away. All was in Allah's hands now. He would have to wait.

>- - - - - >BY SYR RIVER FORD > - - - - - >

"A fine way to spend my wedding night," Leyla scoffed to herself as she filled the water-bag by the river. She allowed the horses to drink their fill. Water would be scarce until they arrived at the grasslands farther north.

"*Mare'ha ba*, hello, who's there?" A call came in a rough male voice through the mist that hung over the river. Leyla moved quickly to lead the horses away. There was a sudden burst of sound from down river: laughter.

"*Ahkel'suz*, stupid fool, there's nobody near the river this time of night. Just some stray horses that'll need new masters."

"Well you had better move fast for they're headed away into the brush. We'll lose them," the rough voice replied angrily.

"Did you have to frighten them by shouting? Now they're running," accused the laugher's voice. "You've scared them away. We've lost 'em."

"Damn you, and your big mouth, we'll have to follow 'em. I'm sure I saw someone with the horses, right by the river bank," the harsh voice affirmed.

"Too much barley beer will let you see anything your heart desires, but you still wake up with a headache," the laugher sneered. The race took their breath away and they concentrated on the pursuit of the retreating horses. The mist still hung on in wisps amid the trees and thorn bushes. The animals knew their way, but the men found themselves lost from the path as the sound of the animals faded. No more laughter was heard, only complaints.

"We'll have to wait for light, we can't push through the thorns in the dark," the harsh voice whined with disgust. "It would have been easy if you hadn't spooked those horses." His only answer was a snort of contempt.

Leyla lay on the far side of the clearing in a thicket armed with her knife and her father's bow. She shivered and wished she were free to sleep by Kerim's side; better a sick husband than a night alone in the woods awaiting intruders.

> - - - - - >IN THORN COUNTRY > - - - - - >

"Where have you been Derk bey?" Yeet hastily asked.

171

His eyes were bright with excitement as they sat around the fire. "How do you come to be out here in the wilderness?"

"I went to visit a tribe of nomads. We have had a bit of trouble with them and we wanted to get things arranged to hurry them on their way out of Dar al Islam. To have our land of peace we must have no kafirs living in our borders. Unbelievers must live in the lands of war."

"Yet you come to visit us and are our friend," Yeet replied.

"Public policy and personal preference are different things, Yeet. You are friends so I stop to exchange news and to help you in your travels. I'm a Muslim who follows The Cow, before the Cow is even found in the recitation. We are instructed that Christians and Jews who believe in Allah and the Day of Judgment are accepted of God, if they do good and live righteously. Your friends do all of those things and live at peace in our society, we can be friends as long as that continues. Our beliefs are two sides of the same coin in the eyes of Allah."

Yeet smiled happily. "We camp here near the spring for tonight. Please honor us and join our campfire tonight and tomorrow as well. We are waiting for friends like you to visit us."

"*Ta'mom*, alright, I have been called home to the west and will by-pass Samarkand and go directly across the desert. I'll change to camels at Khiva on the Amu River." He went to his pack horse under a scrubby tree near the *cheshme*, a fountain and water source protected with a smooth stone basin.

"*Harika*, wonderful! You'll stay and I can tell you how I got this ugly bandage on my head," Yeet laughed as Derk took a small cage from the *hebe* on the horse. He heard the coo of pigeons and their scuffling in a small cage. Yeet peered into the cage while Derk explained.

"These little beauties are my letters home. They are tired of land travel and are in need of food and water before night."

172

Yeet's face showed a shock of amazement. Then he laughed again shaking his head in wonder as he peered into the cage. "You are the Caliph's agent. I should not be surprised by what you do. You have reports to make and send. Your superiors await important information."

>- - - - - - - >KOOSKOO BEY'S HOUSE > - - - - - >
Katchy passed a long and frustrating day. The new widow was inconsolable and would not cease her hysterics to listen to his story. The neighbors came, but they too would listen to only a bare sketch of how Kooskoo died and of Katchy's part in the whole chase. Food for all was brought to the wake. A villager came back from the posse to admit defeat and loss of the trail. He took the Sheriff and villagers' horses back after the funeral. At nightfall Katchy, without a word, left the money in the lap of the widow and departed for his corral. The exhausted woman stared at the coins and said to a circle of neighbors.

"Kooskoo said the goat boy had money to buy some goats and he was going to ask for rent on the land. The boy has given the price of the herd and the land. I'll have to ask the Kaymakan to see to the legal details. He was brave to chase the murderer and to stay by the body all night." They all agreed that Allah would bless him.

> - - - - - >IN THE TANRA DAH > - - - - - >
Bolben sat staring into space his lips seemed to form words that were unspoken. He formed two syllables and then finally whispered them. "Dah'kool, mountain rose," he sighed deeply and moistened his lips.

"*Yap'ma, baa-rok'*, don't do it, leave off. I can't stand any more of this waiting and you're going on about her," Sesli complains. "It gives me goose flesh to think of what is happening to us. They should be back by now. He said it would be only a couple of hours, but it's light outside."

Dawn breaks over the mountains as a small figure darts into sight running at full tilt. Out of breath the boy arrives at the ruin. "*Yakalada onlara*, they caught them," he gasped out. They plied him with questions he could not answer as he sat on a stone to rest. Then, little by little, he replied recounting all the incident.

173

To which he added, "It's true that the Uigurs burned the village and refugees are everywhere in the mountains. The garrison is rounding them up for detention and repatriation. There is a spreading sickness and villagers are not supposed to leave their homes."

"I have to go home," Bolben stated, "my people will need me. I have family and friends who need my help."

Sesli's face was stricken and pale. "There is punishment for me that way, and I'm the only one left of those who escaped. What am I to do?"

Korkmaz spoke up again with a smile. "The lady Nooryouz is with the baby, hidden in town. She is asking about you, but I can't take you there. When the baby is well she will come to you. You will have to stay in the country. Kadir's family lives in a valley near the Issyk Kool Lake, down the mountain. They would gladly put you up. Come, I will take you there. They have started searching for me in the village. I'll have to stay away a while."

> - - - - - >NORTH OF THE SYR RIVER> - - - - - >

The Chipchak camp was set up and guards on duty as the small cavalcade of five returned to the Khan's yurt. The excitement of the day's fights had many up beyond the normal hour of bedding down. There was also more after dinner drinking than would normally occur in a nomad's camp. The riders were quickly surrounded by an anxious crowd of concerned friends. "Where is Leyla?" They asked first. After that a shower of queries followed as the riders passed into the yurt. While the attendants fed their leaders and passed drink among the inquirers the story came out, piece by piece. Each of the five hurriedly contributed some valued part of the whole.

"Kerim, Leyla's savior and guide, was injured in a fight."

"He bested and killed Kynan of the Kaynaklar."

"Leyla tends his wound."

"Mookades married them at sunset."

"We buried Kynan ourselves."

"Kerim's wound was under the arm; a small thing."

"Kynan had been pierced through the heart."

"He died while we were there."

"He had repented and confessed to Mookades."

"We all heard the words of remembrance spoken over the grave."

"Leyla was full of tears and laughter."

They quieted, each settled down to tell their part of the story.

174

Setchkin repeated the words of the interment verbatim and even shed some tears in doing it. She affirmed that her brother had died a brave man who had bested the Caliph's best guards and troops. She insisted that the changes in his character were real and that he had become like one of the tribe's ancient heroes, Kaya. She affirmed that Yesu, the Savior, had won his soul.

Some of the listeners rejoiced that he was dead, others that he had repented and changed for the better. Most of them used the phrase: 'bash'un-uz-a sa'luck, may you be consoled and protected,' to comfort Setchkin, even if they were happy about his death. A few wanted to go and bring the newly wedded couple to the camp.

Twozan, however, forbade it. The river was enemy territory and not to be approached again. Besides, Kerim was determined to return to his own country. They gave up the idea and returned to the kumiss.

> - - - - - >NEAR THE SYR RIVER > - - - - - >
Leyla sat stiff and cold beneath the clump of brush. Her mind, like her body felt numb and leaded. A wave of convulsive shivering caused her whole body to tremble. Every nerve suddenly sent warning messages of stinging fire to her brain. Her mind was filled with a cold burning. It was dark and the freezing wind sighed in the twigs that framed her head. Leaving the strung bow, she staggered out of the hiding place and moved to the place far behind her. There the horses, draped in their leather covers, grazed together with only their hobbles to restrict their ranging.

Kerim lay beneath fur covers: warm and secure by her efforts. She resented, almost despised his happy repose. Yet he was the source of what she craved at that moment. Warmth, food and rest were her dearest need; affection would be a wonderful luxury.

She clumsily lifted the covers and lay behind him. Warmth touched her and she drew closer to spoon and press her cold face against his back. He groaned and turned on his back. A bag of ayran, held against his chest slid forward toward her. Leyla was quick to grab and embrace the warm bag and uncorking it, squeezed out the warm, salty, sour milk into her cold, dry mouth.

175

Beneath the covers, out of the wind, she greedily gulped the fluid. A contented moan signaled her gratitude. She emptied the bag. Her shivering was ceasing and she inched closer to the source of heat. She extended a foot and arm over his legs and stomach. She could smell the blood of his wound and hear his heart beat. She sighed as sleep and warmth penetrated her misery. As she relaxed against him other hungers made themselves known. She put her head on his chest and cupped herself against him. She felt his warm arm on her cold back. She smiled, this is the way it should be; they were married and God would take care of them.

> - - - - - >UNDER GOAT HERDER HILL > - - - - - >

Sevman wakes suddenly with a chill of fear; something is wrong. He listens carefully and thinks he hears a click, as of two stones together. He had slept hidden beneath overshadowing thorn branches. Beyond his bush the moon shines weakly. His tied horse snorts nervously. Sevman's lame leg feels cramped from too much riding.

Sevman had found it easy to rest a day after the long trails he had traveled from the nomad camp to the village. The fast ride from the village with the posse exhausted him. He was glad to take time out and let his horse graze on the green slope. The goats were grazing back in the brush far from his camping place. Katchy had not returned so Sevman had felt confident that there would be no problem. Now he wonders if he had been foolish.

The click comes again from up the hill and a whirring sound precedes the crash of a rock on the thorns above his head. He shrinks closer in his blanket and listens to the shouting.

"I warn you Yeet, you no come here no more. Horse eat all Katchy's grass. Goats suffer hungry winter. I tell you good with big head. Why you come again?" Another stone follows the first. Sevman remembers the pile of rocks on the hill. He starts yelling before the third stone crashes into the bush showering him with debris. He decides to run for the horse.

176

"I'm Sevman, not Yeet. I look for my friends here. I'm going early tomorrow morning, but I'll go now. I came here with the village posse and was told to wait here." The stones stop, the word posse brings fear to Katchy's mind even at a distance. He keeps a stone in his hand, but starts down the hill calling out.

"*Ta'mom*, okay, you look for friends, I no mad you. You go first light, we no fight. Kardesh, Tayze, Yeet go west. Kerim, Leyla go north like you and Atilla bey. Why you come back? Where's the good man?" Sevman saddles his horse and stays on its far side, away from Katchy.

"Atilla bey rides with the posse to catch the murderer. I stay here to follow my friends. The tribe goes north to their homeland. Leyla is with them. I left to bring Kardesh back to his people, but they have gone west, the wrong direction." Sevman's voice carries distress and Katchy understands.

"You stay. We be friends tonight. Tomorrow you see trail better." He drops his rock and instead puts some sticks on the dull campfire. "I tell story now."

In the light of the new fire Sevman sits and listens while Katchy tells him about following the stolen horses and finding Kooskoo bey dead. Both expressed their fear that the posse would return that night. As the cold increases, both boys retreated under the thorn trees to share the blankets.

KATCHY SLINGS

PEOPLE, PLOTS & PLACES IN CHAPTER 16

Erly: knows his way around; brings friends to party.
Katchy: finds he has been, unknowingly, replaced.
Kurnaz: the vizier is frustrated by a merciful escape.
Onat: dispatches three problems to other places.
Secretary: keeps the vizier advised on important matters.
Sevman: rides out to surprise his friends with news.
Sulema: survives in a new place, better than a village.
Tash: is given responsibility and a lecture on reality.
Thieves: find more than they were looking for.

GLOSSARY:
Dee-kot' ol: look out! Beware! Be careful.
Efendim: Sir? Pardon? (When something is not heard.)
ha-rik'a: splendid; great; wonderful.
ha-key'key: right; just; appropriate.
Inshallah: God willing; I hope; may it be.
yet'ter: enough; sufficient.
Yesu gel: Come Jesus; God help me.

LEYLA CAPTURED

Onat bey finished writing the letters, passes and orders for issue of goods and transport for Corporal Tash. The onbasha was healed of his bruises and anxious to leave the border post and return south. Tash knew he would have information for Ali bey that might also bring him additional rewards. He knew that the refugees from Tang China would be a source of interest. They had passed enemy kingdoms and would hold information needed for the expansion of Dar al Islam. This trip was an escape from present danger and would also be a new experience. He would find more opportunities to exploit people and situations to his own advantage.

"Here you have the necessary documents, Onbasha. You will wait in Khiva for the government agent who will speed you on your way directly to Samara and the Caliph's presence. You will be held responsible for the safety and health of your wards. Remember they are not your prisoners. They are wards of the government and the Caliph expects you to take good care of them. They are in your charge. Take horses at the stations until Khiva. There you will switch to Bactrian camels for the desert."

"Sir, I've never ridden one," the youth objected.

"You will learn or walk," stated the commander flatly. Then he laughed, "Don't worry the humps will hold you on. They're easier to ride than the ones you get south of Baghdad, they only have one hump. Now there should be no trouble along the way, the tribe of our Yuzbasha has passed beyond the last river. They are on their way home."

Tash smiled broadly, "We shall be glad we are rid of them, sir."

Onat bey looked the boy over and shook his head with regret. The boy needed teaching.

"You don't agree, sir?" Tash was puzzled. He knew everyone feared the nomads and wild Turks of the north.

"You don't know these people, lad. With them on our side we could take China or the Roman world. Without them we will just hold our own. They look rough and simple, but appearances are deceptive."

"Is that why you keep the Yuzbasha and other unruly tribesmen on duty here? You could have Arab troops from Merv or Khorasan."

"The Arabs are good fighters and determined, brave troops, but they cringe when confronted by the cold, rough, northern winters. That's why we are still here on the outer edge of the agricultural districts. We hold a porous, wavering line of resistance against northern raiders for over 200 years. The Uigurs show the high civilization these Turks are capable of, if they have a suitable climate and a softening religion."

Tash gave a depreciating laugh and repeated his creed. "They must surrender to Allah and our ways: abandon their ways of the ancestors, and idolatry. Only Islam will make them a superior people worthy of our friendship."

"*Inshallah*, Allah grant that we will convert them. But they will never give up their old concepts and heavenly processions. The eternal blue sky and the winter fires of heaven are too much in their minds. The ancient yak tail standards and swan symbols are a necessary part of their existence wherever they live. The religions of Buddha,

Yesu and Mani have touched their tribes, but none have sunk so deep as to change their core character. Their tenacity and skills assure the spread of their presence in the world."

The boy smirked, his face twisting humorously as he spoke, "Sir, Islam needs no stubborn barbarians from the cold north."

"Islam under the civil wars has stagnated. We lose in Iberia against the little Spanish states backed by the Franks. Greek fire stops our navy and Rome holds its eastern borders. The Caucasus Mountain states are resistant. The advance up the Nile and in Tigrenia in Africa has ceased. Beyond Sind on the Indus River the Rajahs defy us fiercely. The Uigurs and Turks of the north hold us back. We need a new people accustomed to face poverty and hardship to expand our borders. We need the Turks.

"They have no wealth or skills that we of Islam need. The men of Khorasan rule the Caliph and his courts. When we destroy the Greeks of Rome we will rule the world." The youth was stubbornly confident.

"Dismissed Corporal, take your charges and go. When you arrive at the Samara palace, notice the royal guard and remember our words this day."

> - - - - ->GOAT HERDER CORRAL > - - - - ->

"You'll find them in a few days Sevman, Allah will guide you good."

"Thank you for your help, Katchy, I wish I had a coin to leave you."

"I wish same thing. I give you cheese now. Look, see if okay. Wait. *Tu-haf' bi'shay*, this is strange, new cheese here. Some one has made cheese. Smell good. Mm... taste good. Here you take mine with you. Milk for ayran here too, you take in bag make ayran by night." Katchy's generosity was now overflowing since he was safely home at his corral.

181

"May the Jesus of light be your provider and protection, Katchy. He will give you all you need because you helped these days."

Katchy nodded, "You tell cart people my story. How I stay up with Kooskoo bey all night. Tell Yeet I sorry about big head, bad mistake. I be more careful now."

> - - - - - >SULEMA HERDS GOATS > - - - - - >

"Kechy, kechy come this way," yelled Sulema. It was her second day of herding and she was beginning to like the work and animals. They were social and intelligent, but a few tended to stray and get into trouble. The milking was something she was accustomed to do in the village, but the preparation of milk, cheese and ayran from the sour milk was much greater than she had ever known. She had started collecting bits of wool and fur in the corral and from the animals and started spinning yarn with a rock weighed spindle she had devised herself. She had a ball of wool now. She thought the goats she now talked to were as intelligent as the villagers she used to know.

"How are you today Bayan black and tan, are your twin babies well today? And Mrs. White foot, how much longer until your full term? Which of these billys is the father?" Sulema felt the answers were as clear as those obtained from villagers. She had seen the villagers returning with the stolen horses. They passed by in the evening, but she had hidden and was not inclined to make herself known. After all, she was appreciated and obeyed in this new society she had found. After the dawn milking, she heard sounds of a horse coming from the high hill. The lame boy who had visited the village and ridden north a week ago was here now, accompanied by the goat boy. Again she hid, watched and listened as they arrived at the corral. Then, she stole away to return to the place she had left the flock, while she finished eating her cheese. She drove them toward the rough country where she hoped the goat boy would not find her.

182

"Where you hide, smart goats?" Katchy said aloud to himself. The signs were sure, the flock had spent the night in the corral and someone had milked them and made cheese. There was no sign of them in the nearby areas, no strays or bleating of lost babies. His shelter had been slept in and changed. The bed was made up and the room had been cleaned and swept. He hardly recognized it as his own. It was a disaster! Jealousy raged in his heart. Someone had taken his job. His thoughts went, naturally, to Kooskoo bey: had he replaced him? But Kooskoo was dead by the river, and the intruder had been here when he died. He scratched his head. The new widow was too distracted to have acted against him. He had done her nothing but good. He ran in a large circle around the many tracks near his corral. Behind his shelter he found signs of goats grazing. He followed them to a dry streambed, where the vegetation was sheltered from the north wind and the sun shown on grass drying into hay. There, the herd had passed. In the far distance he heard the faint cry of the animals. Then he heard it: singing! He listened carefully to hear the words.

Rest sweetly now, the sun rolls past the flock.
The blue sky shines above, clouds drift by.
Come shade my fevered brow. I seek a lover.
Though I wonder; would he ever love me?
Worn, abandoned now. Left to lie alone,
Stolen from my nest. Cast away to die
Beneath the thorns, to mourn and sigh.
Allah, I cry, but no answer comes to tell me why.

The animals listened quietly. The morning sun warmed the cool breeze and the wind -sheltered north bank of the arroyo took in the sun's brilliance. The girl sat spinning her spindle and making thread. Katchy watched in awed fascination. She continued her complaints to her audience.

Rest sweetly now, day past, the sun descends.
A chill breeze fans my face. Blow you wind.
Come cool my fevered brow. I seek a lover.
Though I wonder; could I ever go home?
Despised, rejected. Here to mourn my dead,
Shunned, neglected now. Cast away for sin.
I fear men's scorn. They trick and lie,
'Allah,' they cry, yet God's answer comes:
'You, too, will die.'

REST SWEETLY NOW

Katchy forgot his anger, he forgot his purpose in
coming with his stones and sling. His jealousy converted
to curiosity, this was not a rival, yet she was; and did his
job well. She was as pretty as a yearling nanny, strong
and shapely. His admiration was grudging, but caused

him to be silent and to watch carefully her administration of his flock. He would seize on any mistake. He set himself to his task: to hide and watch.

> - - - - - >NEAR THE SYR RIVER > - - - - - >

The loud, rough voice cut through Leyla's sleep like an icy knife.

"The horses are here, but hobbled, so they can't run away. The Fergana mare we've been following is here."

"Good, but who hobbled them? There's got to be people around. Look for them quickly you big ox. We don't intend to give them up now after staying all night." The high nasal voice commanded, so the compliant voice moved.

Leyla moved too, and was up adjusting her clothes and searching for her weapons. A large, loutish man moved in the morning mist toward her.

"There's someone over here near the trees. Hey, it's a woman," the joy of discovery rang in his voice. "We got ourselves something better than horses."

Leyla took off in a run toward the clearing where she had left her knife. However, the man was quick and in five jumps he had her by her shoulder and arm. He pushed her toward the clearing and she fell forward, near where a man was leading their three horses, now freed from their hobbles. A little old man of indeterminate age stared down at her.

"Well, well now, don't muss her up. She can be for both of us." He looked her over taking one arm while the big man held the other. "Nice and young too! Is she the only one?"

The big man looked confused and angry. "I don't know. Isn't one good enough? I had to catch her. She's fast and was running away."

The old man nodded, chuckled, then commanded loudly, "Go back and search under the trees. More may have been there. Pretty girls don't travel alone."

The big man turned reluctantly. "I found her and caught her, she's mine. You can go find your own."

185

"You do what I say. I'll watch this one for us. She won't get away."

"*Yesu gel*," Leyla panted. "*Dee-kot' ol*, beware," she shouted. The old man twisted her arm painfully as she tried to rise from her knees.

A muffled sound came from the other side of the clearing. Horses were coming, four or five, and men's voices slurred and indistinct. Leyla stood as the men turned toward the sound. All motion ceased in the clearing as the three stood listening. The voices at the river entrance to the clearing came loud but not very clear from a group of four men, all high on *kumiss*.

"I heard a shout, someone's ahead of us," one rider affirmed.

"You sure this is the way in, Erly?" said another rider, sleepily.

"I was left as sentry by the river, but I know this is the right way."

"None of us have seen this Kerim, fellow. How will we know him?"

"We know Princess Leyla and she will be with him. *Yet'ter*, enough, that's how we know."

> - - - - - >IN SAMARA PALACE> - - - - - >

"All is done as you ordered, Kurnaz *efendim*," the secretary bowed low "the plans will go forward as projected." He stood awaiting orders.

The tall aristocratic figure so addressed, stood with a half smile on his broad handsome face; a Central Asian face. "Our gracious sultan is occupied with other urgent business today. I have, therefore, received permission to use the signet for today's affairs."

Both knew that the sultan's urgent business was the inspection of new slave girls, sent from the provinces for the harem. The ruler seemed to have time for little else. In effect the Turkish guards and vizier held the royal palace at Samara with all its power from within as well as from without.

"Yusuf bey, the man from Chang'an, is now in control of his estates and effectively brought his affairs into order and is prospering all his enterprises. All without resort to courts or judges," the secretary reported. "The old steward is effectively curtailed and dismissed, but without the dire punishment we expected. In fact the shameless rogue has come three times demanding an audience with you. He is expecting a pension from us in view of the favors and reductions of accounts in our favor. It seems he has kept accounts of our dealings."

The vizier sighed, "If only it had come to court we could have arranged his end; on the gibbet or behind bars. Now, however, we will have to satisfy his greed or be called into question ourselves. See to it, but don't let the oily scoundrel in here. I can't stand the sight of him."

The secretary bowed his acquiescence, as the vizier continued. "We must find a way to tap this prosperous source of wealth. Taxes or fines: which can we do?"

"The man has a daughter detained and then lost near the border with the Uigurs. Her discovery and rescue will be a source of wealth, if we can get her here quickly."

Kurnaz smiled broadly. "See to it, apply all our resources. Wait, is this connected with the Umayyad ambassador's daughter and her escape?"

"They were together in the harem, both escaped."

"Remarkable, give this full attention, both these women could change the future of our prosperity and rule. We must have them."

> - - - - - >NEAR THE SYR RIVER > - - - - - >
The thieves unfroze and reached for their weapons. Leyla jerked loose and ran for her sentry post beneath the brush where her father's bow lay. She had the bow armed and an arrow notched when she appeared on the other side of the screen face to face with the big man who had run to cut her off from the woods. He stopped and stared at her stupidly. She lifted the bow and motioned him back. She moved into the center of the clearing and took the Fergana's halter in her teeth. With jerks of her head

187

she led the mare to one side of the trees where she had slept. She kept the arrow half-pulled and pointed at the men. They were caught between her and the advancing horsemen who had appeared on the riverside edge of the clearing. The riders' easy conversation stopped abruptly, in the clearing stood two men, and beyond them Princess Leyla stood armed with a bow aimed in their direction. It was their turn to stop and stare stupidly. Erly, the guide, spoke first his voice hesitant.

"Pardon, Princess, it's an early intrusion, but we meant no harm. We came to congratulate you and…" As neither man in the clearing seemed to fit the bill for a successful suitor he stumbled to a mumble at this point.

"We brought *kumiss* to celebrate the occasion," volunteered another.

"We didn't think you'd object to a party," worried yet another.

The princess continued to cover everyone with her arrow. She wore no smile. The men between did not move or say a word. The confused horsemen continued to stare at the scene without any understanding. The princess' long silence unnerved them. They remembered the Khan had vetoed all visits to the river.

When she spoke it was with a quiet, slow cadence as if she were dreaming. "I appreciate your thoughtfulness and good intentions in coming to greet us and celebrate our marriage. I will never forget this hour and your happy presence here this morning. I thank God and bless you with all my heart. However, it is dangerous for you to stay, and so I must request your immediate departure back to the camp." She paused, a half-smile appeared.

"These men came seeking straying horses. I was about to persuade them that they were mistaken in taking ours. I don't want them hurt, but I do want them on the other side of the river. Make sure they cross, please. You might share some *kumiss* with them. I want them to go home wet and warm to sleep late. Three of you should handle that nicely. I'll talk to Erly and send him in just a minute more. Then you can all go to camp and sleep."

They listened in disbelief. These two outsiders had the nerve to try to take band's horses? She didn't want them hurt? Resentment boiled up inside them, but they were not going to tell her so. She held them captive: silent and obedient. Two armed their bows while the third walked his horse behind them and separated them from the animals, He sent a boot into the back of the big man and they hurried forward past the other three. Erly silently watched them go.

She sighed, "One against two is not comfortable with only one arrow. You will tell Khan Twozan that I was so happy to see you and I beg his indulgence for your dawn excursion and good will. Don't let them kill them. We want no vengeful riders following us. You were the first guard I met of his band. Remind me of this some day for I owe you a debt of gratitude. Go now with mine and Tanra's blessing. We, too, must ride swiftly away from here.

"Could I not meet your Kerim? The stories we heard in the camp excite us and the honor would be mine."

She paused before her reply. "Wounded and weak warriors do not love to be seen when at so great a disadvantage. He can call you back if he changes his mind. You must restrain your men, Tanra guard your steps."

Erly nodded slowly, "*Ahn la dum*, I understand," he murmured. "You will follow a close trail for some days. I guard the right wing. If you have any needs: medicine, food, horses, you can call me."

She smiled her relief. "Go happily."

"Go with God," was exchanged. Erly left reluctantly.

SULEMA SPINS

PEOPLE, PLOTS & PLACES IN CHAPTER 17

Abdullah: forwards his successful plans.
Ali: tries to restrain a friend, but is ignored.
Deputy: plays judge and jury punishing a prisoner.
Derk: brings sad news and makes a surprising offer.
Kardesh: is diverted from pursuit of his tribe.
Katchy: loses his work, flock, house and dignity.
Kerim: finds safety in weakness and dependence.
Leyla: continues to meet threats to her happiness.
Magazi: plans further exploits for his employer.
Mansur Ibn el Ari: the hunter becomes the prey.
Sulema: claims the corral house for her own.
Tayze: corrects the rude behavior of her charges.
Yeet: gets news about his mother from an old friend.

GLOSSARY:
ahn la dum: I understood.
bar-awk'tum: I left them.
Bach or'da: look there; look yonder.
bash a nas ah sa'aluck: be comforted; health to you.
gehena-ya: to hell with it.
gel: come; approach.
loot' fin: please.
Te-she- kur ader'-em: Thank you; I give you thanks.

STAG HUNT

The week had passed painfully for the newly
circumcised Chipchaks. They were camped beyond the
desert pass into Abbassid territory with two armies
blocking their advance or retreat. The Khorasan Army
was behind them and the Royal Guards surrounded them,
while the Caliph's Army awaited them across the pass.
Inside the country a reinforced garrison of border guards
kept the men of Khorasan from completing their sworn
task: annihilation of the invaders.

A deep resentment clouded the faces of the men who
followed El Ari. The spoils and glory of besting kafirs was
gone. The conversion of the enemy gave them little or no
comfort. It was especially bad with the rumored prospect
of disbanding the army so far from home. Everywhere
men spoke of it.

"The moment of action is today, beloved friend. The
stars are propitious, the agents are ready and the victim
is unsuspecting."

"Who is equal to you Abdullah? Your new plan covers
every contingency. Nothing is too hard for you!"

"It is you, Magazi, who shows genius in contacting the
actors and the gathering the tools and staging necessary.
You have done it all superbly. How fortunate I am to share
your bed." The conspirators beamed satisfaction.

"I saw one of the Turks riding out today they are
becoming active again. The youth are as good as new,
but the older ones move slowly."

"They'll move fast enough tonight." Abdullah sneered.

"Spread out, men: fifty lengths between horses. Our cast must enclose the mountain." The master of the hunt called in strident bellows.

The noise level continued to rise as the men in line passed the command to their neighbors. The line continued to advance as the wave of expansion and adjustment touched the string of men as they walked forward to beat the mountain-side brush to scare up game. Mounted archers and a few men with hawks followed the beaters up the slope. Birds and small animals flew and ran before the line of rapid fire. The action followed thick and fast as they advanced.

All the officers and important army men had been invited and key workers with special skills and gifts were pressed into the hunt. Persistent reports of stags in the near mountains had attracted the attention of the bored and frustrated commander and his chief men. After the long journey with its depravations a feast of excitement and meat was due. Their idle armament could, at last, be put to good use and taste the blood of those escaping their will. The innocent creatures of the country-side would atone with their lives for the government sin of allowing the guilty nomads to escape the intended vengeance. The frenzy of the blooded sacrifices was on the army at this moment.

"*Bach or'da*, look over there, stags!" A herd has been raised near the broken cliffs and water course. The sound of shared news traveled the line. Those near the discovery strained to see; those far away wished themselves near. Mansur Ibn el Ari pressed forward between the beaters. Only a few of his abler men could follow his impetuous course. Swift as an eagle he rode, down into the cut bluffs to launch his arrows at the climbing bucks on the opposing banks. His aim was sure and one large eight point buck came crashing down into the draw. Another deer of six points took a second arrow in the shoulder, but vanished over the edge, out of sight and range. Leaving his downed beast to his followers the commander pursued the wounded buck up over the edge and into the brush and trees of the chill forest. Up into the grassy alpine meadows he rode toward the snow dappled summit. There a field of boulders, and split rock littered the landscape. The run became a walk and tracking the wounded animal was the only way to trace it in the jumble of fallen rock. The cliff wall was pocked with overhangs and caves. A hoof print in the spots of snow showed the way. Prince Mansur, leaving his horse, threaded his way through the maze. The silence was a contrast to the noisy chase. A sense of foreboding chilled him.

Mansur found more tracks and blood drops, but the deer could have been anywhere before or behind him. He searched in vain, but suddenly saw a man peering out of one of the cave entrances. He moved in that direction hoping the higher ground would give a clue to the deer's hiding place and even as a refuge from the oppressive cold and silence. His aim of companionship was dashed. The man had quite disappeared leaving him clueless as to his prey or the way out of the circling paths. Breathless he arrived at the cave entrance. The figure he had seen left tracks in the sand and rock of the floor. It was warmer out of the wind, but he was shivering.

As he peered into the depths of the cave a hiss and flash was the only warning he had before an arrow buried itself in the center of his chest.

> - - - - ->NEAR GOAT HERDER HILL > - - - - ->

Sulema had another fine day in the brush tending the goats. She was starting to knit a sweater for colder weather was on its way. Spinning, knitting, tending the animals and continuing her animated conversations with some of them, she passed her day. Several times she had felt someone watching her, but could see no proof of her feelings, and so dismissed them. The corral had been cleaned when she arrived there for the milking. The stores of cheese, butter and milk had been moved and processed. The jerky, dried meat had been used. A bag of lentils was hung from the roof beam. Someone had been around so she hurriedly finished her tasks and taking several sharp stones as weapons entered the shelter. She firmly closed the door and put up the cross bar. She would be safe from any lurking thing.

As darkness came on, someone pounded on the door. Sulema listened silently; she would not be the first to speak. If it were the goat boy he could sleep outside with the animals. If it were the posse she did not want to be found. Katchy listened to see what she would say. The pounding disturbed the goats, but neither would speak. There was no sound of horses, she was sure it was the goat boy. She'd never let him into her house. Strangers weren't supposed to see a decent woman's face. Allah didn't approve of bold, bare-faced women. She knew that because she had done it. Just look at the results! Her brother murdered and herself kidnapped by a false lover.

Katchy had no such restraints and when his temper was fully aroused he screamed insults, threats and curses to his vocabulary's limits. He howled like a dog and hissed like a cat; bleated like a goat in pain and even roared like an attacking bear. Sulema listened with smug satisfaction, none of that would frighten her. The door was stout. He could sleep near the door of the pen as the shepherds did in summer days. She was asleep by the time he retired there with his voice used up. The night was cold and he was angry, so he slept little and hoarsely continued his complaints to his bed mates.

> - - - - - >KATCHY'S CORRAL > - - - - - >

"Hai Allah, *gel, bach* Ali, come look what I found sleeping here in the corral gate. Just the guy we're looking for," the deputy's voice rang out.

"Well get down and hold him, he's as quick as his goats," Ali replied.

"Come help, he's strong and I'll need help to tie him up," he panted. The tussle was, indeed, hard, but the boy's screams were muted and hoarse.

"You think he's sick? Maybe got a cold staying up all night with old Kooskoo bey?" asked the deputy. His friend shook his head and laughed.

"He's got enough to answer our questions. Hold his hands while I tie his feet." He tied them together. "Now put the loop over his head so he can't stand. Kneel boy or you'll strangle yourself." They plopped him on his knees and each held a rope around his wrists. "Help me spread his arms up over those branches, a rope on each branch just so he's spread eagle."

"Great job Ali, he can't get away now. Let me get a couple of thorny sticks to apply to his back and soles. We'll get the truth out of him."

"Now you little sneak, who did you steal the money from? Tell us."

"No steal, give money to bayan Kooskoo, stay up all night with bey, protect him." Katchy's voice was a strained whisper. The men doubted it.

"You bought lentils before leaving, whose money was that?"

"Cheese money belong me. I sell at river village fair."

"What about the money you used to buy the flock and land? Where did it come from?" The deputy flexed the long thorn branch menacingly.

"I guard and count money all time, give to *bayan*. She keep good."

"We want straight answers, now. Did you get the money from the quarry man? Stuff he stole in the village?" he insisted belligerently.

"*Hi'er*, no money from bad man. I send him rocks. He shake knife, but I stay away. He run on horses, I run on foot."

Ali nodded in agreement. "Well, he got that right. The boy's got spunk to stay on his tail."

"Just trailed along to see the excitement, it don't mean a thing."

"He got a hell of a lot closer than we ever did," Ali observed.

"The money's not his. He never saved that much in his whole life. He's going to tell me where he got it." The deputy was furious now and hit Katchy across the back. "Speak up, you little bastard," he lashed out again.

"I guard money all time. Kooskoo bey dead, bad man cut him, steal new horses, leave village horses. I send rocks, but too dark. Bad man run away. I tell truth, no steal money, give to bayan. *Loot'fin*, please, Allah witness."

"You blaspheming kafir, I'll cut your feet to ribbons." He matched action to his words despite Katchy's howls of pain.

Ali protested loudly, "You best wait till the sheriff arrives. You got no authority to do this."

"I don't need nobody to tell me who the liar is here." His thin stick splintered and sent a shower of pieces in all directions. "*Gehe'na ya*, t'hell," he complained, as he picked a thorn from his hand. "His feet are as calloused as horn. He's hardly bled at all."

Ali stood away to one side. "I don't think you should do this now. Wait and just ask questions."

"Why should you care if a hump-back, goat-boy gets a few stripes? You've heard him beg for money. He collects for information and sells Kooskoo's meat to anyone," the deputy groused.

His friend shrugged in reply. "So he gets money and all he ever buys are lentils. He's been here almost fifteen years. Only Allah knows where and how far he goes to sell."

KATCHY BEATEN

196

"I still think justice can only be done by stripes just like the law orders. They ought to cut off his thieving hand like the Koran says." He turned his back on the crying, moaning victim. Both men looked up the road, aware that someone was riding their direction. It was the sheriff.

> - - - - - >NEAR THE SYR RIVER > - - - - - >

Leyla stood for a moment as Erly rode out of sight, then the horses, who are social animals, started after him and she had to run forward to gather their halters and lead them to her camp site. Kerim, her new husband, lay apparently asleep, looking warm and refreshed under the wool quilts. She scanned him and the camp resentfully, but remembering her part in his wounds, set about collecting and folding the goods into the packs. She turned to the covers last, and starting at the top removed them one by one.

"I had a strange dream just now," Kerim said with a pleasant smile as she removed the last quilt. "I dreamed you were troubled by animals raiding the camp. I tried to get up and help you, but a strange man stood above me and said: 'Don't bother getting up. Tanra has sent her help. You must rest for the travel today.' So I fell asleep again, and now I wake up to see a beautiful princess attending my bed." She was pleased, but didn't want to show it.

"Lazy husbands are the bane of the yurt woman's life, especially on moving day." She complained as he stood carefully and rotated his shoulders gingerly. It was evident by his grimace that the cut was stiff and sore. He carefully put on his armored vest, coat and shoes while looking around.

"Are we invited elsewhere for breakfast?" He inquired pleasantly.

"We eat on the move, unless your dream messenger has prepared something close by. Otherwise, we eat riding or further along," she replied scoffing. She had the horses ready and he moved carefully to mount.

He paused asking, "You checked everything? Food, bed, weapons?"

She froze in shock. "I, - my father's, - Oh, *Tanram, bar-awk'tum*, I left them." She leaped from her horse and ran to the clearing where, under the brush, she brought out the quiver and knife. When she returned he was on his horse, but he looked a trifle pale.

"Are you alright?" she inquired. He cocked his head and moved his horse toward the side of the meadow where the cart had appeared the day before. He followed the track away from the river without a word. She led the pack horse and they traced the tracks for an hour. Then they saw a hut on a bit of rough ground where a little spring of water made a green oasis in the dry landscape.

Near the hut a boy played with a long stick that he spun suspended from a string of fiber tied around the balance point of the stick. He twisted the string around his finger. He wound it tight so it would unwind in rapid circles. As they drew near they saw the stick was a Chipchak arrow. Leyla was amused and rode closer to the boy. Kerim, however, rode over to look at some brush where he selected some stout curved branches which he cut from the tree.

"You found a pretty toy. What does it point to?" The boy pointed to the spring where the remnants of a frosted garden lay. He took the arrow by the shaft and pretended it flew up and down toward the garden. "Would you like the arrow to fly to the garden?" she asked, intrigued by the display.

"*Gel*, come, we will make it fly in the garden," Kerim said, as he rode up with the wooden frame of a bow appearing under the edge of his knife.

"Let's see your garden now. You show me." The child raced ahead with the arrow clutched in his hand. Kerim followed walking his horse.

"You still have root crops maturing under the ground," he observed.

The boy stood very still and then slowly pointed his arrow at the edge of the field. A rabbit or wild hare hopped slowly toward the crop. Kerim armed his bow and shot it. The boy jumped in elation and other hares leaped too. Kerim brought down two more as they darted and wove through the space before him.

The child, without hesitation, ran to gather the animals as they fell. He used the arrow as a knife to finish one of the wounded. He was full of laughter.

"Good hunters know where to find the prey," laughed Kerim, also, as he rode the edge of the field hoping for another shot.

Back at the hut, Leyla, while watching, talked to the mother who had just appeared at the door.
"Your son found rabbits, bayan," she observed brightly to the lady.

"Your man has killed them lady, and we are all glad. He and his father use rocks, but kill few," the mother acknowledged. Leyla felt a warm glow of satisfaction.

"It is early," the woman observed, "have you eaten breakfast yet?" she inquired solicitously.

Leyla bobbed her head up in a negative move. The lady disappeared into her home, only to appear when the hunters came back to the door, bearing three trophies, which the boy dropped at his mother's feet. She bore two bowls with a wooden spoon in each and proffered them to the pair, still mounted before the door.

Kerim thanked her, "*Te-she-kur-ader'-em* bayan, the blessings of Yesu be yours this day."

"Do you want the animals skinned or will you carry them this way?" inquired the home-owner. "Do you use the skins?" she asked.

Kerim sighed, "The skins will be lost with us traveling, and we are only two. One carcass is enough. We haven't enough time to dry meat."

Leyla spoke up, "Your garden fattened them they should all be yours."

"No, I will give you their equal in dried meat," she volunteered. The lady took the rabbits inside and later returned with fresh meat wrapped in leaves and the dried meat was folded in dry rushes harvested from the river and platted together.

"I think I'll saddle cure some of the fresh meat," Leyla exclaimed. "It can be used on the trip and if you put onion or herbs it tastes better." She took the raw meat and placed it in its package between the saddle and blanket.

"I've never seen it done before," exclaimed the lady. "Muslims make *kibbi*. Raw lamb meat mixed with cracked wheat is beaten into a paste, eaten with bread."

"The heat of two bodies cures ours and the pressure of the saddle and person riding tenderizes it," Leyla was quick to explain.

While the ladies finished their preparations and Leyla got to see the contents of the house, Kerim finished his handwork. The bow was ready and several additional arrows were being made. The child watched everything carefully.

"Remember that a horn and bone bow is better for distance and force. Any bow will work at short range. You must wait for the hare to approach. Remember that dried gut is better than string, and will send your arrows much further," he concluded.

"Where is you father today?" he added, curiously. The boy pointed toward the river they had left that morning. Kerim went to the corral and saw that the horses the man owned were all gone with him.

"Come Leyla, we must hurry there may be more visitors here soon." The ladies had become quite intimate now and they terminated their visit reluctantly. They parted with many expressions of good will. As they rode from sight the lady sighed out-loud. "My husband is wrong. Turks are quite civilized, but just passionate in love."

> - - - - - >MOUNTAIN HUNT IN IRAN > - - - - - >

"Allah, Allah," exclaimed the mountain guide to the men he led, "Treachery has been here before us. The prince, your commander, is dead by a Chipchak arrow. The Turks have their revenge."

The cave echoed with the cries of the men who met this new disappointment to their hopes. Torches were ordered to be brought to explore the cave. Cloaks were stretched and rolled around two spears to make a stretcher to carry the body. The arrow was left to bear evidence of the manner and source of the death stroke. The bearers carefully picked their way through the maze of rocks and turns when another cry was raised. The six point buck was discovered dead behind some rocks. The El Ari arrow marked the owner, who gave life for life; because an enemy gave stroke for stroke. Binding its feet to a spear shaft the animal was carried after the hunter to the base camp where a victory feast of meats from the hunt was changed into a feast for the dead. A huge mass of men from the army surrounded the body of the beloved commander in tears and lamentation. They all swore to take revenge on those who caused his death. The body was put on display before the commander's tent.

Abdullah came swiftly to search for his beloved Magazi. "It's done. No slips or failures so far. The plan, though is changed, matured. The master will be pleased."

His friend nodded as he embraced his conspirator warmly. "But the guilt must fall on the proper victim and leave the tribe as well as the army headless; otherwise we finish only the necessary half rather than a full abundant overflow."

"Wait and see, my love, wait and see," Abdullah laughed.

> - - - - - >ON THE WAY TO KHIVA > - - - - - >

"It seems you have lost your way, and since I must go west you can accompany me. Old friends can share their food and money."

"But Derk bey, we are slow and of small benefit to an important man with official business," Yeet insisted. The lavish meal was appreciated for the money from the quarry afforded little and would soon terminate.

"We thank you for your generosity, but Sevman and Atilla are coming and we may have to wait for them," Kardesh stated.

Derk bey smiled. "They have good horses and can catch us in a few days. I have finished an important mission and can afford the time to travel at leisure."

"What possible benefit could our presence contribute to you?" Kardesh reiterated to their guest.

Derk smiled and made a hopeless shrug. "Yeet has been a friend for a long time and I bear news that I would break gently to him. However, if you will not indulge me and bear my company, I will tell him bluntly and move on."

Tayze spoke severely. "Are these words of welcome spoken by crows? Has the rock quarry blunted your minds and tongues to generosity and goodwill? Does the beggar spit on the shoe of his alms giver?" Her eyes flashed anger. "Such kindness is a gentleman's gift to be treasured, not seriously questioned." She drew herself up proudly, "Some of us remember the station from which we have fallen and the days and manners we enjoyed heedlessly. We beg you sir, forgive these hasty words from youth, unmindful of manners."

"We live in perilous times, bayan; suspicion is normal and protective among humans so immersed in violence such as we have suffered these last decades. But for the men of Khorasan and their Seljuk warrior auxiliaries, the great Abbasids would have been replaced long since. It is the East that holds Islam against the powers of current dissention and division."

Tayze softened and turned. "Never mind lads," she instructed, "He will stay and you will be glad. Our friends will come after with yet more news and we will arrive where Tanra decrees."

The boys continued to look ashamed, but Yeet spoke now, "News is better borne directly than worried about, Derk bey. What is your news?" The man turned to his saddle and took down a small packet.

"Here you have it." A string was tied around a roll of thick fabric, unrolled it proved to be a rug of silk and wool almost the size of a Muslim prayer rug. Yeet gasped at the sign of death in the pattern. It was traced in a single thread: the faint small sign of the head of a wolf. He knew it was his mother's rug finished while he was still working in Kokand.

"She died quickly?" Yeet asked in a broken voice, as he embraced it.

"I arrived too late. She had time to do the thread sign. The rug she had started some months before was cut down, stolen for some reason. She knew beforehand and sent her love and a warning."

Yeet nodded pensively and sighed. "We knew the pressure to serve an evil cause. She insisted I leave, thinking that would solve the problem and relieve the pressure."

"It didn't save her. She didn't give me enough to know how to save her. I picked up the rug and hid it before Ali bey could get a hold of it."

"Thank you for your faithfulness in attending her," Yeet murmured.

"*Bash a nas ah' sa'aluck*, be comforted, she spoke of you often." All echoed his words of condolence. The awkward moments passed and then in the distance they heard the sound of hard riding. It was dark now and the light of the campfire was the only light, yet someone rode at breakneck speed through the gloom.

AMBUSHED!

PEOPLE, PLOTS & PLACES IN CHAPTER 18

Atilla: feels that leaders should stick with the mob.
Aziz: sees changes in his grandson, more are coming.
Derk: is surprised by his Kokand friends' information.
Gerchin: gains victory over a pursuing enemy.
Jon: leaves in chains to take his mistress home.
Kadir: is ready for every contingency and request.
Kardesh: feels too much is happening to understand.
Kerim: although married, must provide his own breakfast.
Leyla: the princess is sensitive: she has the right to react.
Manson: works for Yavuz and is willing to do anything.
Maril: learns from the commander's mother.
Sevman: makes the long trip to his friends' cart.
Sulema: finds that punishment and hurts are shared.
Yavuz: holds evidence against his old partner.
Yeet: is learning more about a friend's secret work.

GLOSSARY:
anne: mother.
evet: yes; agreed.
ordu eve: army headquarters; command tent.
su: water
su-sa-dum: I'm thirsty.
yah: butter; oil.

MARIL'S FAREWELL

"Now you men spread out and look through these ruins. If you see any signs of recent occupation or any goods left lying about you let me know. That kid's been seen coming out this direction lately and I know he's up to something. Old Aziz doesn't fool me. I know he's got his nose into my trade. He's got girls coming over. Well, get to it, don't just stand here listening, Manson."

"I thought I heard hoof beats, boss," Manson reported. Just for a moment, very faint; they're gone now."

Yavuz bey aired his suspicions, "Aziz bey's grandson, Korkmaz, was all over the place and there is talk of girls and Uygurs with him." Yavuz was investigating every rumor.

"Over here, Yavuz bey, there were people cooking in this third room. The ashes are from last night, they're not long gone." Yavuz ran eagerly to the man and pressed a small coin into his hand.

"Good, now can you tell how many?" Manson came to search the floor. He looked in a corner and found a small ball of hair.

"*Bock*, look! Combed out hair: a woman for sure." Yavuz grabbed the wad and pulled some of the hairs out full length. "Long, black and silky, probably a looker, this is the proof I need." The discoverer pointed to the wall with a stone before it.

"A man sat here, see, no dust. His back touched the wall here. A big man! Look here, scuff marks at the door they left fast running: three or four at least." The first man pushed Manson out of the way.

"One is going toward town, the man, I think. The other prints go this other way. I'm not sure how many, smaller I think."

"I've enough proof now," Yavuz held up his ball of hair. "I will confront the shameless deceiver now. When I find him, he will have to listen."

> - - - - - >ROAD TO KHIVA > - - - - - >

The hoof beats came closer as Sevman galloped to the edge of the camp between the cart and the fire. He slid off his horse, nearly falling as he touched the ground. Yeet and Derk hurried to his side. Derk attended the exhausted horse, while Yeet and Tayze helped him to the fire. He was stiff and sore from the long rides. They all talked.

"How are you Sevman?"

"Where have you come from?"

"Are you hungry?"

"Have you come alone?"

"We have soup ready."

He sat heavily. "I left Katchy yesterday morning, and rode for two days and a night to get here. I didn't stop at all. I slept in the saddle." He ate the soup and bread with relish. He finished three bowls before his story ended.

"That is the sum of it," he concluded. "Afterwards Katchy told me what happened by the river. The murderer committed a second murder - Kooskoo bey - and escaped with fresh horses and the girl over the river. Atilla bey went with the posse and I left the morning Katchy came back." The group sat quietly a moment.

Yeet spoke up. "Why didn't you go on with the posse from the village?"

"Exhaustion, fear and a distrust of the men sent to do justice. They were only intent on personal vengeance."

Derk bey, who had finished with feeding the horse, came back to the fire to ask, "What fears, Sevman?"

Sevman looked at him a long minute. "My mother is Uigur. Many feel I belong to an enemy nation. Since I am not Muslim, most people fear I would not be loyal to their interests. I am a distrusted minority, a poor cripple boy

206

who must associate with Christian tribesmen to find companions who do not despise me."

Derk nodded his head, He looked sharply at Yeet. "How do you feel about this?"

Yeet, wagging his head, replied, "My father was a Muslim warrior and although mother is a Christian and I like what she taught. I, by Sharia law, must be a Muslim. My life depends on it."

Derk bey nodded his agreement. "It's the law of the Caliph, state and religion. It must not be questioned or debated. Order and the will of Allah can only be preserved in surrender to what is ordained." There was a long silence following these statements.

> - - - - - >KATCHY'S CORRAL > - - - - - >

"What the hell are you two donkeys up to now?" The sheriff shouted as he rode up to the group. "Cut that poor little monkey down. You can't do that without just cause."

"Aw, listen boss," the deputy protested. "This boy must have stole that money he gave the new widow lady. He's a thief and ought to lose his hand. You can't make that much cash on cheese and meat when old Kooskoo was takin' his part of everything."

The sheriff glared down at him. "Maybe, maybe not, but the lady is not goin' to press charges. He's a hero for stayin' with the body. Kooskoo kept her in the dark about his funds; both gains and losses. She's sellin' the flock and water rights, plus the hillside field and seep." There was a silence.

"She must be crazy. Sell this to a stupid hump-back?"

"It's fit for nothin' but goats and she ain't goin' to ride out to put things right a dozen times a year. She's got a son who'll come take the house on the edge of the village and farm. She's goin' to the city."

"I'll be damned!" muttered the deputy's friend Ali, totally astounded.

"You will be, and worse if you don't cut that boy down and get out of here, before some one reports you to the magistrate." He trotted away.

"Wait up boss, we're comin' too," the deputy shouted as he untied the knots and coiled the ropes. They left him where he fell and rode off after the fading hoof beats of the departed Sheriff.

> - - - - - >THE KHORASAN CAMP> - - - - - >

"Allah, Allah, we have lost our treasure."

"Our great leader has perished."

"Cut down by cowardly assassins."

"To arms, to arms we must avenge his death."

"Kill the dogs that hide in the rocks and caves."

"A star has fallen from Islam."

"Sound the alarm."

"Murdered in ambush!"

"Our glory has departed."

"*Allah hu Ekber*, God is Great."

"Kill the *kafirs*, down with unbelievers."

"Revenge, now," the voices cried.

The Khorasan camp was in an uproar as the body of their leader, Mansur El Ari, was brought back from the mountain animal drive. All the hunters and beaters were massed around the hastily built stretcher made of limbs and saplings. The horns blew long sad notes as the howling mob returned to their camp. Drums and cymbals added to the bedlam. There the shouts became indistinct, only a loud roar, as of a wounded animal, filled all ears.

The sound carried up the mountain pass to the border guard and beyond to the recuperating Toozlu Turks. Even the Royal guard sent to reinforce the border and to escort the new troops to Baghdad and Samara heard it. The call to arms echoed through the camp for the formation of the battalion. Riders dashed between the guards and Royals. The sound of hoof beats and rumours filled the Turkish yurts. Gerchin called up all his able-bodied men.

A MAD MOB

208

Although they had been disarmed on passing the guards a few scimitars and bows appeared among them. Gerchin sent messages to the Royals and guards pleading for the return of their weapons. The mob was moving toward the Toozlu camp. Their anger and hate were clearly heard. The Tuzlu made more preparations.

> - - - - - >THE CHIPCHAK CAMP> - - - - - >

The men and women too, pulled their knives and some took out part of the wood frame that made the supports of the yurt, collapsing them. They held them like batons or sharpened staves in their right hand and the knife in the left. They formed a circle around the Khan's yurt. The women and children withdrew out of sight into this *ordu eve,* the tribes' command center.

The battalion of the Royals was still arming and forming in their camp when the mob pushed past the border. The guards were reluctant to attack the men of Khorasan, so important in their recent history. They limited themselves to pushing and yelling at them.

"You can't pass here."

"This is forbidden."

"The Caliph denies you entrance."

"Go back to your camp."

"You have no permission."

But the mob, hundreds strong, paid no attention, pushing past, they voiced their own intentions without heed or need to listen.

The Chipchaks had formed a circle of young men about their camp of largely or partly collapsed yurts. Each warrior was about a staves distance from the other. Three paces behind them stood the men who had bows. Other men stood beside them with stave, knife or baton. The older men still tender or infected were in a tight circle near the largest, the central Khan's yurt. The young women and children were inside and the older women were behind the older men. Several companies of mature, cool-headed men were formed between the old and the fighting lines to be mobile reinforcements for any sector that gave too much under pressure. The tribe was choosing the instinctive defence found in the natural world among herd animals. There they intended to sell their lives dearly.

The enraged mob, careless of strategy and many without proper armament or weapons plunged toward the camp. The mob leaders were picked off in a shower of arrows by the bowmen as the mob came thirty paces from the first line. As the two groups clashed the first line was driven back to the second line and the bowmen escaped to the third line to rain arrows down on the men's head in the areas of thickest combat. The bodies of the wounded and dead among the downed tents now hampered the attackers. The bowmen moved back to the ordu eve while two companies of reserve moved into the area of attack. Some weapons were picked up from the dead and wounded as the line swayed indecisively. Then the mob forged ahead.

Spilling blood excites. Losing blood cools the temper. The mob was finding the cost excessive. The infidels did not die easily. A flag went up from the Toozlu army headquarters, half the protective circle ran around to the left flank of the enemy. When a second flag flew the other side whirled to advance on the enemies' other flank. The mob was now being encircled. Some, less enthusiastic or slower, realized this and turned to meet the danger. The front ranks of fighters did not realize this and continued to press forward. By great effort they reached the line of old veterans and women who entered the battle ferociously.

Above the Toozlu camp, from the horse meadow, Kemeer led a company of mounted men down in a swoop to cut off stragglers from the Khorasan camp. Lacking bows and scimitars they had sharpened staves and used them as lances. They cleared the area between the mob and the border police. Hoof beats and cries from the rear of the mob reached the ears of those farther ahead in the fight. Panic seized them and those on the front of combat discovered their support gone. Tripping and falling over those dead and wounded behind them, they were pushed back into a tightening, retreating mass of frightened men. Some broke through the thin line of encircling Turks and ran for home, only to face a gauntlet of mounted men awaiting them with the wooden lances.

> - - - - - >ARMY FAREWELL > - - - - - >

"You will send news of the journey and your safe arrival in Baghdad."

"Evet Anne, yes mother," Maril answered meekly. "I will."

"You were so foolish child. I had some excellent Seljuk families in mind with strong, handsome men available. You could have had such a beautiful marriage. The

210

occasion is lost." Onat bey's mother enjoyed the farewell to her guest. Maril was being sent away to her family in Baghdad. She was glad to go, but felt sorry for her lonesome hostess; who longed for the free, open faced life of the herders.

"We mustn't cry over spilt milk," she continued, "but you must promise to write me about life near the capital. My son says we Seljuks must go west some day to save the empire. He understands these things. I would so love to know about the life where you're going. You must keep the young servant at a distance. He's handsome in a rugged sort of way, but he has no inheritance or family; so guard your heart. I think the new corporal's too young for this kind of responsibility, but Onat says he's ambitious and capable. If the journey gets too hard, call a stop. Men can be managed best by tears, remember that. I shall miss you child, you are a bright day for my eyes. I shall worry until I get your news. How fortunate you have learned to write." Maril nodded agreeably to all this talk.

She rose when Onat bey entered and conducted her from the multiple embraces to the door. There Corporal Tash, Jon and a squad of men waited with horses for the forced ride to Khiva. Jon's wrists were bound in a small metal chain with eight links of slack so he can still do some tasks himself, but they were both limiting and identified his position in the squad. Maril, dressed in a riding shalvar, was not required to wear chains. With a motion from Onat bey the mounted group moved off, while his mother cried under his arm. The hoof beats thundered as the company departed dramatically. As the distance rapidly increased between them, Maril realized that, clearly, tears do not always win.

> - - - - - > TURK'S CAMP> - - - - - >

The camp was cleared of dead and wounded by the veterans and women. The wounded Toozlu were taken to the *ordu eve* and tended by the young wives. The Khorasani were piled outside the camp; dead. Weapons and valuables were the new possession of the finders, although they would be picked over by the Khan for himself or confiscated for redistribution to those who merited or were needy of goods. Few of the attackers managed to return to their camp where the funeral of Mansur El Ari was still going on. The officials, officers and men, drawn into an honor guard, were horrified by the news. The defeat would have to be avenged later.

The Royals dispatched notices to the Caliph and moved a company to reinforce the border guard's post. An investigation of the murder of the Khorasani Prince was initiated. The Toozlu weapons were returned to them by cartloads with apologies. The dead were buried in both camps by Muslim clerics. However, feelings hardened in both camps. That evening El Ari was buried and a feast of commemoration held. Everyone left in the camp attended and vowed vengeance.

The re-armed Toozlu horses disappeared with their riders that night. One of the warriors had found a goat herders trail around the mountain and the border posts. At dawn they appeared behind the enemy camp and overran the sleepy guards. With fire arrows and torches the armed warriors charged into the sleeping camp. The thunder of hoof beats was the only alarm as they killed every man in the command tent. Companies of mounted archers killed the troops as they ran from blazing tents. At the end there was no army left only a few frightened men scattering to hide. It was a costly raid for the Toozlu and the leader Kemeer was among the many killed.

Khan Gerchin had remained in his *ordu* eve to deal with the ambassador who came protesting the destruction of an Arab led army. Khan Gerchin was all apologies and excuses.

"You must understand that some of our younger warriors were infuriated by the brazen attack after our surrender to Allah and circumcision. We were attacked only a week later by one of our supposed new allies and fellow believers. Under the direction of one of our esteemed young leaders; they have eliminated the threat to us and to the throne as well. Those men of Khorasan are wilful and determined to rule the Caliph. You have contracted with us to protect him, who is the shadow of God. We have done our best to protect Abbasid interests. You must excuse our zeal."

"We accept your apologies and statements of intent in the name of our all wise sovereign. Since your war commander has died a martyr's death in the cause of Allah we will return his wife and child. I will write our great Caliph of the destruction of his enemies. I am sure of his grateful acceptance of duty done and his gracious understanding and praise." All knew Samara would rejoice.

> - - - - - >ON THE WAY TO KHIVA> - - - - - >

The drumming of the hoof beats increased in tempo and nearness. Someone seemed to be about to overrun the camp. Derk bey armed his bow. Then a man charged his horse into the light of the fire and laughing loudly pulled the horse into a rearing stand before their astonished eyes. They gasped as they stared in amazement.

"Atilla bey," Sevman shouted "You've come."

Atilla grinned, "I knew you had become such a good rider you would be here. I came straight from the search. What a farce, they didn't listen."

"So you ride up like a maniac, shouting and rearing your horse. You could easily have been killed," Derk bey shouted angrily.

"I came quickly to warn you, Kooskoo's murderer is here somewhere north of the river. I didn't go back by the goat corral."

"I was there and left early yesterday morning, Katchy was glad to see the last of us. He got back late the night before and I thought I was in for trouble. But he had his story to tell and wanted a friendly audience. He even gave me food supplies to send me on my way."

Derk bey had disarmed his bow and in a quiet voice spoke up. "But what about the murderer? Where did you lose him?"

"The fools rushed over the river and spread in all directions, but found no trails. I told them we should search the other side, but they were dispersed and would not listen." Atilla looked smug.

"But you stayed with them and argued rather than cross over alone?"

Atilla drew himself up indignantly and looked at each one. "A leader is expected to direct his men to the true path of justice and deliver the law breaker intact to the

213

judge. I know my duty. You and I talked of this at the corral Sevman. I kept my word."

"I'm sure you did," Sevman hurried to say.

Kardesh spoke up, "Where were you before going with the posse, Atilla bey?"

"With Sevman visiting the tribe and the marriage of Khan Twozan to the old Khan Erdash's widow, just a slip of a girl really. I was visiting her brother during the wedding, but Sevman saw it all."

Derk bey rose quickly to his feet. He faced Sevman, his expression severe. His voice trembled as if under some great emotion. "Why didn't you tell us that when you arrived? We had supper together, there was time. Why were you silent?"

Sevman stammered, "I was too full of stories about Katchy and the posse. I was sick and tired during the wedding. I didn't see much. Princess Leyla came and fed me, so I didn't attend." Derk bey's voice rose to double its volume. His eyes bugged as he grabbed the lame boy's shoulder.

"You saw the princess Leyla? She was there with the tribe?"

"Yes, she was there, rescued by an East Bulgar, She talked about Kerim constantly. It's an exciting rescue story."

Derk sagged, "I'll hear this story myself in a moment. But first, Atilla bey, you spoke of the Princess Setchkin's brother. You saw him with the tribe? They travel together?"

Atilla moved his head up in a negative jerk, and smiled almost to himself. He settled himself beside the fire. "He travels alone and saw his sister only a moment the day after the wedding. He returns to the Bulgars alone. I saw it all."

"That's a story I want to hear also. Come I have a bag of *kumiss*, let this sad moment become a night of stories." It seemed a strange thing to say.

The news of the wedding was, evidently, not good news to Derk bey. He was not happy about the rescue of their princess or the journey of Kerim alone to the north either. Why would he want to drink if not to celebrate? Why seek details of some unpleasant news? They were all curious now. Kardesh was eager to hear the stories of his people.

> - - - - - >AT THE GOAT CORRAL > - - - - - >

"*Su, su-sa-dum*, water, Katchy thirsty!" Again and again the call went out. However, the flock was far away, too far to hear.

Sulema had not delayed near the corral. She had quietly slipped out. Driving the flock with tossed pebbles, she had departed the area as quickly as possible. There was no separating of the kids or milking of the mothers. She only escaped from the awful shouts and threats of the deputies. Deep in the thorn brush Sulema passed an anxious day. Would they look for her now? Had Katchy volunteered her presence to escape hurt? What would her punishment be in the village? Was Allah bringing her into judgement and the threat of death and the fire for her sins? Fear and worry haunted her day. The flock seemed aloof and uncaring. Her usual conversations and queries were forgotten. Her new village seemed less friendly. By afternoon she was so fatigued that she drove the herd, loudly and with curses, home to their corral.

She noticed immediately that the place where Katchy had been tied was empty, but blood spots left a trail where he crawled to the hut behind the corral. Her new room was now occupied by that horrid goat boy. She had seen him come and go to the markets since they were both children. She would rather die than go in there. She did the milking full of silent complaints and tears. Yet she was thankful that he, rather than she, had been caught and whipped. It seemed strange to think that someone else had taken what she deserved. Gradually, as she fixed and ate the evening meal in the little open kitchen outside the room, she decided that she owed him something. She took the prepared lentils and put ayran in the bowl. She adjusted her scarf, took it to the door of the room and pounding on it, announced that food was ready. As she

215

pounded the door it came open of itself. She could see the dim form of the boy in the corner where the furs and skins were piled. Not the bed she had made for herself some days ago. She was pleased that he had recognized her rights.

Holding out the bowl she repeated. "Food's here if you want it." He moved, but didn't answer. "I'm sorry they beat you. I made lentils. Can you eat?" He moved again.

"*Yah*, butter, need butter now." He rolled over and indicated his exposed back where dark welts ran across, punctuated with ooze.

"Oh Allah," she gasped, shocked by the sight. "I'll get some." She put the bowl down on a flat stone and ran to the tiny spring and brought out a blob on her hand. She felt the need to make it up to him, and squeamishly rubbed the cool blob over his warm back. The liquid ran into the edges of the welts and changed color. He moaned piteously as she gingerly tried to get it into the cuts. When she finished she looked down and saw his feet. Carefully she spread what dripped from her hands on them. Her hands were now as red as his wounds. She was marked by his blood. Sickened she went to wash and think.

> - - - - - >SMUGGLERS' VILLAGE > - - - - - >

"Kadir bey I don't know what's wrong. My Korkmaz has been acting very odd since our last trip across. He's not normally full of strange requests or mysterious activities. He always manages to be underfoot wanting something to do," Aziz fretted.

Kadir grunted in agreement, "He has taken three of your best horses with only the word that he will meet me at my family home. He took food for an army. He's as tall as his mother was and is still growing. He'll be a big man if he doesn't bankrupt the family first," Kadir quipped with a grin.

"My tall, precious daughter, how I miss her," Aziz exclaimed. "Well, we will humor the boy for her sake. You will leave tonight?"

"Yes, I got another strange request. Baja wants to go with me, and has requested two horses and a pack mule for luggage. She acts like she will move her house to the lake. She's got a relative from among the refugees and doesn't want her repatriated so it's all very hush-hush and after dark."

216

Aziz chuckles an affirmative and began to reminisce in a thoughtful tone. "The border divides families and causes us to publicly affirm different religions, yet it provides a living for both sides and causes us to cooperate closely to make our fortunes and live well. With the refugees and the army alert you must be very careful tonight."

"We will load the animals behind the walls and I have the duty roster for tonight's postings. We will have friends with blind eyes."

"It's good to have such men. However, we have had a lot of betrayals lately. You make sure they look the other way."

"We are taking stockings for our mounts' hooves. They won't even hear the retreat of our hoof beats," Kadir swore seriously.

> - - - - - > KERIM & LEYLA > - - - - - >

"My messenger sent a great breakfast," Kerim teased as they rode north. "You won't tell me why you refused to fix it for me."

"Tanra taught me that I would have to look after myself. You were lazing around with made up excuses for lying late in bed."

"I made up for it by teaching a boy to become a great hunter."

"I helped prepare food for travel while you played games with another little boy. You use a little scratch to beg off helpful work."

"You begrudge my new scar? It's the proof of your virtue and virginity. I shall always treasure it as the hallmark of our eternal loving relationship. You must give me credit for my appreciation. Many men would hold it as a grudge to be repaid in kind."

KERIM ABANDONED

"It's a lesson in morality and a correction of rude behavior. I would hope that any decent girl would do the same," Leyla stated.

"Painful lessons are rarely appreciated. At least I didn't end up like that poor schmuck at the village spring."

Her face flushed angry red. "You... you ungracious barbarian Bulgar, I..." Tears came and she spurred her Fergana mare into a full gallop, leaving Kerim open-mouthed and startled. He urged his black into a gallop.

He stopped after a few moments a mask of pain on his face. He sagged in the saddle and the horse and pack animal both stopped. He whispered to himself, "The pursuit of a princess is a painful, exhausting thing to do. Why do you persist?" but he knew the answer even as he felt the wet of the wound. The hoof beats of Leyla's horse faded into the distance.

> - - - - - >THE TOOZLU PERIMETER > - - - - - >

"I decided to come in and visit the camp today, Erly bey," Leyla called out as she neared the camp-site.

The guard rode forward, his face grim. He reflected the after-effects of celebration that morning. "We broke camp early and are on a fast track. As soon as we made our report, the Khan ordered an early start. I can feel their hoof beats in my head," he complained.

She knew the signs of a hangover. "*Getch'mish ol'son*, may it pass," she said, as she proceeded toward where the main column would be traveling.

"Leyla dear," came the call of Setchkin who rode over with nurse and baby. "How fresh and delightful you look this morning."

"It was a memorable night and dawn," reported Leyla, smiling. She realized how much she liked her.

"Most of us in camp are suffering from late hours and drink. I think my husband is punishing us for our lack of restraint. He woke us with shouts and cymbals. On we march without breakfast," she sighed.

"I've some fresh rabbit meat under the saddle to condition and bread from ours in the saddlebag."

"We're gone long enough to settle my stomach, let me try some of the bread first. Baby is hungry and I'll need something." Marium the wife of Kootsal and other ladies rode up with greetings and a kiss.

"Your husband didn't enter camp did he?" Marium worried.

"No, he's slow and difficult this morning. He'll be along in awhile to call me out." The flat statement raised no eyebrows. The conversation soon turned to more interesting feminine subjects.

> - - - - - >MONASTERY RUINS > - - - - - >

"Wouldn't it have been better to follow the tracks that led away from the ruins, Yavuz bey? Manson asked. "You could catch the girl and boy, bring them for evidence."

Yavuz snorted in contempt, "I have enough evidence and the man going back to the village may lead us to the center and source of supply. Besides," he panted, "we didn't bring horses and those two will have them hidden nearby. Aziz is here, not out in the country." They slowed as they came to the first sentry post where greetings were exchanged. Everyone in the village was known by sight and name.

Yavuz stopped to ask, "Any newcomers pass by today?" He smiled casually.

"The Uygur Bolben is back. Says he's with the refugees now. He's not been around for a couple of years, but he seems anxious to get home. Didn't stay very long, he's going to the Commander now."

Yavuz face went blank and then slowly red, he seemed unable to talk.

"Bolben?" Manson said, "The Uygur who worked the border trade before?" The guard nodded an affirmation.

Yavuz grabbed his helper's arm and pressed on without a farewell. The man, Ali, who found the hair, raced after them. Yavuz was swearing quietly as if out of breath. Nevertheless they ran to the garrison's gate. All three arrived together. They saw Aziz bey standing and waiting there before them. Yavuz's triumphant yell startled the garrison.

"I've got you, Aziz! Now you'll pay.

STAVES SHARPENED

219

PEOPLE, PLOTS & PLACES IN CHAPTER 19

Abdullah: takes advice and escapes to tell his life story.
Aziz: is intent on becoming an honest smuggler.
Bolben: wishes to return to help his burned-out village.
Derk: has urgent information to send off.
Kerim: is overcome by weakness and authority.
Leyla: finds comfort with friends moving on.
Magazi: knows what must be done to escape a wolf.
Manish: is allowed to return, but helps his captor first.
Mookades: represents his people before men and God.
Mooktar: Muslim civil authority; here on police duty.
Onat: is intent on the day's work and repatriation.
Sanjak: gets all the information he has been seeking.
Seerden: shares information with a client.
Setchkin: feels better with a little breakfast.
Twozan: must confront the accusations by a witness.
Umer: faces more hardship and refuses to surrender.
Yavuz: comes to town to accuse and get revenge.
Yeet: learns more about government and secrecy.

GLOSSARY:

Alla hu Ekber: Allah is great; God is greater.
anne: mother.
baba: father; dad.
eeyee'der: he is good; it is good.
de'kot: attention; alert; careful.
deli'sin: you're crazy.
getch'mish ol'son: may it pass away; get well soon.
kafir: unbeliever; non-Muslim.
kahret'sin: curse you; damn you.
lanet'la: a spell or enchantment; under a spell or curse.
nobet'che: guards; those on duty.
ramadan: fast, day time fasting for 28 or 29 days.
shabat: the sabbath, the keeping of the Jewish holy day.
sheker bayram: the candy festival follows the fast.
yasa: the law; any law; here, meaning the Jewish law.

KERIM SURRENDERS

"You there! Keep your hands up and in sight. The *Mooktar* wants to talk to you." Kerim sat up from his slump and tried to clear his head. After nearly falling off his horse he had, evidently, dismounted and slept.

A large company of horsemen was approaching from the south. They were heavily armed and belligerent in attitude. There sat among them a large loutish man almost too large for his horse. One spoke to him. "Well, is this one of them?"

The large man scanned Kerim. "No, I never seen this one before."

The answer disappointed the riders and they cast dark glances at each other and Kerim.

"You're sure?" the evident *Mooktar* snapped.

The big man grunted and looked around almost apologetically to continue. "It's like I said: this woman with the horses and four Toozlu riders, they beat up on us. Then they sent us across the river, after they filled us with lion's milk. My partner never could handle his liquor and drowned. With the river up we was almost swept to the village when it happened. He was a good partner and always paid my liquor and meals."

The Mooktar dismissed his maudlin summary. With a piercing glance and commanding voice he spoke to Kerim. "Who are you and how did you come here?"

Quickly he said, "I'm Kerim of the East Bulgars. I'm traveling home after selling ours and buying Fergana horses. I'm hurrying home 'cause my money's run out."

They looked at him, suspiciously and then at the horses. "Say, them horses looks like the ones I got this mornin', but they got took back." The lout got down to look them over. "Yeah, sure, these are the horses all right. How'd you get'um?"

"They got them from me and I got them back this morning. One of the Toozlu gave me this wound under my arm." He pointed to the enlarging stain. "They don't give anything back without cost."

"One against five, you must be quite a man." The mooktar's voice was cutting and sarcastic.

The lout spoke up for Kerim. "They was drunk and still drinkin' at dawn. They surprised us or we'd sure have whipped'em."

Kerim smiled, pointed and added, "It only takes one sober enough to get a knife point in under the arm and in spite of armor you spring a leak. I got two horses back and I'm going home to heal." Kerim's arms were growing heavy.

"It doesn't look like you'll make it at the rate you're leaking now," the Mooktar observed. He motioned one of the men down. "Help him get back up on his horse. There's a village up the road where he can rest a few days and recover his strength."

Kerim discovered that he was dizzy and mounted with difficulty. He was watched closely by the men and the Mooktar rode to his side.

"You're not a Muslim," he stated, "nor Toozlu. We know little of the Bulgars. Where is your home?"

His query surprised Kerim. "We live northwest of here, above the Aral Sea near the Ural Mountains. We trade with the Kazars where the mother of rivers meets the Caspian Sea." He wondered if they would imprison him.

"I hear that it's an abomination. A kingdom of Jews, but we know Allah has cursed them to be servants of others." His voice carried scorn.

"They're honest tradesmen. We get value for goods and money. Our fathers dealt with the farmers at the Amu River mouth on the Aral Sea when they were Christians, but after the conquest it became less joyful. Now we avoid them."

The Mooktar frowned, "But surely they are honest and give value? Does their zeal offend you?"

Kerim wondered how he could change the subject. "Christians persuade, and are less forceful in winning converts. The old festivals were full of fun and plenty, they say, and the hospitals were efficient and full of the kindness of sisters and nuns."

"Full of Icons and idolatry, barefaced women showing hair and flesh to tempt men. Weak, immoral societies deserve to be taken over by the strong. Allah gives success and demands rectitude from His worshipers. He does not love sinful ways: neither permissive freedom to do wrong nor images used for worship."

Kerim guarded silence, the desire to sleep was persistent.

"You're Christian. Is your tribe also of the same opinion as you are?"

Kerim shrugged, reluctant to continue nor able to keep silent. "Most guard the ways of the ancestors. Some are persuaded to follow Yesu and others the *Yasa*; the law and *shabbat*. Those who move south must follow Islam."

The Mooktar lashed out, "Your grandchildren will be Muslims," pride filled his voice.

"Yes, if it's their free choice," replied Kerim softly, while thinking to himself: 'You've been saying that to people for hundreds of years. People will always resist force where persuasion and example alone can win the day.' A village came in sight ahead.

"Do you feel the need to stop here? I don't know if they'll receive an unbeliever."

Kerim smiled wanly, his voice weak, "I'm in no condition to meet Toozlu."

The Mooktar smiled, "There is more tolerance in Islam than you know. Wait while I make the arrangements." He was gone only a minute and returned smiling. "You're promised food, bed and even a healer," he reported.

"*Allah hu Ekber*, God is great," Kerim said aloud, and '*Yesu gel*, God help me', was in his heart as he slid weakly off his horse.

> - - - - - >ONAT BEY'S OFFICE > - - - - - >

"Well onbasha, tell the yuzbasha Sanjak that we are at last ready to return the refugees and to get that boy, Manish, ready to go with them. I've sent one group west, now we'll deal with the ones going east."

Onat bey came from his office happy with the state of affairs. Quarantine and curfew, plus the extra work for the garrison, had brought a feeling of discipline and activity to the soldiers and respect from villagers. Smuggling was down. Moral and self-respect were up. He needed to make contact with his opposite among the Uigurs to return those who had fallen into his hands from the burning village two weeks before. His sources told him that the Uigur commander from the palace had returned to his master. The local officer would quiet the border and resettle the village. After all, a dead village pays no taxes. The story of the escaped harem girl would be retold for generations with differing views on what happened, but always with one fiery ending. Mention could be made of bodies of villagers that turned up in diverse places - not all killed by soldiers.

"There's an Uygur refugee to see you sir. His name's Bolben, used to be a big operator around here," the corporal returned to report.

"Call him in. They'll take all my day." Onat ordered, but as the man entered the office a scream of anger outside interrupted the meeting.

"*Kahret'sin*, curse you, Aziz, You're in on this aren't you? You brought back the competition after I warned

224

him off. Now you're procuring girls for the soldiers. I knew you were lying when you swore you never deal in flesh," Yavuz shouted while hammering the larger man with fist and feet. "Curse your eyes! May the evil Jinn carry you away! I help make you an honest living. You betray me."

"*Deli'sin*, you're crazy! You crazy old man, stop or I'll hurt you," Aziz shouted, as he held the little man at a distance. "What's wrong now?"

"I heard about Bolben being here and came to see. Look!" Yavuz pointed, "There he is."

Commander Onat and Bolben came out to join the fray. "*Nobet'chi*, guards, subdue those men. Bring them here," ordered Onat. "Explain yourselves, why do you come to fight at my door?" The two sometimes-partners were pushed forward by the soldiers. Onat bey looked them over with little respect. "I know you smugglers, defilers of the border and of Islam. To deal in concubines is one thing; to feed the army on alien flesh is another."

Aziz objected, "Not me sir, I handle commodities only: silk, perfumes, spices, tea from the merchants of Tang China. They are avid for metals. I give employment and aid the village economy."

Onat bey laughed, "So, our merchant is honest? Then I will send an appraiser to your warehouse and assess the taxes owed, otherwise time in jail will be the penalty."

Yavuz was not listening. His hate gleamed in his eyes and twisted his small, mouse-like face. "*Lanet'la adam*, damned man, foul *wigar* sneak, I'll kill you." Suiting action to words, Yavuz suddenly held a *hanjer* which he darted toward Bolben's face. A soldier slapped down the hand and Bolben extended an arm to protect himself. The result was a cut through coat and sleeve to the forearm. All stared in shock at the sudden violence and Yavuz was shaken like a rat by dogs as the soldiers took away his knife and held his arms extended.

Bolben staggered back. His arm gushed sudden blood.

Aziz was startled, amazed at the completion of a threat by his erasable little nemeses. "I never saw him do

225

anything but talk before," he said. "The donkey brays, but never kicks. He's a harmless, foul-mouthed fool, that's all he is. He never hurts anyone."

Onat bey looked skeptical and turned to the sergeant. "*Chavuz*, call the doctor for the victim, and put this crazy man away until I return. Call the assessor to accompany Aziz bey to his..." the commander paused to find a word, "depository to collect due taxes on import goods. Where is Sanjak bey? We need the boy, Manish, and the rest of the refugees that go across the border with me today."

> - - - - - >SEERDEN IN IRAN > - - - - - >

"Your information was correct and the agents have been detected. Justice will be done on all the perpetrators by the Sultan's orders, privately, lest his thing become public and reflect badly on the government. The sultan commends your wisdom."

The local hereditary prince accepted his praise graciously and modestly invited his guest to tea and treaty terms.

"It is, as I said, Seerden bey. We must accommodate those who will accommodate us. No one enjoys eating green quince. My people were enriched when the Toozlu cleared the Arab camp and in haste left to take their long road back to their camp carrying their dead. We have profited in other ways also. I will provide troops, if they are needed.

"Your payments suffice for now, great prince. I have promised you information about the source of our intelligence and extent of the web spun by the Gray Wolf Society. They undermine the Abbasid authority, but it's difficult to ascertain for whom they work and where the head lies. Some claim it is in the north outside Islam, but a few think it more central and closer to power." Their heads were very close together now as they whispered of things too dangerous for even that.

"We know that much without your help, but you must be precise as to place and persons. The woman killed in

226

Kokand, why a humble weaver of rugs? Who is their local agent?" A head nodded.

"I know the man who investigated that. It was in connection with an invasion plot. The woman was a leader in the Christian community in that city and probably too influential to be allowed to continue. She had an aura of confidence and spiritual power that kept them resistant to conversion. The Society warned and stopped her. She has a daughter and evidently a son, they disappeared about then. From there we move north to the Kaynaklar, a sept of the Chipchaks a powerful tribe of the Altai Mountain region. The Khan is weak and without an heir. The Wolf seems to be working there. A son of one of their most important men has escaped from a base near Kokand and eluded all efforts to capture him. How can a man escape the clutches of Islamic armies and agents without special secret help?"

"And now in my very own lands a prince is killed and before my face a Khorasani army is destroyed. How was this instigated?"

A chuckle, "We have that information and are following the two perpetrators and their instruments of execution."

A sigh of relief, "But the money: its resources seem endless. Where is the source of this wealth and where lies the goal? Where will they take us?"

"They work for the dominance of Islam, but seem to weaken the Abbasid's government while they destroy the Khorasani or perhaps alienate them. Islam has stagnated and the empire is too large to manage. Iberia remains under Umayyad princes and prospers. Perhaps we, like Rome, are divided into two parts," Seerden speculated.

"Our empire is Allah's empire. It can't be compared to that of unbelievers or end. We have weak leaders and bad government. Replacement can remedy that. My family and people are ready and willing. Islam must not break into small fragmented states. Our civilization is glorious; not in decay. It unifies and is self-renewing, eternal." The client drew back, committed, but added piously, "I only speculate. Allah's ways are past knowing. To Him belong the straight paths. He guides aright all who surrender."

Seerden smiled and added: *"Allah hu Ekber."*

> - - - - - >UMER'S PURPOSE > - - - - - >

Umer woke with a start and regretted the waking. His stomach immediately started complaining of negligence. The famished feeling returned to haunt his waking hours. He had dreamed of food. Visions of *Sheker Bayram* were the theme of his sleeping moments. The Ramadan fast was over and the preparations at home were for the customary sweet treats that follow the month of day-long fasts. A tear started uninvited down his cheek at thoughts of home. Although he considered his *baba* a fool and lout, he remembered a few of his better jokes and words now. How his *Anne* had scolded and advised, but he had not been interested in taking a woman's advice. Let her tend to her pots and stews. Now home sounded too wonderful not to cherish. He licked his lips. His horses stomped, they were hungry too. He would have to find an alfalfa field for the horses today. He could not leave them to graze freely at night. The food from Sulema's village would supply only one meal a day for the next week. Living with hunger was to become a part of his life. A pigeon flew by with a whistling rush of wings on still air. In the distance he heard sounds of worship. The distant chanting called memories of home. Religiously indifferent he now thought of Allah and shuddered. He had chosen the path of evil doers and could expect no mercy until he surrendered and returned to the true path. He rejected that hard road and turned his thoughts to escape. They were still searching for him. If he went north out of the Amu valley region he could run parallel and re-enter to the north and return south to Samarkand or Boukhara. He needed to rob a village to get new supplies for the trip. But the pursuit was too close. He would have to wait. His thoughts returned to the sound of worship, it demanded investigation. It was too weak for a village mosque. A thin child's voice issued the call to prayer: *Allah hu Ekber.*

> - - - - - >ARMY JAIL > - - - - - >

"Is it true, Sanjak bey, I'll be restored to my people today?" Manish pleaded a favorable response from the yuzbasha.

"Yes, boy, you will finally go home, but you had better have good answers for the authorities there." He gave the boy his staff.

"A shepherd boy will take them no time, unless you tell them I brought people expelled by the Tang from China."

Sanjak replied, "I can't take you back because I brought people from there and was expelled after they seized my wife for the harem. Your two friends were sent on to Baghdad this morning."

Manish perked up, "Jon and Maril were sent to her family today? Praise Yesu, He heard me. He'll get them home."

Sanjak froze, mouth open, then asked, "Jon and Maril from Tang China? No one here mentioned their names, I would have known. Did they say anything about my dear wife, Nooryouz? Do you remember?"

Manish now stared, shocked. "Yes, she and the baby were lost trying to cross the mountains when we parted. But they got here safely. The boy told me."

"Baby? She has a baby? The boy that spoke to you at work, he told you this?" Sanjak was in a trance, - happy - not yet able to believe his good news. "Where have they hidden her?"

"The boy said she was safe with an aunt Baja, and they would move them out soon. They must have decided to rescue Maril first. That's when they caught Jon, I guess."

Sanjak's face glowed with joy. "I traced the boy, I know his name is Korkmaz, I can find him."

"You must be very careful, she is still hunted."

Sanjak nodded, "She loves me and has come here. Tanra *eeyeeder,* God is good. I'll find some way to get her out and home. No one must steal my treasure now that she is near."

A loud voice called out his name. "Yuzbasha? Sanjak bey? We've come for the prisoner. We're ready to start."

Sanjak looked happily on his small charge asking, "Do you have any money for the journey? You may need it." He dumped coins out of a small bag from his waist. "Here, take it."

"Not gold or silver, three copper coins is enough, they'll keep anything larger. I'm just a shepherd boy."

The outside voice yelled, "*De'cot,* attention, lieutenant, respond."

Sanjak yelled back, "Present and prepared for travel, corporal." He handed the boy a small packet of dried meat and flat bread, standard travel rations, and pushed him toward the door in a hurried manner proclaiming, "We clean Dar es Islam of *kafirs* and all who defile our pure land. The law of Allah alone rules here. *Allah hu Ekber.*"

>-------->VILLAGE NEAR IRAN PASS > - - - - - >

"Abdullah, wake up, we must leave this place now, immediately."

"Why dear friend? Are you frightened? What has upset you?"

"I heard the growl of the Gray Wolf and saw his teeth gleaming in the moon light. I'm afraid for our lives." Abdullah laughed heartily, "A bad dream, nothing more. They brought us here to save our lives on the day of Mansur's death and burial. Why would they deliver us to death now?" He knew Magazi was being unreasonable.

"I don't know, but I feel his threat. I want to leave for Baghdad now. Why should we wait?"

Abdullah stretched lazily and sighed, "Because our instructions are to wait for further contact."

"I don't want to wait. We've received our reward in gold and personal satisfaction, why remain?" He draped himself around Abdullah's neck.

"There, there, don't cry now" Abdullah comforted, "Where is my brave, little man? Look, you took care of Mansur's executioner neatly. They'll cease the hunt with the murderer beautifully identifiable."

"I hated taking back his money. His family will need it, with the shame on them."

Abdullah held him off, shaking his head forbiddingly, looked his beloved full in the face. "That money would lead to another trail, ours. We changed the plan because his hatred was the best motive since everyone knew."

Magazi shook his head. "They'll wonder if others were involved, what if the Wolf made us clearly identifiable?"

Abdullah scoffed and turned away. "We will speak of this no more, it smacks of disloyalty."

"The Wolf, in times of need, turns on its own. I'll saddle the horses and pack. We must hasten on to Baghdad."

Abdullah shrugged, turned away again in disgust. He couldn't change Magazi's mind and yet didn't want to be left behind.

> - - - - - >TOOZLU COLUMN > - - - - - >

"Leyla hanem, your new husband delays, did you exhaust him?" Setchkin's old maid servant teased. "Or did you find him lacking in staying power and discard him?"

Leyla was cool, "I tucked him in, took care of all his duties, but made him hunt for his breakfast. A new husband needs care, but must know who is boss."

The ladies all chuckled in their appreciation. It was nearing mid-morning and the column sped along the trace northward toward the Chu River.

Setchkin gaily took up the banter mischievously. "The man has rescued you, pursued you, fought for you, and been wounded for his efforts. Did he have the strength to satisfy you? Has it been an unfulfilled night with a promise still to be kept?"

"I found he doesn't snore which satisfies me. He promised meat, which you have sampled. Our night was filled with visitors. He is always near in times of need. Late or early why should I worry?"

The evasive reply pleased all the women and they were laughing as a rider appeared suddenly through the low thorn brushes.

He shouted loudly. "*Decot, decot*, attention, alert, a troop of horse approach." A guard rode into view of the column. He made a motion to indicate the direction and rode away. The warriors, arming bows, rode after him. Khan Twozan flashed by from the head of the column. The women armed bows and separated into groups near their packed yurts and trunks of goods; because it's better to die with your home than without it. A quiet descended on the travelers as all listened. Then they quietly sang an old tribal prayer of protection:

> Father, guard Your wandering children;
> Keep us though we go astray.
> Enemies against us gather;
> Death pursues us night and day.
> Yesu come, your faithful gather;
> Keep us safe from danger's harm."

231

"Why do you come with a troop of twenty men? State your business. We pass with the approval of the Sultan's commander Onat bey." Twozan and Mookades sat their horses on a hill where they could see and be seen. The troops were drawn up hidden by the hills.

"I am the Mooktar of the Upper Syr River. We seek five Toozlu riders who caused the death of a Muslim."

Mookades spoke next. "How did your Muslim die?"

The lout spoke before his leader. "He was drowned. Drunk and drowned, damn you." A laugh started on the hill and seemed to echo behind them.

The Khan spoke, "My people pass rivers and endure rain, but otherwise spend little time with water. You must look elsewhere."

The leader spoke, "They forced prohibited alcohol on the men and sent them into the river to die. We will identify the guilty."

Twozan smiled broadly, "Your one witness, who was drunk, will identify the guilty?"

"We already hold one of your men prisoner."

232

Mookades spoke, "No one is missing. Who have you captured?"

"Kerim of the Bulgars, a wounded man."

Mookades replied, "Your Muslim justice is to make a Bulgar pay for the supposed Toozlu error? Did you wound him in the capture?"

The leader snarled, "One of your men did it when he recovered two horses."

"We have lost no horses. We do not share our liquor with good Muslims. We have permission to pass. Let us pass unhindered."

"We will identify the culprits. Troops forward all, Allah, Allah, *Allah hu Ekber!*" The impatient squad sprang forward with this one cry.

Twozan raised his hand in command and a line of ready warriors rode into view and released a flight of arrows. The first line of the advancing horsemen toppled. The wounded and remainder turned away. The Mooktar rode away with a shoulder wound. The lout lay dead on the field with three others.

Twozan called a halt and cease-fire. "Let them go, we want no further trouble from these people. Half the troop goes back to lead the column and half to the rear. I hope they leave us alone in the future."

He rode back with news of Kerim. The women would cry and hope, but he esteemed him as good as dead. He wondered that there was no feeling of satisfaction that an heir of the powerful Kynan clan was finished before the Toozlu were. But there was only sadness that the two should face extinction before powerful enemies. The lone survivor and the weak returning clan, both were at their cruel enemies' mercy. Only Tanra could save them: *Allah hu Ekber.*

> - - - - - >CONSPIRITORS LEAVE > - - - - - >

"Abdullah, look down at our street." Magazi had won the day for the retreat. They hurried on their way, but he stopped above the village to see a detachment of soldiers about the house they had so recently departed. The door was being forced and they were entering.

"Dearest friend you have saved our lives, you were rightly led, *Allah hu Ekber.*" Abdullah marveled.

"Animals, especially wolves, are not to be trusted, even when they pay well," Magazi whispered.

"Quickly now, beloved, we must hurry, they will not rest and the hunt may become official when they realize we know too much."

They walked the horses over the hill being careful not to allow their silhouette against the sky.

Abdullah hastened to ask, "Why go to Baghdad, the center of officialdom?"

Magazi laughed, "To hide in the shadows of their backs while they search the world." they walked their animals and Magazi quieted his mare and continued, "You will have to exercise your profession there. Money paid for aiding evil doesn't last. It's only to get us safely started" Abdullah nodded, "The smell of blood is honest to a butcher, even if less profitable. You'll be a tinsmith again?"

Magazi laughed quietly, "A mender of pots and kettles, friend, don't try to glorify my humble status. You'll bring in the money and the meat, while I'll buy the bread, sometimes."

Abdullah too, relieved to be free and away said, "I don't regret our agreement and situation. I've done worse."

"You don't ever wish you had married?"

Abdullah's lips pursed, "Women are expensive and there is the bride-price to pay the family. Children are pests and their mothers become complaining whiners and noisy naggers. My father had three wives when he could only afford two. Us kids fought constantly and the girls reported everything the boys did. The mothers threw it up to each other and told father. He was a harsh, angry man. I had my fill of women there. Later I sampled a few for money, but it made me feel dirty. How about you?"

Magazi sighed and shook his head. "I too, grew up in a large family, but I spent my time with boys and loved their qualities, even the babies showed the difference. Boys were complete, girls were not. They lacked something essential. Boys were important with father. Girls were a burden even when bringing in money to the family. I saw that boys reinforce: girls diminish the family. They take other names, new loyalties. So I loved other boys, I think I was born that way."

They rode for a while in silence. Then Magazi spoke again. "The funny part is that my customers are largely women. Some flirt with me and others see I'm not interested in women and trust me with family secrets." Both men laughed together.

Abdullah added, "Ironic isn't it. A skirt-chaser would be ecstatic; with you it's a burden. But you watch your step with the men who come by."

> - - - - - >DERK BEY'S DILEMMA > - - - - - >

"Fly now, little messenger, fly away home," called Derk as he lifted the bird above his head for release. It caught the breeze and soared in freedom over the small cart where Derk and Yeet were side by side near their prayer rugs readied for dawn prayer time. They faced southwest toward Mecca. Yeet watched in concern as the bird flew off south eastward not toward Baghdad at all.

Derk laughed at his concern. "News goes to Merv, Samarkand or Grozny first and then is sent on or acted on in a direct manner. How could you catch bandits or trouble makers if it all went to Baghdad first? Dar al Islam depends on the faithfulness of its civil servants and local authorities. If they fail, all fails. If all are alert, faithful and dutiful; all works as the Sharia demands. Allah's rule depends on the efforts of each, so all are judged. *Allah hu Ekber!*"

MESSENGER SENT

235

PEOPLE, PLOTS & PLACES IN CHAPTER 20

Atilla: likes to argue, but has a hunter's eye.
Derk: must apply pressure to spur action.
Gerchin: leaves a wreck for an assured, rich future.
Katchy: finds healing and new situations irritating.
Kerim: seeks new strength in difficult circumstances.
Leyla: assumes the best conditions and seeks a stray.
Mookades: speaks to both seekers and strays.
Mooktar: is wounded yet zealous in his duties.
Setchkin: tries to help and do her part for all.
Sulema: finds scolding easy when sure she's right.
Twozan: masks weakness with growing strength.
Umer: makes plans and continues his defiant ways.
Yeet: learns more of Dirk bey's character and work.

GLOSSARY:
Chabook ol: hurry up; be quick.
kootsal: holy; sacred.
pahzar goo'nu: Sunday; the day of bazaars.
Rabi Chooba'num: the Lord is my shepherd.
tau: the Greek word for the letter T. A T shaped cross.
Yesu gel: Jesus come; come help us; God help us.
yuf'ka: dough of flat bread stored in rolled out layers.

COMMUNION SERMON

"I was angry. I don't like to be reminded of ugly moments in my life. Tanra knows, I've had a lot of them." Leyla cried as she spoke and Setchkin listened with sympathy. She too, had such a life.

"It's natural and easy to react, but your man is a support of your joy of life. They are sometimes stupid as to your needs and inner feelings, but still... one must endure a lot... it's essential to be happy."

"But what can I do now that I've abandoned him when he was sick and wounded. They say he's a prisoner. He'll hate me for it."

"You mustn't blame yourself. Would you have fought twenty men? I think Tanra saved you from the same fate. You rode swiftly ahead. He lingered and was caught."

Tanra was becoming more dear to Setchkin. Her return and marriage to Twozan had not only saved her baby's life, but produced a happiness she had not known since her childhood. She had started keeping the prayer times with the chapel: gratitude drove her.

Leyla, on the other hand, had largely used Tanra to complain to; when her brother, father and financial circumstances came to mind. Now that paradise was lost, she was seeking reasons and dealing with new pain.

"Will Twozan do anything about Kerim?" her lips trembled as she voiced her dearest hope. Setchkin searched the horizon, as if she expected a troop to come surging over the hill. Finally she turned, "We are still in reach of troops. I understand that they go beyond the Chu River only on raids. We are too weak to face an army. We have left the thorn country behind and will see only the alkali sand from here to the Chu River. Once into the sand we will suffer until we pass the Chu and the salt flats to the uplands where grazing is possible. To stop is to die. To turn back is to die. We must speed on to survive."

There was a long silence then Leyla cried, "I hate these zealots who accept the testimony of thieves and liars because they are of their religion and ignore that of any number of honest unbelievers." Despair touched her. "I should have stayed and died with him."

Setchkin reacted sharply and retorted, "How could you know that you'd die? Gang-rape is as possible, and a sure death for Kynan ... ah, Kerim bey." She looked around to see if any had overheard them. "Have faith in Yesu and pray. Twozan says that they have no evidence against him. He's stubborn and, once decided, he'll carry through." This was her parting shot and she spurred ahead to ride with Twozan.

> - - - - - >KATCHY'S HUT > - - - - - >

"You haven't moved in four days. Your back has stopped bleeding and your feet are clear of thorn spines you could try to walk about some and wear a shirt if the flies bother you." Sulema insisted loudly.

Katchy looked at her sullenly. She had taken over his house and work, and now was treating him like he was a baby kid, orphaned from his nanny. It was true, he was hungry now and wanted to be out caring for the flock, but the shirt hurt and he knew from experience that the flies would feast and blow on any wound, animal or human.

"I sit outside tonight. Full moon rise early, no flies, no shirt."

She made a resounding hump as she stopped by the door to say, "Even the days are cold now, you'll get something worse than fly bites if you go out with no shirt. Don't think I'll take care of you, if you go coughing and sneezing all around. In the village they'll be gathering firewood for the winter. I'm knitting a sweater for myself, but what are you going to wear when it freezes all day?"

Victorious, she slammed the door and began to lead the flock toward the deeper sand beds where the warmth would accumulate. He sat at home, chill now, resenting an unjust world. He must try to decide how to improve his present situation. He eyed the rough wool shirt and faded jacket suspiciously, as if they had malicious intentions against him. He recalled that Sevman prayed every morning. Just wake up, bow and talk with Yesu like a friend and helper. Different and more intimate than his proclamation of *Allah hu Ekber* and himself to the flock every morning. There would be comfort in having a heavenly friend.

>------->THE CALIPH'S ORDERS > - - - - - >
"There must be no more delay, the Toozlu Guards must speed on to Baghdad with the Royal Troops. Sore or not, the whole camp must move immediately. There is danger of local retaliation if they remain here."

The ambassador pontificated, "It has been a fitting lesson for local strong men not to press demands on the Caliph, as those from the east tried to do. Local problems must not be allowed to trouble the ones responsible for obedience and the wise nurturing of Islamic schools and foundations for the needy. Your duty is to comply now."

>------->AT THE TURK CAMP > - - - - - >
The Toozlu were glad to leave. The camp was a wreck, anyway, after the riot the yurts were in ruin. Their new habitations would be rooms and buildings more substantial than felt and wood frames. Their war and travel accommodations would be Arab style tents and inns for transients. These new structures would still be called by the old names of yurt and caravansary.

"Leave the felt and frames here," Khan Gerchin ordered. "It will serve as a memorial of our suffering, to prove our devotion to our gracious Caliph. From this day and this place we will be under his care and comfort every day of our lives."

However, some carried their sharpened stakes to remember the time when, deprived of protective weapons, they had defended their camp with such primitive tools. The stories of the invincible Turks would find a source there.

> - - - - - >THE MOOKTAR RETURNS > - - - - - >
"Is the prisoner in his room?" The Mooktar dismounted, and staggered slightly, before the village

house. The village authorities met him at the door. One reached out to steady him.

"You're wounded sir. What's happened?" they asked.

"An ambush; it's slight. You have a healer? We have use for him. Send for him: I have men who need immediate attention. Send him to the *Kade*. They stopped at the municipal building. I asked about the prisoner I left yesterday. How is he?"

They hastened to answer, "He's asleep sir. He has an oozing wound under his arm. He was thirsty, but not hungry. There was fresh meat in his saddle pack and bread. The pack horse was carrying a woman's goods."

"Not mixed with men's things? Just a woman's pack?"

"Yes sir, bedding, clothes and private things."

The mooktar thought for a moment before speaking. "There aren't any contradictions in his story so far. The Toozlu pretended ignorance of the man or the loss of animals. The witness said that there was a lady and three horses with the four riders. But I still can't believe he downed five, drunk or not."

"When we talked about the wound he said she had good aim and got through his armor. We found the leather piece. It was strapped on top of the lady's load."

The mooktar sat heavily, and carefully took off his coat and shirt. The wound revealed was a nick on the muscle. His chain-mail had turned the arrow. It had bruised him.

'I'll stay for a day and talk with him tomorrow. But why would drunk men, leave the woman? Everyone knows what those bare-faced hussies are used for. There is something here we don't know." They all agreed that tribesmen were worthless thieves as a messenger rode up at a gallop and a corporal salaamed respectfully.

"Headquarters sends a report of large numbers of men and some families on the move north from the villages. They require an investigation and information."

The mooktar agreed reluctantly, "I have lost men and the wounded need time. I'll see to it first thing tomorrow.

I have a prisoner to interrogate first." He painfully rose and entered the house and went to the prisoner's room.

"You must have slept well, did I wake you?"

Kerim smiled to answer. "I heard a multitude moving. They were both happy and sad, but I don't know why. A voice told me to rest and be trusting."

"Good advice from whatever source. We must talk some now."

"You will send me on my way today? I feel much better now."

"We need to get a few things straight first. You said you were in the Fergana Valley for horses. What did you buy?"

Kerim sighed, "A gorgeous mare that took every cent I had. She was a three year old who had been trained by a Turk and knew the commands."

"Describe her to me. They used to export them to China, but the market under the Tangs is not good, nor is Hindustan any better."

"This one had a black blaze on her white face and black stripes on her white rump but the neck and front were a dark color and the feet had white socks on the dark legs. She is a beauty. I will not find her equal again, for the woman rode off on her, leaving me short by a treasure. A double treasure if you would believe it."

"So, it was the woman that wounded you? I suspected as much. You were ashamed to admit it that morning."

He nodded, "Yes, she hit my weakest spot. I never saw the Toozlu riders they talked about. It happened while the Turks were passing the river and none of them were drunk at that time. I watched them and all was lost before I knew it. The next day I ended up with the two horses, while she rode away with my heart," he sighed again.

"You inflicted no wound on her?" The mooktar was intrigued.

"None visible, Toozlu women are competent and tough."

"Can you describe her?"

241

Kerim looked curiously at him. "Your witness should be able to do that. Where is he?"

"He died in our encounter with the Toozlu."

There was a moment of silence while Kerim thought carefully and spoke; "She had scars scattered across her face and an angry expression when she stabbed me. Her words were angry when she rode away. If you had entered the Toozlu encampment you would have found her."

The mooktar nodded, an anguished expression passed his face as he moved his arm. His wound was stiffening.

"You are free to go tomorrow, but you will remain here tonight. *Pahzar goonu*, Sunday, you are free to speed on your way"

Kerim watched him with concern. He rose and looked at the arm seriously. "You ought to let me put some alcohol and oil on that bruise or you won't be able to move that arm tomorrow. You use chain mail but the point still scratches and mashes the metal into the flesh."

"There are reports of refugees moving about. I have to see to it tomorrow early. I can't afford to be ill."

Kerim agreed, "I have a bag of kumiss, with my pack, it's alcohol to rub on the area and oil for healing. Will you let me bring it?"

"It would seem to me; a sensible way to use that drink. Even if it burns, better the flesh than the brain." Both men laughed.

> - - - - - >AT THE CART > - - - - - >

"We have every reason to leave now and speed on to our destination. Everyone is here at last. I've used my last pigeons, we must get to Khiva and meet the rest of our party. The Caliph's business demands promptness." Derk bey was issuing an order, not inviting a discussion. Only Atilla dared object, but he did, strenuously.

"I cannot fathom such a change of plans. We are upon the killer. Some of the posse is still on the other side of the river. There are still no results. He has to be on this side and in a few days we'll have his trail. It's dangerous to leave that kind of man at large."

Derk retorted, "Are you the only man north of the river? Others are already searching. Local men will be turned out in force toward Samarkand. Leave it to them, he won't get past them."

The group reluctantly prepared to leave, and only Atilla continued to grumble about it. Hidden in the brush scarcely a hundred yards away, Umer snarled, in a whisper, his comments on all he had heard.

"The silly fool shows more wisdom than the Caliph's man. Now, you will show me the way to Khiva, and I'll get even more than that if you give me the chance."

Tayze called out, "Which of you men have been into the rations? There's goods missing from here and some *yufka's* spilled on the ground. One of you worthless vagabonds has been messing with my kitchen. If you're hungry you're to tell me, not help yourself. I never saw the like of it," she complained as she repacked the back of the cart.

The listener said, "She has more sense than the whole lot of them. I must watch my step with her goods. But I have enough for three or four days."

"I'll help you, Tayze," Atilla bey affirmed easily.
He looked over at Sevman who was limping to saddle his horse. Then at Derk who had mounted his horse. Yeet was harnessing the cart horse. Kardesh was coming back from a morning call by following the sound of Yeet's voice. Atilla then looked carefully at the ground behind the cart and shouted, "You speed on and ride ahead. I'll catch up later. I have a call of nature that's urgent." He watched them disappear.

> - - - - - >AT KATCHY'S HUT > - - - - - >
"I told you you'd freeze if you came out at night without a shirt. Bring the wool blanket. I'll put the muslin cloth between you and it. You'll stay warm and it won't hurt much. Winter is here. The frost is browning everything. Your hill pasture is drying into hay."

Sulema was always proud of her way of putting things bluntly. She had decided to treat the 'goat boy' in a manner to which she thought him deserving. In spite of the fact that she was the intruder and that nothing, where she was, belonged to her.

Katchy responded, "You bossy nanny, always yak, yak, full of easy advice. You no hurt, you escape posse. You 'fraid t' go home. You eat my food."

"You can't work. You'd be eaten up by blowflys and have lost half the flock if it wasn't for me. Who'd put salve on your back? I'm Allah's blessing to you. You're an invalid, hardly out of bed."

"You one bossy girl. You leave too much milk for baby kids. You use too much butter in lentils and on bread. You buy flour from grocery merchant when pass. Make soft bread, not good hard, dry bread like I have before."

She slammed her stone bowl down on the table, and put her veiled face close to his eyes and laughed at him. "You eat enough of both to pass anything I ever eat. You'll get stronger babies if you leave enough for them to be full at pasture time. Then, they don't bother the nanny as much while she grazes. You don't know as much about goats as you think." She stung his pride.

"You think you smart girl; no show face to merchant. He think you modest. I know you ugly." Now, he stung her pride and tears came.

"You'll never know. I can go home any time I please."

"Good, you speed on home, or I tell posse, come get you."

"You're a stupid goat boy who can't even talk right."

"I no stay now, I walk to hill." He stood up and threw the muslin cloth over his shoulders and the blanket over it. Then, with a face of agony and pride, he left the hut.

She slammed the door after him and hunkered down to the dirt floor angry and hurt. It surprised her that she was crying. She got up, furious now, and barred the door and lay in bed to stew and cry some more.

> - - - - - >WITH THE TOOZLU COLUMN > - - - - - >
"Today is Sunday. *Kootsal* will talk about the lost animal and the herder. It's one of my favorites. Twozan has ordered a break in the trek

to have worship and prayers," Setchkin reported. It was dawn of a new day of travel with a stiff, cold north wind.

Leyla agreed, "I always loved that story when I was a little girl learning to ride herd. I always wanted to be the brave herder riding out to save the lost one. Riding back with the poor little lost one across the saddle to celebrate its safe return."

Setchkin motioned to come, "*Chabook ol*, hurry up, the sun's warm. Some are already there praying. The singing will start soon." Both continued together to the spot where a cart held a small alter where the tau cross was standing. It was a carved bone cross with the cross bar capping the upright post. Mookades stood beside it as the singing started. After songs and prayer they sang an old hymn that prepared the listeners for the theme of the morning. The Ninety and Nine was sung with hand drums, flutes and *saz* accompaniment.

NINETY AND NINE

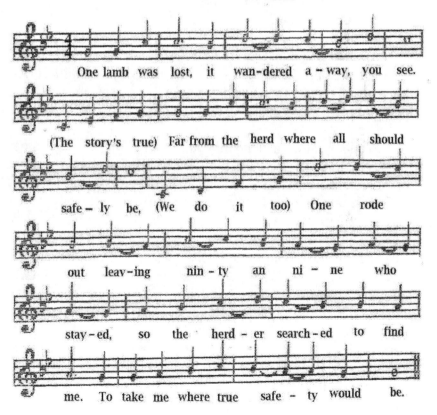

One lamb was lost, it wan-dered a-way, you see.
(The story's true) Far from the herd where all should
safe-ly be, (We do it too) One rode
out leav-ing nin-ty an ni-ne who
stay-ed, so the herd-er search-ed to find
me. To take me where true safe-ty would be.

One lamb was lost, it wandered away you see.
(The story's true)
Far from the herd, where all should safely be.
(We do it too)
One rode out leaving ninety and nine
Who safely stayed.
 So the herder searched to find me;
 To take me where true safety would be.

2 One ran away, the crowd didn't care at all;
   (This could be you.)
Danger was there, but nobody heard his call.
   (This happens too.)
One rode out leaving ninety and nine
 Who safely stayed.
So the Savior died to find me;
To make me what true righteousness should be.

The congregation was led in the recitation of 'Rabi Choba'num',
the 23rd Psalm. The priest, dressed in a black gown, with a green
scapular hanging from his neck, spoke to the assembled tribe. The
fervent sat close to the speaker. Others mounted or standing were
further away.

"Animals stray, every herder knows this. They may see greener
grazing and wander away. Curiosity can beguile some. The attraction
of another herd or need to escape unwanted attentions can drive them
out. But herd animals become victims very soon; for they lack the
ability to live safely alone. Predators of many kinds: reptiles, birds and
beasts all seek the stray. So must the herder who values his animals
be alert to seek. We live around the animals and we know they have
personalities even as people do. They become friends whom we know.
Their lives depend on how their herder treats them. The qualities of
the herder are shown by his care of the flock.

"This song tells of Yesu and his love for each of us. If we belong to
His flock, we are part of Tanra's herd and He will not let us go astray
and be lost. Yesu is the herder who tends us and takes care to feed
and protect us. He guides us to good pasture and guards us. Life on
earth is short and full of troubles, but He will take us safely to His
kingdom when this life is over. He will have a place for us there. We

must occupy our lives as citizens of His kingdom. We must do those things which please Him and are of benefit to our souls.

"We must obey Tanra first and always, remembering that Yesu gave us a new commandment: to love one another. Greater love has no man than this: to give up his life for his friends. Yesu calls us friends. To die for the tribe is the privilege of the protectors. Yesu gave his life for us. One perfect life for many sinners: a calculated sacrifice. It's an example of how one life can save others."

"We have the example of the extremes to which love will go in the famous ancestor of all Chipchaks, Kaya the Great, who, in the time of the Huns, traveled from the Ordos of China to the heart of Hungary in the far west to rescue his promised bride. We are the chosen bride of the Messiah Yesu. Let us, like Kaya, be true to our pledge to Tanra. His words invite us to trust in Yesu's love and salvation."

There was a flurry of sudden noise and activity behind them. A guard rode in, rearing his horse, to shout. "De'kot! Attention! Many horsemen approaching! Men are coming to the camp!"

Women screamed and grabbed their children. Twozan passed riding, "All men armed and to the rear. Women to the baggage, get ready to lead the march on command." He left a scene of chaotic activity. Setchkin gave the baby to her old nurse and armed her bow. Leyla followed suit while Marium stood hands on chest praying.

Behind them the noise increased as men ran and rode to the archer's line forming there. Mounted men loomed on the horizon: a multitude.

"Our only option here is to pray. They are too many for us." Twozan's face reflected amazement and concern.

Mookades responded, "We need a miracle or we will be in the slaughter house. We are His herd and He will have to save us."

Twozan's face hardened, "I don't intend to go down without cost to them. The whole invasion and rescue attempt was my folly. I'd rather not outlive this clash, although I have more to live for now than for the last twenty years." He started counting heads and dust clouds on the horizon.

"Sir," shouted Erly" They aren't armed for battle, they come with families like refugees." Erly was on the outer perimeter of camp. The line of archers relaxed and some laughed with relief as their own eyes confirmed the declaration; a few cheered.

As the multitude came within bow range they slowed to a stop. One man pressed on with his hands forward in appeal.

"We watched your invasion with hope, when you were defeated and divided we groaned within. We saw part of the Toozlu go to Baghdad to serve the Caliph. News comes that they have destroyed a Khorasan Army that pursued them. Yesterday you defeated a Mooktar's troop. They are afraid of you even weak and in retreat. They sponsor your departure and speed you on. You can't free us from the tyranny of government and religion now, but you can let us come with you."

"We're with only enough food for our own needs. How can we take more?" Twozan's voice spoke to the first ranks of people.

"We brought our own food and enough for more," someone shouted.

"We need your protection and help to leave and return home to the north," another cried loudly.

The leader spoke again. "We tire of corrupt officials and tyrannical clergy. Let us go with you to the freedom of the steppes. We will pledge ourselves to serve the khan and tribe." The listening crowd cheered and agreed heartily.

"Most of us came here for a better life. When we didn't find it they wouldn't let us return. They said we would become apostate to Islam and merit death."

"The Persian farmers don't like us. They hate all grazers."

Others nodded in agreement and spoke out. "We are for Tanra and the everlasting blue sky."

"My tribe followed the teaching of Mani and the Jesus of light."

"We followed Isa, that is, Yesu with the Nestorians."

"We obeyed the Yasa, law and Shabat, Sabbath, like the Kazars."

"We used to dance in the heavenly procession, but now we have to do the whirling ceremony in secret."

"I don't mind serving Allah, but I don't want their religious police breathing down my neck."

"I just want a chance to start over somewhere."

"Too much religion is bad for business."

"The Seljuks have the best grazing and best jobs, but even they don't obey all the rules of Islam."

"Yeah, there's no room to expand or to move freely."

"My children are often hungry here."

The complaints were many and varied.

Mookades was whispering in Twozan's ear. He nodded agreement, "We will accept your offers of food and will receive it into one store where it will be distributed so all will have enough, in the weekly ration. When we pass over the Uplands where the rivers run north and the grazing is adequate you may divide in groups and speed on toward your home grounds. Those who wish to join the Chipchak nation may enter into negotiations with the High Khan. You and your stock must be quarantined, so the Toozlu will camp on the east-side ready to lead north or defend south of your people.

Assemble to the west of our camp. At noon we will depart with those who are still determined to go." Khan Twozan finished.

Mookades spoke as he looked over the families with small children. "Measure yourselves people. The pace will be brisk, the weather cold, each must do his part. Stragglers will be left behind. Go home quickly, if you change your mind."

The crowds' spokesman said, "Some of us have come far, we will be penalized or killed if we return. Our hearts are set; we return to the steppe. You are our safest way to go, be our shield in the desert and on the upland plains. We plead this favor and mercy."

Mookades gladly responded. "We pledge you our best efforts, but no guarantees. We are in Tanra's hands. *Yesu gel*, God help us, we'll do this thing together."

Erly led the people to the west side of the camp while the Toozlu women watched open-mouthed.

Setchkin held her baby up to see. "See darling, all the people coming to help us get home? The Caliph will not care to touch us now. Even my daddy would be afraid..." She paused and then shouted, "Daddy will be forced to come to terms with such an army. *Yesu gel*, we have a miracle."

Leyla too was full of excitement as she watched the people still coming as the sun moved toward noon. It was obvious that they would not be able to move on that day. She got her horse and sped on past ever more new arrivals.

A MULTITUDE

249

PEOPLE, PLOTS & PLACES IN CHAPTER 21

Baja: finds pain in all her activities and values it.
Derk: hurries every one to Khiva for an express ride.
Kadir: discovers truth about his travels and future.
Karga: pretends piety and enjoys tragic conditions.
Kaplan: the tiger learns the fate of Kynan his son.
Katchy: must agree to his new partner's conditions.
Kerim: gets free with the Fergana mare; is it worth it?
Kurnaz: seeks recompense for his expenses.
Leyla: is detained and dispatched to Baghdad.
Manish: gets his trip home with a promise.
Mooktar: a Muslim civil authority, wounded in battle.
Nooryouz: travels by night, but sings a lullaby.
Onat: makes promises and assignments for all.
Sanjak: gets the new venture with a lecture on Allah.
Setchkin: worries about Leyla's safety.
Sulema: gets all her demands by a lock out.
Tash: is facing new experiences unprepared.
Twozan: now leads a large but inept army.
Yusuf: gets good news and a direct offer.

GLOSSARY:
Allah is'mar laduk: God commends my leaving; bye.
bach: look.
dough roo: correct; exactly.
evet: yes
hanjir: a sharp pointed knife.
hoja: a Muslim title; one who has been to Mecca.
iblis: the devil; Satan.
iz'ler: scars; tracks; traces of tears.
so'ook: cold.
ta'mom: alright; okay.

KATCHY COLD!

"Here is the boy, Manish, Commander," said Yuzbasha Sanjak.

Onat reassured the boy. "Don't worry, son, I'll put in a good word for you to your commander," He turned to address Sanjak, "You'll take the supply wagons on to the Lake Balkash area. Our advance posts will need their winter rations. I'll be back tomorrow, if all goes well across the border."

Sanjak said amiably, "The supplies will get through, Sir, don't worry. I promise a safe delivery."

Onat looked carefully at him, he nodded at his words. This was a good test of his reliability.

"You will pass the River Talas where the armies of Allah destroyed the presence and power of Tang China and drove them from these lands beyond the Tien Shan, the mountains of Allah. Victory is the sure sign of the blessings and rewards of Allah on His prophet and the believing people. The Uigurs took the basin and mountain lands between Dar Al Islam and the Tang. There are Christian and Manichee people where we both are going, so guard your self as I will also."

"I'll pray for your safety, Sir."

Onat's head snapped back. "I submit myself to the will of Allah. I don't ask for favors. Only Christians think that Allah would change his plans for their pleading. You must learn to surrender to Allah's will."

"If evil comes will we attribute that to Allah's will?"

"Evil is man's interpretation of those things that occur. Allah is merciful and all-knowing. It seems one way to us, but He knows the true value of all that happens. We submit our will and self to Him."

"You absolve yourselves of responsibility in human affairs? You make Allah responsible for everything that men may put into action?"

"Allah alone has all power, to Him be glory. You must learn these things to become a good Muslim."

Onat turned to his sergeant and nodded his readiness to depart. "*Ta'mom*, okay, let's get this Uigur crowd moving back where they came from. Form the column. Apply the whip when necessary, Sergeant. None must lag or stop."

> - - - - - >KATCHY'S HUT > - - - - - >

"*So'uk*, Katchy cold, feet hurt, no mad now. You good help, put salve on back, watch flock, big help make cheese. We be friends now."

"You called me bad names," she replied from safety inside the barred door. "You'll call the posse from my village to take me back." She continued, "You must tell me you are sorry for your insults and promise me not to tell the village."

There was a long silence as the message penetrated his numb mind. His voice became humble, "*Ta'mom*, okay, you right, Katchy not tell village, not trust posse anyway. We be friends, share work. You forget bad words."

"I can't forget insults, I want an apology. I can't forgive you without an apology." Her pouting voice hid the triumph she was feeling, the desire to milk the moment.

"Katchy forget bad words, you tell me which words bad, I forgive them all."

Sulema gave a huff of disgust. He needed help. "You said I was a bossy nanny and ugly, that I ate your food."

"You work good, eat food you earn. You strong, pretty nanny when you sing. You good boss with flock. Katchy cold here. Open door please."

A flash of triumph split her face. She flipped the bar so the door would open. He burst in with a blast of icy wind behind him. He moved to the center of the room where he shivered. He still clutched his blanket over the muslin cloth. She saw that when he lowered the blanket the cloth was stuck to his back. She slipped outside into the cold and brought back some butter. It would be a painful separation, but it would be worse to wait till morning. He groaned as the warm hands pried the cloth from the chilled skin. She applied the oil of the butter which she melted on her skin, held cupped in her hand to take away the stiffness of the product. Now she was sorry for her delay in admitting him.

When she was finishing the job she turned him around with hands on his shoulders. He bent his neck to kiss her hand. She stroked his face, the beard was soft and ticklish, but then turned away quickly. She felt him move closer and kiss her neck. She gasped and moved toward her corner of the room. His cold body pressed against her inviting warmth and she fell forward to kneel on her bed as he nibbled her ear, bleating softly like a billy. She giggled at the tickling sensation. A sleepy, agreeable warmth swept through her. He was tenderly stroking her. She sighed as he bared her back for his kisses. As he pressed closer, she knew her triumph was complete. She had found a safe haven with all she ever wanted.

> - - - - - >WITH THE CART PEOPLE > - - - - - >

"I think the assassin must have visited our camp for food and he had a fire in the wadi, last night, but where is he now?" Atilla bey asked himself in a whisper. He had cast a large circle around the camp after following the foot prints from the cart to the brush nearby. Had the man continued downriver or cut into the interior. The horses' tracks were clear in the sand and dirt of the wadi bottom. It was more difficult on the thorny plain and casting circles produced nothing that a few goats or karakul sheep could have made while grazing. Hours later he set off in the direction his friends had taken to the northwest, the shortest way to Khiva. There had to be important events on hand to agitate Derk bey into such hurried action. He gave up the wide pattern of search for a direct line of approach following their tracks.

> - - - - - - >TASH'S SQUAD > - - - - - >

"Onbasha, *bach*, look Corporal, There are people on the move everywhere." It was noon of a new day of travel for a weary Tash.

"Yes, but they all move away from us when we approach to try to talk or ask questions." Tash answered, frustrated, "they run away."

"Look Sir, there's a house, the people are out watching them."

"Good we'll go ask them. Be brisk, move at a trot, but don't frighten them. We need to know what's happened."

Tash salaamed, "Peace, the blessings of Allah be on your house. Can you tell me why the people run when we approach? Where are they going?"

"Salaam," she repeated, "They go to join the Toozlu Turks. They want to leave the Syr Valley and return to the steppe," she explained. "Life is becoming harder in the valley and they want to return to the old life, away from the villages."

Tash was indignant, "They can't just up and leave home and Islam like that. They belong to the Caliph. They must be stopped."

She laughed, "You catch one bunch while twenty others escape. The Toozlu won a great victory over the Mooktar, and at the river crossing. The people will use them as a shield for their return to the steppes."

"Look, Sir, a woman on a Fergana horse is approaching at a gallop. What shall we do?"

Their informant, waved a hand, shouting, "She is a friend, don't shoot her."

Tash took in the situation, "Down bows, she isn't a danger to us. We take both of them."

"Did my husband return here?" she asked the lady of the house, ignoring the soldiers and their prisoners, "He was lagging and feeling his wound."

The lady's head made a negative jerk. "When my husband came home that night, he said your man was a prisoner in the village. He said that the Mooktar had suffered a defeat by the Toozlu. He's in the village now."

Tash intervened taking command, "We are going to that village to see the Mooktar. You must come with us. Tell me who you are."

She looked at him coldly. "I am the Princess Leyla of the Chipchak, I will see the Mooktar first, catch me if you can." She turned her mare and was in a gallop before the surprised onbasha could answer.

The whole cavalcade was shortly in hot pursuit. Groups passing nearby watched, but the soldiers never caught up.

Leyla enjoyed the thrill of the chase. She remembered giving the village a wide berth when riding alone, now she rode directly for the center. She stopped before the *Kade* building, Mayor's office, near the mosque. The people stared at her in shock.

"I must see the Mooktar here," she demanded.

LEYLA ARRIVES

255

A wounded soldier tried to stand. He spoke up in anger. "Why would a cursed, bare-faced Toozlu bitch want our Mooktar? Our leader will be riding your horse and you too, when we finish with your tribe."

Leyla stared him down in contempt. "Is there no one in charge of this rabble?" she inquired.

Begging your pardon Miss," exclaimed a sergeant, "the Mooktar is in that house on the corner."

She was off in dash before the cavalcade in pursuit arrived. Her horse plunged to a quick stop at the door. She spoke to the onlookers.

"Bring out the Mooktar, we must talk," she demanded of a guard.

"He's inside Lady. You can go in, he'll take care of you," he sneered.

"No, he'll come out to me," she corrected. "I know what happens to tribal women who go into a house." She waited while the pursuers drew nearer. The Mooktar appeared at the door.

"I'm the princess Leyla of the Chipchak nation. I have some inquiries to make."

The Mooktar was staring, then, he spoke, "I have heard of you Princess and I recognize your horse and your face as it was described to me, the little scars."

She stiffened, "*Izler*, scars? You know me by scars?" Her chin went up. "I think I know your source."

He laughed as the pursuit drew up around them. The guard reached up and took the reins from her hand and she slashed out at him with her *hanjir*.

"The princess has a temper, men. Keep your distance or you'll be scratched," laughed the Mooktar. He continued, "Where from and where to Onbasha?" he asked Tash.

The corporal salaamed, "From commander Onat's ordu-eve on the border. I'm going to Khiva and on to Baghdad by express. I have two important prisoners recently come from Tang China."

The Mooktar was now in a very high mood. "You have just acquired a third prisoner and one the Sultan will reward you for, if you deliver her intact. Four guards and yourself should be enough. I will retain the rest of your troops to restore order here. I have wounded who are useless for that now."

Tash objected, "The binbasha, gave me army men for security and protection. You don't have army status or command."

The Mooktar grimaced, "In times of emergency a civil governor can take precedent. However, I will give you four more for protection if you insist." He looked at the sergeant a block away and yelled at the top of his voice. "Chavush, get me four wounded men who can still ride and guard. They must be ready within the hour the onbasha is on an express journey and can't stay for reports." He turned to Tash, "Two women and a man in chains should be no trouble for a man with eight men even if some are wounded."

Tash was speechless. Leyla spoke, "Why do you send me away as a prisoner? What have I done?"

"As princess you are a political hostage and as a woman you stabbed a man. And now please dismount.

"We will get another saddle and put it on a horse for her. Guard, you see to it." He turned and entered the house. Leyla sat her horse until another was led up. Then she leaped into the saddle without dismounting. Her face became sullen and resentful. The four soldiers who wanted to go to Khiva led them away. The ones who chose to stay joined the sergeant. Four men with slight wounds rode up and Tash led the troop away.

"Why didn't you come out when we took the Toozlu woman prisoner?" the Mooktar inquired solicitously of Kerim.

He laughed, "I was frankly afraid of what she might say or do. I didn't dare face her."

The Mooktar nodded agreement, "A powerful woman, that's certain. Well, you get your Fergana horse and saddle returned."

Kerim sighed and shook his head. "You have been most generous. What can I say?"

"Say nothing, except to affirm your promise to pass by the Aral Sea and visit the area. See that Islam has improved not destroyed the level of happiness and prosperity. The Sharia, properly obeyed, brings prosperity. They have reason to be zealous."

"I will see, *Allah ismar ladik*, God willing, I'll go now."

"The sergeant's bring your horses from the stable now. He saddled your black and put the spare saddle with the pack horse. You may have to sell the women's things in the pack."

Kerim laughed, "Not to worry, there's always family to give it to."

"They'll love you for it," the Mooktar predicted confidently.

"I wish I could be sure of that," Kerim said as they salaamed.

> - - - - - >NOORYOUZ WELCOMED > - - - - - >

"Brace up Baja, we are making good progress and we can stop at dawn to take a long breakfast."

The journey had been through the night. They had left quietly enough and the guards had all been otherwise occupied and perhaps chose not to notice the departure. Old bones however feel any change of routine and Baja was all aches by the time midnight had passed. The baby, on the other hand, had taken to the journey with coos of joy and excitement. His mother was an old hand at travel and fit in doing all the necessary jobs normal to such activity.

Kadir led the threesome but only by a horse's head. He was fascinated by the mother and child. He knew everything about her life in Tang China and the harem of the Uigur Emperor and her journey across the border before dawn. He was in a holiday spirit and they told stories and jokes as the night advanced.

"I should have known that boy was up to something, when you trailed us. I was too preoccupied that the last trip be a great success to note anything. I thought *iblis*, the devil, was harassing us."

"I think he must be now, for the baby is starting to complain and he won't drink more. It's time he went to sleep. Let me sing a Shepherdess' lullaby. He usually likes it." She proceeded to sing quietly:

Sleep now my babe you need your rest,
You grow a lot each day.
You're growing strong; you'll need your rest
To herd our sheep some day.
To play all day. You'll have such fun of it.
Come sleep and get your rest now.
When you grow up you'll dance and play.
You won't have time that day.
You need your sleep.
You'll have to live with it.
You can't stay up all night, yet.
You must not try. Go to sleep!

SHEPHERDESS LULLABY

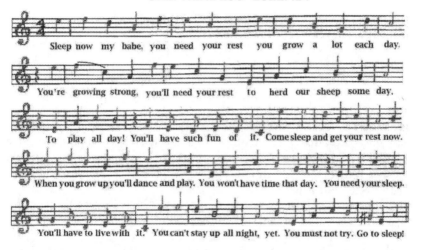

Sleep now my babe, you need your rest you grow a lot each day.

You're growing strong, you'll need your rest to herd our sheep some day.

To play all day! You'll have such fun of it. Come sleep and get your rest now.

When you grow up you'll dance and play. You won't have time that day. You need your sleep.

You'll have to live with it. You can't stay up all night, yet. You must not try. Go to sleep!

The baby was asleep by the time she had sung through twice.
"Your music is effective, bayan: I almost went to sleep too."
"It's the long hours of night travel, Kadir bey. Poor Baja would love to sleep, but hurts too much to even relax." She turned to her friend, "It's nearly first light now are you good for another hour?"
"That's like asking if losing two fingers would not be better than one. Go on with you. If my time has come I'll call on Yesu and leave you to finish without me."
Nooryouz leaned over to kiss her. "Don't say that Baja, I love you too much to leave you even dead. Let's stop for breakfast now, Kadir bey, baby's asleep, but I can use a pick up, it's so cold even sitting on a horse with blankets around us."

259

"There is a house ahead where Korkmaz is waiting. He will have something warm for us. It's only a little while to dawn, hold on."

"Just don't trot, I swear my bones will break into a thousand pieces if we move any faster." So the walk continued a long time.

The boy named fearless didn't wait at the house. Well rested and energetic, he came charging up at a gallop.

"Breakfast is ready. Hot soup is waiting for you. Sesli's a great cook."

Kadir led Nooryouz away at a gallop. He shouted back, "You come with Baja. I want to meet this Sesli that Nooryouz has told me about." Nooryouz laughed with the exciting finish to the long night and the baby never woke up even once.

> - - - - - >IN SAMARA PALACE > - - - - - >

"Yusuf bey: the councilor Kurnaz will see you now" the court messenger was courteous, but not overly cordial. He valued his position.

"Lead and I will follow," Yusuf responded with a bow. As an important leader of a minority people he had his position to uphold.

"Welcome, Yusuf bey, I am happy that you have returned safely from the Tang dominions. I trust that Allah has prospered your holdings here in your home city." The man was graying now, so different from the man who was just maturing on his last visit years ago.

"There are always adjustments and slack to be taken up in an enterprise left to hired help. The miller is now my overseer."

"A wise move, the man has merit. He has prospered everything you left him, hasn't he? I think your prophet has something to say about treasures left to underlings; a well done to the faithful and good servants."

Yusuf nodded his acquiescence to the complement paid to him and his position as a Christian leader. He wondered where this extra warmth was taking them.

Councilor Kurnaz continued, "Your illustrious father was extremely capable, but perhaps, over dependent and trusting of some men of dubious character."

"Mercy is ordered by our God on all his children in relation to workers, even though not always profitable. Human weakness is universal; our sin finds us out sooner or later."

"But you have recovered command of all your interests nicely. Your prosperity continues with Allah's blessing."

Yusuf objected, "My personal needs are simple. My chief concern is for my daughter detained in the Uigur Empire."

The councilor smiled, "On this subject I bear you welcome news. She is safely in Dar al Islam and is being dispatched with a serving man to you by direct express."

Yusuf's face wore a look of shock and incredulity. "When did this happen? I've heard nothing to this point."

"We have the means of speedy communications."

"When will they arrive, *Hoja*?"

The councilor grinned, "You should be able to enjoy the summer together."

"I don't know what to say. How can I thank you?"

"Don't try words, there are more effective ways of thanking one. It's a substantial expense. It is a measure of our esteem for you by the throne. Our gracious Sultan extends his parasol of favor over you and yours." They had now arrived at a subject which Yusuf expected. Taxes and gifts were a basic part of the government's web of intrigues and favors, to promote friends and down enemies.

"I hope a small chest of gold will be accepted as a gift of gratitude and sincere devotion from his most humble slave."

Hoja Kurnaz stroked his beard, and replied with an oily smile. "Gifts are so much better than taxes. They cement friendships and speed hands to needy work." He laughed and continued, "It's a pity you aren't a Muslim. The Royal family seeks a daughter, a new bride for the youngest son. We could put in a word. As it is, one of the Turkish men in administration will probably win out. The girl is really fabulous, but dull. She lacks travel and the wisdom of a broad education. I know yours reads and writes among all the other normal female skills. Your wealth and abilities would be added incentive." He scanned Yusuf out of the corner of his eye. "I just thought I'd ask."

Yusuf bowed himself out as graciously, as if bribes and suborning enticement did not matter or even exist. 'The devil has put a high price on my soul,' he thought.

> - - - - - >SETCHKIN SEEKS LEYLA > - - - - - >

"Leyla is still missing. I'm sure she went back to look for Kerim. I hope the silly girl is alright."

Twozan, lying on the bed made on a double line of trunks, listened to Setchken's relating all the day's occurrences. A litany of events with fragments of conversations recited. He was dead tired and had his own long day, but he heard her out. The Toozlu led the afternoon march, but the rear, where Twozan had remained, had been unable to move with the press of new people. The newcomer's personal rations were not given over, but some groups had such a clear surplus that

261

they could take over those provisions without too much protest. He feared an attack while so many were underfoot. No defense could be properly organized. The numbers of people was impressive, but that did not guarantee a good fighting force. He turned over restlessly on the firm though padded bed to speak.

"Tomorrow we must take all who have arrived and leave the stragglers to come as they can. The head of the column is almost a day's march ahead of the rear as it is. We have to get over the alkali and salt flats west of Lake Balkash to the grazing lands beyond."

"We cross the Chu River first don't we?"

He chuckled softly, "If it's still flowing, It could be a string of pools or even dry."

"That silly girl will never catch up to us."

He grunted, "I remember a silly girl that caught up: disappointed and abandoned. She still found love. Another silly girl can be under Tanra's care also."

She reached out to stroke his face and murmur, "I pray she does as well as I."

> - - - - - - >IN THE CHIPCHAK CAPITAL > - - - - - >

"You are late in your attendance this morning," growled Kaplan, the Tiger. He had spread his weight on the divan he loved to occupy. "Business should not be the concern of sleepy heads. What's wrong? What have you been up to?"

"The last communication from the Toozlu eye, it came by pigeon last night or perhaps this morning. The bird was badly worn. It was the last in her possession."

The tiger pounced, as was his habit, "You will, no doubt, describe its color and breakfast before the message which I long to hear."

The Crow's eyes gleamed mischief, "I was rather uncertain how to break bad news to a faithful father."

"You refer to the marriage of my daughter and the Toozlu chief. It doesn't matter. Her child has been displaced by our northern heir and candidate. The eye will close her child's possibilities soon. It could also be a way to move the man toward our position. But even that is too late. We have the harsh winter and spring attack to eliminate the opposition he has offered."

The crow was having trouble controlling his face. He shrugged and chuckled, "If you know the news concerning your son, I can burn the message." He moved his hand toward the brazier near the divan.

"What? My son? Speak up you cursed fool. What is my son into now?" The Tiger heaved his bulk up.

The Crow allowed his smile to show. "He fought a Bulgar at the Syr River Ford for the hand of the Princess Leyla."

"The boy never ceases to amaze me. He has audacity and enterprise. That would put us in a double position to get power. He may amount to something great yet. The escape and now a wedding."

"Your daughter reported to our eye that the sought Princess wed the wounded Bulgar, and they buried Kynan." There was a long drawn out hiss of anger and exasperation. The man rose to his full height and his mass diminished the scrawny Crow to tiny insignificance.

"You are sure of this, Karga?" He glared into the man's eyes.

"The report is here. There were fights at the river crossing and with pursuit later, both were Toozlu victories. They've left the Sultanate."

"Where is the Bulgar? He travels with them?"

"He stayed behind with the Princess. They return alone to his country."

"Send a general message to all our eyes near and far, everywhere: I want the Bulgar found and killed without delay – immediately! Did they include his name? I must have the name."

The Crow's voice quavered, "*Evet*, master, He is Kerim of the East Bulgars."

"Send me his head."

PREACHING AWAY

263

PEOPLE, PLOTS & PLACES IN CHAPTER 22

Baja: finds travel painful and arrival not much better.
Gerchin: is determined to make a big impression.
Hakim: finds good advice un-welcome.
Jon: helps defend the order in riotous villages.
Kadir: answers questions of curious visitors.
Kerim: joins the squad transporting his wife.
Leyla: finds a wealth of emotions hide in her heart.
Maril: rides through danger on an express trip home.
Mehmet: takes his place as a voice of caution.
Nooryouz: finds new freedom in the country.
Sesli: discovers that suffering brings sympathy.
Tash: must improvise in his travels to the west.

GLOSSARY:
Dough'roo: That's true; correct.
yoh: negative; not so; not that.
You'rue: walk; move ahead.

TASH CLASHES

Kerim started off in a slow trot, but beyond sight of the village, he picked up speed. Within the hour he had drawn near the reduced army squad led by onbasha Tash.
A man had stopped and was slumped in the saddle. One of his companions was giving him water.

Kerim drew up close, "You have problems Corporal?"

Tash's face was flushed. "The man is unable to travel, his wound opened."

"Send him back to the village with his friend. I'll join you until we get to Khiva."

Tash looked confused and examined the rider and horses. He saw the unsaddled Fergana horse on a lead.

"How did you get that horse? My prisoner was riding it."

"*Dough'roo*, correct, she rode off with it two days ago. I have it returned now. The Mooktar got it back for me. He's sending me to Khiva and I thought I might be of some help. I'll travel with you if you like, as far as the city." Tash looked doubtful. Kerim shrugged. "Well, you can decide later." He rode back to the wounded men who were bringing up the rear of the party. He leaned over to speak to one.

"I'm Kerim of the East Bulgars, I heard you're one of the wounded."

"I'm Mehmet, I got a cut on my thumb. I can't use the bow now. The sergeant sent me because I'm no good for fighting."

"But you can guard," Kerim asserted. "What's wrong with your friend?"

"An arrow grazed his leg and killed his horse. I carried him out on mine."

Tash passed hastily to take his position at the head of the column. It seemed important for him to demonstrate leadership in this way.

Kerim nodded and inspected the other rider closely. "His leg has a wet spot on it and it's spreading. Look, there." He pointed to the man's lower leg. A long streak of dark red was dripping to the ankle. Mehmet reached over and motioned his friend to a stop. All three inspected the source of the flow. Kerim pulled a cloth from his pack and gave it to Mehmet who bound the wound tightly. They looked at each other and back where the other two men were still in sight on the horizon.

"You can ride back with them. The surgeon will certify your departure from duty. They'll have to move slowly, so it won't open again."

The man nodded doubtfully, but Mehmet insisted. "You go back with them, there's only a man and two women to guard and we're still six."

Kerim smiled confidently at them, "You have seven. I won't leave you short handed, I can do guard duty. You can tell the Mooktar I'm helping."

The man rode slowly back while Mehmet and Kerim hurried to catch the squad.

> - - - - - >NEAR LAKE ISSYK KOOL > - - - - - >

"Why do you think we'll be safe here in the country near this lake if it is in dispute between the Uigurs and Islam?" asked Sesli.

"This is grazing or farming country. The grazing is Uigur and the farming is somewhat Christian or Islamic. All are too weak to police it. The commercial and smuggling areas run east and west, part of the Silk Road. They largely pass to the south of here. There are only two or three army outposts up here and the

Uigurs let their bands protect themselves." Kadir was defending his choice to the travelers.

Nooryouz spoke up, "I love it here. I don't have to worry about the baby crying or the neighbors catching some trace of us,"

They were waiting for Baja. Kadir continued, "The Issyk Kool is a warm lake as its name indicates in our Turkish, the cold nights produces mists that warm the entire valley and pours like rivers down its slopes toward the lower, dryer lands. Figures move like ghosts through the morning fog. It would shroud all movement, until the parting mist reveals what is passing by."

"Here she comes," Kadir called; glad to distract the questions of Sesli for a moment. Korkmaz came dutifully accompanying his aunt.

"Welcome Baja, the food is prepared, come in and rest." Kadir ran out to help her dismount. She could hardly stand and staggered as the young people gathered to her aid. They laid her on a divan and adjusted the cushions. She panted as she talked.

"When I was young I fasted and whipped my flesh to bring it under control. It didn't help much, but I thought it would make me holy. Now, I pamper my wants to keep lively. Today I have allowed my body to know how old and painful a burden it has become." She continued despite all the denials that she was old or a burden. "I pray the Yesu of light that I shall not have to suffer a rebirth to another life. I can't reach his standards, so it will have to be an act of mercy. Mani can encourage our striving to holiness, but I never made it."

"We love you Baja, you don't need to change. We want you to be just like you are," Nooryouz, Korkmaz and Kadir assured her, but she continued.

"We tend to ignore the Yesu of flesh, victory is so much better, we think. But now I feel more akin to his sufferings on the cross: to Yesu's exhibition of what our sinful flesh deserves."

Sesli stared in wonder at the strange old woman's circle of loving and comforting friends. She had never had that kind of concern, except from her friend Nooryouz who treated everyone like that. Envy touched her, "Come and eat, everything is ready," she announced in a louder than necessary voice that demanded attention.

> - - - - - >TRAVELS WITH TASH > - - - - - >

"Are you really a Princess of the Toozlu Turks? The Chipchak are Christians, aren't they?"

Leyla looked at the girl prisoner riding next to her, then she looked away vexed. She was so angry, she was ready to cry. She had started back to rescue a tardy, wounded husband; to find the lost sheep, and triumphantly carry him into the camp. The story had gone wrong and now this slip of a girl wanted to talk. She snubbed her, but the girl didn't have the sense to recognize the fact.

"The leader who brought out the refugees from Chang'an was a Toozlu Chipchak. He was called Sanjak. When we passed through the Uigur lands the girls were taken to the harem and we never saw him again. His wife was the daughter of an Umayyad ambassador. She was carrying his baby, so we arranged to escape. We lost track of her in the mountains, but we heard that she found her way across and was hiding near the border. I got caught in the border village and when a local boy and Jon here tried to rescue me from the *binbasha's* home. I was caught again. Now I'll never know what happened to them." She chattered on heedlessly while Leyla tried to ignore her.

Gradually Leyla started to listen. She had heard of Sanjak who quarreled with his father and ran off to the reconstituted Tang Empire, now greatly reduced in size and stability. Leyla recognized the self-pity expressed by her fellow prisoner. Her own expiring anger was moving her in the same direction. She had been betrayed by love. Instead of being cherished and loved by a husband, she would be the prey of soldiers. Her deep fear surfaced.

"Have you been molested by these army dogs?" she asked the refugee. "Did they take you into their houses?"

Maril was perplexed, "I was in the *binbasha's* house. His mother was my friend and treated me like a daughter. I was in a smuggler's house where I was caught by army searchers, but Manish, our Uigur guide, protected me. The commander told Tash, the corporal, to treat me with respect. Jon is here too, he won't let them - bother me."

Leyla saw his chains. He would be a limited protector at best, she thought, but she had none. The Mooktar had recognized her by scars on her face. Who else could have told him that bit of news? He, who had already run off and left her once, had betrayed and abandoned her again. She kept her head high and averted, so they would not see tears. She started to pray. She didn't notice that two soldiers had dropped behind. Tash turned back too, but the riders continued at the same fast pace.

> - - - - - >GERCHIN RIDES TO BAGHDAD > - - - - - >

"Sir, You are out-riding the Royal guards, they are now hours behind," observed Hakim.

Gerchin khan's cocky smirk revealed his satisfaction. "*Dough roo*, right, We'll get more good food without competition at the inns and supply stations. They can eat what's left. We'll enter Baghdad without escort or with one so far behind they'll look tacky. We'll straighten out this empire so it runs right. This working for the Sultan shows great prospects: riches and fame."

"The walls have ears, my Khan. He can have your head if he is displeased. That powerful a man deserves an attitude of respect."

Gerchin looked up with disgust, "You're starting to sound like Kemeer, Hakim bey."

"You need a restraining influence, my Lord. You are hasty and at times careless of consequences."

Gerchin turned with a snarl, "Have you still more criticisms for your leader, Hakim? Are you being hasty and careless of consequences?"

Hakim bowed "Yes my Khan, but I speak out of love for you and our people."

"Speak more softly in the future. I want no harsh words even from a friend."

Hakim bowed again, and asked to leave. "*Is an isle*, with your permission," he left on the Khan's nod.

"Will you despise the advice of friends?" inquired his wife.

"And interfering wives as well," he turned angrily. "We are now under Islam and I'll add some additional wives if you don't shut your mouth."

She shrugged and turned away with a comment, "Then you'll get up to four times the criticism you hear now."

"With four times the pleasure I have now," he growled.

"Your pleasure is in how fast you can run by day and how much you can drink by night. Life on the steppes was better."

"Go back then, you could become the wife of a camel driver on the Silk Road. Or even the wife of an impoverished Khan with sheep."

"Better a sheep than a man who hears no voice but his own."

269

"Others have pressured us to change and live new lives. I will not live at the bottom of their ways. Even as a slave I'll win the top place."

"Your slavery will take a deadly course down within, though you may rise up to power among men." She left him alone.

> - - - - - >KERIM'S ROAD TO KHIVA > - - - - - >

"If you don't mind, would you lead my pack horse and my spare Fergana beauty, and I'll go up and talk to the corporal," Kerim asked Mehmet.

The man grinned and took the leads from his hand. "Sure friend, I'd even trade you for the spare, any time."

"Some things would strain a friendship," laughed Kerim as he rode forward, leaving his animals to his new friend. He rode to the next man in the squad on the left side, trailing the prisoners.

"Hi soldier, I'm Kerim, the Mooktar knows I'm helping, Mehmet back there's my partner. What's your name?" He nodded.

"Selim, I'm looking forward to the city, I've always wanted to go there. This is the first chance I've had."

"With a horse and army pay you'll get to see most everything."

"I'm counting on it."

Kerim left him for the forward left rider. "Hello, are you the squad's first? Selim said you were next up to the onbasha."

The old soldier voiced his complaint loudly, "Dang right, I'm the oldest and most experienced at the base and I ought to be up there in the lead. I got relatives near the city and I need to see some of them. I'll take back enough to make a few coins for my pleasures." He laughed, "That kid's a political appointee, got pull from somewhere. I'll get him so drunk he'll not know his way home or my name's not Hasan Izlerje."

Kerim smiled agreement, "So are you a tracker or a maker of scars, old timer?"

"The name don't mean neither one for me, just something the boys hung on me at the base."

Jon the nearest prisoner was listening. "Who's your prisoner here?' asked Kerim. "He doesn't look bad."

"Got in trouble trying to run off with a girl from the binbasha's house. Turns out the girl's home folks want her in Baghdad and the boy is a family servant. They're going to sort it all out there."

"Why's he in chains if he's going home? Doesn't he want to go?"

"Beats me, must be the onbasha's idea to make the mission look good and impress everyone of his importance."

Kerim nodded to Jon, "I'm helping the squad, I hope we have time to talk later at the journey's break. I'm Kerim."

Jon smiled and nodded in a friendly way. Maril was listening to this strange man who was talking to him.

"I'm Jon and my master's daughter is Maril. We are refugees from Chang'an and were forced to escape from Uigur hands to pass the border. Her father's in Baghdad."

Kerim made a salaam to both. "Who is the other lady with you? She doesn't look at us at all."

"We don't know. She rode the horse you led when you joined us back there, when part of the guards left us."

He answered. "The Mooktar gave me the horse. I think she's a political prisoner. They're having trouble with the Toozlu Turks now."

"She's beautiful," Maril replied, "but in distress; she cries."

"Yes, who can know a woman's heart?" Kerim said, as he rode to the onbasha's side. He was ignored for a while until Kerim spoke.

"The Mooktar regrets the depletion of your forces, but the emergency is near a disaster. The Toozlu could easily overrun the country with the reinforcing of its ranks by the departing discontented."

"What of our protection? With the families migrating the movement will bring out the thieves and robbers to profit themselves at everyone's expense. Look there's the river. You see what's happening there now?"

Kerim saw people fighting by the river he had crossed only days before. A group of departing families were hard pressed by village people as they crossed the river. Women were screaming, children crying and men shouting as they strove to hurt one another. The fight continued as they descended the Syr River bank.

"Batons at ready," called Tash, "use the flat of your sword if necessary. Troop forward," he commanded. He led a charge into the riverside fight.

The prisoners found themselves in the midst of it. Jon leaned over and clobbered a man with the chain on his wrist. He hit a second man with a helmet and the chain fell free. He descended to recover it and used it doubled in his hand like a whip. Kerim used the butt of his whip swung round his head.

The villagers fled shouting insults. "Death to all *kafirs*."
"Throw out the Turks."
"Down with the Seljuks, give us back our country."
"Destroy all turncoats and spies, *Allah hu Ekber*."
"Go back to your country."

The women had ridden through the fight without damage, but several soldiers bore bruises and blood.

Tash didn't pursue the defeated. He turned instead to the people drawn around the carts. "You people should never have left your homes. You can still return, the Mooktar will forgive you. Don't abandon Dar al Islam. You share in its greatness by staying."

A wounded man came forward, "Most of us were originally steppe dwellers and new-comers here. The villagers resent us. They"re attacking houses of men that aren't in favor of joining the exodus. Villagers attack to rob and loot our properties. They're forcing us to leave."

"You will be protected by the authorities. There's Sharia Law."

"Tomorrow soldiers will come and authorities will act. Today we run the risk of robbery, rape and death. We won't live through the evening and night. We can't delay. We move while it is still day. Tonight *Iblis*, the devil, rules. There'll not be any chance of return."

Another man spoke "It's being said these days: that a prince was ambushed and killed near the Caspian Sea; with him, an army of Khorasani has been destroyed. The east is hated by the Sultan. Prosperity won't return." The men were now moving forward to follow the carts.

"Thank you Onbasha, you did your duty and Allah will bless you."

When Tash joined his squad, Jon had wrapped the chains around his wrists and everyone rode forward silently leaving the river behind. They noticed the smoke of fire in a nearby village.

"The pillaging has started," Kerim remarked to Tash.

"What do you expect me to do? I only have five men."

"You have seven if you include me and the prisoner who fought for you at the river. You can do what Allah would expect."

"Do I have the mind of Allah to know that?"

"You have a conscience made by Him at birth."

They rode in silence for a moment. Tash sighed, leadership is costly, but he had decided. "Attention troop! We ride to the village. You, prisoner Jon, take off the chain and take a weapon of your choice. Fight if you want to get to Baghdad. You women come after us, but ride straight through, you have *hanjirs* for your personal protection," Tash was angry, but firm. The squad's aspect changed to respect.

"Mehmet bey, let me have your bow, I'll take the horses too," Kerim shouted as he dropped back to retrieve them. He passed the bow and quiver to Jon. "I hope you know how to use this," he remarked. Then he took the leads of the horses and handed them to Leyla. "Here, take the horses and try not to get separated again."

She had not seen him until he rode in front with Tash. Since then a real kaleidoscope of emotions flooded her: relief, anger, affection, resentment, hope, irritation, joy, passionate love, and the desire to kill, mingled in fleeting array. Tears ran down her blushing face to snarling lips.

He smiled happily as he passed her the leads and rode forward again, drawing his sword.

PEOPLE, PLOTS & PLACES IN CHAPTER 23

Adjutant: left in charge, panics in Onat's absence.
Bolben: seeks shelter from danger for the night.
Hassan: though wounded travels with the squad.
Jon: is a prisoner and protector of the squad.
Leyla: travels as a political prisoner to Khiva.
Manish: reports to his master in his home country.
Manly: takes control of the north-west frontier.
Maril: succeeds in making a friend of the princess.
Onat: meets his opposite number in Mani's country.
Sanjak: is affected by accidents and emigrants.
Seerden: must recognize a failure and travel again.
Sergeant: faces new problems in supplying the forts.
Tash: shows courage as he faces risks.

GLOSSARY
Ah-fee-yet ol'soon: Good appetite; enjoy your food.
Ben'de: Me, too.
barish: peace; no aggression.
Chavush: sergeant; man in charge.
dough rue: correct; you're right.
esenlik: tranquility; rest; peace.
hoe'sh ge/'deniz: We're happy you came.
hoe'sh bul duke: We're happy to find you.
Mer'haba: Hello; greetings.
ordu-e've: Military Headquarters.
Tamom: Okay; I agree.
Tanra Dah: Turkish for God's Mountains,
Tien Shan: Chinese for Heavenly Mountains.
you'rue: move on; walk; go ahead.

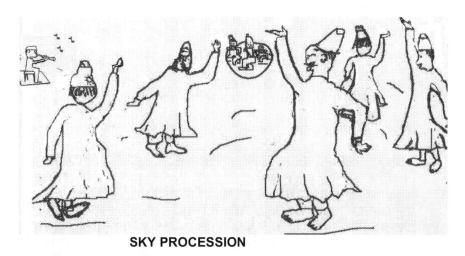

SKY PROCESSION

"*Hoe'sh geldin'iz*, welcome to our land, Binbasha Onat," greeted a man in an impressive uniform.

"*Hoe'sh bol'duke*, happily we found you, we brought your people back." A column of several hundred tired, hungry people were arriving at the burned-out village in the valley.

"They are welcome home again. We are preparing a supper meal for them. We will be happy to feed your troops as well."

"They have their field rations. It will be enough, thank you."

"That's excellent for combat training, but we are at peace. Let us eat together as friends. We have prepared mutton with lentils, leeks and hummus with bread. We know what is pleasing to you. Any Muslim can partake."

Onat bey hesitated; he knew his men's needs. "Granted then, we will eat together.

"We welcome our villagers back with a heavenly procession tonight. It is an old practice from the homeland. You are welcome to attend. It is in honor of Tanra the creator."

"It is practiced by our Turkish troops in secret, but I accept. You are the new border commander, appointed by the Emperor?"

He smiled, "Your humble servant has taken the eye of the highly placed and heaven has smiled on me with an expecting wife, home above Aksu city, on the skirts of the Tanra Dah."

Onat's smile expanded, "We have good reason to celebrate such an auspicious occasion. *Ben'de*, I too, have reason, I have been relieved of a burden, restoring a girl and her servant from Chang'an to the father, now in Baghdad."

Both bowed and smiled while fitting the known information into what was already assumed by rumors.

Manly decided to venture a bit more. "We had three lost lambs from Tufan. You could have returned one to us for reward. We find it strange that none other is found."

"Alas, the father in Baghdad has means to pay a higher reward. I have reports of the rest of the group and have put a hound on the trail of the lead. We expect results shortly."

They walked together to a large tree located just outside the ruins. "I have sent the key man out of the base to see if he will lead us to the lamb all seek."

"You mean the Umayyad woman, don't you? Will you treat with the Iberian branch of the family? They hold distant Spain outside Abbassid control."

Onat bey hesitated, had he said too much? "The Sultan may have something like that in mind. Allah knows that Muslims should not be divided. That is weakness and ultimately the destruction of Islam. Only in unity can we rule the world." Oh no, he had said it, but the prince did not seem to be surprised.

"We, too, work against rapacious tribes. They are anxious to obtain the lands of others rather than develop what they have. It's the law of the demerge, Jehovah, at work, The flesh corrupts always, leading us to rebirth and the downward spiral. The Yesu of light must be our example, the road to true life and freedom."

Onat made no answer.

The noise from the end of the column now gave way to the rejoicing of the weary travelers at the sight of cooked food. Mobs rushed forward to stand around each boiling kettle, while the cooks dished out vegetables into their bowls by huge spoonfuls. Others took hunks of meat from the whole roasted sheep and putting a piece between their teeth cut a bite off using a knife with an upward slice that always seemed to threaten a severed nose, but never did. Families sat together around the food each sharing what they managed to acquire. Uigur soldiers patrolled the area keeping order. They had been fed earlier. Under the large tree an area had been separated for the authorities who sat around food trays where boiled grains were piled up high and smaller bowls of delicacies rested nearby.

"I notice you eat no meat, only the grains and vegetables, Manly bey? Is something wrong?"

Manly laughed and moved his head up, "Not at all, we ate horse and all other meats long ago when we were Christians. Then when our leaders decided to follow Mani, we learned to avoid flesh which holds us prisoner to the baser passions of the world and to deny ourselves that which debased us."

"There is meat that debases, Muslims are forbidden pork and pawed animals, but, thank Allah, other meats are approved for us."

"When you hunt the fierce wild boar, fattened on the acorns of your oak forests, what do you do with the carcasses? Who eats the meat," Manly asked?

"We give it to Christians, who have no regard for Allah's prohibitions. They say all foods are legal for them and should be received with thanks to God."

Manly smiled wryly saying: "We still have the Nestorians among us, but they have no nation or empire as we do, only a few tribes in the north and commercial people in the villages. They are few and harmless."

"We have many more in the west and are afraid they will join with our enemies farther west. We use many enticements to compel them to convert, but they are noted for stubbornness."

An attendant approached Manly with a whispered message. "*Ah-fee-yet ol'soon*, enjoy your meal, and excuse me, there's business to attend to. Just for a moment..."

Onat speculated on what that might be. Over where the kettles cooked, Manly found Manish waiting. The boy had eaten and was able to bring his master up on what the situation was over the border, including the presence of Sanjak.

"They are all safely over, but scattered into four parts," he concluded.

Manly nodded in satisfaction and summed his part. "We here are re-established at court and I am married to one of the emperor's daughters who still sends occasional messages to her father, but she grows more concerned now over her child's future and our promotion. Our support of the refugees from Chang'an has proved a source of Mani's blessing, more than mere asceticism or fasting."

Manish smiled and bowed his approval but replied, "I have had a revelation from the Yesu of light. I did not find my jailing a burden. By my confessing all the details of our escape, except for your part, I found a satisfaction and a cleansing. I have decided to train for the elect and go to Barmani to become a monk."

"He was expelled from our old possessions in the Fergana Valley. He always hoped for an Uigur return. He has sent a child, Maniette, to live at the Titan court. She delights the heart of my wife and we have decided to educate her as our daughter. The astrologers have predicted a son for our house. I will send you to Barmani at Aksu as a return gift for our God of Light."

Manish bowed low and sighed relief, saying, "The Commander Onat continues to press north toward the Illi and Chu Rivers from the Issyk Kool Lake and other's fight in the lower Syr River Valley. They continue to take all the agricultural areas, but leave the grazing between for the Seljuks."

Manly's nod was with keen understanding, "A worthy opponent, but the civil wars marked their end of unity and empire. Their strong men will now divide them into states. Soldiers of the same creed will kill each other for treasure, land and local masters. Their expansion will be piecemeal and largely uncoordinated. You must pray for our unity. Our empire can stand only while we are one against the tribes that continually press from the north."

> - - - - - > SANJAK'S SUPPLY TRAIN > - - - - - >

"*You'rue*, move on. Take up the slack in the line. Keep the carts close. Don't straggle." Sanjak's shouts were loud and continuous.

"Chavush, sergeant, what's the hold up back there? Why is he behind?" Sanjak rode back to the last cart in line and saw it. "Damn, you've got a broken axle. We're only half a day out and now this."

"I'll stay with it sir, and bring it up later."

"Sanjak laughed, "How, Sergeant? You'll cut down one of these little trees and put the green wood in the place of mature oak?"

The sergeant sighed, "What can we do then? We can't get it back to the base."

"Dismiss half the squad of guards. Load a bag of wheat on each horse and each guard will walk and lead his horse."

The *Chavush* objected, "The area is not subdued for Allah, what if we are attacked?"

"If Allah wants these people under Sharia, he will have to protect them."

The sergeant called the troop and dismounted enough men to accommodate all the large sacks on their mounts. They worked grudgingly, grumbling. "The armed Uigur irregulars are all over the Lake Balkash and Chu River areas. Why make us walk into danger, Sergeant?"

The man faced them down, saying, "Would you rather die suddenly and nobly as a martyr for Allah, or starve to death on garrison duty as a martyr to your negligence?"

278

The line of horses and men joined the noisy carts as they threaded through the valley, moving west and then north. Distant herders on the slopes disappeared before they could be identified. The track was devoid of travelers. They spotted occasional bands of people moving north over the high ridges, avoiding the lower ground.

"Something is strange today, Sergeant, it doesn't feel right."

"Sir, the people are moving directly over the high ground, whole families. They don't act like herders at all, not much stock."

"Spread the mounted men over the front end, three to the rear. There's supposed to be a village, by the river, just ahead."

"Careful sir," called the Sergeant as Sanjak rode ahead.

"*Mer'haba*. Hello, anyone here? It's deserted, some doors stand open. They haven't been pillaged, everything is too orderly."

"Maybe they're hiding in the brushwood. Maybe frightened by rumor; something they've heard. Look they haven't taken all their stock."

"*Bar'ish, es en lick*, peace, tranquility, send a man out to talk. We are from the base and are passing through. We are friends." There was a motion in the distance and an old man came out to talk.

"We will protect you, friend," said Sanjak as he walked to meet the man. "What has frightened you?" The man pointed to a group on the mountain side. "Who are they? Where are they going?"

"Turks, leaving to go home. Some villages down below have been looted for food and stock. Some are killed for their goods or their words." The man was shaking and wide-eyed.

Sanjak assured, "You're safe with us. No one will attack you."

He shook his head, "You're passing through. You'll be gone in an hour. They've been moving all day and not likely to stop." The man started back, "If you need something help yourself."

Sanjak spotted a cart. He yelled, "We'll borrow the cart and return it when we come back." The man waved his approval and the Sergeant had his men load the cart and hitch up a horse. They were shortly out of sight.

> - - - - - >AT THE ARMY BASE > - - - - - >

"What are your orders, sir," the Sergeant inquired. The Major, in commander Onat's absence was now in charge at the army base. He was showing signs of shock. He sucked in his breath, shook his head as if in a dream and quietly whispered, "Double the men on the perimeter. Turn out all the troops to set up an inner line, and send a message to Commander Onat to get back. We don't know how bad the emergency really is, but it's big enough to warrant his prompt presence. Send a mountain guide afoot and a rider, separately. It's dark out now and will be harder traveling – either way - on foot or horseback." His voice trembled.

The Sergeant pressed on, "The Mooktar requests troops sir, How many can we spare?"

"Chavush, we have troops delivering refugees. Others are distributing food to the northern garrisons. We aren't up to full strength. We may need all for defense. Praise Allah the refugees are gone, no extra mouths."

"Shall the messenger return with a denial sir?"

"*Yoh*, no, we can't do that, it's bad for our record. We have to do something for them. Send twenty of the old hands. Tell him we're expecting an attack." The major was sweating, his appointment was political; his father-in-law hadn't mentioned the danger of dying.

"Sir, there are two civilian prisoners here. Do we keep them until the commander returns?"

The major remembered the fight. "No, let the Uigur go tonight. Leave the hot-head until tomorrow morning."

The major moved away, but the Sergeant asked,

"*Efendi*, Sir, shouldn't we send some reinforcements to the supply train? They have only just started, and it would assure us of success in restocking the garrisons." The major laughed hysterically. "That Yuzbasha, Sanjak has stories about his herding refugees from Chang'an. If he's half as good as his brags he'll survive without our weakening ourselves."

> - - - - - >TASH TRAVELS ON > - - - - - >

"Well, that was short, but sweet," Kerim said to the veteran, Hassan.

"Dang right it is, but they ran too soon. I like a little more blood in my victories." Hassan was speaking loudly glaring at Tash, who had called them off when the looters started to run away.

Kerim looked at Leyla to mummer. "A sweet victory is long remembered." She looked quickly away.

"We aren't here to kill villagers, just to discourage looters." Tash insisted coolly. There was a happy confidence about him that spoke well for the experience. Tash came back from the people who had thanked him for his intervention. They waved as the troop left.

Cheered by the reception the troop moved briskly. "Did you see how brave Jon was? I was afraid every moment," declared Maril to Leyla.

Leyla agreed, recognizing the symptoms. "He must have done many brave things on your travels. You mentioned a Sanjak. Tell me about him, too."

Maril was only too glad to oblige as they rode on the south side of the Syr River through village after village.

Tash took on himself the duty of warning the people that rioting would not be tolerated by government or army. He sowed a quiet and settled atmosphere wherever he stopped. The troopers too, seemed to acquire stature in their own eyes. They were welcomed as heroes and saviors everywhere: especially in villages that were still Zoroastrian, Christian, or Manichee. All came out to celebrate the presence of order whether they spoke Farsi, Turkish or market Arabic.

Kerim rode beside the proud leader. "You have won the people's hearts, Onbasha."

Tash looked severe, trying not to show his pleasure as late-blooming, garden-protected flowers were presented to him along with food, pressed on the willing troopers. The two ladies were receiving special attention from the village women who thought the soldiers were an escort for them and the two men who had no uniforms.

Hassan was delighted, "Dang, if the kid ain't hit the bull's eye with this royal progress. I got more food and gifts than I seen in the last ten years."

"It slowed us down, but it sure is time well spent," Selim added.

Kerim had made friends with the other two troopers and was well integrated into the group. They stopped to spend the night at a municipal guest house in one of the larger villages where the mayor himself welcomed them. The ladies were given their room and Jon and Kerim had another. The troops stayed in the police barracks, whose men were out patrolling the area. The day of turmoil had given them a night of ease.

In bed Jon blew out the light asking, "Do you have a wife, Kerim bey?" to which he answered,

"Yes, a tribal Turk, much like the Princess Leyla, proud and difficult."

Jon sighed thoughtfully, "I would prefer a city girl. They seem modest and quiet. The ambassador's daughter, Nooryouz, and Maril are like that."

Kerim answered, "They can be that at marriage and develop fire afterwards." Both laughed and silence descended.

In the other room the girls talked, "Are you married, Leyla hanum?" asked Maril to her new companion. The feeble lamp gave little light as they covered up.

"Yes, as a debt of gratitude, to an irresponsible joker."

"Oh how difficult for you! Were there no other available possibilities?"

"There was a sweet boy I liked very much when I was still a girl with father and brother to contend with in

282

Kokand. We could talk about anything and even found some secrets to share. He was a lot younger, just a child, but such fun. We lost contact when I left the quarry with father. After that life became a harried chase always escaping and running away; days full of pain and anguished decisions. I married at such a time."

Maril was distressed, "You do love him though?" she asked.

Leyla shook her head, "The answer is yes and no. I don't really know, He is a lot like Kerim bey, talking and joking with everyone, but with little serious to say about the future. Life is no joke, and I think knife throwing lessons from Yeet were more interesting than travel with a careless husband." She was sobbing now and Maril patted her shoulder.

"There, there, Yesu has been my comfort at such times, and His Mother comforts the hearts of maidens with secrets to share."

> - - - - - >A SPY REBUKED > - - - - - >
"Two birds have flown, Seerden bey, fast and far. They know all the plans and person of the prince's end. You said they were in your hands."

The accusation came in the growl of the wolf. The accent was different, but the sameness was enough to identify a society member. Seerden felt his hair rise on neck and arms.

"They were, but someone must have tipped them off and frightened them, but I'll have them soon enough." Whisperings followed, "The plan to reveal the assassin's plot remains incomplete, the hand is cut off, but the eye is not yet blinded. Investigations will continue. Their blood-hounds follow our trails. Avengers grow closer."

"And so will I. I have the inside track." Fear seized him.

"We have the inside track, you have to travel."

"I've done nothing else for months."

The voice chuckled, "We don't pay for idleness. You will go back east to Khiva."

"That dump? It'll take months. What am I to do?"

"You have a reward waiting there. You'll be reached."

"I'll start tomorrow if you wish."

A whisper came, "Go now, this very hour and remember obedience brings life." A door closed somewhere in the inn. There was a noise in the stable area. Dawn pushed a feeble ray of light under the door. He rose to dress. He checked the facts he knew with this late development. He thought he saw the pattern: it was all within his grasp now. He knew where the two ends of the society rested, how and to what end it functioned. The only questions now were: Is this move toward or away from the seat of power? And who is seated there?

> - - - - - >IN THE UIGUR VILLAGE > - - - - - >

"My Lord Onat, an emergency at the *ordu-e've*, they require your immediate return. Tonight two messengers have reported, It is fact." The adjutant on night duty was firm in spite of his commander's protests. It was first light: the time before sunrise. Due to the lavish festival there was no adherence to schedule. Soldiers overeat when the special food is free and there are always other diversions of the flesh to distract them late into their freedom. Hangovers are the common denominator of such occasions.

"This had better be a real one." Onat grumbled.

The adjutant whispered in his ear.

The general whispered the words back louder, incredulously: "Insurrection, immigrant families abandoning land, houses and Islam to return home. Others are fighting authorities to be freed?"

"*Chavush*, Sergeant get those troops out and moving," he yelled. "Horses, Sergeant! You bring the men. I'm riding ahead with the staff." Now the camp was awake, Uigurs and Muslims alike. Some thought the other side had attacked them and there were a few fights and wounds where the two camps rubbed shoulders. Fatigued soldiers were awakened to a new day of march. Starting without breakfast underlined the urgency of their movement, although most had no idea of the reasons. The horsemen were off first with the Binbasha in their midst. The marching escort who had controlled the refugees formed up and started at a slower pace.

"Get my staff in here! I want to know more about this new emergency," ordered Manly who had not been ready to receive a departing salute from his equal. Bits and pieces of information

284

were put together to give a general idea of what was really happening. Spies reported as the Muslim troops withdrew in haste.

"Yuzbasha, Captain, take a squad of four hundred horsemen and get to Lake Balkash and re-enforce the irregulars that are stationed there. Get the irrigated land if you can, but get the grazing lands, especially the high country from Lake Issyk Kool to the Chu River. Don't attack regular troops. Just make your presence known. The local people will do the rest: Manacheans will rise, Christians will try to stay neutral, and the Muslims will fight or withdraw. You aren't there to start a war, just to let what is happening happen. It'll be two weeks to get there. The Muslim troops will be even later; evaluate and act. Withdraw where it's prudent. You have your orders now; ride swiftly."

"Yes, my Binbasha, do I take captives?"

Manly signaled no. "Only for your own uses, Captain."

> - - - - ->SMUGGLER'S VILLAGE > - - - - ->

"Friend, put me up for the night, it's too late to travel tonight." Bolben pleaded with his old friend.

"I've been searched three times since you hid here last. You bring nothing but trouble. We had stuff confiscated as contraband."

"I won't come again and my house in the village will be open to you and any you send. Don't be mean, it's only for tonight."

"*Ta'mom*, okay, Bolben, but you need to stay away, there's men in the village that hold a grudge against you. I don't want trouble with them." The door opened and Bolben slipped in as quiet as a shadow. The door closed quickly, but watchers were out in the dark.

"So you take shelter while my little boss sleeps in jail. You brought girls over the border and cut in on our market. You'll be dead before you leave this village." The night was dark and cold, but evil, spurred by hatred, never sleeps.

DISPATCHED NORTH

285

PEOPLE, PLOTS & PLACES IN CHAPTER 24

Baja: likes girl talk, but not men in the kitchen.
Bolben: has an unexpected meeting in the village.
Jon & Maril; arrive at Khiva to change and continue.
Kadir: gets more questions from travelers.
Kardesh: meets an old enemy at a bad time.
Katchy: goes from an object of contempt to praise.
Kerim: drops out at the Khiva market to wait.
Korkmaz: a successful hunter is sent from the kitchen.
Leyla: enters Khiva in style on the Fergana mare
Manson: spies for his boss to murder a rival.
Marium: waits to watch a multitude pass.
Mookades: takes the wide view with historical facts.
Onat & adjutant: leave the border and return to the base.
Sanjak & sergeant: go to an abandoned border fort.
Sesli & Nooryouz: tell tales of harem life in the palace.
Setchkin: worries as they plan for the refugees.
Sulema: makes sure that they go to see the Mooktar.
Twozan: faces problems on the departure of Turks.
Umer: finds his life a burden that he can't lay down.
Yavuz: finds an outlet for his frustrations and anger.

GLOSSARY:
ba'rak: leave it; quit it.
ber'aber: together.
bir dakika: one minute, just a minute; slang, bi'daka.
dede: grandfather.
de'kot: attention; alert; be careful.
e'yee: good; wonderful.
kil'lim: woven, patterned rug, cover or wall hanging.
Nereye?: Where to? Where are you going?
ordu ev'e: army headquarters, a building or tent.
Sultan valide: ruler of the harem, the Sultan's mother.
su'suz kum: waterless sands.
Ta'mom!: Okay! Agreed!

BOLBEN'S VISION

"Yavuz bey, we got important news, we know where Bolben stayed the night. We may catch him there if we hurry," Manson yelled. Yavuz was in an ugly mood. He had slept little and eaten less during his stay in jail.

"E'yee, good, burn the house, that'll bring 'em out running. We'll root out the competition and village opposition with the army too busy to notice. Let's get 'em." The house was outside the second perimeter and they took some time to arrive.

"Come out, we'll burn you out if you don't." Yavuz was past caring that the house belonged to a prominent villager. He threw the torch to the roof and stood snarling before the house.

"*Barak*, leave off, don't burn the house, I was just leaving, I promise never to come again. I was helping refugees and I'll go home and help them." Bolben's hands were extended pleadingly as he came out of the door.

With a scream of rage Yavuz rushed forward. "I told you what I'd do if you came again. I don't forget or forgive anything!" He plunged the knife to the hilt in Bolben's chest. "You can see the smile on my face when you die." He shoved the man against the wall and glared into his victim's agonized face. "Look at me," he screamed, but Bolben wasn't looking at him. He had raised his astonished face, "Dahkool," he murmured, "You've come back."

He slumped and fell. Screams issued from inside the house. Yavuz let the body fall. His men were urging him to come away.

The torch had been tossed and the people were running out: front and back. The army took up the alarm. Cymbals clashed and a horn rang out.

"Boss, run, I left horses near the cave." Shouts and screams followed them. Soldiers rushed to the perimeter to repel a dawn attack, but the village saw nothing of an incoming enemy.

> - - - - - >NORTH OF THE SYR RIVER > - - - - - >

"A dawn start is always best for really eating up the distance." Twozan reported to a sleepy wife. She yawned, "Marriage to you is one way to keep a girl on her toes."

"Toe or hoof everything among the Toozlu moves at dawn." She watched him ride away, with graying temples he was still the most desirable man she had met in her life. She wondered if that was the reason she had resisted him at first. Fear of deception, he was too good to believe. She finished securing the last rope on the cart. The trunks were secure, ready to travel.

The call soon came and the line filled with those ready to form the column. There were now too many people to form one camp. Like beads on a string they stopped at night and awoke at dawn. Most had provided for their water to pass the *Su'suz Kum*, the waterless dunes. Those who exhausted their supply were helped by others. They had a week to make it to water, two weeks would be over-stretching it, cattle and people would be dying. Life rests on the narrow edge of the blade.

"Gives you the feeling that Moses must have had when he took the children of Israel into the Sinai. Will the water supply live up to the needs?" Mookades proclaimed, half in jest.

Twozan answered, "Tanra, has put this duty on us, like it or not. The certainty is that, like the Israelites, there is no turning back." The count was hardly believed, ten thousand men was the estimate, but not the published amount. Men were selected as leaders by the different bands. A Toozlu rider was the official contact with the Khan.

"It will demoralize the people if we state the extent of the migration. Better just keep it vague." Mookades advised.

Twozan was not happy with the advice. He had seen greater tribal movements, "It's not much for the steppes, bigger tribes than this move with the seasons."

"But it's grass and water most of the way. We have two deserts to pass. We face this little one to the Chu River and then pass the Bet Pak Dala: the Starvation Steppes -- full of poison and salt pans. Only

288

then can we reach the higher steppe-lands." They rode silently for a time.

Twozan made a decision, "Let's ride to that small hill beside the trail and see the people pass." They stopped there and dismounted to rest, eat and refresh themselves. Marium and Setchkin spread the *killim* to serve on. They ate and rested an hour, but the line of people never slowed or ended.

"It stretches from the south to the horizon in the north," whispered Marium, "How can there be so many?"

Setchkin was cleaning up after the breakfast. She fretted and trembled, "It's too much, we will never get there with so many." They stared at the line.

Mookades patted Marium encouragingly, "Tanra gives the tasks, He must also see to the results. We will trust, pray and do our best. He will have to provide."

Twozan replied, "*Beraber*, together, as others do when facing difficulty, see it through or die in the attempt. Mookades, pray now for our passage."

> - - - - - >FORT SUPPLY CARTS > - - - - - >
"Two weeks and we've only supplied the first stockade," said the sergeant, riding beside his officer.

Sanjak smiled broadly. "Next, today, the Illi River fort and last the Chu River where both flow out of the mountains on to the plains. I see the last fort as a key to connect the Syr River to the Balkash region. But why retain the Illi River post? We don't control the area up river or down."

"I understand, Sir, that the garrison is stationed in an old Chinese fort, erected by the Tang when they ruled here. We drove them out at the battle on the Talas River, I suppose it's so they can't come back and occupy it. I've always wanted to take this trip to see it."

Sanjak looked perplexed and stopped his horse. "I thought you'd done this circuit before, Chavush. Is it all new to you?"

The sergeant looked back to see that no one was close. "No, sir, I just talked it over with old Hassan *Izlerjee*. He's a veteran that knows all the routes."

Sanjak laughed and asked, "Where'd he get that name, Is it tears from eyes or scars from cuts?"

"Both I guess, Sir, he's a devout Shiite as you would guess by his name. Cries and lashes himself on Kerbala's day when they all remember Hassan and Hussain's deaths or martyrdom as they prefer to call it. He has scars to prove his zeal and his tears are real too."

"Both tears and scars leave their traces. They are tracks of life's experiences. I'm amazed that they continue to follow a faith that they believe made a major mistake in killing the prophet's descendants in political murders to put the Umayyads in power. What can they do about it now? The Umayyads are gone except in Spain and so are the descendants of the martyrs."

"Allah's truth must be known and accepted sir. Acknowledgment of sin is the first step in reconciliation."

"You sound like a Shiite yourself, Sergeant."

"I lean that way, sir. In true Islam all men should be equal as they are also equal before Allah. Men invent genealogies to be descendants of the Prophet and claim the right to rule."

Sanjak paused, thinking, the study of Islam was interesting, if not personally very convincing.

"You are a Kajerite, then? You hold to an open democratic state?" Chavush looked uncomfortable,

"I wouldn't like it put that bluntly. I lean that way."

"You're a cautious man, Sergeant."

The man agreed, "Habit sir, I wouldn't talk this freely with most superiors."

"You're safe, Sergeant. I'm still a Christian. I'm tolerated, but my words are worth little in the mosque courts." Both rode silently for a moment.

"I know sir. I wondered if you would tell me something about Isa... that is Yesu. The Koran speaks well of him, if badly about his followers."

The sergeant stopped his horse and looked down the slope, "We've arrived. Hasan said we should be able to see the fort from the hilltop. Yes, there," he pointed. The roof still bore the upward curve and dragons of China, but the gate was open and its courtyard looked deserted.

> - - - - - >AT THE LAKE > - - - - - >

"Well done, you bake like a professional," said Baja to Sesli.

"I'm glad you find it so, I was assigned to kitchen help when we were separated from the refugees. I wasn't approved for more intimate possibilities until the head baker pinched my bottom and I protested with a wooden bread paddle to his hard head."

"Really, what happened then?" exclaimed the laughing Baja.

"When I was taken before the *sultan validey* she realized my potential and I was trained for satisfying the flesh that they are supposed to ignore. A job of satisfying repressed men, who for religion ignore their wives for anything more than procreation. The preparation is quite thorough and includes dress, music, manners and all forms of enticement."

Nooryouz agreed, but put on a teasing smile, "The baker continued to send us fine delicacies, I think you impressed him."

Sesli raised her eyebrows and shook her head. "I hit him hard enough. It must have established my virtue."

"Some men require that and more." laughed the ladies. Korkmaz came in holding a pair of dead rabbits and a duck, taken from the fall migrants that filled the lake. He held them up for the ladies to see and admire. Kadir followed from the stable to join the congratulations.

Baja, however, took a different tone as they stood about commenting.

"Get those dead creatures out of my clean kitchen. Go clean them outside. I won't have them where the bread is baking. Kadir you smell of horse, don't you come in here without washing up first. You men get out!"

Korkmaz left with his trophies hanging low. "Do I have to cook them myself?" he asked Kadir.

He replied, "Ask Sesli when the kitchen is clear, she won't mind."

"Do you think *Dede* Aziz will stop smuggling? It's nice not having to worry about breaking the law. These two weeks have been such fun with the Chang'an ladies here with Baja."

Kadir agreed, he had met hurried army men, dispatched from the base, on the road and all carried bad news. "The army has its hands full these days and we are blessed to be out of it. There are a lot of bad things happening now around us."

The noise of horses came to their ears and turning they saw a squad of soldiers coming along the road. The black flag of the

Abbasids came first. The men were dusty and tired, but they had no wounds.

"*Nere'ye*, where to, Captain?' asked Kadir.

"*Ordu eve'ye*, to the base, friend. Our Illi River stockade is not supplied, and is exposed to attack. We have decided to retrench."

Kadir frowned, "You leave us exposed to the irregulars here, Yuzbasha."

"I know you Kadir bey. You have a house in the village. You'd better come there with us now. You'll be safer."

Kadir bit his lip, "You go ahead Captain. The enemy won't dare follow closely. We'll come later. Do you have news of any other fort?"

The Captain's head jerked up, "I expect the Chu stockade is still intact. They have friendly farmers, people who will sell part of the crop. On the Illi River our only neighbors are enemies."

"God commands," He called as he left.

"Happily go, we'll be in touch." Kadir stared long at the backs of the departing troops. "They'll report on us when they arrive."

> - - - - - >WITH KARDESH NEAR KHIVA > - - - - - >

"*Ta-mom*, okay, I can go by myself now, Yeet. Thanks, I'll get back on my own." Kardesh moved forward slowly, and squatted to answer a call of nature. Two weeks of hard travel was telling and the food rations had been shortened because of the loss of provisions. It was dawn of the last day of travel to Khiva.

He heard the footsteps of one coming his way. So he called out, "*Bi daka*, just a minute, I'm not through yet." The approaching sound stopped and instead a quiet but familiar voice spoke to him.

"It's me, Kardesh, don't call out, I don't want to hurt you. I've hurt you enough as it is. I just want to tell you something. I'm Umer."

"I knew your voice, Umer and I heard about you from Yeet, by the goat hill."

"I got over that, but I got in trouble again. Every time I run I get in worse trouble. I'm the one who stole from you, food enough to get me through. I want to get a new life, Kardesh. I can't go home and I'm not willing to die for what I've done. The old guy at the river wouldn't let go. I couldn't shake him so I stuck him so he'd let go. I hit too close to home and he died. Believe me; I didn't want to

292

do him in. Now I've killed three, but they keep coming after me. If they'd only leave me alone everything would be okay. We've arrived near the valley again. I heard it last night, people and animals. I won't keep following you anymore. I truly regret that I started this with you. Allah, I'm really sorry. I wish there was a way of starting over. I can't tell the other three, but I wanted you to know. Goodbye, Kardesh. I won't see you again, but if you'd forgive me for what I did -- and I guess it would be too much to ask you to pray for me. I feel like I need it. I don't know what to do -- and all I know about Allah are rules. Say you'll forgive me. Christians are supposed to forgive, aren't they Kardesh? That's what I've always heard."

Kardesh spoke, "I forgive you Umer. May Yesu have mercy on your soul." There was a sob and the sound of feet running away.

> - - - - - > NEAR THE MOOKTAR'S OFFICE > - - - - - >

"Walk slower! Stop looking around at every noise. I'll stay right behind you if you don't dart away at any move."

Katchy stopped. "There be too much noise here," he complained. Sulema was tired tagging after him and was out of breath. She puffed her burka from her face. It rubbed her nose, tickling. They had spent his hoarded coins to get clothes fit to meet the Mooktar. Katchy was nervous. He suspected some trouble that might get him whipped again. She was insistent and now he was here almost without money. They had left the dried winter jerky at the meat market where it would be sold and the butcher would pay him after taking his share of the sales.

They moved toward the imposing government palace slowly, now that the market was past. The new clothes caused Katchy to roll his shoulders and make faces as the fabric irritated his still tender back.

"You say again, why we called by Mooktar." His voice showed his worry. He was ready to return without the visit called for by the Mooktar of the Upper Amu River Valley. All his previous experiences with authority had been painful.

293

"Kooskoo bey is dead, You don't know who will take his place, what the conditions of work will be. They will be glad you stayed with the body. They might even thank you and be generous."

"More generous sell me three nannies."

They entered the imposing building. Showing the guards his written pass, they entered a great room.

"What is your business here? The Mooktar is very busy today." The adjutant was very brisk and cool. He looked at the new, but cheap clothes and the aspect of the herder and wife with contempt.

"Mooktar call Katchy come office. I here now!"

The man sniffed, "Yes, you would have to be the goat herder. He warned me, but I forgot about it." He led them to a corner of the waiting area, "You will wait here until I call you."

They passed the afternoon waiting. Rich men entered and departed with smooth words of welcome and farewell by the adjutant. A few other ordinary citizens came to wait for a time, but were called in eventually. Katchy and Sulema continued to wait.

"You can't come in now. It will take too much time. He's tired," the adjutant stated brusquely. It will be better to come back tomorrow." Smiling he showed them out.

"Me, you call from work. You make wait. Now say 'come back'. No, you tell big man he come my work. I give him bread, milk and cheese. No send home hungry. No make wait for talk. I walk half day to come; half night go home to milk goats sunrise time."

Contempt filled the face of the adjutant as he opened the door set in the larger front gate. As he did so a handsome, turbaned and expensively robed authority appeared. He had been aroused by the shouts.

"You didn't mention another appointment waiting. Would this be the goat herder I've sent for?"

The adjutant squirmed and answered. "Yes, but it's rather late, I was sure it could wait until tomorrow."

The Mooktar said, "You will wait, I'm anxious to see this man." he turned and motioned toward a door invitingly.

"I feel it is an honor to have such an important visitor. I want to hear your story of the night you followed the quarry man. You may not know that I have news of the widow's grant of her rural property and water rights to you. The murderer of Kooskoo bey has not been found. However, we will spy him out eventually. Justice is the concern of Allah, for this we have Sharia law. I have some papers to authorize your possession of the animals and lands given over by the widow. Come we have much to occupy us. My cart will carry you home afterwards. My young helper will bring tea and, later, supper. Allah blesses the reception of guests."

> - - - - - >AT THE ARMY BASE > - - - - - >

"It looks like they are ready to throw back an attack, Binbasha. It's a defense in depth." The commander looked down on the Army base on a hill nestled on a flattened little valley below the pass.

"Yes, but where are the attackers? I see nothing on the opposite mountain or plain."

The adjutant was eager to arrive home, "Perhaps they have not yet arrived Binbasha. We can get back without fighting our way through enemy ranks."

Onat bey snorted, "I've heard no reports of attacking armies. It's an insurrection: the desertion of Islam and the rejection of Abbassid authority. The Uigurs are not attacking; they let us leave in peace. There's no army behind us, or before us. The Toozlu nomads have permission to leave. There is no news of their arming or returning to make war."

"You mean that the major has made a mistake?"

"Don't be quick to judge your superior officer. We don't know what information and requests have come in. The situation is obscure and reports may be scarce if there is a general rioting. Promotion, reproof and commendations are done after all information is in and analyzed. Some-where there will be heroes to reward and blunderers to reprove, but all in good time."

"What next, sir?" The adjutant was careful now.

Onat grinned, "Mother's cooking, a hamom steam room massage, and then a long siege of reports and conferences with personnel."

The adjutant smiled, as the general motioned his horsemen forward. "It sounds wonderful, Sir."

The commander shouted back, "Hurry, or I'll be the first to arrive," so they raced.

> - - - - - >AMU VALLEY NEAR KHIVA> - - - - - >

"I put your saddle on the Fergana mare this morning Princess Leyla. I thought you would like to ride her when we enter town. She carries a message from you to the commander of the garrison and the others in authority."

She put on her coldest face and tone. "What message would that be?" she paused, "Bulgar."

"That: a Princess of the Chipchak Nation cannot be held." There was general laughter by guards and prisoners alike. After two weeks of desert crossing they knew each other. The lady was a repressed, cold fish; pretty but dangerous, best kept at arm's length.

"You'll remember that when you return to your own nation," she retorted.

"Use her happily, that mare was selected by a horse master without equal among the tribes."

She paused, swallowed, and said, "Yes, I believe you're right," in a kindlier tone. She mounted, "Maril and I will ride to that little hill, beside the road, alone. We'll return in a few moments." All nodded acceptance as they rode away. All of them knew the ways and word of the princess. All were mounted and ready when the ladies remounted and returned to join the squad. As usual, the women rode together. Kerim led the spare mount beside Selim. Much later the town loomed on the horizon.

"Well, it's been a hard trip, but we finally got here." Kerim said to Selim, as they rode together, into the town nestled in the irrigated valley of the Amu River. Khiva's day of grandeur had not yet come, it was an agricultural center prospered by a good irrigation system and diligent farmers. Most of the inhabitants were of Persian origin and some remained secretly Zoroastrian in belief. They have worked the land for generations. The emigrant disturbances of the frontier on the Syr River rarely touched them.

"What will you do now that we have arrived safely, Kerim bey?" Selim asked.

Kerim's smile was beatific. "I'll travel home with a friend I have to pick up here." Selim persisted. He was intrigued by the Bulgar Christian who helped them.

"Your friend lives here in Khiva?"

Kerim's negative was clear, "No, my friend arrives too."

Selim was puzzled, "Where will you meet?"

Kerim shrugged knowingly. "At the market. What are your plans these next weeks?"

"After a celebration, I hope to go back to the base. We have passed enough desert for me. I wouldn't want to face the Kara Kum south of here."

Kerim nodded thoughtfully, "I had best say my good-byes to the prisoners you protect. They'll go on to Baghdad and her father. It must cost him a lump of gold." They laughed and wished they were as rich.

He rode over beside Jon. "I wish you well on your trip home, young man. And you, too, my lady." Maril and Jon thanked him for making the trip safer and lighter.

He looked across at Leyla and said, "I'll wait for the mare, late this afternoon." She acknowledged his statement and he rode up to Tash. "You have done a remarkable job Onbasha, I hope your trip to Baghdad will be all you expect. I'll drop off at the public market for a meal that'll be memorable and wait for my friend's arrival."

PEOPLE, PLOTS & PLACES IN CHAPTER 25

Adjutant: the Captain receives information and prisoners.
Jon: meets new people that hold a family party.
Kardesh: finds his sister and new friends.
Kerim: the groom can't talk to his bride.
Leyla: finds her family and friends unexpectedly.
Maril: loses a friend and gains a valuable mother.
Mookades: leads the grateful in a song of thanksgiving.
Setchkin: finds her faith and endurance small in trial.
Sevman: meets his leader's sister again, in Khiva.
Sulema: knows how to use white muslin cloth.
Tayze: encounters her niece in a strange place.
Twozan: endures suffering to encourage others.
Yeet: meets a dear friend in time to say goodbye.

GLOSSARY:
Bock, ordu gel'eyor: Look, an army is coming.
Booy' roon: Behold; this is it; look here.
hich: never.
Hy'er: no; definitely not.
Koo mool dah ma: don't move.
saz: a stringed musical instrument with a long neck.
to haff bir shay: something strange; a difference.
yany: that is; I mean; in other words.
yav'*room*: my baby; my little one.

A PARTING KISS

"Onbasha Tash reporting sir, we are escorting three prisoners for delivery. The order for the lady and servant from Binbasha Onat and the Princess Leyla of the Toozlu Turks by order of the Mooktar of the Upper Syr River. I'm supposed to continue from Khiva with camels." Tash stood awaiting a response.

"Relax, corporal. The man you're to escort is not here yet. Check in and take some time off. But first tell me about things on the Syr. We've had no violence here, but some people have left quietly."

"There was rioting and looting in some villages where families of nomadic background left to return to the steppes. Sometimes homes were attacked on a political basis. We found it possible to quiet things by direct intervention, police work, where people were being attacked. I heard reports of insurrection, but saw nothing like that." Continuing he reported, "Binbasha Onat has returned Uigur refugees to their country's authorities. The Toozlu Turks have kept moving north. The Princess came back to find her wounded husband, reported to be in the hands of the authorities. The Mooktar said to bring her here as a political prisoner, but gave me no papers."

The Captain nodded agreeably and started to read the orders, "Well done corporal. You're free of duty, but the post gates close two hours past yatsa prayers. We'll talk again tomorrow." The captain walked to the door.

"Send in the prisoners," he ordered. The three entered. "You are Jon, servant of Yusuf of Chang'an and this girl is the daughter, is that correct?" He held up some papers from Onat bey. They agreed.

"My father sends to bring us to Baghdad," Maril said.

"We crossed the border secretly to escape the Uigur authorities who wished to detain us," Jon added.

The captain agreed, "It's all written here," he explained, "you would be free to go your own way except for the special order to get you home the fastest way. So, tomorrow we will dispatch you on a camel train. You can occupy rooms in the city caravansary tonight. Your corporal will come there for your early departure. Now," he turned slightly and eyed the lady traveling alone. "The corporal called you princess?"

Leyla had steeled herself for this moment. She held out a letter, "I have instructions from the Mooktar of the Upper Syr River, if you would receive it now?"

He took the page curiously and read. "Why was this not sealed? It's open where all can read it."

"It's a general pass, not a private communication."

"It says the bearer will be free to travel to the Aral Sea Delta, and must be taken on tour of the district and afterwards be released to travel north with three horses, one is a Fergana mare. Where did you get this?" The lady looked cold and disapproving,

"It was delivered to me by a friend of the Mooktar."

"The corporal called you a political prisoner," he eyed her suspiciously, "What did he mean?"

She shrugged, "I was detained, perhaps as a guarantee of Toozlu departure from Abbassid territory. They are gone now. I am free to depart as instructed. Perhaps a

Christian's word was not enough, so I'm sent out another way. So the Toozlu won't know and change their minds and return. I'm uncertain of the Mooktar's motives."

He doubted, "How do I know your words are true? The document is open."

"My words are all correct before Tanra. You know the Mooktar's writing. You must correspond with him constantly."

"The corporal mentioned a husband."

She laughed, "He's waiting outside, impatient for his supper."

The captain hid his disappointment and thought for a moment. "Our Mooktar is traveling north, so I can't consult him. You will have the chance to meet him there however. I'll send a couple of soldiers to guard you on your travels." He made a salaam of dismissal.

"I'm not sure how my husband will like having others along on the trip. We have usually traveled alone," she worried.

"The guards will come to the caravansary tomorrow. Don't forget to wait. You'll be watched while here."

"May I have my letter please?"

The captain smiled, "They'll bring it tomorrow morning, Princess." "Guards," he cried, "take three guests to the caravansary. The husband may be waiting outside, He, too, can sleep there. Stay for their security until I relieve you tomorrow morning."

> - - - - - >GOAT HERDER CORRAL> - - - - - >

"Why you cry, big baby? You no like I kill little Karakol for skin?" Katchy scolded scornfully.

"Mothers should be allowed to birth their kids," Sulema protested vigorously. "It's not fair to abort them to sell; its blood money." She gestured with hands down.

"You like pretty things for 'come in six months' baby," he reached to touch her tummy.

"It's still not fair," she fussed, moving out of reach.

"Take only one of three nannies, every three years each lose only one. Not much. Always slaughter half-grown kids at six months, males mostly. Why you fuss about babies?" he wrinkled his forehead.

"We'll have our baby in the summer. It's like we're tempting fate," she concluded exasperated.

"No worry," he finished, "Kardesh say Allah good. Allah send angels to watch babies and mothers. Like good Shepherd story, Sevman tell. Allah look out for lost lambs and babies. He keep us safe. You see."

- - - - - - - >THE KHIVA SARY > - - - - - >

"This is the caravansary, Leyla hanem." The guard reported.

"Thank you Onbasha. We can manage from here." He salaamed, "We are ordered to provide security during the night."

"My husband is delayed and I will sleep with Maril hanem. See that we are not disturbed." Jon took a place in the adjoining men's rooms.

"How exciting, your husband is coming, I saw you looking everywhere on the way here."

Leyla's smile was weak and evasive. "I was sure I would see him, but he kept out of sight. He will appear when things are ready; He sent me the paper for my trip tomorrow and will appear somewhere there." She sat heavily.

"I remember the paper just under the saddle when we were on the hill today. How wonderful for you. Jon was so surprised when you showed it. I had to hush him." Maril giggled.

"But we'll go separate ways tomorrow. I'll pray for you as you go home." The girls embraced. Leyla decided to tell Maril about Kerim, but noises out in the corridor interrupted.

Maril squealed, "Listen, I hear Jon. It sounds like Kerim. He's arrived and is with Jon in the men's room. They're laughing." She ran to the door. "Kerim is describing the market place. He's bought food for all of us. He's inviting the guard to join us. He's asking permission to send us two portions." She had her ear to the door as a knock came. "He's got it. I'll open the door: you stand to see out." They did so with eager smiles. The covered bowls of food were passed in and the door closed again.

"Set them outside when you've finished." Kerim said. "Everything will be taken away tomorrow. Good appetite to you." There was more noise in the hall as more people came in, but the women's door was shut. The girls were being thankful when the door opened again. An old woman was allowed entry. When the door was closed the woman walked to the light and sat on a bed. She stared at Leyla. "Leyla, child, is that you? Are you here in Khiva?"

"Tayze, how did you come here? Who is with you? Is Kardesh here?" They hugged and both started to cry. It would be a night to remember.

> - - - - - > SHERIFF'S VILLAGE OFFICE> - - - - - >

"Sheriff, I done seen a woman again at that little hump-back's corral. I think you ought to look in on him. Find out what's going on there."

"Deputy, you are a nosy donkey. She's been there for months and is at least some months pregnant. She hides every time she hears some loudmouth ride by."

"I don't tarry around there Sheriff. My horse picked up a stone in his right front hoof and I stopped to borrow a wedge to pry with. I smelled fresh baked bread and found a mud-brick oven by the corral hut. It was still warm and there was goat pills and thorn branches to burn piled near. While I was looking a woman come out of the hut. Before I could say somethin' she saw me an' screeched. She pulled up her veil and ran like the devil. I yelled, but she wouldn't stop for nothin'. With my horse bad I couldn't follow."

"She recognized you. You raised hell with the goat boy even after he was a hero."

"I still think... anyway, she had two weeks worth of bread inside. I took a pida' snack and came to report it."

"She obviously doesn't want to see anybody, and I think nobody, especially you, should bother her."

303

"But Sheriff, who is she? What's going on anyway? Ain't it your responsibility to know about it?" The deputy's voice was demanding and loud.

"I know about it and am smart enough not to tell those who don't need to know. The village property, house, of the murdered man has been taken by the kaimakan for a mosque school. The field is for village commons. No one appreciates the delays caused by the discovery of an heir. The woman doesn't want to be discovered, questioned or found by anyone. So leave it alone!"

"I'll bet they ain't married!" the deputy snorted.

"No, and they don't read or write neither. But we'll buy their cheese and jerky and pay for a kid to roast when we celebrate. She had her choices, so leave well enough alone."

> - - - - - >LATER AT THE SARAY > - - - - - >

"You can come and go as you please, Bayan, but the two ladies with you can't leave the room until the relief guards come and one is taken to the Mooktar. The others go by camel express tomorrow."

"One lady, Leyla, has a brother and two friends that need to talk to her. They are here in the men's room." The answer was definite. "*Hyer*, no, it would not be acceptable. They cannot enter nor can she leave her room."

Tayze knew the limits permitted and said, "They can talk through the door. It can even be open. You are the guard and will see that all is proper."

He agreed reluctantly, "Only one at a time, the brother first. I will sit at the end of the corridor and eat the food, Kerim the Bulgar has purchased for us." He left.

Tayze whispered, "*To haff be shay*, it's strange, I feel like I should know the man that brought food. Why?"

Leyla smiled and pushed her out the door saying, "Go bring Kardesh here, then talk to him. You must remember to guard your tongue. Maril here will travel on the camel train with you and she knows something of our trip here with him."

304

Tayze called, "Kardesh come to the door, a surprise awaits you." She helped seat him with Kerim's help. He winked at Leyla, who blushed.

Kardesh spoke first, "Kerim said you were here Leyla, I can't see you, but I heard your voice just now. I hoped you and father would get to the tribe."

"I did, but father went for food and never returned. Kerim found him dead and buried him."

Kardesh moaned and tears flowed, "I failed him and you Leyla, I thought I was so smart with the gang, but I caused our going to the quarry. I caused Sevman's injuries because of my pride and failure to look after family interests. How can I atone for such sin?"

Both cried as she comforted him. "You have friends who love you and will help you. Yesu died to get us forgiven. I was selfish and self-centered. Father protected me in my worst fears. Now I have a husband, but it's a secret here, they must not know who he is."

"We all know, Sevman was there when Twozan married Setchkin. He said you loved a Bulgar, you told him all about it."

"He's more -- *yany*, that is, different from what he seems." They looked up as Kerim, who had borrowed a long necked *saz* started to sing:

#1   All families start with only two;
            Just one like me and one like you.
            They start and add first one, then two,
            Love's count is always left to you,
            To do what God wants you to do.

#2   Most families grow before they're through;
            With some like me and some like you.
            They grow so fast while you make do,
            The oldest ones will do it too,
            Your flock is larger than you knew.

#3   Your herds increase, they need room too.
They do what any herd will do,
They spread as God will give them grace,
To fill a larger bit of space;
With joy increase the human race.

ALL FAMILIES

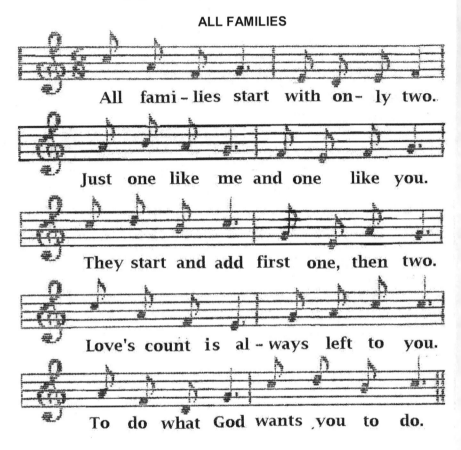

All fami-lies start with on-ly two.

Just one like me and one like you.

They start and add first one, then two.

Love's count is al-ways left to you.

To do what God wants you to do.

There was general laughter at the end of the number and the guard took up the saz to play some home old melodies with background strums. Several conversations started, Maril stood on tiptoes beside the door to listen in on Jon's group.

Kardesh tenderly said to Leyla, "Tell me about all your adventures now." So she did. It took a long time and when they finished, Sevman was ready to talk. That didn't take as long for she had seen him at the Toozlu camp and got a lot of his news. But she heard some more about Katchy. Then, came Yeet!

"Oh, sweet Yeet, how I have missed you. You were such a dear comfort to me back in Kokand." She was crying, "How I have wished for our talks. It seems so long ago now, the Fergana Valley and the quarry. Almost like a favorite fairy tale."

Yeet wiped his eyes, "We did have some fun times. You made me feel bold and forget my nervousness, having a real princess as a close friend."

"I wasn't like a real, that is, a rich princess with attendants, I had to do most things with Tayze's help." She looked at him carefully, then with an exclamation touched his head. "What happened to your head Yeet? There's a lump here – and your ear..."

He snickered and blinked away tears. "Katchy thought I was an intruder and got me with his sling. Isn't it ugly! I wonder if it'll ever go down to normal size? Tayze says not to worry, looks are not very important to a boy. But I wear a turban now to hide it, and rub it with bitter herb twice a day."

"It will be okay after a while. You are still the best looking boy in the gang. Do you know what? Tash is the leader of our army squad. He's a corporal now and hasn't recognized me. I never had much to do with the gang and I have these dreadful scars on my face."

"Let's see," Yeet lifted her face with a finger and held the lamp close, "Yes, but they're not deep tissue, the skin is clear, they'll match the other color soon, the tracks will vanish." The guard made a warning sound and they realized that they had broken some rule.

"Oh, thank you Yeet! You're such a comfort. I had a crush on you back in Kokand."

Yeet put the lamp down, understandingly said, "I know. I was going through a transformation with the gang and needed love and comfort; a temporary, but real need. I will always love you for that." His face was in the shadow, she quickly met his lips. Then he was up and gone before the guard could be sure of anything.

Kerim, however took a sudden breath, "I would like a word with the lady," he said to the guard.

"You are a stranger, as far as I know. It is not proper or allowed. It's dawn outside and the guard will soon be here." He yawned and stretched his full height, "I'll tell the grooms to saddle the horses." At that moment the new guard walked in.

"How did your night go?" he asked.

The sleepy guard replied, "You wouldn't believe the party we had, like a visit home with relatives. They kept bringing in food. I didn't catch a wink of sleep all night." He turned to go as he bid his charges a good journey.

His replacement laughed and turned to speak, "You who go to see the Mooktar must be ready now." Leyla kissed Maril and Tayze and walked to the door.

She asked, "You have the pass and letter?" He nodded an affirmative. "May I have it please?"

His negative was a defiant sneer, "I was told to hold it and put it in the Mooktar's hand."

"I'm the husband, Kerim, by name, I go with you."

"I thought he had not appeared yet."

Kerim smiled grimly, "He's here to stay or go, but not to be separated again. Bring the Fergana mare and the black," he called to the grooms.

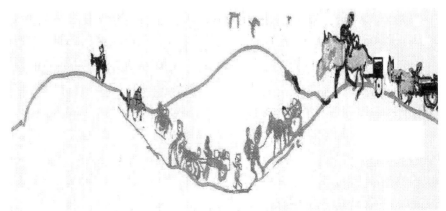

THE LONG DUSTY ROAD

"Where you going now Sheriff?" inquired the deputy hopefully, longing for action.

"Where you're not wanted deputy. I'm going alone. So don't start prying, understand?"

"I know you bought a bolt of muslin cloth at market. You got it loaded there. What's it for?"

"The wife of an important man is expecting a new baby. Women like to have soft cloth to make up for wrappings and little clothes. The work occupies them while they wait. Does that have your approval?" The Sheriff enjoyed taunting his men.

"You sure favour that humpback and his bitch. He stole to get ahead and you make him important."

"I'm sheriff because I'm smart enough to see who Allah favours and who merits attention. She'll deliver alone with only the man present. He's had lots of experience with his goats. The Perikanda Mooktar wants to know how they're doing, so I'll leave the cloth and best wishes, then go on to the city. Now you curry our mounts and think about the consequences of hasty action. You may make Sheriff yet." The big man rode off.

"*Evet pasham*, Yes boss, give my *tebrik eder' em*, congratulations to them, too," the deputy shouted.

"We're late, the caravan is ready to leave now, hurry." Tash called to the two remaining in the caravansary. Jon and Maril had been ready when the man called Derk had entered to call out Kardesh, Tayze, Sevman and Yeet. He acted like he was a part of the family. Derk said he had spent the night with his own family before departure to Baghdad. He seemed distracted and worried. The garrison's commander had traveled, and so he was denied the information he wanted about the insurrection. He had hurried Tayze and the three men out with few words. Jon and Maril had waited for Tash and left last in the same manner. Only the empty dishes, waiting to be collected, remained as evidence to the safety found during the night, which had refreshed and stimulated all the participants with sweet memories and endearments.

> - - - - - >GOAT HERDER'S HUT> - - - - - >

"Sheriff bring soft white cloth. No good for wear in thorn country. I say *tamam* anyway." Katchy's voice was filled with scorn. "He want me know he watch me always. Sevman, he say: 'Yesu, Isa, love and die for all. So, you do good to all people.' "Allah hears all talk, He like warm words.' Kids like warm milk. New baby will like warm milk, *ullook sute*, sweet talk from Nanny." He bobbed his head and leaned over to look at the pile of newly acquired blankets, woven baby clothes and squares of cloth she had stacked in a box.

Sulema paid no attention. "Katchy," she finally said, "hand me the cloth. I know what to do with it."

> - - - - - >WITH REFUGEES > - - - - - >

"Where is this famous River Chu? Is it dried up or lost?" wailed Setchkin. After two weeks they were still in the waterless sand dunes trudging north, while animals died and people's mouths cracked and skin chapped in the cold winds that picked up salty sand and dust to throw in their faces. The Khan had taken the lead of the column.

"The river is where it has always been. It is taking us longer than we expected to reach it. People left hastily without proper preparation. Most took the wrong things. The breakdowns and lack of enough water is costing us lives; animals and human." Twozan recited it in a dull, cracked, matter-of-fact voice. He rode stolidly on.

"When will we get there?" Desperation filled her voice.

"When we have traveled the required distance."

"How much longer?"

He reached over and touched her face tenderly, "Until you learn to endure."

She cried in sobs, but they rode on amid the sand and the wind. She shook her head, "I want to die!"

He shrugged, "You have only to stop and stay. To move is life."

" I can't move any more."

He shrugged again, "I can't stop. I lead a people to life. If I stop, we will all die. If you love me, move. I can't stop for you."

She looked angry, perplexed and pleading all at the same time. "You wouldn't stop to help me?"

His head bobbed up, "If I stop all die. The many value more than the one - even the loved one. I cannot stop."

She did stop, to stare at him. She shook her fist at him and screeched her protest. "The herder leaves the ninety and nine."

"They are safe and have what they need. It's safe for them. When the herd is safe you can go out to help the needy."

"No, the one is as important as all the others," Setchkin insisted.

"Tell that to a man whose wealth is his herd. Ask God," he replied.

"You're a fanatic and a fool!"

He nodded, she caught up, he continued. "I have faith. I know it's there. All I have to do is move until we get there. Then those who have this faith and see my example will live. We will reach water."

They crested a hill and below lay the most beautiful scene anyone could wish in the desert. Pools of water were in their sight, endless like the column, leading back toward the distant mountains. There, autumn rains had started to swell the Chu River before it would freeze into a string of ice ponds: pearls on nature's necklace.

Word spread down the column of sufferers like a flash of light: a wave of sounds and shouts from parched throats. Message flags waved, metal shields flashed sun brightened signals to friends farther back. Within a few minutes everyone, even to the last stragglers struggling forward, knew that the river had been found.

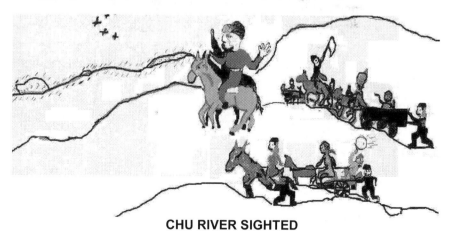

CHU RIVER SIGHTED

`The head of the column had arrived, the column's tail hurried forward with the body of thirst-crazed, frenzied, joyful travelers rushing to surround the pools of life.

The water was cold, but clean and each drank and filled skins and barrels with the life sustaining liquid. They were wading into the water of the Chu River to splash and drink, wash and cry with passion. Many were praying and shouting praise to whatever God they and their people favored.

Twozan and Mookades rode up the opposite, north bank of the river, with the men who had been outriders of the column. They fought their horses to bring them up before they became water logged and useless for riding. The animals and people alike were crazy with thirst.

The lead group on the north bank started to sing a well known hymn of thanks to Tanra, which some in the water joined.

Father, thank you for your mercies:
Sparkling water, daily bread.
By your bounty and provision,
All are comforted and fed.
Yesu, we have shared your suffering,
Faced temptation too.
By your love and perseverance,
Help us keep on serving you.

The hysteria and shouting ceased. The river bank and shallow river bottom were filled with tired, grateful travelers. Life was the reward they had hoped for. Death, braved on the road, was cheated of its potential victims.

The Gray Wolf would howl his loss of control of these herds of people. His management through fear was gone. Mercy was found in the flood that flowed from Tanra's Mountains to the desert, bringing refreshment to all who persevered and found it. These were the brave, who had dared a painful death to be free.

312

SPARKLING WATER

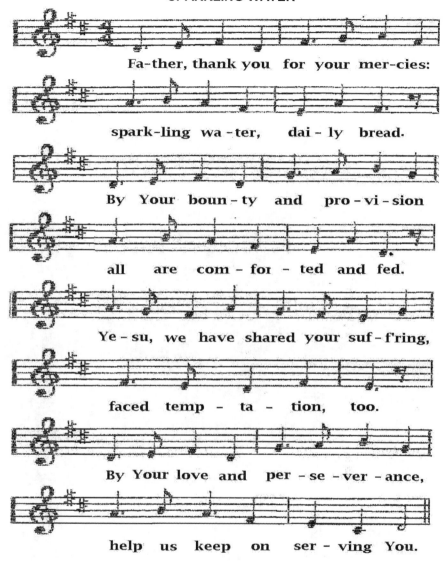

Fa-ther, thank you for your mer-cies:

spark-ling wa-ter, dai-ly bread.

By Your boun-ty and pro-vi-sion

all are com-for-ted and fed.

Ye-su, we have shared your suf-f'ring,

faced temp-ta-tion, too.

By Your love and per-se-ver-ance,

help us keep on ser-ving You.

THE HOWLING GRAY WOLF